BONE
DIGGERS

Tiffany Rose &
Alexandra Tauber

ISBN-13: 978-1724412195

ISBN-10: 1724412191

Dedicated to strangers
you meet online

LOADING...CHAPTER ONE

Owen felt like a jerk for coming to these meetings. Like a predator who had evolved, over millennia, into an asshole. These people were technically his people—video gamers—but they wouldn't exactly be welcoming if they knew what he did for money.

"Hello, my name is Grant, and I dream of 16th century Age of Shadows." The current speaker at the podium was young. Anywhere else would have carded him.

"Hello, Grant," Owen said, tiredly and in unison with everyone else. He was sure Grant's story was good. The stories were always good. But Owen doubted many people could really follow along, since Grant had picked up a poor French accent. Not the type that comes with being a native speaker, but the sort that sticks after hearing it spoken for a while. Occasionally, one of Grant's words would slip completely into French as if the English variant had been forgotten. The man had problems. That's probably why he joined the group.

Not understanding the man wasn't Owen's problem. No, just the opposite. Many people in game changed their controls to the Native Speaker option. You'd never find an arena player doing that, but serious roleplayers claimed it was more authentic. Owen wouldn't argue with that logic. He did it too, after all.

Help, however, wasn't why Owen was sitting in on the meeting. He'd be able to afford rent this month by simply figuring out if this particular video game addict was still playing or not. His bread and butter was made off of paranoid mothers and private investigators who needed computer classes. People like him were like called bone diggers—players who dug deeper past the pixels until they found the bones behind the controls. This particular hunter sat with an elbow propped on the armrest and his fingers trailing up to his temple in a vain effort to fight off a growing headache.

"Thanks, Grant," the room around Owen chimed. Grant stepped away from the group, lured by the refreshments laid out in the back of the room.

Owen took this as his chance and pushed himself up off the chair. He waited for Grant to fill a little paper cup, and pretended to divide his attention between the last speaker and the current one. "French faction?" Owen whispered.

"It's obvious, isn't it?" Grant said, with a sudden frown. "You too?"

Owen shook his head, and waited for a slight lull before replying. "I've spent a lot of time in that region, though."

Grant nodded, one of those small, meek nods that contain nothing but bitter understanding. He paused, looking at Owen more critically as his eyes narrowed trying to recall him. "I don't remember seeing you here before."

"I tend to come and go." Owen admitted. He offered his hand in introduction. "Name's Owen."

"Nice to meet you," Grant said, as they shook hands.

"Thanks Grant," Owen smirked, and Grant coughed a laugh. "So, when is the last time you played?"

Grant paused with his water cup pressed against his lips as he shot a look across the room to his sponsor, Jimmy. "Last week," he confessed, and shifted his weight to the other foot. The truth always has a way of making people fidgety. "You?"

Now Owen was the one averting his eyes. "Last night..."

"Ah, that explains your sudden appearance."

But, it really didn't. Despite playing Age of Shadows daily, he hadn't experienced any of the unintentional side effects. His new headgear was far less likely to have bugs, and he didn't consider himself to have an addictive personality. Simply a part of the majority of Americans who played without any real world problems.

Jimmy walked over. He was an older guy whose steps had a limp, though Owen had never been able to figure out why. Owen moved out of Jimmy's way so he could reach a tray of cookies. Getting a nod in greeting, and possibly thanks, but no other words were exchanged. Likely because it wasn't polite to talk until the speaker in the front of the room finished.

Grant skirted away to sit down. Owen didn't mind—he had the information he needed. He would be able to tell Grant's mother that yes, her son was playing. And yes, he was trying to get better. If his mother was worth her salt, that's really all she could ask from an addict.

Owen headed out before the next speaker was up. Leaving a meeting and going straight to the game always unnerved him, so instead he'd go home and close the case first. Finishing a job was equally, if not more, satisfying than any quest. It had taken Owen weeks to track Grant down, and he was ready for payday.

He stared at his phone with the new text screen open and the mother's name and number seemed to be waiting too. The job didn't always make Owen feel like a professional tattletale. Grant seemed like a nice enough guy. Why couldn't he be cheating on his wife, or politician using slurs in the game? Owen's thumbs twitched above the letters before he shook the feeling off and texted everything he learned.

Thinking about it any more would cause him to refresh his emails a dozen times, or obsessively check his texts. He wanted to play, but unfortunately his friend Neal said he was going to come over, so it was more logical to just wait a little longer. One text from the mother and two compulsive refreshes of his email later, there was a knock on the door.

"Sorry, I'm late," Neal said as Owen let him inside. He ran a hand through short messy hair that suggested it was windy outside. His clothes were baggy. They didn't sag around his hips, but were a clear fashion choice.

"No worries." Owen locked the front door before returning to the couch. "Not sure how interesting watching me play is going to be."

"It's fun," Neal said, "Plus, it gets me out of the house."

"Whatever does it for ya." This time, Owen's tone was more dismissive as he hoarded the couch. Neal took the chair by the desk. The TV went ignored since the headgear took up his entire field of vision. Unlike older game systems, this one didn't need a controller or keyboard. All you had to do was think and the headset picked up the brain's requests.

Tech like this had been attempted dozens of times, but Age of Shadows was the first game that proved it could be done properly. No limited controls, no eye strain, and a game that let you breathe in an open world only alluded to before in pixelated imaginations.

For Owen, the boot up always started with his hand. He'd heard other players describe it differently, but for him, it was the feeling of reaching out a hand and spreading his fingers against a nothing that almost felt tangible. If he looked up fast enough lights outlining shapes could be spotted before they blurred like fast-moving traffic that gave way to a fully rendered city.

Footsteps beat gently against digital streets. This fake Spanish city had almost become a second home. Friends made here felt just as real as the ones made in person. Excitement rose up through Owen's bones like a wave of heat as he walked closer and closer to the target of his current quest. The mark was talking with some other men as girls danced around them like cherry blossoms in the wind. There were enough NPCs and players around that, given enough care, this all could be done cleanly.

"Why don't you take the path to the left?" Neal interrupted.

"I don't need a backseat player." Owen groaned, ignoring the suggestion. "You break the immersion. If you want to play so bad, load up your own character."

"I like watching your story more," Neal said, with the ease that someone might use for why they liked watching football more than playing it. Age of Shadows had been designed to avoid this sort of thing, testing personality type and giving each player a story arc and missions they'd enjoy. But maybe Owen had spent so much time with Daniel as his avatar that the character was no longer flat to Owen or Neal. Daniel had a whole life to share with them.

After a quick check to see if the coast was clear, Daniel moved over stone railings as easily as a pebble skipping over water, then jumped to reach the edge of a windowsill that would allow him to climb up the roof in a fashion that would make parkour enthusiasts envious. It was one of the perks of being part of the Thieves Guild.

Players could choose between different class types. Each had its own social perks or status upgrades, but Owen would argue this was the best way to go about things.

The headgear gave the player a rush that was close to the real thing, but without the stray looks that flipping over benches could get you in real life. Daniel ran across the roof and slid to a stop before reaching the edge. There was no room for error. The toe of his boot hung off the edge.

Owen's fingers twitched as he watched his target below him. The movement echoed to Daniel before he reached for a throwing knife. With a mixture of art and timing, Daniel flicked his wrist, and the blade flew to sever a bag from one man's belt. The loot dropped to the ground, the knife holding it safe for now. The men carried on through the street without notice of the trouble they could have been in.

"Perfect," Daniel said to himself.

"See, I can't do cool shit like that!" Neal added.

Owen grinned. This time the headset picked up that he wasn't responding to in-game stimulus. "Well, that's what you get for joining the Knights. I told you the Guild is the way to go." A different stat boost and logged playtime that tripled Neal's also played a factor, though. Daniel jumped off the building and rolled safely to a stop on the street.

"Oh, now you're just showing off," Neal said.

Owen opened his mouth to reply, but he noticed a man in armor was eagerly headed towards the item drop. The blue tint of the name that popped up instantly showed that he was another player-controlled character. Johnny wasn't the most period accurate name, but the game allowed it. Stealing someone else's loot wouldn't get you a lot, but you could sell it all the same. It wasn't much to gain compared to what Daniel would lose. Unlike offline games, there'd be no reload if his quest got hijacked by another player.

"Back off," Daniel warned.

Johnny the Knight stopped a few steps away as the shining glint of another throwing knife caught his attention. He didn't look worried as his hand hovered over the mace hanging from his belt. The spikes were a far more imposing weapon than a throwing knife.

Daniel looked past the knight to the crowd behind him. He tracked a figure moving between the people before playing with the blade in his hand.

"Are you going to fight me, thief?" Johnny asked.

"No."

That brought a crooked grin to Johnny's face, and his hand fell away from his weapon. He seemed more than ready to grab the loot and be on his way.

"But, he will." Daniel nodded over to a man who now stood behind the knight.

Johnny looked over his shoulder, almost nicking his neck on a fine sword that had been drawn on him. This man looked more like Owen himself, with a quiet confidence that sat on a smaller frame than Daniel's. Unlike other NPCs with their names listed in black, his was grey.

Johnny grumbled an insult.

"Meet my companion, Lance." Even with his charm, Daniel's taunt was obvious.

"Take your prize then. See if I care." Johnny said, as if he hadn't wanted it in the first place. An act that Daniel didn't believe. He kept wary eye on Johnny until he left the area, likely to go rain on someone else's parade.

"What did I tell you about having adventures without me?" Lance said, but didn't sound like he was broken up about it. He bent down and picked up the loot for Daniel. Owen's inventory updated when Lance handed it off.

"Thanks," Daniel said. "I was worried I drew too much attention after all."

"I got your back."

Owen smiled at Lance, at his freckles where others wore war paint. He wasn't sure how he was lucky enough to snag a companion. They were rare. Some even suggested it was a bug in the system, despite the game's creators proudly claiming it was all part of their personality system, that nearly anyone could decide to join you if it suited the NPC.

"Do you have another adventure planned?" Lance asked.

"I was only planning on this mission."

"Hélas," Lance said, showcasing a bit of his programmed native language. "Until next time, then."

LOADING...CHAPTER TWO

"Relax," Michael said, "I'm a photographer."

Despite his very real skills at photography, he always came off as a bit of a creep. It wasn't like he was a jerk around the office, stealing people's lunches or drinking too much at the Christmas party. No, Michael was a dick—or rather, it was clear he thought with it.

The NYC Today wasn't a big production, so Owen could watch from his desk as Michael tried to nip and tuck the model like real-life Photoshop. The model, who may or may not have been called Ashley, kept shifting between professional mirth and contempt between takes.

He could imagine clearly what Daniel would do in this situation. He'd get up without further thought and tell his co-worker to sod off, and the model would thank him with a realistically unreasonable amount of gold.

But this wasn't a game, this was real life. Doing the best thing for everyone wasn't so cut and dry. Who knew if Ashley just wanted to finish the job, let alone the crap he'd hear from his boss for possibly ruining the shoot.

"Owen!"

He jumped in his seat, barely catching a pencil cup before it fell over. That would be his boss, Frank. Owen took another glance over to the others before he walked over to Frank's office. The room had a mounted TV in the corner, as if it was meant to keep someone company idly in a waiting room. In truth, it stole far more time than anyone intended.

Frank looked oblivious to Owen's presence as Owen stepped into the room. On the TV, two Age of Shadows arena players were going at it like gladiators in the coliseum. It was a brutal match broadcast close enough to the sweat and blood so you felt you were on the ground with them. A burly avatar cleaved a shining axe into the shoulder of another man, causing enough damage that the feed cut to show the players underneath. Their faces pulled into masked expressions that the Greeks would have been familiar with.

The celebration of the audience was mirrored in the mirth Frank had as he cheered his favorite on. But the tragedy of the other player was closer to the cringe Owen gave over the collective volume.

"That's a win for the English faction," an announcer said, taking over the discussion. Behind the two speakers, one could make out the players who ended their match much like boxers would. The talking heads debated what this meant for the next arena match.

Excited from a win that was debatably his, Frank finally turned to Owen who lurked in the doorway. "I knew that warrior didn't have it in him. It's nearly impossible to fight a knight straight on if you haven't taken the oath yourself."

Owen nodded so slightly it was almost a one-man play in sarcasm.

"I take it you don't play?" Frank laughed.

"Uh..." The answer should have been easy, but what Frank was really asking was what he wasn't saying. He meant: Do you play Arena? A yes would lead Owen to nights out with his boss, watching matches and downing sodas to keep from being unprofessional in front of his employer. "No."

"Ahh!" Frank waved his hand as if there was a fly about. "For the best. This stuff will rot your brain out."

Owen's eyes flared a bit wider in an effort to keep them from rolling. That must have been said about every medium when it first came out. "So, what did you call me in for?"

"Oh, right, yes!" Frank leaned over his desk to grab a sheet of paper. "Here is the list of the candidates running for council member. Research them all and see if you can find anything good."

Owen crossed the room in a couple strides and took the print-off. He scanned over it, but didn't recognize the short list besides the man who was already in office. "Sounds fun," he said with a shrug.

Frank grinned at a silent joke.

"What?"

"And, you think I find fun in weird places."

Owen chuckled and tilted his head a little to concede. "Yeah, but I get paid to do this. And I'll do almost anything for money."

"Let's hope one of those candidates does the same thing."

"Right? Nothing sells papers quite like skeletons coming out of closets." Owen took another look at the paper. "I'll let you know what I find."

A lot could be found if you simply looked. A stray like or favorite could get someone in trouble. If you pulled on the wrong string, the whole tapestry of a carefully organized campaign could unravel.

Many people forgot everything you could look up freely. That your name could be tied to an email that you used to post an opinion years ago that perfectly highlighted bigotry. It no longer surprised him how shitty people could be. Normally, Owen's job focused on looking up things that the internet wasn't quite equipped for. Mostly obscure fact checking and reviewing figures, but after a freelance bone digging job discovered that a charity's funds were going towards in game Age of Shadows purchases, Frank always gave him these assignments.

By the end of the day, Owen hadn't found anything newsworthy, or even remotely interesting, besides one of the candidates who upvoted a ridiculous amount of Advice

Animals. He must have clicked through a hundred of them by now, nearly praying one would be horribly offensive.

Owen groaned and put his head down on his desk.

"Going that well, huh?" Michael asked. Owen picked his head up to watch as his co-worker pop open a soda with a sound so crisp it almost caused him to drool.

"Did you bring that one for me?" Owen joked. His smile wide and friendly.

The noise that came from Michael was more of a snort than anything else. "That was a stupid question for a fact checker," he said.

"A monkey can do your job." The insult trailed after Michael as he walked away, but wasn't said with enough force to catch up. In part because Owen didn't believe it. He saw Michael's photos, they unfortunately were pretty good. It made the fact that he was asshole worse. If only talent bred kindness.

At least for Owen there was one thing that never failed. Daniel.

In VR, even the simple things that were the equivalent of being an office gofer were far more rewarding. He traveled with Lance over cities to deliver papers and family heirlooms to thankful NPCs for pockets of gold and EXP. He tabbed over to the leaderboards, seeing that he was a close second to the weekly top players in the northeastern region of the U.S. He'd been solidly at third without any real extra effort, but recently he pushed and was getting closer and closer over the past month. Someone with the log in Tiansheng had held the number one place for what seemed like forever. They relentlessly hoarded the spot. There were good prizes for the top players, so it was worth the extra effort.

On Daniel's way back home, a herald caught his attention. Or rather, his voice raised over everyone who had gathered. "The Duke has left us hungry, and without coin in our pockets! We no longer have to stand for this atrocity! His caravan comes this way. Good people, let's act now and stop it!"

"I don't know why the Duke thought he could live such a lavish life without facing any consequences," Lance said.

Merchants who could pack up their wares did, and others who were in the streets decided to clear out before there was trouble. Leaving the town square empty for players to risk what they had on the event in hope for more.

"Wasn't it only a month ago that he earned that title?" Daniel asked.

"Mmm. Took it at the edge of a sword, too." A few more people from within earshot had gathered like them, but for the most part, the group was shrinking. The Duke wasn't an NPC, but taking him out would most benefit that group. Lance's lip curled up in disgust as more people passed them. Every time good people did nothing, he wondered why he left his own country for this one.

"Shall we give it back?"

"Let's." Lance grinned, and drew his sword.

They fought in tandem against the guards that protected the Duke's caravan. Feeling no desire for position or power, Daniel left that target for whoever had a vendetta against the man. He was aiding in the raid simply because he had been a witness to the plight. A good ally didn't steal the spotlight.

The versatility a sword allowed Lance to set up anyone for failure before they even reached Daniel. He, too, could use a sword, but favored the daggers for speed and the ability to get up close and personal with men in armor that would otherwise give them both trouble.

With his chest pounding, he looked at the battlefield. Fallen bodies were piling up now. That heads up gave everyone plenty of time for an ambush. A few people were still fighting, including the Duke, but all the help his title gained him had run off or had been killed.

In the chaos, a woman stood apart. She was watching from the sidelines. Her small frame and the six inches in height Daniel had made her stand out even more, like a daisy among weeds. Curiosity captivated him as strongly as attraction ever could.

Daniel glanced over to check on Lance who was pulling his sword out of the chest of a man. "Are you going to be fine on your own for a moment?" Daniel asked.

"Bien sûr." That man breathed confidence as easy as air.

With his worry sated, Daniel headed over to her. "Greetings, miss," he said. Her chestnut brown eyes seemed striking against pale skin. "My name is Daniel Ortiz. I'm sorry if this violence has startled you still."

"Amilia." Her hand twitched, but anything that manners normally would have called for was lost to the moment. The name displayed in black like any other NPC. But he wasn't given time to wonder about why she was here. "It would take a lot more than that to scare me."

"Well, I guess you aren't going to run off on me too quick, then," Daniel replied easily.

A small sly smile stretched across her face, and stirred butterflies in his stomach. "Not unless you give me me a reason to," she said. It was such a fair and honest answer that Daniel chuckled.

The sound of a guttural groan cut through the air. The Duke was in a pile on the ground, red spilling out from behind fine leather armor. "Well, finish it then," he taunted, ready to take the death penalty and reset his character.

"Wait," said a bard from the group of fighters. "I bet if we turn him in there will be a bigger reward. It isn't as if he and the king are on the best terms." They debated for a moment before agreeing that it was the best choice. Lance excused himself from their party once his sword was no longer needed.

"You two fight as smoothly as ghosts," Amilia said once Lance neared. He shot a look over to Daniel, equal parts amused and flattered. "I'd like to learn."

"You... want to learn how to fight?" Daniel repeated as if he didn't understand.

Amilia nodded. "My father was a part of the thieves guild. I fear my family's current path isn't...just anymore." She ran her hand through brown hair that fell back into curls. "It must seem funny. A thief trying to be noble."

It's almost magical when you hear a stranger repeating a personal truth back to you. "No, actually, it doesn't."

"You'll do it?" Amilia asked, brighter than the midday sun. "There is a festival tonight. I could meet you again there?"

"Sure." The word slipped out of his mouth without further provocation. Too fast for his liking. "I'll teach you if you can prove you have the heart for it."

"I promise I won't disappoint you." She curtsied, and bowed her head to the both of them before excusing herself.

"Won't that be fun," Daniel mused to himself before turning to Lance. "What do you think?"

Amilia's excitement was undeniably intoxicating. It held the promise that he could share everything with her. It might be a foolish or tedious venture, maybe even selfish in ways. But her story intrigued him. What did he have to lose?

"We have a term for women who death follows," Lance said, *"Femme fatale."*

The night was filled with color. Under the candlelight that lined the streets, Daniel's mask had a metallic tint. Black lined his cheeks and nose, while red swirled around his eyes like flames. The same shimmering red was carried to the sides of his eyes where three black stones lay.

There were two things on his mind as he walked around the masquerade. The first was to find Amilia, but his thoughts also hovered over the mission the guild was running tonight. Big crowds always brought out important people. An official had come out to play and the guild was itching to scratch him off their list.

A man fell in stride with Daniel, his mask matching with reversed colors. Lance was on the prowl, but wouldn't be alone for it. It didn't take them long before they spotted the chubby official as he moved his hips out of time with the music. The dance had an odd sort of wobble when he did it, but the women dancing with him were trying to follow along.

Lance was something else when he hunted. His movements were precise and calculated as he broke off and worked through the crowd. His stealth would have been enough if one of the girls didn't trip over the official's feet, revealing Lance's approach. Fear painted the official's face. He pushed the woman aside and bolted through the group of people. Lance let out a curse and darted after him.

Distracted in the search for Amilia, Daniel didn't spot the problem until people started running. If he moved toward the next street, the official would run straight over to him, not even aware of their connection. Daniel stepped out, blocking the path as he pulled out his blades. The bureaucrat stopped short, staring as the metal gleamed in the moonlight.

The two were in silent stand-off for what must have felt like hours. The staring contest was ruined as the man's eyes went wide with shock before blinking back pain. Standing behind the bureaucrat was another man—his dagger coated with blood. Lance grabbed the bureaucrat before he fell and helped him discreetly slump against the wall.

"Thanks." Lance's expression softened as he looked to Daniel. "I was worried that I would draw attention."

"I'll always have your back."

Lance smiled as he stood up. "And you have a meeting tonight."

Daniel scoffed at his word choice.

"No? What would you call it? Something more?"

Daniel was quick to say no, which only made Lance's grin shine brighter. "So, where are you headed?" he asked changing the subject.

"Thought I'd give the guild good news," Lance said. "I can tell them of the valiant work you did as a roadblock."

A cough erupted from Daniel's throat. "Sonnets will be written about our adventures."

Lance skewed his face up to the side as he imagined how those would sound. "Maybe we'll find a bigger adventure before we get the poets involved." He patted Daniel on the shoulder before retiring for the night.

The immediate addition to Daniel's to-do list was to move away from the body. More time passed and he started to grow concerned that Amilia had yet to appear. Maybe she changed her mind about the whole thing. Daniel walked around until he ended up back where he started. He sighed. There must have been something he missed.

"Señor?"

He turned, expecting to find Amilia standing there, but instead was taken aback by another woman standing there with a goblet in her hand. Her outfit suggested that she was a barmaid, and reflexively Daniel reached for his coin purse.

"Oh don't worry, its covered," The woman said. "You just looked like you were in a need of a drink."

Daniel blinked hard at the wine now in his hand, mumbling a surprised thanks before the woman left.

It was a strange enough occurrence that Owen toggled the controls so he could see the items details. The small crest like emblem was displayed next to the objects name. "Are you kidding me?" Owen said to himself. "It's a plot item." In the real world it would have been a no-brainer to just toss the drink. But in here?

Daniel lifted the cup to his mouth, taking a sip. With a pleased little hum, he took another. The festival was full of giggling, excited people. A woman who was dancing like a top got a little overzealous in her spins and nearly fell into him. The more time he spent enjoying the party, he more he wondered if it mattered whether Amilia would ever show. And now that the wine Owen was sure was tainted took its effect, the details around Daniel were becoming muddy. He abandoned the cup as he made his way to a chair, crashing into the cushions without any attempt to be graceful. The controls lagged, and before any more time passed, a woman had seated herself next to him on her own chair.

She leaned in Daniel's direction, like she was waiting to say something if he gave her the attention. His eyes lazily moved to look at her more directly, taking in a golden filigree mask, inset with small crystals. He noticed black tulle that also stretched under the mask, pulling all her dark features together in contrast to her porcelain skin.

As if on cue, she smiled brightly at him and leaned further in to whisper. "I saw you haven't been dancing, and was wondering if I could fix that?" she asked, acting oblivious to his condition. With a small shake of his head, he watched the eyes behind that beautiful mask finally grow concern. "Oh, are you alright? Do you need some help?" Her hand reached to brush his cheek.

Daniel licked his lips, his eyes failing to track the spinning dresses in proper time. The effect was actually enhanced by the drink in his system. It made the pools of fabric move in slow motion, making their skirts arch in stunningly beautiful ways. His mind grew hazy, but one thought was clear as he realized what had happened. He blinked up again, focusing on one long dark curl that laid softly against the neck of the woman who was almost looming over him now.

"Oh, you're more handsome close up than you were across the room," she said. "I could take care of you, if you'd like? I promise, I'll keep you safe."

He simply swallowed as she initially spoke, not for lack of words, but more lack of ability to use them. Daniel's breathing became more ragged as his will crashed against the effects of the drugs. He suddenly wished that Lance had not retired for the night. He needed to take a breath, he needed to find his voice. "Okay, dear, take me with you," he breathed.

The woman took his hand and slowly guided him outside of the festival. She braced him up with an arm around his waist. As she led him out a pathway, they came up to a carriage led by a horse. The driver smiled after an exchange of coin and drew the reins.

Daniel jolted awake as all of his facilities were returned to him within a single frantic second. His arms hit a tug of resistance. Panic now tinted his vision as he looked up to find them bound in fabric to the bedpost behind his head.

His eyes darted around the room trying to absorb it all in a single moment. The sight of Amilia caused him to freeze up again.

"Of course it's you." A sigh accompanied a slower look around the room. Weapons were stacked on the table in an intimidating fashion. Or they would have been, if they weren't his.

"I needed to show you I had the heart for anything," Amilia said. Her expression was completely blank, not letting emotion betray her will.

Daniel had a line of wit ready, but it fell short as he spotted a knife in her hand. His muscles tightened as she stepped closer, concerned with what she planned to do with it. When she reached up to one of his hands, he relaxed enough to provide enough slack on the ties.

His first hand was cut free with a breathlessness between them. She leaned over him to reach the other hand. A freedom that lasted a moment as he grabbed her waist with one swift movement, flipped her onto the bed, pinning her hand with the knife above her head. She let out a small yelp, her eyes flaring wide as she looked up at him.

"Do not ever trick me again. Understand?" The threat in his voice more rough and serious than her weapon.

Amilia nodded through the suddenness of it all. "I'm sorry."

"Not as much as you should be," Daniel mumbled. He pulled away from her to sit up, rubbing his wrists, though they were unmarred compared to his pride. "But I can't deny your success."

"I know you're furious," she said, and he shot her a look. "But, if you can regain your calm, I think you'll understand the point I am making."

"Get rid of the knife."

Amilia looked down at her hand, realizing she had been gripping it tightly all this time. Without the upper hand, she was afraid of retaliation. She pushed up from the bed and dropped the blade on the nearest dresser. Without it, she didn't have the nerve to be near until she could predict him.

Daniel ran a hand through his dark brown hair, trying to understand. "Who even are you?"

It wasn't the most elegant question, especially when the safest thing would be to just leave, but it was the most pressing on his mind.

Amilia's breath came out shaky. "I'm someone that was blind to what my life was before. You told me to prove myself to you, and to that extreme I have shown you what I'm capable of. But I need training, real training." She paused as she glanced out the window to the morning and city around them. "I want to know who I could be if I had the skills to defend myself—to fight."

His hands ran down the front of his pants before he stood up. There was a raw sincerity in her words.

"Fine," he sighed, and Amilia raised a brow, not following yet. "It's against my better judgment, but I believe you. I'll teach you." Her lips parted as if she was about to utter surprise, but pressed them tight and nodded instead. "At least change into something..." Daniel gestured over to her dress. "Appropriate to run around in."

Her dresser was close by and she stepped over to it, digging through her clothes for a moment before realized that Daniel hadn't budged an inch from where he was standing.

"Are you going to give a lady some privacy?"

Daniel looked up from the golden mask he spotted sitting on an end table. "No." His expression hinted that he didn't trust her enough to give her the benefit of the doubt that she wasn't planning on any further tricks.

"Wonderful. I'm a prisoner in my own home." Amilia dropped a bit of fabric she was holding with an annoyed little push.

"Turnabout is fair play, my dear." Daniel grinned from ear to ear as he crossed his arms over his chest. "You are the one who insisted that I come over."

Refusing to back down from a challenge, Amilia started to boldly change in front of a man she'd barely known for a day. Daniel ended up glancing away as a blush threatened his confidence.

"There," Amilia said in triumph once dressed. "I bet that was faster than you could have gotten ready."

Daniel cracked a smile despite himself. "That's because I'm prettier than you." Amilia's only response was a small eye roll before Daniel gestured to the door. "Let's go."

Amilia led the way, the text of her name shifted from black to gray to show she was now an NPC party member. The shake of Daniel's head was indistinguishable from Owen's. As impossibly rare as this was, he wasn't sure if fate was smiling at him, or setting itself up to give him the finger.

LOADING...CHAPTER FOUR

Screens that were once dedicated to every ESPN channel were now filled with snipers, boots scraping against prized digital ground, and other sounds of war. First person shooters may have lost their crown, but still held strong. Their clans mirrored the NFL's football teams and their seasons filled with fans just as loyal.

Only two members of team AK-aos were left defending their base. One was camping at the heart of it and virtually safe as long as they didn't move. The second was crawling around from vantage point to vantage point in hopes that he could pick off the other team one by one. It was a slow process as the other team went around picking up all the weapons and vehicles they could. But then, faster than a blink, the sneaking player got a rocket launcher to the face.

"I do envy how often FPS-ers can die without penalty," Owen commented as he sipped on his beer.

"It's not that bad," Neal said.

"Of course you wouldn't be afraid, you've died more times than Sean Bean," Owen joked. He tipped his drink towards Neal, who looked away towards the rest of the bar for support, but none was found as their friends broke out into a fit of laughter. "An inventory reset and drop in HP is basically your default character."

"It's an inspiration that you haven't given up yet. At the very least you'd think something would have rubbed off from watching Owen play," Emily said. She stood out from the group, not because she was the only female in the trio, but because her pregnant belly was so big that no one even asked if she wanted anything besides a refill of her caffeine free soda.

"Come on. I'm not that—"

"To Neal!" She raised her glass and Owen mirrored the gesture.

Neal fought the fake praise before he caved to bask in it. "I'm not handy with a knife, but I can whip you both in lore. And to that I will drink!"

"Oh, oh, keep it down for a second, I want to hear the halftime report." Emily leaned forward so she could focus on the TV in the noisy bar. No matter how big the screens were, it could still be hard to focus. The esports bar was close enough to Times Square that light from giant flashing billboard screens intruded through the windows.

"I'm Hank, and it's time for The Rundown." His words were broken up by the segment's title cards. "Developers of Age of Shadows have confirmed that one lucky player has reached a new milestone in game. No, the level cap hasn't yet been reached, but the record for NPC's has been broken. One player in the Spanish faction has somehow snagged himself two companions," Hank reported, before he turned to discuss it with the other gaming experts on the panel with him.

"I'm no MMORPG expert, but if today's game has taught us anything, it's the importance of teammates. I'm not sure how this guy snagged two, but kudos to him," said Jose, Hank's faithful co-anchor.

"Or them," Aaron, the third gentleman, corrected. His wardrobe was different than their suits. Being a former pro-gamer he got to wear his jersey. "Unlike other games, Age of Shadows doesn't show player information. They didn't confirm the player, did they?"

"Nope," Hank replied. "Meaning it's likely a roleplayer. All of the arena players are quick to announce themselves. The promise of sponsorship is just too good. Could you imagine a three on one match? It would be no contest."

"I know, I'm looking forward to tomorrow's analysis of it during #Rehashed," Jose said, before the ad break.

"Two?" Neal repeated. "Looks like someone is better than even you."

Owen said nothing. Even turned his head away to try and hide the sly smile that was demanding realty on his face. His hand soon pulled over to cover his mouth.

"No..."

Emily paused, looking at them both for a moment before her jaw dropped. "You didn't." When Owen didn't look back, she placed her hand on his, which was enough to make him look. "You did! Oh-my-god. You have to tell us everything!"

"It's no big deal," Owen said, failing to play it off, if he had even been really trying to.

"No big deal? You are on—" her voice dropped off so her increasing excitement wasn't heard by every person in town. "The news. How did you manage to pull that off?"

"I think I might have actually glitched myself into it?" Owen paused, not really wanting to tell everyone the embarrassing story. Amilia wasn't like Lance. It wasn't like when he simply asked for Lance to join and he did. Amilia was...perplexing.

"Lore doesn't do me a lick of good when your glitchy ass is so fortunate," Neal grumbled.

Owen looked over to him, scrunching up his face with a bit of worry, before Emily, with great enthusiasm, flagged down the waiter.

"I need a round of shots!" she called. The waiter leaning against the bar looked over, his expression shifting to horror when he noticed who was calling. Emily rolled her eyes. "Maybe I should just give you the money instead of me trying to order."

"Geez, Em," Neal laughed, his bitterness not lasting long. "You're going to give him a heart attack. Poor guy will have to worry about his tip or his ethics."

Owen got up from the bar stool. "Don't worry about it. I think I learned my lesson about accepting drinks from people." Neal and Emily shot each other a look as their friend went over to the bar, hoping the other could fill in whatever story they had clearly missed.

Several shots and a cab ride home later, Owen sat in front of his computer. He was too drunk to play, so looking into things for work seemed like the next logical choice. Owen couldn't tell if the first few candidates were actually clean or not, they simply were old enough that they didn't have a very big digital trail. If they had secrets, they were hidden the old fashioned way.

The fourth candidate, Suzanne, he found on Twitter. Her tweets were mostly really boring political comments linking to even longer, more boring topics. But, when he dug back enough to find more casual things like silly photos of animals lazing in a manner similar to his own, he found exactly where she ruined her whole campaign. Either haphazardly, or not caring at the time, Suzanne had turned on the location marker. Most showed she was tweeting from out of state, and if she lived outside of New York, it would disqualify her from being elected. Sure, it wasn't hard evidence, but enough to make news, and enough that her opponents would bring up a complaint and demand they officially check into it.

Owen's excitement was dashed as he groaned suddenly. He leaned back in his chair as a deep pain in his stomach hit. The other names on the list would have to wait. The once friendly buzz had shifted. Without much grace, he twisted out of his chair and stumbled into the kitchen to get some water. He leaned against the counter, and massaged the headache that was trying to settle in his temples. His room wasn't far, but the trip there felt like it took forever. The bed was a relief. He didn't bother to struggle with getting under the sheets. For now, this would do.

He rolled into work at the barely morning hour that was 11 am. Falling into his office chair more than sitting in it,

Owen tried his damnedest to look up the rest of the names, but his headache was making it hard to read anything.

"Owen!" His boss' voice was an air horn going off next to his ear. Wanting to completely give up on the respectable adult thing, Owen put his head down for a second. He took a deep breath as he gathered the strength to get up and collect his papers.

Frank didn't look at him for more than a second before narrowing his eyes. "Are you hung over?"

This question was completely ignored. Owen saw no sense in addressing it. It would only send the conversation in a direction he didn't want to go. Instead he held out the folder, which Frank took. "Suzanne hasn't been a New York resident long enough to run for office. Right now, it's only speculation, but it's enough to start an official investigation."

After a few pages were flipped through, Frank looked back up at Owen. "Does anyone else have this?"

"I dunno." He turned his hands up. "It's all out there for people. I don't know if anyone is sitting on the information or simply hasn't put it together."

"This is good. We'll include this right away."

Owen took an eager step towards the door, but once again was stopped by his boss calling for him. It was enough to make him cringe slightly. "I'm amazed you can come in here like that," Frank said. His boss gestured to the whole of Owen, making him worry he badly needed to find a mirror. "And still can find me this. What happened?"

This time, Owen thought a bit longer about answering the question. "If your pregnant friend says you are 'drinking for two,' do not take that as a challenge."

His boss laughed, and Owen returned to work.

For much of the afternoon, Frank went on about a package that needed to be here right this second, until finally Owen volunteered to head downstairs and wait for it. To save a few more seconds, he watched the doors for the bike messenger while drinking his black coffee. Courier services swarmed the streets of midtown Manhattan, assisting every business in its 'here and now' mentality.

He walked over to the front desk's water dispenser to fill his empty mug. Probably better for him than the coffee, anyway. When he turned around, drawing a hand through his short, dark hair, he saw what he guessed was a bike messenger, dressed in thermal cycling tights and a chimney collar sweatshirt, making her way towards the front desk. He jumped to action to intercept her so he could sign off on the package and get back upstairs in his somewhat comfortable desk chair.

"Hey. I'm the one picking that up."

The girl turned on her heel, shifting her backpack off her shoulders. "I.D.?"

"Yeah, sure."

Once he handed it off, she swiped it on the little scanner she had attached to her tablet before visually confirming the badge. Her lips twitched slightly. "Nice picture."

Owen raised an eyebrow at her before pocketing his I.D. again. His hair was near buzzcut in the photo, with an expression that hinted at both delight and horror that his photo was being taken for a press badge. He eyed her for a moment while she did something on the tablet, taking note of the piercing in her nose and the height of her cheekbones. Her features weren't strongly one race or another, but he guessed she had Asian heritage somewhere.

"Sign here." She handed over the tablet before pulling the package from her backpack in anticipation of trading the items.

He searched for a name tag, thinking one must come with the job, but came up empty. After looking over her face a second time, he tilted his head as if she was a puzzle he hadn't stopped to see the pieces of before. "Do I know you? Maybe from another life?" Owen mused.

"Does that line get you laid often?" she asked with a straight face.

"You'll be the first to know."

That one managed to get a chuckle out of her. "You think you're cute, don't you?"

"No," Owen countered. "But you might."

She rolled her eyes. "I really need to go and actually do my job. Can you just sign and take this?"

With a scribble, he signed an unrecognizable version of his name. He held the tablet out now tiredly as it was swapped for the package.

"Thank you for using Minute Messengers," she droned, likely for the thousandth time.

Owen barely lifted an eye from the package as the girl stuffed the tablet back into her bag. Without further word, he headed up stairs to deliver whatever this heavy thing was. Freedom of Information request, he assumed. Which meant this package would end up on his desk after a once over.

"Mail's here," he announced as he popped into Frank's office.

"Oh, good! Hand it here." Frank might have been a child on Christmas if he hadn't been glued to his seat focused on writing up an article. Really, the only thing that held him away from the promise of a lead was one he was already working on.

Owen hesitated in the doorway for a second, shifting his weight from one foot to the other. "At the risk of sounding like the worst employee ever, can I run out and get lunch? I could bring you back something?" He put an innocent little sing-song tone in it.

Frank glanced at the time. He had blown past lunch hour. "Nah, that's alright. You can go ahead though. A man cannot live off booze and coffee alone."

"We should get that on a plaque for the office." Owen turned to a blank space of a wall that was nearly filled with framed articles. His hands spreading out to show the perfect place for it.

"Get out."

Owen laughed, and left the man to write in peace. On the elevator ride down, he debated whether he wanted to walk all the way to Subway or just stop at the halal food truck on the corner. His decision completely forgotten when he spotted the same bike messenger standing outside the lobby's glass doors.

"You're still here." The statement was laced with confusion as to why. "I thought you really actually needed to do your job."

She turned, smoke trailing out of her mouth as a cigarette kept her hand company.

"Ah, never mind," Owen added, getting it now. "Don't let me disturb you." That left the where to eat question. He glanced down the street to some food carts, but it was difficult to tell if they were actually busy or just obscured by foot traffic.

"Hey, wait."

Owen paused, looking back with a brow raised. She looked unsure. Maybe surprised herself that she had even said anything. It wasn't a bashful expression, more calculating if she wanted to take it back. "Name's Andreah."

"Pleasure," he said halfheartedly.

Instead of frowning, Andreah took another drag of her cigarette. She decided he was cuter when trying to be friendly. "Would you like one?" she offered, trying to coax out more than a word from his lips.

"Why not?" He shrugged, and held his hand out.

Andreah smiled at the progress and pulled out the pack, passing them along before patting down her pockets for a lighter. She found it by the third pocket, but paused as Owen stared at the unlit cigarette in his hand. "What?"

"I was trying to think of the last time I had a cigarette," Owen said. The memory actually was pretty clear. He was standing outside a meeting, trying to gain the trust of a bone digger mark and asked for one as an excuse to talk to the guy. You get a lot out of someone if you shared their vice.

"Don't tell me," Andreah started filling in her own story. "You started to rebel as a teenager and this was the 'coolest' way you could think of that would piss off the family."

He gave her a dismissive nod that didn't quite confirm that was the case. "Maybe, I just didn't think I could pull off piercings as well as you."

Andreah took it as the compliment it was meant to be, and handed the lighter over without further tease. Well, for a moment at least. When Owen closed his eyes to take a drag she simply had to harass further. "I don't want to be a bad influence now."

Owen shot her a sideways glance. "Don't flatter yourself."

She let out a near impatient huff. "When do you get off work?" Andreah asked, innocently enough that it seemed like a new look for her.

"Uh..." Owen felt like he knew the answer he should give if he wanted to learn more than just her name. Frank was a cool boss, but he wasn't can-I-ditch-early-because-I-spotted-a-hottie cool. "I don't know actually. The news never sleeps and whatnot."

She lifted her chin to nod. Not really getting it and unsure if she fully wanted to. "And what do you do for the news, Mr. Press Badge?" Andreah asked. For an ID, it barely gave any information at all. "Hotshot writer who came to New York to make it big?"

That idea was quickly shaken off with a laugh. "Nothing like that. I'm a researcher."

Andreah's incredulous look now seemed permanently plastered on her face. "A fact checker?" While she wasn't blushing, she looked around with the same unbelieving and flushed manner. "Should I have invited you to a bookstore instead?"

"I feel so incredibly cool right now, you have no idea." Owen fiddled with the cigarette in his hand as it burned away on its own. "Do you want to get coffee tomorrow?"

Andreah didn't look all that convinced, so he rambled on. "A drink? Dinner? A line of coke? What I'm saying is, do you want to hang out with me later, or should I go back inside?" By the time his ramble was over he was blushing a bit at the level of ridiculousness, but didn't feel much shame for it. The nice thing about strangers in New York was that the odds of seeing them again were practically nonexistent unless one made a concerted effort. Easy to cut your losses if things didn't work out.

Behind a half-bitten lip, she chuckled to herself. "Alright, but only because it doesn't seem like you'd be the boring sort."

Andreah put out her cigarette with the aid of a trash can before digging in her bag for a pen. "Call me later for one of the first two. It's my general rule of thumb not to risk jail time around people I don't really know."

"That's a totally reasonable and normal rule to have," Owen said, unsure if she was still joking around like he was.

"Keeps me out of trouble." Andreah handed over a torn page from a booklet of forms with her number written on it. "Until we meet again."

"Au revoir."

LOADING...CHAPTER FIVE

It had been days since Amilia joined Daniel's team, and it was soon decided that he'd take his new recruit out to see how she could help. Under a rustic sky, they ventured along recreated historic streets towards the start location.

"What sort of mission is it?" Amilia asked.

"We are protecting a witness."

"Oh." It sounded noble and hopefully trouble-free enough. "Is that something the thieves' guild does often?"

"The powers that be will really take almost any mission that follows their tenets," Daniel candidly answered.

Amilia remembered them discussing this at a café a couple nights before. "Do not raise a hand against another, for we take care of our own. Bring no harm to the innocent or poor."

Daniel hummed an agreement. "Both morally sound, and a good way to avoid making unseen enemies."

"That just leaves..."

Daniel looked over with a smile, wondering if she'd get the third one or if she needed a hint. They passed a few buildings before he offered the answer. "Take only what you need."

"That's a funny rule," Amilia mused. Daniel tilted his head. She shrugged. "For a bunch of thieves, that is."

"It might be if we weren't a guild. Greed leads to corruption, which leads to abuses in the ranks. I would rather be part of a morally gray group that hasn't forgotten about its pack than blindly following all the laws set without much say."

It hadn't been long, but Amilia was starting to feel an odd tenderness towards Daniel. She wanted to know what he specifically thought about the world. "I'm in."

Daniel pulled out a map of the city, spreading it wide so Amilia could look over his shoulder. His eyes traced the path they'd take. "The Knight we are escorting is wanted in court to testify soon. Whatever his story, it is imperative he gets to tell it in one piece," he explained as the corner of his mouth twitched up. "Most likely boring, but has the chance to be something dicey. Any worries to confess before we go?" he teased for the sheer fun of it as he folded up the map.

"I guess not," Amilia said, and looked down at her hands. She had no real weapons of her own, like the arsenal Daniel carried. "If things do get messy, what am I supposed to do?"

Daniel chewed on his lip as he looked Amilia over. What did he have that he could share? A dagger would only be good in short range combat, and the idea of someone being that close to her without the proper training made his stomach uneasy. "Do you know how to use a sword?"

"I know which side to hold."

Amilia's eyes grew wide as Daniel pulled out a sword and handed it over with an everyday casualness about it. "Th-thank you," she said. With wonder, she blinked at the rather beautiful rapier while Daniel pulled off the belt that had secured the sword to his waist.

The two headed towards the north side of town, to a cantina. "Amilia," Daniel said, and nodded towards tables across the street. "Do you see that man outside eating? Don't believe a word he says, nor fall prey to his charm."

Amilia looked over, expecting the serious words to match who she saw, while Daniel's expression was one of amusement. When she glanced again, she actually thought it looked like the man she saw with Daniel before.

He walked straight up to the man, not only stealing a seat next to him, but the remaining half of his sandwich. "We must protect that figure of yours, dear Tarlé."

"As always, Danny boy," Lance replied, making Daniel twitch at the name. Amilia followed behind, entertained by their exchange. It was a disregard of proper etiquette rarely seen in this age.

Lance wiped his hands against each other as he stood. "You've brought the beautiful woman from before," Lance said, offering his hand to take hers. "And I'm certain you are far more than that."

Lance gently planted a kiss on her hand so soft that his lips hardly touched her. At the last moment, Lance looked over to Daniel, who crossed his arms over his chest.

"Shall we?" Daniel's tone was shorter than before. He took a step to a nearby table with an older man picking at his food, too jittery to commit to the meal. The man, nearly twice Daniel's age, jumped as he neared, but settled back once recognizing who it was. Daniel must have said something encouraging because the man nodded, and looked back at his plate.

"Lance Tarlé," Lance said, introducing himself properly. "Excuse my friend's manners. Daniel isn't used to being set with the recruits, especially the cute ones. The man he is currently talking to is named Joseph, and our duty it's to protect him." He leaned against the table, glancing at them. "For today, at least."

Amilia peaked at the man sitting at the table.

"So, tell me," Lance said, pulling her attention back to him. "Are you here for business, or because you like my friend."

At the question, Amilia sunk down in a chair. Once the surprise washed over her, a small smile returned. He seemed like the playful sort, so she took a risk. "Well, he does have a nice behind," she whispered. There was something about the light, joking aura Lance gave off that made her relax. It was hard to feel like the terrified little child that she feared they'd see her as.

Lance smirked. *"Vrai.* But you've yet to see mine." He walked over to Daniel as if to give her the chance, even though, truth be told, he just wanted to get moving.

Joseph kept a watchful eye on Amilia. She hadn't noticed at first, but sometimes he'd just stare until one of the boys moved in a fashion that accidentally broke the line of sight. It was unnerving, and sent twitches through the whole group. His eyes drifted to her—or rather Daniel's—weapon. For support, her hand rested on the hilt.

The group traveled through the city in silence until Lance spoke. "I heard what you did the other night. I'll be sure not to leave my drink unattended around you."

Amilia opened her mouth to defend herself, but realized he was likely looking to amuse himself. "I had no idea that news had already made the rounds. Being a topic of discussion makes me feel notorious. I'm flattered that it was impressive enough to become a story."

"It wasn't that impressive," Daniel grumbled.

There was a limit how far Lance would go for a joke, and that line was drawn at making Daniel uncomfortable.

"Nous avons ennuis," Lance said with words unfamiliar to everyone except Daniel. He came to a perfect stop on the beaten path they had been traveling. There, in the shadows, he could see someone shifting their position. It was black on black, but he could just barely make out the shape. Daniel and Lance spread out, widening their group for a better defensive stance. They didn't make it much farther before more questionable men walked onto the street, no longer caring if they were hidden.

By Daniel's count there was now someone at each cross street, plus the original man that spotted them further back. Joseph started backpedaling, glanced over his shoulder, and looked for an escape. Lance caught the man by the tunic and tugged him back into the center of the group.

"I don't think he wants to stay with you," replied what the boys assumed to be a mercenary.

"People tend to run off once they see your face," Daniel taunted.

"It took all my willpower not to run away myself," Lance added.

The man smiled, but the hard-set look in his eyes showed he was not amused. "Hand him over, and we can go our own way."

Amilia unsheathed her sword, extending it in front of her just as Daniel and Lance had done. She heard someone clear their throat, like they were trying to cover a chuckle. Her eyes moved toward the sound. When her eyes locked on the man, she went pale. A fight broke out before any more words could be thrown about.

The thieves held them off with parries and evasive maneuvers, which caused the mercenaries to get tangled up in each other's movements. All Daniel had to do was wait for them to eagerly jump out of the formation that would have otherwise protected them. Lance had positioned himself in front of Joseph, but, during the fray, ended up back to back with Daniel, both itching to strike in opposite directions.

As Daniel looked around the battlefield, their foes had all fled. Amilia was standing guard over Joseph, who had crouched behind barrels, just barely visible from Daniel's angle. She seemed focused on where their enemies had retreated to.

"I know we are good at this, but I've never seen mercs run away before," Lance said, refusing to let his guard down just yet.

"Something isn't right here." Daniel nearly spun around as he assessed the pieces on the board. The ones weighing the heaviest on him were Amilia and Joseph. He had taken a stray punch, but the both of them looked otherwise fine.

"I think it's her," Lance said. He lifted his sword towards Amilia, but their distance made the gesture unthreatening.

The comment went ignored as Daniel walked over to Joseph, who was too scared to run away now.

"Do you want to chase them, or get him someplace safe?" The question was pointless to ask. The logical answer of completing the mission was clear.

"If you'd only use your head, instead of—"

"Enough," Daniel said, harshly enough that Joseph took a step away.

Lance glared Daniel's way for a second before tilting his wrist to lower the sword. Joseph was left feverishly confused if he should follow Lance or not as he continued on down the street. In the end, he cast his lot in with Lance.

"This was a bad idea," Amilia said. During the fight she had only grown paler to the point that it looked like her stomach might betray her. "I shouldn't have come."

Daniel's arms were loose at his sides, wavering for a second as if he might shrug off her comment too. In the end, his hands ended up on his hips. "Don't tell me that wild heart of yours ends at swordplay."

"It's not that." She flinched slightly. It must have been something other than the sight of blood since her eyes were unfocused on any spot in front of her. When she worked up the courage to look up she nervously chewed on her bottom lip. "Are you sure about this?"

"No." Amilia's quick frown was so exaggerated that it made Daniel smile. "I merely meant, the mission isn't a bust so we should finish it before it no longer matters either way." He held out a hand to help get her moving again.

Tentatively, she took it. The small bashfulness that found her added color to her face once again. Daniel allowed her to take the lead in catching up with the others, not wanting to lose any of his party.

"You have great trust in your friends," Joseph said, once they had caught up. "It's an admirable trait."

Owen could now see the marker that indicated the drop off point, a green floating diamond only he could see. "Trust has to begin somewhere." But that wasn't fully it. He simply wanted to believe in people.

36

Off the cuff, Owen found himself dialing Andreah's number on Friday night. He had some idea of where to take her, just needed to make sure she was up for it.

"Hello?"

"Hey, it's Owen." He stared at a fan that slowly turned above his bed as he laid back. He had been home a while before deciding it was time to finally get that date.

"Wow. Hi there." She sounded genuinely surprised, which made Owen lean up onto one elbow in uncertainty.

"What is it?"

"The only person who ever actually calls me is my landlord, and my mom. How old are you? I'm really not looking for another old dude again. Always so controlling." He could hear the grin in her voice. Her tendency to mess with him never let up, it seemed.

"Are there perks to dating old dudes otherwise?"

"Well," she trailed for a moment, clearing her throat. "There are some."

Owen paused for a good moment, assessing what had just happened with a purse of his lips. Not something he

37

wanted to talk about just before officiating their date. "So, are you busy tonight?"

"Mmm, nope. Just opened up my order of Chinese, though."

"Well, good. You'll have some extra energy to burn."

"Oh?" Her voice was ringing with a smile again, and Owen knew exactly what went through her mind at that moment.

He could feel the redness traveling up his neck. "There's this alternative fitness center in Brooklyn. Would you want to meet me there?"

"Isn't that like a gymnastics center?"

"In a sense, yeah." He fidgeted with the comforter on his bed, and wondered if it was a good idea at all. She counted as the athletic type, right? It shouldn't be that bad.

She let out a small hum, and he could hear her fork pushing around on the plate he imagined in front of her. It was interesting trying to place her somewhere personal. Apart from the chaos of New York and settled in an apartment somewhere, probably with a rescue cat. He could imagine her with a cat.

"Sure. What time?"

He pulled his phone back to check the time quickly. "How about eight? The place is open till midnight, so we'd have plenty of time."

"Sounds good. I'll see you then."

"See you soon," Owen said before they hung up.

The gym wasn't really that far from where he lived. Walkable even, if he wanted to cross the Brooklyn Bridge. But being late to a first date, or whatever this was, wouldn't be a good idea, so he got ready and opted for a cab.

Owen waited outside the gym, nervously checking his phone once or twice before Andreah walked up. "Hey." She smiled briefly upon seeing him, and tucked her hands into her coat pockets. Andreah's eyes drifted over to the generic name of the place as she raised an eyebrow. "So, why did you pick here?"

"Well, you said you didn't want anywhere boring, so I thought I'd show you one of my favorite places."

Andreah shot him a cautious expression before pulling the door open and heading inside. What she expected was various kids standing in line for the pommel horse and uneven bars, but what she saw was an energetic free for all. People, mostly their age, were flipping off faux rooftops, and free running over small dividing walls that were painted to look 8-bit. There were some of the things she had expected, like an open floor for gymnastics and a foam pit, but both were used as an excuse to get more jumps in.

"Is this—?"

"Parkour?" Owen grinned. "Yeah."

She turned back to look at Owen with clear surprise.

"You can do that?" Andreah asked, gesturing, but without really looking, towards a guy who cat-leaped onto a wall before climbing up. Owen nodded.

"Hmph," she said. "Impressive for a fact checker."

The tease flickered his otherwise bright expression like a candle. "Let's see if you can do anything besides ride a bike," he said, and moved away towards the others.

"Wait." Andreah had to do a quick double step in order to keep up. "Aren't you going to show me how first?"

Owen looked over his shoulder, back towards her. "Only if you say please."

For a fraction of a second, he reviewed what he'd just said and winced. Too cocky? Too pushy? Would she read it as a joke? He had to hope it came off as intended, because stopping midstride to correct it would ruin the casual tone he was trying to set.

He jogged up to a wide wall divider that was waist high and supported himself with his hands as he swung one leg completely over and back, before the other. When it looked like he was going to repeat the move his hand placement changed and he spun around to sit facing Andreah. Collectively, it all only took a few seconds before he contently waited with his hands under his chin.

"Alright, show off." Andreah's hand was up by her mouth, but it didn't muffle her words. "Please show me."

Owen stood up and gestured with a nod for Andreah to step up there with him. She pulled herself up on the ledge that was big enough for the both of them to stand comfortably. "The most basic thing I can think of is a precision jump. Basically, it's as simple as jumping from one object to another." Owen walked over to the edge and jumped over to a divider a few feet away. "Like so."

Andreah pursed her lips as he hopped off. That didn't look so hard. She jumped and, with a wobble, made it over.

"Close," Owen said, "Your arms were in front of you as you jumped, and swung back. You aren't a rowboat. Momentum dictates forward motion."

Her sour expression suggested she either didn't picture what he was talking about or didn't like the correction. Either way, Owen shook it off with a chuckle. When he demonstrated again, he emphasized his arm movements. Tucked back, then swinging forward. "Try again."

With a tight expression on her face, Andreah angled herself to jump back to their starting point. This time it looked like she was telling herself where her arms should be. The wind up for the jump took much longer, but she was landing with less wobble now. She tried a few more times back and forth as Owen entertained himself by flipping off a nearby bar and keeping an eye on Andreah. Soon her jumps were solid and steady.

She landed and looked to Owen. "Ta da," she said in sing song.

"Top of the class."

Andreah stepped off to be level with him. "Now what?"

"Do you want to play in the foam pit?"

"Are you even an adult?"

That tease brought a smile to Owen's face as he walked off toward the pit. "Sometimes."

They climbed to the highest mock roof in the gym and looked over the sea of foam. While Andreah wouldn't ever admit it, her wide eyes made it clear that the height was getting to her. Owen moved so his toes were at the edge. He jumped off with seeming carelessness and smoothly turned over in the air so that when he landed he was cradled by the foam.

"Yeah..." Andreah said, as she looked down at him. "I'm not doing that."

Owen tilted his head back so he could look at her from the flat of his back. "Oh, come on." He rolled out of the foam pit to make room for her. Her hands fidgeted liked she was trying to think of where they should be now as well. She was still looking straight down despite the fact that Owen was now standing along the side. "Andreah, just jump."

She swallowed hard and jumped straight off. The foam cushioned her fall as she landed chest high in the pit. It took her a second to register that she was fine and another to enjoy the rush. Only then did she try to move and realize the foam had nearly swallowed her whole and didn't seem to want to let go. Andreah reached forward to pull herself towards the edge, but all her strength only gave way to an inch. She tried a new tactic of trying to kick forward, but that was even less effective.

Owen stared wide-eyed for a second himself, but his expression dissolved into a laugh. Andreah shot him a dirty look that made him choke out another chuckle as he tried to control his amusement.

"I swear to god when I get out of here I'm going to hit you." She adapted a more swimming-like motion. Better, but still wasn't close enough to grab the edge.

He crouched down as if it was all too much for him, but instead of cracking up further, he reached his hand out to help her. Andreah blinked, looking to Owen silently for a few beats of her heart before grabbing it. Owen pulled her towards him until she was back on her feet.

"I'm still going to get you back for that," Andreah nearly whispered since they were suddenly so close. The twinkle in her eyes made the comment promising.

"Won't that be fun."

Andreah let go first. Quickly becoming very aware of her hand after it slid out of Owen's. She reached up to her hair as if to check if it had turned into a static-filled mess after fighting an almost losing battle against the foam.

"Don't worry." Owen smiled. "You're still very cute. For a hardass." She drew in a breath and glanced down at his lips in a fashion that made Owen's heart stutter for a second.

Andreah stepped around him, and he turned to watch where she was wandering off. She didn't go far, since it was too easy to get caught up watching everyone as they ran around with almost inhumanly fluid movements.

She exhaled sharply as a guy ran towards a wall, and instead of climbing up, he flipped backwards. "Can you do that?" she asked, and glanced back at Owen.

He nodded, watching someone that looked like one of his friends do a similar flip that used the corner fully instead of just one wall. "Yeah, it's one of the first things I learned."

"Why?"

He tilted his head at the question. The tone was hard to place. It wasn't the easiest trick, but it didn't sound like she was being insincere. "I thought it was cool."

This time when Andreah looked back, there was a clear smile there. "Could you teach me?"

"Can you do a backflip?" Owen made a face that caused lines to crinkle around his eyes.

"No."

Owen took a few steps closer, leaning in as he passed her. "Maybe later."

There was more there. Andreah could tell he was holding some sort of joke back. He might not have been comfortable enough to say it, but she could almost feel the mischief radiating off of him.

As if to prove his word, Owen moved towards the wall, waving a hello to someone as he waited for others to clear. He ran towards the wall, one step started up the wall and the next reached higher than his head giving him the power to gracefully jump off. Before doing another standing backflip for good measure.

"Stop being a tease, show-off."

"I live to impress."

Andreah laughed, and placed a hand on her hip. "Liar." She didn't peg Owen for the type that lived off other's admiration. If anything she figured she could write him off this very second, and he'd merely raise a brow before heading to hang with whoever he greeted moments before. It seemed like an inextinguishable confidence.

"You know what they say..."

"Takes one to know one?"

Owen hummed an agreement. He glanced around, looking for something, and caused Andreah do the same as she was at a loss for what he was looking for. "Are you hungry?" he asked suddenly.

"I could eat."

"Awesome. I really want a smoothie from next door."

"You are pretty ridiculous," Andreah said, tucking her hands back in her pockets, and prepared for the cold wind again.

Owen paused for a second, before rolling his eyes. "Liar."

"Maybe."

If Owen wanted to avoid getting on the news again, skipping the arena would be best. It was overhyped, and far too removed from his normal world. But the place did have one person he fully respected; Sal. He hadn't figured out who in the world played the barge of a man, but hadn't tried to out him, since so few arena players didn't freely give their name.

"Ah, Daniel, it's been too long!" Sal said, his voice booming cheerfully. "What brings you by?" He stood with his arms crossed, making his square shoulders seem even more so.

"I wanted to see how much fight this one has in her." Daniel gestured over his shoulder to Amilia, who had been silently trailing behind like a shadow. She didn't venture forward at her name, too absorbed by where she was.

If historical minimalism was possible, a screencap of the arena is what would appear in textbooks as the example. Unlike Daniel's usual hunting grounds, details were smoothed over to handle the influx of people. It was hardly missed since it wasn't what most of these players looked for, but Amilia seemed to. While her eyes carefully looked around, Daniel watched her with enough curiosity as if seeing an eclipse.

Sal cleared his throat before speaking. "Sure thing," he chuckled, before speaking directly to Amilia. "It would be a pleasure to set that up for you." He bowed his head, remaining taller than her even then, before he left to arrange the matches.

"He's going to put you up against people who'll get progressively harder as you learn," Daniel explained, as he started after Sal. "Remember your greatest asset against them is being light on your feet."

Amilia swallowed hard, then nodded. "I'm ready."

The short hallway opened up to a new area with a sparring ring at its heart. The first adversary stood waiting, his idle stance looping quickly since his whole existence was that of a punching bag that could throw one back.

Sal was standing in the corner, conversing casually with someone, but found himself curious of Daniel's experiment. The man in the ring cracked his knuckles, a smirk grew on his face as Amilia stepped in.

Daniel leaned into the railing. "He's not talkative, but he'll go straight for your jaw if given the chance."

Amilia shied to look back at Daniel. Her face puckered up, but when she couldn't find any real reply for the warning, she turned back, trying to wash away any emotions that would get in the way. Her hands balled into fists as she raised them. "Ready," she whispered to herself this time.

If there was meant to be a bell, she didn't wait for one. She jolted forward to strike first. The jab was quick, but he dodged sideways and took the opportunity to throw a punch at her torso. The rush of air he forced out caused Amilia to stumble away to regain her breath.

The man stood back, grinning like he had a remark, but didn't venture saying it. Amilia's hand twitched towards her ribs, but she willed herself not to baby them. Her ego wouldn't stand going down after the first hit.

She straightened up soon enough, and turned to fight. This time waiting for a punch to be thrown at her. After a shuffle of feet and a tease of a jab, she learned to read his movements better. A punch came at her face, but she knew exactly what she had to do to avoid getting hit. Amilia spun, and kicked him square in the chest. He stumbled a step, but regained his posture automatically.

Adrenaline seeped into her veins. Her thoughts sped up and her focus solidified. Another punch came, but she stepped out of his range. Amilia moved close again to land a kick to his stomach. He reflexively grabbed his sides, and once she thought his guard was down, Amilia swung for his head.

The man caught it, and pulled her off balance enough that she spilled onto the ground. He kicked down at her, but she blocked it with her forearms. Effective, but the grimace on her face suggested it still hurt a lot.

Not having much choice, she waited for the perfect moment. He recoiled, and she kicked with her whole body at his knee. It collapsed, and he awkwardly crumbled. She bounced up to her feet, expecting him to do the same.

Instead, he groaned and held a hand up to quit. Amilia stared down, with her fists ready as if she didn't believe.

"That's my girl!" Daniel called, giving her a start. Amilia looked over, the surprise dissolving into pure excitement. "Keep it up."

Amilia nodded and turned back. She blinked at the empty spot before catching the movement of another man stepping into the ring. His movements were organic enough to be real. She wiped at the dirt on her face, then returned to a fighting stance.

This man didn't look much different than the first, so it took a second for Amilia to realize it had been the person that Sal had been talking to before. There were enough muscles lining his arms to suggest that all he did was punch things all day.

He moved towards her, closing in for his first attack. Amilia kept Daniel's advice in mind. Being light on her feet was key. More time than she would have liked was spent dodging, but she jumped at the first chance to knee him in the nose when he stumbled too close.

It wasn't a knockout, but it sure looked like one for a second. Annoyed, the man came back with force. He returned a kick that left her breathless. Without time to recover, the man reached for her hair. He pulled her towards him and Amilia bit back a cry.

His free hand moved to grab her by the neck. The grin made him look more sinister than the others. Amilia stared at him, helpless for a moment, before an idea came. She tucked her chin down and managed to bite.

Reflexively, he dropped her before landing a strong fist against her jaw. Amilia stared down as the small stones that made up the ground blurred. The brute looked Daniel squarely in the eyes. "Your bitch bites!"

"Quit your yelping, runt." The muscles in Daniel's jaw twitched after he spoke.

Amilia spit blood out of her mouth as the man traveled over to Daniel. "I'm sorry to tell you, kid, but your girl just isn't strong enough." The grin on his face dared Daniel to do something about it himself. The vulgarity stepped up a notch as Daniel cussed at him, the fact that the two weren't friends became clear to anyone around.

"She is quite a looker though." The brute ignored Amilia as she pushed herself up from the dirt. "I'd recommend you keep her in your chambers nex—"

Amilia was on his back before he could finish. He reached back trying to rip her off, but she only tightened her grip. He had no leverage. The second he stopped trying to shake her off, she wailed at his head until he dropped to his knees.

She jumped off before he could try to crush her. "This bitch will also kill," Amilia said, and spat blood at him. He wobbled, and rolled over to his back like a dying bug.

Daniel had stepped into the ring, but froze when it became clear he didn't need to. Sal was staring wide eyed. While it wasn't unusual for players to join in, normally they showed better manners to fellow fighters. Amilia continued to glare, as if she missed all the details around her besides the man she just took down.

The first person in the ring to move again was Daniel. He walked past Amilia to the man who was slowly blinking up at the ceiling waiting for his stamina to return. Other bystanders had gathered, and Daniel glanced them over before crouching down. "See what lack of respect got you," he whispered. "You look pretty foolish now."

Sal gestured to a few of his men to clear the ring of the trash. Two men came over, helping the guy up and escorting him outside. "Impressive," Sal said seconds later, but it was unclear if he was talking to Daniel or Amilia.

"Clear out," Sal called. Some of the remaining crowd grumbled, citing that arena matches were open to the public.

"This is my gym," Sal roared. "Leave or I'll ban you."

Daniel was too focused on Amilia to care what whiny PvPers wanted. "Are you okay?" Daniel asked. She nodded. Unconvinced, Daniel's eyes narrowed as he looked over her again. Not able to find anything wrong, he tucked a tuft of hair behind her ear. "Good." Daniel smiled softly before his hand dropped to his side. "I'm sorry about all of that. Sometimes...sometimes people are horrible."

"You did pretty well today, all the same. What have you been feeding her, Daniel?" Sal asked.

"She is like a flower," Daniel said, "I simply turn her in the direction of the sun and she grows on her own."

"The name was Amilia, correct, *señorita?*"

She nodded. "*Sí*, Le'Russo," she said, holding out her hand for a more formal greeting.

Sal lifted her hand and gave it a small kiss. "It was a pleasure meeting a...a friend of Daniel's."

"Could I borrow the room?" Daniel asked.

"Certainly. Just don't kill each other, all right?" Sal winked before leaving.

"You have one last person to fight today." Daniel started to peel off his armor and weapons.

Amilia stood there, dumbfounded for a moment, not following until he stood there in front of her in a loose white shirt. "What—you? No!" That snapped her back into the real world. "Daniel, I don't think I can hit you."

"That's sweet of you." Daniel couldn't help but feel like he was flirting with her. Even if the idea seemed crude in this setting with insults being thrown around. "Maybe I should have done this in the first place. If we are going to be fighting together, I need to know how you fight. That...comfort with each other is why you called Lance and I ghosts."

Amilia's arms were crossed over her chest, still not wanting to give this round a go.

"Come on, that is a horrible stance." Daniel added, "Fight me or I can become all sorts of bratty. I'd prefer to stay my charming self."

She smiled a little, and took a real stance before Daniel reached out and reposed her arms. "You sure this isn't payback for the other night?" she ventured. He looked amused, but kept a loose stance completely unlike hers, and the other men she fought today.

Amilia threw out a jab, and he dodged. Her kick landed against his forearm, and might have hurt if she hadn't been trying to get this over with. Daniel had the dexterity to grab her leg and knocked her off balance as he pushed her back. "Am I not worth the effort you gave to the others?" Daniel asked.

He was about to continue taunting her when the fire in her belly seemed to reignite. Amilia kicked again, which seemed to be her attack of choice. It landed, sending a spike a pain along his side.

"Make sure to use what is around to your advantage," he said. Daniel delivered a powerful kick of his own to her chest, forcing Amilia to stumble back into the railing that encased the ring. She barely caught herself.

He backed up, giving her space and time to come back to him. She tried another round kick, but he was always a second ahead of her. "In the practice ring, you might get hits in, but out there you need to lead your attacks a bit more. I'm a moving target, you need to plan accordingly."

Daniel jumped back from a punch, and ended up directly in the path of another. This time his recoil was pure instinct as the hit tested his jaw. He winced as it complained. "Like that," he mused. "Maybe I'm too good of a teacher."

Amilia tried to spin away like a dancer, but Daniel caught her arm, pulling her back against him, twirling her with a force as sharp as a whip. He shuffled his feet between hers as he kept her close, weakening Amilia's stance. She tried to stomp on a foot so he wouldn't be able to trip her up, but his boot protected him.

He made sure she didn't fall after all, or at least not much as his arm supported her back. Amilia tensed up as she looked over her shoulder, thrown off as he steadied her instead of finishing with an attack. "Follow what I teach you, and I will always have your back," he added words that seemed too soft for the ring.

"Is that a promise?" she asked, finding a smile again.

Daniel licked his lips as if thinking about it. "It is."

Owen folded the paper that lined their food trays, creasing it one way a couple of times before shifting it around to fold it another. "Maybe Amilia gets a boost from Daniel," he said. Neal looked up from his food and across the table to Owen as he went on. "Otherwise, she should be a complete novice, right? It would be pointless to add party members if you just have to end up protecting them."

"It's cute that you think I know." Neal finished his last bite of food before crumpling up the wrapper and tossing it onto the tray.

The movement caught Owen's eye. He looked towards their shared tray like Neal had just illegally walked onto the field, but didn't cry foul. "It's not like I have anyone else to talk to about it. I haven't even told the guild about it yet."

"Why not?"

Owen shrugged. He stared down at the paper football he made and spun it around between the tips of his thumb and index finger by its corners. He wasn't sure why he hadn't told the guild. For the amount of time they collectively put in, someone was bound to know. In part, Owen just wanted to hold onto something that was just his. Telling the public, or anyone besides his close friends, would be putting it out there for the whole world to speculate on.

"What's her name again?" Neal asked, and held his fingers up against to table to make goal posts.

"Amilia Le'Russo." Owen set the paper football down on the table before flicking it. It flew in between Neal's fingers and landed in his lap.

Neal picked it up, lining up a shot of his own. "Check the Wikia." The paper landed on the seat next to Owen, who shot his friend a look as he reached for it. "Oh, come on! There are people dedicated to updating that thing."

"Like you?"

"Some people have religion, I have video game knowledge," Neal said as he gathered the trash onto the tray.

"Good to know I'll have company in hell." Owen barely had enough time to toss his own trash on the tray before Neal took the whole thing to throw away. Owen headed for the door, incidentally holding it open for a mother of two as he waited. "So, L train, or do you want to get a cab back to my place?"

"Train," Neal said, "I hate trying to get a cab in this neighborhood."

It was almost scary how safe he felt in Daniel's home. The buildings in this section of town were stone and felt as if they would withstand any siege. Despite how unlikely an attack would be, it was still his own personal fortress.

Books and papers were piled on the desk across from a fireplace that was lit year-round regardless of the weather. From by the door, where Amilia was standing, one could even see into the bedroom, though it was only a glimpse of the blue trim at the foot of the bed.

Trinket-lined shelves hemmed the room with items saved from quests. They weren't all rare or particularly valuable, but each had a story attached that had earned them their place. Daniel shifted uncomfortably on his feet as Amilia looked around his private museum.

"This is quite the collection." Amilia had been slowly edging closer and closer to them, likely without even realizing it. Before her curiosity got the best of her, she turned to Daniel. "Have you been collecting for long?"

"Little over four years."

Amilia seemed to nod a little before asking another question. "How far have you traveled?"

Daniel leaned against his desk. That was a question he hadn't expected. Siguenza was about three or four days south of the coast, and almost right in the middle of the country. Many cities like this one filled up during the day, but most lived in capital. "Uh..." He tossed his hands in the air. Unsure how detailed of a story she was looking for. Learning about her would be far more interesting than repeating his own story. "Almost everywhere around the country, I guess. Barcelona, Santiago, Madrid. Even France a number of times."

"I guess you would have to go far for such treasures."

Daniel smiled, his chest warming as if he'd accomplished something grand. "How about you? Do you travel?"

"My family moved here from Barcelona, but that's it." Amilia was looking away, towards the mask Daniel had worn before that sat amongst the collection. Maybe seeing it before gave her the courage to reach up and examine it closer. "I've heard of Santiago..." Her voice trailed off until her eyes found Daniel again. "I've wanted to go there, but I have never had the chance."

"Maybe I'll take you," Daniel said, very casual for what seemed to be a serious matter to her. "Of what I remember, it's a lovely city."

"Wait, wait, wait," Neal said, his voice interrupting the game. Owen grimaced. Despite the good intent, the outside voice was jarring. Owen was ready to almost ignore the comment when Neal went on. "She's lying."

Owen pushed the head gear off his eyes. Blinking hard at the overhead light as Neal came into focus. "How so?"

Neal spun the desk chair around, away from the screen to face Owen. "She was born in Santiago. The page says it so."

"Maybe someone typed the wrong city?"

"This isn't an edit, it's an automated listing complete with name, birthday, and city of birth. Doesn't even register her as a companion character like Lance."

"Huh..." Now he really should ask someone. Why would she lie? He wanted to call her on it, but the game kept metagaming in check and simply wouldn't allow him to. Owen repositioned the headgear and Amilia smiled over at Daniel as though he had simply spaced out for a moment.

"One day perhaps." Her expression wavered as if she didn't quite believe that day would come.

Daniel knew he had missed something. That there was more that she wasn't saying, but the questions died upon his lips as she moved closer. His hands found the desk and leaned back as Amilia's expression shifted to one that made his mouth feel dry.

"Today, you, sir, are the most curious thing in the room," Amilia said softly. "How does it feel to have two companions now?"

"I—uh." Her comment seemed out of place in the atmosphere her expression created. The desire in her eyes seemed more for information, rather than for him. "It feels...good, I guess. Just don't go asking who my favorite is."

Amilia's expression hovered for a second over his face before she reached for the desk. Daniel tilted his head and watched as her hands were placed just outside of his. Very narrowly missing a casual touch that could have meant something greater.

"You must be getting pretty popular. I'd be surprised if you weren't the talk of the guild."

"Maybe. But, I like keeping what's mine as mine."

Daniel's posture caused their eyes to end up level to each other, with their mouths at the rare, perfect height with each other if one so dared. "Oh, is that what I am?" Amilia chuckled. "I'd think the admiration of it all would be too much to conceal."

"Lance and you..." he started, but stopped short. If anything, the tension was too much. Her eyes had slipped to glance the length of his neck, and he was simply glad she couldn't register his pulse jump. Daniel picked her hand up, and wrapped his fingers around hers. "It isn't about conquests."

"No?" Amilia hummed a quick thought. "Then what?"

"Maybe you should tell me." His tone picked up a serious edge, but he didn't pull his hand away.

Amilia smiled. A small but bright gesture that suggested she knew more than he did. Something Daniel would willingly believe. After a short shared silence, she pulled out of reach. Amilia took a few steps for the door, looking back. "Glory would look good on you, but maybe we'll save that for another day."

Daniel nodded a confused agreement before she left his home. He thought about going after her to ask just what she meant, but found himself pinned in place trying to sort it out on his own.

The biggest hurdle right now was the fact that he didn't have time to find the answers he wanted. Owen pulled the headgear fully off this time, and placed it up on the table. The same confused expression was echoed here. "I think I missed something," he mumbled to himself. There had to be something more he hadn't picked up besides her place of birth.

"Yeah, a kiss scene." Neal was awkwardly tugging his shoes from a standing position. Despite advances in VR, the world changing around Owen did nothing but throw him off further. "And we are going to be late to meet up with Emily if you don't hurry up."

"What?" Owen pushed himself off the couch with gusto. "Why didn't you warn me sooner?"

"I wanted to see if you were going to get a kiss scene. What? Don't give me that look!"

Owen shrugged on his hoodie, the hood catching on the crown of his head. "Let's get a cab this time. I definitely don't want to explain to Em that we were late because you wanted to watch me almost make out with fictional women."

"Oh yeah, that's a horrible excuse."

When they got to the bar, Emily was already waiting in one of the few booths available. Her brow was knitted in a way that only an annoyed boredom seemed to cause. "Hey, sorry to keep you waiting," Owen said as he slid into the seat next to her.

"That's okay." She idly spun her phone around in her hand, the true cause of her apathy. "Online is just really dead on Friday night."

"It's not so bad here, though," Owen said. He had been glancing over Neal's shoulder as he sat in a fashion that made Neal look back as well. A man was stumbling around the pool table, leaning over to line up a horribly unlikely shot. The pool group wasn't much larger than Owen's own, but no one in Owen's group was unsuccessfully, and obnoxiously, trying to hustle his friends.

Neal snagged a fry off the plate that Em had pushed closer to his side of the table. "I don't know why you keep picking bars, though. Can I slap some sense into you if you are one of those parents who try to relive their youth by taking their baby to the bar with them?"

"Cut me some slack. I can't drink anything even slightly unhealthy. I don't have time to play anymore, because I'm either trying to baby proof the apartment or fighting off morning sickness. And being at home gets so boring. Plus, I miss you guys."

"What about the second-hand smoke on the way in?"

Emily scoffed, ready to spit out a retort.

"Geez, Neal," Owen commented first. "Cut her some slack."

"Thank you," Emily said. He gave a slight nod before laying his head down on her shoulder as a sign of support. She reached over and affectionately ruffled up his hair. "Why were you guys so late, anyways? Train delayed again?"

"Owen was trying to kiss pixel girls," Neal said matter-of-factly.

"The hell, man?" Owen sat up suddenly, and tapped against the table. "On the ride over, we thought of at least three decent excuses. Just had to go with that one?"

Neal looked like he was an inch away from sticking his tongue out but considered himself too proper for that. "I believe the words you are looking for are *Et tu, Brute?"*

"Wait, I thought you had a real girl to make out with?" Emily asked.

"I wasn't trying to make out with anyone." Owen stretched out across the table, sitting for so long made him feel stiff. "And, who? Andreah?"

"Yeah."

He shrugged the arm he wasn't leaning his head on.

"I bet she is really cute. Look her up. I want to see where this piercing is." Emily was gesturing vaguely along her cheekbone waiting for confirmation of just where exactly her piercings were.

"Oh no. We aren't talking about this." Owen shot up to his feet as if he could escape the conversation. "I'm going to get a beer before you invite us on a double date with a married couple."

Emily caught Owen's hand before he managed another step. He rolled his eyes, but glanced back at her with a smile. "Text her."

"Maybe afterward we can go to the library and pick out a girl for Neal?" he suggested with mock excitement.

"Hey—" Neal objected sharply before adding, "can we though?"

Before he got caught up in anyone's love life, fictional or otherwise, Owen headed to the bar to order. As he waited for the bartender to fill up a line of shots in logo-emblazoned glasses for a trio of girls, he did find himself thinking about a girl. But it wasn't Andreah. It was Amilia.

From day one, he wouldn't have denied that there was something about her, but tonight was different. It was almost like she knew it was a game, or maybe she was playing at something else entirely. He did like her. Maybe the game was just picking up on that.

The sound of shot glasses being slammed down, followed by the chorus of laughter, snapped him out of it. He glanced over again, feeling rather silly about everything. Come to think of it, there wasn't any reason he shouldn't text Andreah. Owen pulled out his phone and quickly checked for the bartender before sending off a text.

To Andreah:
We should hang out again.

Simple and sweet, he told himself.

"Sorry to keep you waiting," The bartender said as he finally made it over. "Usual?"

"Please." Owen shot a quick look down the counter. "Busy night?"

"Gotta love birthdays." The bartender popped the top off of a beer bottle and handed it over.

When Owen walked back over to the table, Emily and Neal were debating something.

"It will be fine," Neal insisted. Em leaned back in her seat, looking unconvinced. "Ask Owen, I'm sure he'll agree."

Owen took a sip of his beer, lost to whatever they were talking about. "What?" he asked, without any elegance.

Emily glanced over. "He wants to play pool."

"Oh! We should." When a sigh from Em followed, he chuckled. "Come on. I'll help you take the shot if you're uncomfortable taking any."

The minor encouragement was all she needed. Neal racked the balls, and after a few careful shots Emily seemed comfortable in her skin again. Owen babied his beer and watched them play. Neither of them were really that good, which actually added to the suspense when they had a two ball streak. The chime of his phone distracted him and he pulled it out to see who texted.

To Owen:
Sure maybe I can be the one to show you something this time

To Andreah:
Sounds fun

Owen looked up to find Emily staring at him with a smile on her face. His eyes narrowed slightly as he looked over to Neal, who also was smirking. "What?"

"You're grinning." Emily wiggled a finger at him, and the expression fell off his face.

Owen sighed. "What do you want?"

She held the pool cue out for him. "Help."

Owen glanced at the shot, which was a tricky one. Actually, he wasn't sure if it was just a hard shot or if Em's belly actually just got in the way of taking it. "Oh," he breathed. "Well, you should have said something."

The first shot Owen took knocked the nine ball in for Emily, and earned a cough of disgust from Neal. The 11 was resting awfully close to the pocket. He lined the shot up, but midway through, his phone rang again. The distraction proved to be enough that the cue ball bounced uselessly off a side wall.

He turned to give the stick back to Emily. Not only had she stolen his seat, but was biting back her amusement. "Not a word," Owen said, shaking his head. "Or I swear I'll swap teams."

To Owen:
Tomorrow, 5 pm at Jackson Square Bring a helmet, I can bring my spare bike for you to use if you don't have one

Owen stared at the text. Biking around didn't seem like much of a second date, but to be fair, a parkour gym hadn't been a traditional first date, either.

To Andreah:
I got one, see you then

When he looked up, he saw Em giving him a glance like she was waiting to catch another smile. He scrunched his face up ridiculously, skewing any real expression, which made her wink before looking back at the table she and Neal were making a mess of.

Owen rummaged through his closet looking for a helmet, swearing it should still be untouched in a box since moving in. Luckily, it was. His bike sat outside on the tiny balcony, tucked tightly against a chair from an long discarded patio set. The cover collected so much city grime that he coughed while pulling it off. God only knew how long it had been out here. But today, it had a new purpose thanks to Andreah. Even if he wasn't so sure of the details just yet.

Owen walked the bike out of his apartment, balancing the helmet precariously on the handlebars as he locked the door. Thankfully the elevator saved him from dragging it down four flights of stairs. Once on the street, he clicked on the helmet. It felt dreadfully clunky and he would have risked not having one at all if Andreah hadn't demanded he bring it. The insistence seemed out of character. She seemed the sort to boycott helmets completely outside of work.

He rode under half a mile to the address Andreah gave him. At the arched mouth of a park, Andreah stood with a few others who were perched on their bicycles. "Hey," Owen said, as he pulled up to them and dismounted. Andreah had on a black hoodie with thin gray stripes, her brown hair pooled into the hood that rested on her shoulders. "I don't think I've ever seen you on a bike without your cute little reflective vest."

Andreah leaned forward, one foot still outstretched to serve as a kickstand. "Brought my other bike too. Doesn't even have a dumb sign from work on it."

He hadn't even realized until she mentioned it, but she was right, it was nice in more ways than the missing advertisements. Actually, the lot of them had nice bicycles. Owen smiled, really as a means to hide his nerves as he glanced over the others with her.

"So uh, what did you want to show me?" Owen wrung his now free hands before steadying himself on the handles again. His guess of them riding around in Jackson Park, while cute in an old retired person way, now seemed weird with two other guys joining them.

"Have you heard of alleycat races?" asked one of her friends who sported an undercut.

Owen shook his head, glancing to Andreah for help. The fact that he didn't even know the names of her friends made him nervous. Any second he felt like they'd comment that his Walmart bike wasn't good enough to ride with them.

"We race around, passing various checkpoints and using, or doing, anything we can to get there faster," she said. Owen gave a half nod, not fully getting it still. "It's like parkour, except on a bike, and instead of flips you break traffic laws."

"Alright." Owen grinned. "I'm game."

"Yeah?" asked her other friend. He had strayed a little from the group doing small hops as he rode a few feet and back.

"Totally."

Andreah's piercings caught the last of the evening sunlight as she smiled with pride in her choice to invite him. "The first checkpoint is Madison Square Park. You have to reach there before you can finish at Manhattan Mall. Skipping the checkpoint is a no-no."

Owen nodded along as his eyes drifted to see who all was participating. There was more than just the four of them. This was far more organized than the random outing he expected.

"Don't worry," Andreah interjected, causing Owen's attention to snap back to her. "This is all for fun. And you're not the only newbie, so you probably won't come in dead last." She winked.

"Least you don't have any foam pits to get stuck in this time."

Andreah let out something reminiscent of a giggle. It sounded so out of place coming from her. Owen grinned back, enjoying a small slice of the night that was just theirs before the racers joined in around the starting line.

Everyone had to place their bikes against the fence before entering the gate. The race would start off inside and they'd have to sprint back to their bikes. Procedure he guessed, since lining up in the middle of the road wasn't going to happen. Manhattan was never empty. When the whistle was blown, Andreah jogged backwards for a second making sure Owen followed before feeling confident enough to bolt along with everyone else to her own bike.

From his bike, Owen searched for where Andreah was, but he didn't spot her. So he rode with the crowd for most of the way. 8th Ave was the major route everyone took, using the bike lanes between the two parks. He rounded the corner at 23rd to take the straight shot to Madison Square. Something from DOT's Don't Be A Jerk campaign must have stuck, since he made sure to be extra careful of each pedestrian, even if it was adding extra seconds onto his time. He wiggled his way past any mishaps, making it far enough to get a stamp as he stopped at the first checkpoint.

Strangers started pedaling towards Broadway, but before he rejoined them a bike sharply cut him off. Andreah appeared as everyone else pushed on past, going around them like a river would around a rock.

"Nuh-uh. I'm not going to let the person I invited make a newbie mistake," she said.

"What are you talking about?" Owen wasn't sure which details he was more confused about his near "mistake" or how she showed up out of nowhere.

"That way is a minefield. You'll never make it out of there alive. Come on, follow me."

She sat up on the bike to get a strong restart as she headed towards Madison, and Owen followed. Andreah ventured a glance over her shoulder whenever she got the chance, making sure he was still there. They both wove between cars, but Owen let her lead the way, trusting her judgment would keep both of them from ending up under someone's tires.

What he hadn't judged was how close he was getting to her at some points. His front tire caught her back tire. The opposite motions caused his front tire to stutter while her's kept going. The friction acted a lot like abruptly hitting only the front brakes, and ruined the once smooth ride. The crash into the pavement was shit, but thankfully they had cut over to what counted as the shoulder so he didn't have to worry about any oncoming cars. He tucked his arms in to protect them from serious damage. The skid scratched exposed skin and left his shoulder tight and sore.

"Fuck," Andreah called over her shoulder before hitting her brakes. He was sitting up by time she jogged back to him. "Are you okay?"

"Yeah." Owen winced as he tested his shoulder. "I see the purpose of the helmet now. Just wish I knew what to look out for."

"I'm sorry, I should have made sure you weren't too tight on my tail." Andreah knelt down to help him, mentally checking off injures he had or didn't have. Her careful expression made him wonder if she had seen this a number of times before.

Owen couldn't help but laugh it off. "It's okay, I'm fine. Maybe I was just distracted by the view."

A cab honked before swerving around them, and Owen realized his bike was still sticking out into traffic. He hooked the tire with his foot and dragged it back.

"Come on, you nerd. Get up." Andreah smirked softly before bonking him softly on the helmet. "Does your shoulder hurt?"

"It's not bad."

"Well good." Andreah smiled to herself like her next comment already pleased her before she even said it. "I can help with that later, if you want."

Lacing almost anything with an innuendo seemed to be her hidden talent, making Owen glance away sheepishly like he had been the bold one. "Shouldn't we keep going?"

"Eh, I was thinking we could skip to the after-party early instead."

"After-party? Instead of finishing?"

"Yeah, nothing too big. It's just at a bar on 34th. And it doesn't matter. This is more about fun and donations than who wins." She gave him a gentle tap on the arm before going back to retrieve her bike.

Owen moved to lift his bike from the ground and walked it towards her. "Lead the way, then."

Andreah smiled and tossed her leg over her bike. The good thing was that now barely anyone would be on their route, so the gaps in traffic wouldn't be filled with an influx of racers.

Once at the bar, they chained their bikes together around a No Parking sign outside and headed in. Owen recognized one person from the start of the race, making it clear they weren't the only deserters. The bar was a relative hole in the wall, but a warm and friendly atmosphere keep it alive. On the blackboard was a list of bike-inspired cocktails, giving the place up as a frequent hangout for cyclists.

Andreah turned on her heel to face him abruptly. "Whatchya want? I'll treat first round," she asked, stripping off her jacket.

Owen caught the hint of more piercings, barely peeking out from under the strap of her tank top along her collarbone. For just a moment, his mind wandered to what else she had hidden. "Just a beer, thanks," he said a beat off and looked up at her face again.

A flirty smile shined through before she trotted off to the bartender. He watched her pull her hair free, the bleached golden ends dancing along her shoulders, before glancing around the room. More people came in that looked like her crowd, even though not all looked like participants in the race. He pulled out his phone to check if anyone had sent him anything interesting, and by the time Andreah came back with drinks she had a friend in tow.

"Owen, this is Drew. Drew, Owen," she said before handing off the beer bottle to Owen with a small clink against the neck of hers. Owen lit up simply because he had finally caught a name. Drew had dark, rich features with neat, skinny dreads pulled back into a lazy bun that suggested he'd been hanging out here for a while.

Drew offered to shake, which Owen quickly did once he switched his drink over to the other hand. "I heard you took a bit of a scuff."

"Ah, yeah. Beginner's mistake, I guess?" Owen turned his left hand over enough to look at the small gash on his hand. He couldn't see it all, because doing so would risk spilling his drink. "Let's just say I'm better on my feet."

"To be fair, I kind of didn't tell him it was a race," Andreah said, "So at least he didn't start pedaling the opposite direction when I told him."

"So you were testing him on how he'd handle your frequent lack of details?" Drew smiled.

Andreah shrugged, and checked her phone. It was close enough to the truth, so why fight it? Plus, she was having a bigger battle clearing the low battery messages that popped up every time she did anything. "I wish this thing didn't have such a shit lifespan," she grumbled to herself.

Drew ignored the comment for the sake of conversation. "So, what do you do, Owen?"

"I work at NYC Today. Well, I intern as a research specialist. I hope to do investigative reporting someday. Or maybe report on specialized media, like video games, since that's ever so popular lately."

Drew nodded. "I remember a TV station when I was growing up shutting down because no one was watching shows about video games when they could just play them. But here we are. The new American pastime. I'm assuming you're big into games?"

"Age of Shadows, mostly," Owen shrugged.

Drew glanced over at Andreah. "Isn't that the game you had me—?"

"Drew's a total computer nerd," Andreah interrupted. "But he says he has no time to actually play games."

Owen nodded before taking a sip of his beer. "What do you do with computers?"

"I'm a developer at a software company. Coding isn't too exciting for the average person, but it pays the bills well enough."

A girl who was in the middle of unwrapping her scarf approached the group, bumping softly into Andreah with a friendly grin as she curled her arm around Andreah's hips. "Hey there, cutie."

"Hey," Andreah said, with a smile that reached towards her ears. Her eyes lit up with a new joy at the arrival of this fair and petite girl. The genuine interaction between the two suggested they were family, maybe sisters, even, despite them not looking the part. "Owen, this is Abigail." She gestured between the two of them with the mouth of her beer.

"Pleasure to finally make your acquaintance, Owen," Abigail said with delight, but still kept snugly next to Andreah. "It's so damn cold outside."

She tried to neatly keep her scarf tucked into her arm but it wasn't cooperating.

"Calm down, Ms. Florida. It's like, fifty."

"It feels like it's freezing!" She bounced on her feet for a moment before Andreah rubbed her back, a slight attempt at warming her friend. "Hey Drew," Abigail said, as if she had just noticed he was there. "You agree with me, right?"

Drew went rigid suddenly, like the cold outside had crept up his neck and made him uncomfortable. "Sort of," he said, "Uh, I'm gonna go get another beer, be right back."

The fact that Drew's current beer was still half-full didn't go unnoticed as the group exchanged looks.

Once he was out of earshot, Andreah slowly released Abigail before giving her a sigh. "He's going to act like that till you let him take you out." She glanced over at Owen, hoping that he'd excuse the hiccup.

"Yeah, yeah, but he needs to stop acting like we're twelve. It's like he's scared of me."

"Abby, he probably is. You're a tornado of energy."

Abigail shrugged lightly. "What about you, Owen? Were you scared of Andreah with the whole..." She stopped to gesture over her friend like she was the subject of a "Real Life Aliens" documentary. Andreah punched her arm lightly, smiling despite however annoying Abby was being.

"Uh," Owen stalled, trying to quickly catch himself up after tuning out at what seemed to be a personal conversation. "Not really? But, that might say more about me than her."

Andreah smiled, wanting to make a comment about his possible poor judgment, but refrained. "Didn't you say you wanted to call Jerry? About a source for your story or something?" she asked Abby, looking for an excuse to be alone again.

"Oh shit, yeah. I need to get that for tomorrow's meeting," Abigail said, and stuffed her scarf into her jacket pocket before extending her hand to Owen. "It's nice to finally meet you."

"You too," Owen said, grabbing her hand for a light shake. Wait, finally? He realized that was the second time she said that. Andreah hadn't spoken about any of her friends while on their first date. The most he'd gotten out of her then was where she was from and where she liked to order pizza. He watched Abigail break off from their group, leaving them alone again. "So, how do you know those two?"

"Drew is a buddy I made through Keith, the race organizer. Abigail and I go back a long ways." She glanced over at Owen and fell silent for a moment. "What about you? Any friends?"

"Do I have any friends?" he repeated with a laugh. "Most days?"

Andreah stuck out her tongue. "Do you want another?" she said, swishing her mostly empty beer in the air. "Or, we could go...somewhere not here."

Owen tried to make a face that was both coy and friendly. "We just got here."

"Well, I don't like staying in one place for too long."

With the cock of his head, he set his drink down and they headed for the door. He spotted their bikes still locked up, and glanced towards Andreah. "Maybe I should lead the way, it seems dangerous when you do."

The ride over was fast, and wasn't until the elevator ride up to Owen's place that he started feeling twitchy about inviting her over. Andreah decided to leave her bike locked up on the street as Owen wordlessly brought his upstairs. His hand tightened around the handrails, hoping the unease in his stomach would go away.

Owen and Andreah shuffled into his one bedroom apartment. She took a few full strides into his small living room as he slid his bike up against the first clear bit of wall he found. Owen dropped his keys on a fiberboard side table near the door before flipping the switch. Andreah hadn't ventured too far when the evening was flooded with light. He was about to shrug off his jacket when she walked towards him, leaving him breathless as he stared at her in this new setting.

Andreah's hand looked like it might move to touch him, but instead it fell on the light switch. Her deep brown eyes traced over his face for just a moment before she turned the lights back off.

He made out the smile she had as her hands grasped at the front zipper of his jacket. Her breath was steady. She wasn't at all nervous. Owen, on the other hand, was wondering what led up to this exact moment. Andreah's lips found his before he figured it out and he pulled her closer. He had admired her lips from time to time; the pucker they created before she'd smile, the damage she caused to them when she was nervous at the gym. He could even picture the shade of lipstick under the dim bar lights. Having her lips against his was far better than the passing thought earlier that night.

Andreah's hands moved up to his collar, pushing the jacket apart, encouraging him to take it off. While she helped, Owen felt a tight pain pull at his arm and caused him to twist back and wince. Andreah instantly stopped moving her hands, the whites of her eyes catching the dim light in the room as she looked up at him. "Does that still hurt?"

"Forget about it."

"Let me help. It'll feel a lot better."

"It's fine," he whispered, leaning forward to find her lips again.

She chuckled under her breath and dodged his kiss. "I'll give you a massage. Even dead-fucking-last deserves a prize." Owen let out a breath as he pulled off the jacket. "The bedroom would probably be better," Andreah continued. "Also, shirt off."

"So demanding. Would you like some oils? Or I can go get some stones from outside and we can heat those up." Owen joked, and adjusted his steps to head to the bedroom now.

"Shush."

He took off his shirt, and noticed the hint of a smile on Andreah's face as she looked him over before bouncing onto his bed and tapping on the open space. He had expected Andreah to inspect his room. Comment on his taste in design and cleaning habits, or silently judge his movie collection. Instead he held her sole focus, a feeling that was far more intoxicating than anything they might have had in the bar.

He expected her to sit on the bed and move around back to work at his shoulder from the side, but instead she wiggled her finger around. Without a word, Owen tried to figure out what she wanted. Slowly he pulled himself further on the bed and rolled onto his stomach.

Laying like this still allowed Andreah to sit next to him, but instead she straddled across his lower back and ran her hands over his shoulder, gently kneading into it.

He melted at the pleasure, despite the rare half second twinge of pain as her hands rolled over a sore muscle.

"How are you so comfortable with anything?" He shifted his head up from against the pillows in an effort to look back at her.

"I'm not always. But it's no secret now that we're attracted to each other, and I enjoy giving massages. Are you not enjoying it?" Owen sighed with contentment as she put pressure under his shoulder blades. "I don't like wasting time. But if that makes you uncomfortable—"

"No," he breathed out sharply. "I'm fine. It's just, weird."

"Thanks," She chuckled and re-focused on giving a massage. The activities of the day made him feel worn out and he closed his eyes as it all caught up to him. "Owen?"

"Hm?"

"What is *that?*"

From the corner of his eye he could see she was pointing at something, but couldn't tell what. He started to roll over, and Andreah moved onto the bed not to impede him. He chuckled, and flipped over to his back. On the wall in front of the bed was a series of hexagonal mirrors arranged to make a creature with eyes where two mirrors weren't placed. "A Space Invader."

"Yeah, but why is it there?" Andreah said, and stared at the fellow.

Owen's brow pulled tight. His bathroom was annoyingly small for anything, and thus, he had ended up with a mirrored Space Invader hanging out in his bedroom. But he decided not to explain that. "Where should it be? The ceiling?"

She didn't say anything else and Owen couldn't tell what she was focusing on. "Andreah," he said, forcing her gaze back to him. "You see, at Ikea. There is this package of mirrors." Owen placed a hand over hers. "You can make all sorts of things with them." He lifted a hand to tilt her chin up towards his mouth. "Beehives, abstract shapes, checkered patterns." The words were meaningless, Owen glanced down at her lips, forgetting their use, or forgetting that words came from them as he kissed her again.

The first was tender, like slowly dipping your toe into a pool of water. It built like a tide until he wanted Andreah to crash down against him again. When she didn't lean into his pull, his hands fell free. He searched for words to bridge the gap again, the effort clear on his face. "Maybe you should tell me what we are doing."

Andreah's mouth slacked as if she was going to say something, but then locked whatever the comment was away. She got up from the bed, and smoothed her shirt out. Which had been untouched, despite the direction things had been heading. "I'm going to go home."

Owen didn't object, he just stared trying to understand.

"Maybe next time, Romeo."

He smiled. At least that sounded more like her. Andreah got up, and Owen followed her out to the living room. She made quick work for the door, but Owen placed his hand on it first. "Does this mean it's my turn to get you into trouble again?" Owen could have played this off as nothing, but if she wanted to leave, he'd at very least let her know she was wanted.

Her quick solemn mood brightened a bit. "Maybe nothing that involves falling this time," Andreah said. "For either of us."

"Nix the bikes and foam pits." Owen pulled away from the door with a grin. "Noted. I'll try to think of something good."

"I'm sure you will." Andreah opened the door and paused. She looked from the hall, to the floor, then back to him as if she wanted to steal a kiss before she left.

Owen smiled, but didn't push. She was telegraphing a bashfulness that just wasn't usually her. "I'll see you later."

///////

LOADING...CHAPTER TEN

A long day at work and other random oddities were tugging at the back of Owen's mind, which made it all the more relaxing when he could slip into the game. No need to think beyond the world provided for him.

Unfortunately, this world wasn't problem-free either. Lance's suspicions about Amilia rattled around his head like a catchy tune no one liked. The need for answers gnawed at him like a dull hunger. He could ask the guild, but Amilia was an oddity, not their goal. Simply a distraction standing in front of their real objectives.

When he finally had free time from guild duties, he had no idea what do with himself. Daniel walked around town half hoping something would grab his attention. He smiled politely as he passed a group of women outside a brothel who fluttered small fans around and over their faces.

"Daniel, my love," a woman called as she folded up her fan to reveal her face. Her long soft orange hair was pinned up in large curls. She had a strong nose that made all her expressions look harsher when she so chose.

"Lily!" A smile the day had stolen from him returned as he spoke. "Isn't it past your bedtime?"

"Maybe you should take me there."

72

Simple as that, he did. Lily was sitting on the end of Daniel's bed playing with the random trinkets that he had. Daniel was leaning against the headboard reading, while Lily went on about something that he wasn't paying attention too. They had a strange sort of friendship that, if asked, would simply have been described as looking out for each other. While also NPC, Lily was different from Amilia, and more importantly, the exact sort of company he wanted right now.

"I always love coming over. You have the best things to play with."

"Mm," Daniel said, hardly paying attention.

Lily made a quick pout before she crawled over to Daniel, and stopped as she loomed over the book.

He glanced up. "What can I do for you, dear?"

Instead of using words, she leaned in and answered with a kiss. Lily moved to kiss down the side of his neck. Daniel put up a silent show as he tried to focus on the book, but was only able to read a few more words before he closed his eyes to enjoy the moment.

She pulled at Daniel's shirt, but he suddenly caught her hand in his to stop her. His was the sort that suggested nothing innocent. Lily didn't back down. It was a look she'd seen a number of times, and every time it caused her to bite her lip in anticipation.

His mind blissfully went elsewhere for a while making it hard to track the time that passed. It moved in a relative way at home, and with only minor syncing, night could easily turn into morning. A hollow, echoing sound woke him and after a moment he realized where the sound had come from. Daniel sat up in the bed, swinging his feet over to the side and hoping that he didn't wake up Lily.

Halfway to the door there was another knock. However, when he opened it the person standing there was a surprise. "Amilia, uh, good morning," Daniel said. He ran his hand through his hair, and feverishly tried to remember if he forgot that they made plans.

Amilia glanced down at his bare chest, eyes flaring wide before she forced herself to look back up. "I guess I was wrong about you being a morning person," she joked. The lack of invite in caused her to fidget with her nails. "I was thinking we could perhaps pick out a weapon for me today," she suggested weakly and glanced back toward the street. "Should I come back later? Pardon my rudeness for waking you."

"Uh, actually—"

There was a hum from the room behind Daniel. The soft floaty sound silenced the rest of his comment. Amilia's mouth fell open and let out a small sound. "Oh."

Daniel scrunched up his face as he debated if an explanation was needed. "You can come in if you wish," he stalled, and stepped away from the door. The tips of his ears felt hot. Normally this situation wouldn't have caught him off guard, but the innocent surprise on her face triggered a bashfulness he hadn't felt about such things in years.

The expression was shaken off as she shook her head. "It's fine. I can just go on my—I'm sorry. I should just leave," she said with a nervous laughter.

If he had called out for her to wait, she was moving with such focus that she wouldn't have heard it. The goal was to move as fast as she could to put space between them. Even storming past a few shops before she realized how far she had gotten.

With a grimace she settled and was left with a sour taste in her mouth despite smelling the bakery nearby. Amilia pushed on towards the blacksmith's, who gave her curious and downright strange looks as she eyed their goods.

"You know I'm a trained tracker, right?" Daniel said. Amilia jumped, and spun to see Daniel dressed and a few feet away.

"Did you have to give me a start, though?" Amilia objected.

He shrugged. "Leave a girl with money and where does she end up?" His intent had been to joke around, but when Amilia's eyes fell to the floor, he frowned. "I'm sorry. I didn't mean..." He sighed. "You wanted help with weaponry?"

Amilia bit her lip, completely different than what he had seen just recently. This time full of worry and uncertainty. It made Daniel want to kick himself for being the cause of it. "Yes, please."

Daniel gestured for her to go first, moving away from men sweating by fires to fix cracked armor. They walked in silence towards shops that sold already completed weapons.

"Did I—um..," Daniel started, but now that he had opened his mouth he was unsure if he wanted to finish the thought. "Embarrass you this morning?"

Amilia turned back to him, and this time she was able to look him in the eye. While some nervousness subsided, she still seemed unsure as she tucked her hair behind one ear. "It was awkward. I don't know I'd go as far as to say I was truly uncomfortable. I guess I was more concerned with embarrassing your...girlfriend?" She paused and shook her head. "Either way, it didn't really matter."

"Friend," Daniel corrected before he realized what he was doing. He had to stop this. Stop the enjoyment; stop the endearment that was starting to sprout. It wasn't like she was going to swoon over him not being taken.

Daniel decided to play the whole thing off, for his own sanity if nothing else. "If I didn't know better," he said, leaning close to look over daggers, axes, and swords. "I would have guessed you were jealous." Despite his tease, he didn't wait to see if a nerve was hit. Instead, focusing on the fine wares in this part of the market, items that were forged in blood, sweat, and tears. Rather fitting considering their use.

"Well, it's a good thing you know better, then," she said after a moment.

Daniel looked up from a collection of daggers that lined a vendor's table. This time he ignored their banter altogether. "A lighter weapon would be good for you, something with a lot of reach," he said. He wandered a little, trying to find one that would be right for her. He could afford the best they had to offer, but nothing at this table was catching his eye.

In the back, bows were lined up in a careful row. He reached out to pick up one carved from redwood. Steel extended up and off at the ends at a sharp point, becoming a weapon of its own. It seemed perfect for her, with use in both close range as well as at a much longer distance.

Amilia fell into place next to him. Eyes bright like a child's who longed for something they knew they couldn't have. "But I've never even handled one before."

"They are beautiful and strangely satisfying once you get the hang of them." He admired the bow for a second more, before his hand fell away. "I could teach you," he continued. The bow fit her; possibly wicked, but equally enchanting. "If you don't get it, I will."

Amilia reached for it, faster than if she had been given a physical push towards it. Her fingers lovingly ran along the string before gripping the handle. "My apologies, but it doesn't seem like it's going to be finders keepers this time."

He broke off to pay the shop owner for the bow as well as picking up some arrows and a quiver. When Daniel handed the extras over, Amilia's smile grew even brighter. "Well, I'm plum out of 'manly' things to do," she teased.

Normally, a thank you would have been called for, but this somehow made him grin more. Maybe it was because he deserved it after his misplaced joke. "Pity," he laughed. "It was starting to look good on you."

They started to walk back to his house, if for no other reason than it was a direction to go. Amilia bounced from one foot to the other and nearly did a little spin as she moved to stand in front of Daniel. "Can you start teaching me now?"

"Why not?"

They headed over to the archery range to give it a spin. After an hour or so of practice. Amilia turned and declared. "I've decided my bow arm is my right." She lifted the bow, and pulled on the string as if she was going to shoot an imaginary arrow. Which was pretty much the extent of her current skills.

The game didn't allow you to think away all the little details like it did other things. Hitting the mark took more than wishful thinking. "Oh, did you now?" Daniel smiled.

She nodded. "You're as good as I first guessed." The target in front of Amilia had two arrows that stuck out of the ground like they were afraid of their mark, while Daniel's were firmly nuzzled up next to the bull's eye.

"Thanks," Daniel said, admiring the shots before turning back to her. "Just promise you won't get better than me. The whole 'pity the student who does not surpass his master' is overrated."

Amilia shook her head before they got back to the lesson.

"One of the first, and most important things, is how you are standing," Daniel said, "If your stance is off, it will throw everything off. Make sure to line your toes perpendicular to your target." Daniel positioned himself in a square stance to give her a visual reference of what he meant, using his hands for emphasis. He went over the basics again such as nocking the arrow, how to draw the string, and where the arms should be at various points. Using himself as an example, he fired off a few shots. "It might feel odd at first, but with practice it becomes natural. Be careful not to practice without proper stance, or you'll be stuck doing it wrong for the rest of your life. Give it another go."

Amilia lifted up her bow and arrow, mirroring the proper posture as best she could before loosing an arrow. The first try was a flop. It wiggled recklessly and fell pitifully short. She pulled out another, adjusted her fingers, then let go again. This time it made it farther, but missed the target.

"Don't shoot," Daniel said. Amilia froze awkwardly mid-shot. She held her position as Daniel moved close enough that he could smell the sweet lemon scent she used in her hair. "You need to wrap your fingers around like this." He gently pulled her incorrect fingers back, and guided the correct ones into place. His hand fell away, and lifted her elbow a bit higher. "Pull the string back just enough to where it meets your mouth."

Amilia swallowed as she tried to focus on corrections and not how close he was. She pulled back on the string slowly.

"Perfect." Daniel stepped back to be clear. "Give that a go."

Amilia breathed out slowly and let go of the string. The arrow flew in the air and thumped into the target. Despite barely hitting the outermost ring, she felt triumphant.

She pulled out another arrow eagerly and aimed, trying to copy each little thing Daniel had just shown her. She then let go again, and this time, it hit higher, but to the right. The string recoiled back, snapping against her arm. It stung sharply since she hadn't expected it.

"I have a feeling this is going to take a lot of patience," she mumbled under her breath. Despite the urge to grumble, she laughed to cover up her embarrassment.

She didn't give up. Occasionally, Daniel offered instruction when he thought she needed it. But, for the most part it was all about getting a feel for it.

"See, you are already getting better," he encouraged. A bow and arrow wasn't a simple weapon to master. It would be a lot of work, but an archer was a valuable ally.

Amilia took a few more shots, but her arms felt shaky, which did nothing for her aim. "Let's make a bet," she said, as she opted for a break. "If I can, in reasonable time, hit a bullseye on a test, you have to take me to Santiago whenever I decide to go. I'll even let you pick what you get if I don't make it." She grinned, letting the words air for a second. "Wait! But, you have to promise to make it a fair test."

"All right." A little friendly bet couldn't do any harm. "You have to be able to hit two moving targets within two months and I'll take you anywhere you wish." Daniel put his bow down and crossed his arms over his chest. "If you lose..." When Daniel started he didn't have an idea of where he wanted to go with the bet, but simply looking at her made him want to be closer. "You owe me a kiss."

Her face had a flash of surprise before settling into a small smirk.

"Ah, but be careful." Amilia said, "Cupid's arrows hurt too, my dear." She plucked the string and it hummed in the air.

"Mmm, then let us hope you have better aim than Cupid."

Daniel's daily archery lessons dissolved into messing around and trying out trick shots. "I can put a candle out with an arrow," he claimed.

"What?" Amilia squinted suspiciously. "No, you can't."

"Yes, I can. My dexterity is high enough." If being part of the thieves' guild had unlocked any special talents, this would be one of the more ridiculous and fun ones among them.

Amilia set her jaw. "Prove it."

"I don't carry a candle on me."

"Uh huh, just what I thought," Amilia said. While Daniel was claiming lofty things, she was still working on merely hitting the target with any sort of consistency. "Better go get a candle to prove it, hot shot."

"Your lack of trust wounds me," Daniel laughed. "I am a man of my word. You stay here, practice more, and I'll be right back." The market wasn't far. It only took a few minutes to run and get one. Frankly, he was just glad the store was automated, because buying a single candle made him feel awfully silly.

When Daniel returned, he made a show of it. Presenting the candle with flare that would make future game show hosts jealous. Amilia laughed, and took a seat on bushels of hay that separated them and the rest of range.

Daniel crouched down to set the candle in front of a target. Once nested enough to stand up on its own, he lit the wick. When he walked back over, Amilia's lips were pursed with a mixture of amusement and disbelief.

"I don't think I even saw a bow in your home. If you are so good, why don't you use one all the time?" Amilia asked.

"I'm used to fighting in close quarters with Lance. I don't feel comfortable covering from a distance. Now stop trying to distract me. I'm aiming to impress." Daniel readied his shot, breathing out as he let it fly. The arrow whizzed over the candle a few inches, making the flame flicker, but nothing more.

"What was it that you were saying?" Amilia grinned, a laugh threatening to bubble up.

Daniel's face twitched at the still-lit candle and he gave Amilia a second to figure out if that smirk was going to turn into something more.

"I was saying," he started, looking at her the whole time he pulled back the string once more, and without stealing a glance he fired off another arrow. He wouldn't have known if he had been successful or not this time if Amilia's jaw hadn't had dropped open. Now, Daniel was the one smirking. "Dexterity is key."

Footsteps of someone else towards them caught his attention, and he looked up to find Lance coming. "Ah, speak of the devil," Daniel said.

"I've been looking all over for you," Lance said. His brow was pulled tight, but he tried to greet Amilia with a small nod and smile. "Is this where you've been hiding all day?"

"Suppose so?" Daniel glanced up towards the sun to gauge what time it was. They had been out for much of the afternoon, but he hadn't even noticed until now. "What is it?"

"You missed the guild meeting."

"Oh." Daniel puffed his cheeks out thinking for a second how he managed that before exhaling. "Oops."

Lance shook his head like he didn't understand the word. "Gael wants to see you."

"Duty calls," Daniel sighed.

Amilia had been looking from one to the other, curious if something more was going to break out, but when Daniel looked over, she smiled. "Until we meet again?" she asked.

"Soon, I hope," Daniel said.

She pushed herself up to her feet, and bowed her head respectfully. "Thank you for the lesson, and...everything else."

"My pleasure," Daniel said.

Lance crossed his arms low on his chest, tilting his head as he waited for them to finish up. The bored expression remained until Daniel patted him on the shoulder.

"Let's go," Daniel said.

"It was nice seeing you again, Miss Le'Russo," Lance said, before the two of them turned to leave. Amilia gave him a quick nod of agreement.

The thieves' faction was located just out of town. They met in a building that was a stronghold in its own right. A grand entrance surrounded by tall stone gave off a timeless feeling. There were a handful of men walking around the halls that left Daniel alone beyond nodding as they passed. He walked through the lobby and up a wide set of stairs.

Their leader, Gael, had set up a small office on the second floor. The man briefly looked up from his chair, and then almost instantly back down to his papers. "You were absent today."

"Apologies."

Gael looked up, trying to study the expression on the other player's face. "Little Miss Le'Russo has proved herself useful recently." Daniel's face paled at the mention of her name, but left his question unasked. "I'm surprised you still think there are secrets for those who hide in shadows. I was briefed all about the possible conflict of interest during your escort mission. You should bring her in. It's something we could further use to our favor."

"She isn't one of our own," Daniel protested.

"You will do what I order you to," Gael said sternly, as if Daniel had crossed an invisible line. "I know what is best for the thieves, and how the pieces will come into play. Her family ties may be of use."

Daniel's jaw tightened. He wanted to leave Amilia out of it, for her sake as well as his. Sharing was only welcomed when not forced. "As you wish," he said, the guild's man as always.

"This isn't the first meeting you've missed recently. There have been other missions skipped, and now there is a rumor you are getting distracted," Gael said. "Is this true?"

"Of course not," Daniel said, and forced the end of the conversation as he headed back down the stairs. No names were listed, but he knew who started the rumor. Only one person knew him well enough to have guessed such a thing.

And that person was currently standing by the doorway waiting like a guard. Daniel completely ignored him and stormed by without even a glance.

"Daniel," Lance said, trying to get his friend's attention, but Daniel kept walking. Lance moved faster to catch up, grabbing Daniel's arm to force a reaction. "I'm sorry. Don't be upset. They asked, and so I told them what I thought."

Daniel glanced around the courtyard, wondering if he wanted to have this conversation here or now. "Next time, you talk to me first," Daniel warned. They weren't wrong, he promised time to the guild and despite distractions would be a man of his word.

"I was trying to keep you safe," Lance countered.

The clarification didn't help. Daniel felt like he had been sold out, like his convictions were being doubted. Maybe they were right. It couldn't hurt to learn more about the person he was spending time with.

On his way home, he decided to cut a path to Amilia's. He wasn't sure what he hoped to accomplish since he couldn't walk in to demand answers, but hopefully he could lead her to explaining herself, and the deeper reasons behind her need to be taught their ways.

He rounded the corner to her small home, but before his hand lifted to knock, he could hear an unfamiliar voice rise with a demand. "You will not do this, Amilia. This family has lost enough to those thieves."

Daniel took a moment to consider drifting away, and letting whatever situation he had stumbled upon continue without his ears so close, but the mention of his faction made him far more curious than polite. He noticed from the small window into her kitchen that she had returned in a hurry; today's gear was scattered on the counter. The white curtains kept his view limited, but also hidden among the shadows.

"This is what we need!" Amilia's strong and convincing voice continued, "If I can keep us a step ahead by knowing things from the inside, we can rank among the nobles. We can reclaim what's ours."

Daniel vaguely recalled she mentioned her uncle being among the company of royals, weaseling his way into their good favor with gold plated stories. Yet, when she spoke of it, she seemed ashamed. 'Abandoned what her father once stood for,' she cited before. Daniel clenched his jaw as he leaned in to listen more closely.

He could see the person he was assuming was Amilia's uncle move about, chest puffed out with anger he presumed. "You don't know the first thing about being a thief. Neither did your father, and that's why—"

"I can learn," Amilia interrupted, "It will take time, but I will succeed. Don't try to bring up my father's shortfalls to me."

Amilia's parents had always been a sore topic when Daniel asked. She had mentioned her father was killed by criminals when she was young, and her mother had passed away from what she explained as a broken heart. But this? This all was new.

"This is what you want?" her uncle said with an even tone, standing tall over the girl who was like his daughter. Amilia nodded.

"No. I simply can't let you do this," he said.

"You don't have to. But I still will," she said, and crossed her arms.

"I don't want you to be a part of this. To risk your life for this," he said, with a fatherly tone. It was a clear change in how he set his shoulders. "You aren't doing it."

She was silent for a moment, noticing the difference, but didn't back down. "Please, Dimitri."

"Amilia, I said no," he said, raising his voice this time.

She lifted her chin. "And I said I will."

Dimitri's posture puffed up again, and Daniel figured this must be something that scared her when she was younger.

"I'm going to do this!" she repeated, her voice raising more than ever before. "Even if I have to die for this just like Father did."

The words seemed to cut. Dimitri's expression fell from wide-eyed and angry to solemn. His hand reached up to cup her cheek and she pulled away, not wanting sympathy. His hand fell with a sigh. "Amilia, you're like my daughter. I don't want to get you in this trouble. It's not your place."

"My father started it," Amilia continued, finding a comfortable steel in her voice. "I want to end it."

Her uncle straightened up. "Fine," he said willing to at least talk about the subject, "But I need to tell the others of this. They are angry with what happened the other day." Daniel couldn't stand another second. His feet lifted off her front doorstep as they carried him away in a rage. He had been blind to everything by thinking she was innocent. It likely would have been wise to finish listening, but his heart couldn't stand anymore. He hadn't gotten far before he noticed a man that looked all too familiar, walking in the direction of Amilia's home. One of the men from the ambush, he was sure of it. That's why they had backed off.

The thought of going back to the guild now sat like rocks in his stomach. He didn't want to tell them of Amilia's connection simply to be told again that she could be of use to them. If anything, they'd want to use this even more. An in with another faction could open up more for them.

There had been one person, however, that saw the danger that Amilia could be right away. He hadn't listened at the time, but Lance would still hear him out now. Daniel found a horse and booked it over to his place across town.

Stopping by wasn't unusual, but there must have been something in his expression that tipped Lance off early. He set down a water jug along a window sill where non-native flowers grew. "What is it?" Worry lines creased his forehead as Daniel neared.

"You were right," he announced.

"Well, I'm glad to hear it," Lance said. "About what, though?"

"Amilia." Daniel licked his lips worried that this story would warrant a judgment, even though nothing else had caused Lance to waver in his support before. "You know those mercenaries we fought in the street? I'm pretty sure one of them actually lives near her."

"Well, that doesn't prove—"

"They are bards," Daniel added. "With estranged family history involving the thieves' guild. She has something to prove and I no longer know to whom."

Lance looked to the flowers he had half watered, before sighing and picking up the water jug again. "Come inside. We shall talk about this."

Daniel nodded, and the two headed into Lance's home. The brief silence felt like holding his breath. He fell onto the lounge in a moment of tired exasperation he let few see and leaned his head against the back. "What do I do?"

This was no easy question, and Lance took a moment and thought it over. "Test her loyalty."

"What?" The comment surprised Daniel enough that he sat up to get a better look at Lance.

"Bard or not, the guild will want to use her as a spy. Training her seems to have fallen to you, and to join, we were all tested to see if we could follow the tenets. By that same logic, the duty of testing her fidelity is also yours."

Without thought, since all of it was dedicated to considering Lance's suggestion, Daniel picked at the dirt that had wiggled under his nails. "That's a good idea." Daniel managed a small nod. "I could do that."

"Glad I could help." Lance smiled, and Daniel looked up, finding himself mirroring the grin despite his mood.

"Are you sure this is a good idea?" The question almost sounded like he was doubting Lance, but it was more than that. He was doubting Amilia, doubting his choices in the matter. Maybe he shouldn't have been so curious about the girl in the first place.

Lance stood and moved towards the kitchen, but paused as he walked behind the lounge to place a reassuring hand on Daniel's shoulder, who turned his head to look at him. "Well, whatever happens, you know where my loyalties lie."

He did know. Lance was with him, no matter what choice he made, correct or otherwise. *"Merci beaucoup."*

The town's church was large, like many in their time. The steeple reached high into the sky like it could touch heaven with its point. Daniel walked in with his head down. His shadowed face made him look even more reverent. The sun shined through stained glass windows, leaving spots of blue, green, and little bits of red on his white cloak.

Mass was already in session as Daniel took a seat in a back pew. He had to put Amilia to the test before he could trust her, and this was the most culture-clashing way he could think of doing it. On the altar stood a priest giving a sermon, backed up by statues of the saints. They silently prayed under a large stained glass window. While the church was well loved, the man was not. He was funneling funds into stockpiling weapons for the knights, and often supported bards who constantly outed thieves in the area.

Amilia had broken off from Daniel a while back. He approved, since this mission was all hers. She had slipped into the confessional near the front, deciding it would be a good spot to hide until mass ended. Allowing her to both keep out of sight and remain close to the inner rooms.

When mass was over a short time later, she snuck out like she didn't want even God to see her—or the bow on her back. Amilia ducked around a hallway that some altar servers walked into, catching a door that lead back to the room the priest went into first. She waited long enough for them to clear before ducking inside.

"How could the money not be ready yet?" the priest called from another room. A quarrel broke out between him and some other deep voice, but their voices were jumbled. The occasional word could be made out, but they were unfit for this hallowed place.

The mission had been to stop the priest by any means necessary. Preferably by taking the donations that were destined to become weapons, but Daniel had hinted that if it wasn't possible, other measures should be taken. Without the money being here, Amilia anxiously pulled her bow forward. Did that really only leave killing the man?

Amilia pressed herself against the wall as the priest stormed out of the room. Thankfully away from her, which was a mixed blessing. She wasn't caught, but her target was getting away. A choice had to be made. Now.

She pulled an arrow out and readied her shot. Breathing out slowly to steady herself as she released the string. A shallow gasp came from the man as the arrow entered his neck, and a spurt of blood fell to the floor. The man slumped to his knees as he failed to grab the arrow. Amilia stepped out of her hiding spot, feeling like she should catch him before he fell, but only ended up twitching where she was when he did.

Amilia crept back the way she came, even though her heart jumped around in her chest, urging her to run instead. She headed straight for the exit, unable to even think about looking for Daniel. Dread filled her to the brim. All she could think about was getting away.

While a bard could kill, ending someone who could help them would never appear on a list of acceptable behaviors from her uncle. They could have her head for this. For turning against them. Amilia didn't even want to think about what she just did. She was upset on every level for putting so much on the line. Maybe she should have taken to the rooftops, but she walked straight into the crowd, wanting to lose herself in everything.

Daniel had followed her from the second she passed. "Hey, slow down," he said once in earshot. "I know the first time is unnerving, but you can't keep running away from me."

Amilia didn't look at him, just kept making her way into the crowd. Finally boiling over, she turned into a seemingly empty alley. Spinning around to face Daniel so fast that he had to stop short so he didn't run into her.

Her jaw was tight as she stared at him for a moment longer, trying to keep herself from saying things she might regret. But it was no use. "Tell me something!" she yelled. "Why did you decide to let me be a part of this? Why did you decide to teach a stranger how to do this?"

"Because you asked!"

"Did you ever question what you were getting someone into? Do you enjoy making someone a killer? Do you believe turning someone into a monster is for the greater good? Whatever that is." Amilia shifted on her feet, only letting a moment pass to give the appearance of allowing him time to speak before she added even more. "You are a thief! How is killing even acceptable behavior?"

Each verbal assault made Daniel grimace. His eyes shined with the same sort of fire she was spitting at him. But he willed himself to stay silent until she at very least finished her rant.

She paused for a moment as her lungs seemed tight, but didn't stop. "Do you ever consider that people don't even recognize or care what you might have done? A crime in your guild's name. At best maybe a few will be happy one *bastardo* is gone."

"Why do you keep assuming any of us do this for the glory?" Daniel asked, unable to hold his tongue anymore. "Do you see any of us bragging about all the things we do?"

Despite Daniel showing up for the fight, she refused to back down. "Even stealing from the rich and giving to the poor doesn't fix anything. You don't even have faith or stories to back your guild's deeds. None of this changes even if you take the lives of the damned!"

Daniel groaned, fists balled up as if he wanted to shake her. "My name may never reach fame, but never, ever underestimate how important one person can be. You changed the lives of many people today. That church might even be able to do some good now that their donations aren't being stolen from within."

"If the thieves don't get to them first," she spat. Daniel's expression darkened in a fashion that only made her feel worse than she had before. Yelling and getting things off her chest was supposed to make her feel better, but all she could feel was hysteria and hate. Emotion was a powerful tool for a bard, but she struggled to get control over it.

Daniel patiently looked at her as a mixture of annoyance and concern tinted his expression. "Are you done?" he asked softly.

Amilia exhaled trying to let every emotion finally settle, until only a strong hint of sadness showed. Her eyes became heavy as if she was picturing more than the day's events. "Does everyone deserve to die?" she whispered.

"No," Daniel said breathlessly. "No, not everyone." He wanted to comfort her, and after fighting himself for a moment, reached out to touch her hand. "You must think of those you love and care about, and decide what you want to fight for. That will give you resolve to do anything you need. You made the choice though, Amilia. No one else. All I can promise you is that with us, you won't be forced to do anything you don't decide to."

Amilia's fingers moved to interlace with his without even thinking about it. She nodded, even though her head was lowered. The knights, bards, mercenaries, were all controlled by a strict set of rules laid down by the person with the most influence. The thieves, however, were free. They weren't confined to a black and white world.

"You just have to pick what you want," Daniel said. No matter what the guild wanted, or her family, he wouldn't force her to side with them. That wasn't loyalty at all.

The way he was looking at her now made him wonder if there was something more than the desires of others that brought them together. Amilia looked up enough to catch their hands that were still together. With a start, she pulled her hand back. "I..." she started, expression flinching at the war within herself. "I'll stay by you."

LOADING...CHAPTER THIRTEEN

"That is the second biggest stack of pizza boxes I've ever seen," Michael said definitively.

Owen had been trying to not bite at the various statements Michael threw out. Each had been getting more outrageous than the last, but this one successfully spiked his interest. He narrowed his eyes at the stack of nine boxes the delivery man just dropped off. They were uncomfortably tall. Owen took one from the top and spread them out over the table. The last thing they needed was an overzealous kid running in and knocking them all over. "How many was the biggest stack?" he asked.

Michael had been dropping bottles of water into a bucket of ice, but stopped altogether at the question. "So listen, I was friends with this guy, well he was really a friend of a friend...anyways, there was this guy who was throwing a party," he started, and Owen crossed his eyes, regretting the question.

"I don't want to say he was a hoarder, but the man was a fucking hoarder. We went into the kitchen and pizza boxes were ev-e-ry-where. We must have counted at least twenty hanging out. I swore we'd find more instead of dishes."

"That's funny," Owen said dryly. He started dropping water bottles into the bucket deliberately to clear them off the table. From this distance they created a splash, but Michael didn't notice as he seemed to be daydreaming about that party.

He snapped out of it a second later. "Yeah, we started drunkenly using them as shields."

"What did you use as a sword?" Owen asked as he bought back into the story again.

"You know, I don't remember! Salad tongs? No, that's not right." He waved the whole thing off, and got back to setting up for a very different type of party they were going to throw for the little league team.

"Hello?" Andreah called as she cautiously entered the room. She stood by a receptionist desk that had never been used, eyeing the empty spot before pushing further into the room. Normally she never had to go to this floor, but Owen was here. "What in the hell is that?"

Owen walked over, eyeing a column of mostly golden balloons, except for the black bottom that was meant to be the handle of a baseball bat. "It's my boss trying to appeal to kids and their influential parents." He stole another look at the pillar again before shaking his head and smiling over to Andreah. Her outfit was partially covered by the reflective work vest she had to wear. "What do you have for me, babe?"

She reached for her bag.

"Wait, wait," Owen said, and guided her by the arm over to his desk. "Alright, hit me."

Andreah gave him a funny little expression as she pulled a padded envelope out, and handed it over. The expression deepened with confusion when Owen gave it right back.

"It's for you." With a grin, he leaned back to sit on the front of his desk.

"You had me bike all the way here for something I already technically had? I might actually boop you now." She hit the bubble envelope against his arm. "This was the only package I had on this side of town."

"I know, I'm the worst. You got paid to come see your boyfriend who had a surprise present for you." Andreah rolled her eyes.

"Open it," Owen insisted.

She started to pull at the glue that held the opening's flap down, carefully eyeing him more than the package. "This isn't like a weird one-month anniversary gift is it?"

"Wow, you are impossible to buy things for. Noted." Owen reached out, pulling on her jersey to have her step closer to him. She stepped into the space between his knees as he sat. "No, you dork. I just wanted to see your face, and possibly make out with it in the break room. That part is totally optional though."

Andreah smirked. There had likely been a comeback, but it was lost when she dumped the packages contents into her hand. "The world's tiniest gas can?" Not including packaging, it was a little bigger than a quarter, complete with a black cap. The label read Fuel Charger.

"You said your phone kept dying, so this can hang out on your keys until you need it," Owen said.

"This is the cutest, and tiniest, thing anyone has ever gotten me." Andreah pulled on the collar of his pea coat, pulling his face a bit closer. "Thank you."

He nodded, eyes locked on her until he leaned the rest of the way and kissed her. She moved her hands off his collar to rest around his neck, while his hands slid around her waist.

"Nu-uh," Frank scolded, sweeping into the room like an on-the-ball teacher's aide. "Take that somewhere else. There are going to be children here soon. And they can't see...that."

Andreah pulled away first, mostly because she hadn't expected anyone besides Michael, who was still by the food like the smell alone was a siren.

Owen pushed himself off the desk and tapped Andreah on the behind to get her moving. "Come on, we can hang out in the break room until you have to get back to work."

She shot him a look that said that's not what he meant, but followed without comment. The room was small, with a microwave that was overused and a coffee pot that was virtually ignored. The table would have been big enough for four if one of the sides wasn't pressed to the wall. In the back, there were shelves with old editions of various newspapers. "You know this is my last delivery again today."

"Saved the best for last?" Owen asked. "People in this building need to use your fine services more often."

"Really though, I could come make out with you mid-day more often."

"I'm liking this plan more and more."

Andreah glanced back towards the other rooms. The small window in the door showed her only a square of the empty hallway. "You know, your boss is super cool."

"Yeah." He leaned over as if he could see the others. "Makes up for how little he pays me."

"You goof," Andreah said, ready to swat him on the arm again. "You shouldn't have bought me something if you're tight on money."

"Don't worry about it. I just got paid on Friday." What Owen left out was Frank wasn't paying him until the end of the month. He had gotten his payday from a bone digger gig. A woman had wanted to know if her husband was visiting the brothels. He was. Kind of boring, actually, but the gigs involving sex, or some other illicit betrayal, always paid the best.

"I could make it up to you," she said. Owen raised an eyebrow, but the expression was washed away as Andreah stepped up, and kissed him roughly. She kissed him until he felt dizzy, then moved on to his neck.

His eyes fluttered, catching the yellow of her work vest. The first time he met her, it had been hidden under her sweater, but now it just was a neon reminder of work. "Andreah," he breathed, ignoring what was taboo or not for a few seconds longer. "You should stop, or take off that god awful vest."

"Huh?" Andreah glanced down at herself and chuckled. "Oh."

Owen smiled before movement behind her caught his eye. "Or maybe just the first thing," he grumbled. Andreah looked over her shoulder as Michael walked in.

"Hey, guys," he said, mostly to Owen. "So, this is the girlfriend?" Only then did he turn to look at Andreah. A small nod in greeting looked like he was sizing a prize he wanted at a carnival.

"My name is Andreah. It's nice to meet you...?"

"You mean good ol' Owen hasn't mentioned me? It's Michael. To be fair, he didn't really bring you up either." He smacked Owen's shoulder, who uncomfortably jerked an inch forward. "Maybe it's because I wouldn't have believed that he could snag such a babe."

Owen looked like his eyes might fatally roll of out of his head. "What do you want?"

"Boss said he needs you so I can man the camera for the event."

"Thanks for the message. Could you give us a minute?" Andreah said, suddenly cheerful. Owen crossed his arms over his chest.

Michael glanced from her to his co-worker like he knew what was going to happen when he left, despite Owen's discomfort apparent to anyone with a hint of sense. "Alright."

Andreah waited silently until he closed the door. Her demure swapped back with the shake of her head. "I've known that dude for like two seconds, and I hate him already."

"God! I know, right?" Owen looked brightly at her, like he wanted to gush about how much he liked her from that statement alone. "I've been here for like a year and a half, and I want to tape his mouth shut every time he opens it."

"Maybe next time I should deliver you some duct tape." She paused as if imagining how that would play out for a second. "Anyways, I could stop by your place at like eight if you wanted."

"Sounds good. I'll miss you until then."

Her face scrunched up. "Don't get all sappy on me," she said, but it was hard to take her too seriously. "I'm going to let you get back to work."

"Don't let the pre-teens get any cooties on you on your way out." Andreah stuck her tongue out, which only played into his point.

LOADING...CHAPTER FOURTEEN

His eyelids were heavy, but his heart was light. Daniel and Amilia were standing outside the guild headquarters after their mission, wasting time. It was almost dark, but they continued swapping stories that they'd hadn't gotten to share yet.

"Señor Ortiz! I need your help please!" the woman cried in a panic.

Amilia looked over to the woman rushing towards them to Daniel, who didn't appear to have a clue what was going on either. As she neared, he realized she worked with Lily.

"Please, one of the girls was poisoned. We know who has the antidote, but we don't have the...skills needed to get it," she said. "Please, will you help us?"

"All right," Amilia agreed, and glanced over to Daniel, who nodded in turn. The woman brought them back to the brothel. The place was full of people at this time of day. Most drinking and flirting in an environment that catered to them. Their guide pointed towards a man who sat smugly on a couch.

There were two women already parading around a man, trying to get his attention, willing to trade for medicine. The women kept a respectful distance; when one dared to move closer, he waved them away. Maybe waiting for a bigger prize to come along, or getting kicks from posturing.

"Hold these," Amilia replied, handing off her bow and quiver.

Daniel blinked at the items, eyes widening as she stripped down to her slip. "Wait—what are you doing?"

"Playing the part." She sauntered over to the man, leaving Daniel wondering if she meant the part of a thief or courtesan.

Amilia had a sly smile as she walked over. "Now tell me, why did you do it?" she asked.

The man looked up at her. "The girl wasn't delivering. Had to make sure she got what was coming to her."

Daniel felt like something had died in his mouth. Maybe it was better that Amilia was testing her abilities, because he would have forgotten the pickpocketing and just intimidated the man into submission. These ladies deserved respect no matter what.

"What would you like?" she asked, whispering near his ear.

He let out a deep laugh. "My money's worth."

Amilia's lips curled up, and she moved closer as if promising just that. His arms uncrossed, welcoming her as she moved to straddle his lap. Her hands first started at his shoulders then one made its way to his lap. She rubbed his inner thigh for a moment as her lips touched his neck.

Daniel's eyebrows went up. Couldn't she just pick his pocket without getting all up in there? He wouldn't admit it, but he was becoming visibly uncomfortable in this den of skin.

When Amilia's hand moved over the man's pants he seemed to considerably lose concentration. Amilia could feel the antidote was in his pocket and worked to slide it out without being noticed. The distraction, however, wasn't enough. He grabbed Amilia's wrist, twisted it away, and pulled a dagger. "Want to rethink that, love?"

Daniel didn't wait to see how he'd use the knife. He pulled Amilia off the man's lap, so fast that she stumbled back into a nearby lounge chair. "Excuse me," Daniel seemed to say to the both of them. He pulled a sword, and kept the man pinned in his seat unless he wanted to skewer himself. "Today's lesson is, if you can't be slick, be blunt," Daniel said to Amilia, before demanding the man drop the knife.

"Now the antidote?" Daniel held his hand out.

The man didn't look like he was going to comply, but maybe the set look in Daniel's eyes convinced him it was this or his life. He leaned back to grab the antidote and carefully stretched his arm out to avoid nicking himself on the sword.

Daniel tossed the small bottle to Amilia, who awkwardly caught it. "I guess you will have to find women the old fashion way, because if I catch you here again I'll kill you. Now leave." Daniel lowered the sword, and took a single step aside to let the man pass.

The wannabe killer seemed to check his ego against challenging Daniel, but decided to bolt in the end.

They were whisked over to the sick woman in one of the side rooms. Lily sat at the bedside of another woman who looked warm and sickly despite the cool rag on her forehead. Without a word, Amilia handed the bottle over to Lily.

"Miracles do exist," she said, with a new hope as she tipped the medicine into her friend's mouth. Once empty, she gestured everyone to leave the room and followed them out. "I don't know how to thank you enough for what you have done. The head of the house is away. I should have been responsible for handling the situation but..." Lily's hands went to her carefully pinned hair as if needing to fix a stray hair somewhere. She could handle many things, but this situation had spiraled out of her control. She exhaled deliberately to center herself. "Please stay. Relax, maybe have a drink. Our hospitality is the least I can offer you."

Daniel stayed silent, wondering if the girls felt the same tension that he did. Then it dawned on him; they hadn't actually met that morning.

Someone else called Lily's name. She turned to look and let out a sigh. "I have to take care of something else, but please stay. The night even, if you want."

Daniel turned to Amilia with a slight shrug. They had run two guild missions together, and this impromptu one. "Would you like to stay?" He grinned. "Maybe we shouldn't. I'm not sure these women would be a good influence on you."

Amilia shifted her weight slightly as she looked at Daniel. "If the thief's guild doesn't work out, perhaps I could try being a courtesan. Holding a sword to clients seems bad for business, though. But, we should stay and hopefully avoid any more trouble."

There were many guilty pleasures that could be found here besides ones that needed a bed. Gambling and drinking among them. "Sounds good." He gestured towards a corner. Two couches sat across from each other with a shared table. Daniel picked up the deck of cards he found and promptly started shuffling. "Do you have any games in mind, or should I just deal the first thing that comes to me?"

Amilia had been looking over to various men and women. Her expression was tight, like she didn't fully approve of people spending time here, but seemed to be trying. "Whatever is fine."

After the cards were dealt, they were brought glasses of wine. The waitress gave a practiced smile before leaving them be. Daniel didn't flinch at the drink this time, making Amilia curious how often he was here. When he noticed she was staring, he slid his drink away making her laugh.

"It's a good thing we are not playing for money," Daniel said after a few hands. "You'd be beating the pants off of me." He took the cards back from her, giving the cards an extra shuffle this time as if that would cure his string of rotten hands.

Amilia leaned back against the couch, and her mind drifted to think about all that had happened lately. She had killed a man. Killed. "Daniel, how many people have you...dealt with?"

He looked up from the cards, unsure what she meant until he saw the dark expression over her eyes. "I don't know, Amilia," Daniel said, with a soft sigh. He wasn't trying to hide the answer, it was just easier to do his job if he didn't count how many people it cost. "I wish we lived in a world where killing wasn't the way people got what they wanted,"

Daniel continued, "Think of it this way, if you asked someone how many people they slept with many can easily think of an answer. They might be embarrassed to tell you, but they know. The courtesans, however, feel different about it. They might not have a number, but they aren't ashamed of themselves for what they do. Some people may look down on them, but they don't buy into it. The act doesn't define them."

Amilia looked up, setting her cards face down as she became uninterested in the game. She could understand what he was saying, see the point he was trying to make, but wondered if he was also trying to avoid a number for her sake.

"Come here." Daniel patted the bit of couch next to him. "Maybe I can explain better."

Amilia looked at the spot skeptically, before getting up to take it. "You didn't answer why you do this. There must be something more than a desire for freedom when it means you not only steal, but sometimes kill as well."

"You see over there?" Daniel leaned in towards Amilia, and nodded over to a woman who was dancing as a musician played the flute next to her. The edges of the woman's skirt flared and reached as far out as the dress would allow. A night together might be for sale, but she seemed truly happy. That spirit shined through every move she made.

"I suppose I do this for the same reason she does," Daniel continued as he watched, "Because I like it." He finished off his drink, and licked his lips clean of the taste of wine as he laughed to himself. "I guess I'm not as noble as you believed."

"You're a saint as far as I'm concerned." Maybe their cloaks resembled monks for a reason. Their shoulders brushed as she leaned into him. "It's late, I'm pretty tired," she declared. She got up as if to do something about it, but the world had a strange wobble to it. Maybe she shouldn't try to head home right now. "You sure they wouldn't mind us staying here?"

Daniel blinked up at her. "If there is one thing I know about Lily, it's that she says what she means. I'll go check with her which room is open."

He found Lily again standing at a podium with a large book placed on top. It looked like a desk might have better suited with the number of papers. Maybe they were just piling up since she was currently flirting with a man in front of her.

Daniel waited by the sideline, but the man seemed determined to stick around. He cleared his throat to get their attention. Both of them looked over, but Lily looked back to her new crush. "I'll talk to you later," she said, with a wink. The man seemed disappointed, but wandered off. "What can I do for you, love?" Lily said not turning off the charm as she spoke to Daniel.

"I didn't want to go hunting around to see which rooms were free, mind telling me?" He felt flushed, and was quick to blame it on the drinks instead of the topic.

Lily looked at him curiously, before looking to where he had been, finding Amilia there. There was a clear question in her eyes, but she was formal enough not to ask. Instead, she looked down at the book. "Upstairs, third room on the right."

"Thanks." Daniel headed back to Amilia and repeated the information, even holding up three fingers to emphasize.

Amilia walked upstairs, glancing back at Lily for a moment before going in. Only then did she realize that there was only a single bed. She swallowed hard. She should have thought of that before.

Daniel piled his weapons on the nightstand, before he noticed Amilia's hesitation. "Do you want me to go downstairs?" While it was cute, in a way, to see her flustered, he had been tired before they started this mission, and now was more so.

Amilia shook her head. "No, it's fine." She slipped into bed and shivered under the cool sheets, before Daniel joined her on the other side. A moment ticked away, before she turned her head back to look at him. A small smile crossed her face in the low light. "Goodnight."

Daniel had tried lying on his back, but he flipped over so they were back to back, finding it wasn't much better. He held in a grumble, and wiggled around until he faced the same way as her. "Amilia?" Daniel whispered, as he looked at the back of her head and wondered if she had fallen asleep already. "I'm glad you came with me today."

The sun spilled through the cracks between the curtains. It was mid-morning when Amilia let out a slight grumble, and turned her face away from the light, burying it into the pillow. Daniel woke to the sound, still half asleep. He tried to move his arm, but found a weight there as Amilia's arm keep his tight against her side. It was far too easy, to just let this fragile moment exist.

It felt like he only closed his eyes for a second, just enough time to exhale, but when Daniel stirred again the bed was empty. What had he expected? That Amilia would just stay here with him? That they'd start the day as one? He sighed and started to collect his things.

Amilia came back in as he tugged on his last boot. "Morning," Daniel said cheerfully, but his smile faded when he was only met with silence.

She placed a tray of food on a small desk, and picked one of the two plates as she sat down on the foot of the bed to eat. A wordless annoyance radiated off her like the morning sun.

Daniel rolled his eyes even though he doubted she could see. He didn't understand the attitude all of a sudden. He grabbed the second plate, and tried to ignore her mood as he sat down at the desk.

He hoped she'd warm up after a meal, but instead the sourness seemed to leech into the food, making the whole thing unappetizing. Soon, he abandoned the plate entirely. "All right," he sighed. "What's wrong?"

"It's just..." Amilia stared down at her food. Her jaw set tight as if having trouble explaining. "Just tell your friend not to have the wrong idea."

Wrong idea? What friend was she even—shit. Lily. "Come on, are you really letting a rumor mess with you? Considering where we are, it isn't even a surprising one." It didn't seem to help. He had the urge to hug her, reassure her that everything was fine. But maybe that was exactly

103

what she was worried about. "It's just one person, anyway, who I'm sure you set straight."

Only after the comment did he realize he lied. Both Lance and the guild had questioned him for something similar.

Amilia sighed, shifting on the bed to cross her arms. "Well, I'm just saying," she reiterated as she stood. "I should head home. I'll see you tomorrow for training."

Daniel opened his mouth to say something, but she left the room before he formed any real words. He tossed his hands in the air before getting up to follow. What did she want? For him to hunt down rumors along with his normal targets?

She gave a quick wave to Lily as she stormed out of the building.

"This is why I'm single," Daniel groaned. He stopped in front of Lily, who was manning the front again. He glanced over to her before shaking his head at the door. "I clearly don't understand people."

"How did you manage to strike out at the brothel?"

Daniel glared at Lance before he glanced back towards the rest of the guild that was gathered for a meeting.

It didn't matter if Daniel didn't find amusement, Lance sure did. So much so that everyone's side conversations were lost. "You can either pay for company," Lance said, weighing the choices on his hands. "Or apparently, you can bring your own now."

"You know that silk pillow on your bed?" Daniel asked.

Lance tilted his head trying to figure out where that came from. "Uh...yeah?"

"Good," Daniel said. "Because if you go on, I'm going to smother you with it."

An offended gasp reshaped Lance's mouth without much force. He pulled his hand up to hold his heart. "I'm starting to see why you weren't so lucky now."

Gael moved to the center of the room, and cracked his fingers. It was more of a nervous tick than anything. "Don Ambrogio Spinola Doria has come into town. As part of the Order of Santiago, I can't emphasize enough how important this event is. Unlike the rest of us, leaders like this nearly seem to vanish into thin air when not out mixing with the people. It's our duty to find out why he is here. His tie to the knights is apparent, and if he is planning anything, we need to know beforehand." He paused, gauging the room for interest, worry, or any other reaction. "I can't promise there will be any good drops to have, but I'm requesting volunteers all the same."

Daniel leaned forward in his seat. Silently considering the offer before tilting his head to towards Lance. "Shall we?"

"I do love annoying the knights," Lance said.

The day turned from sunny to gray. Daniel watched the clouds as the handful of thieves gathered around. Not everyone could, or even wanted to group up. Despite being a big guild, they generally worked in small groups, but those who did volunteer gathered again that evening.

The thieves blended in with the staff or shadows whenever they could. Daniel, however, had a different idea. There was a balcony that everyone else seemed to ignore. Why hide below when you could get a top down view? One simply had to get up there. Easy enough. Daniel folded his hands together, holding them low so he could boost Lance high enough to reach the railing.

Lance pulled himself up to the balcony before spinning back around, and reaching a hand down. Daniel took a few steps back to have enough space to run up the wall, and grab Lance's hand.

After being pulled up, he bounced to stand on the solid ground of the second floor. "Go team."

Lance smiled. *"Allons-y."*

The advantage of being up here became instantly clear. This floor looked over the first part of theater seating. Servers were buzzing around like busy bees from one patron to another. The knights didn't have the most members, but they definitely had the most money. It showed in how free the wine was flowing. Some drank up, while others just used the shimmering glasses and decadent food as a show of class.

Daniel focused on finding Ambrogio Spinola. As he searched the crowd from above, he spotted a woman with a green corset with black flowing skirt. Hadn't he seen that outfit before? A man walked up to her offering his arm, dressed to match. Daniel felt like he'd seen him before, too.

Then it clicked.

"Amilia." He felt like the word had been ripped from his lungs.

Lance fell in line with Daniel, line of sight following his friend's. "And the Don."

The man at her arm appeared too young to be the same person. Daniel forced himself to look away, soon finding another man in his mid-thirties. This one was old enough, and wore armor suggesting a military background.

The group was brought over to a table, where someone else was already sitting. Daniel couldn't place him, and Lance didn't offer any more help in the matter. The first man, a brother maybe, considering the way he touched Amilia. Close, but not lingering like a lover. He whispered something, then left her alone amongst men who greatly outranked her.

"It has come to our attention that you are working with thieves," Don Ambrogio said, and watched her carefully. "Is that true?"

Amilia shook her head. "No, sir, that is not."

"Care to explain to us then?" The tone was careful, as if he was only giving her a single thread to walk along.

"I apologize for what happened at the church, but in order to carry on the façade, to act the part, I had to do it."

Daniel turned his head away. He should have signaled to the others, but couldn't even spare a thought if they were still looking for Ambrogio or if everyone else was distracted by the coin purses of others.

"Why did you choose to learn their ways then? When your family has an existing deal with us?" the second man asked, as Ambrogio edged on boredom. If he dealt with bards before, he didn't seem to care for them.

Amilia turned her head towards her shoulder, almost as she knew she was being watched, but didn't turn enough to spot Daniel as he watched from above. Slowly her eyes found her way back, giving the question the seriousness he desired. "I'm doing this for the knights."

"And the boy?"

Her head twitched to a tilt before she righted it just as fast. "He's of no concern, sir."

"Good." His tone didn't sound fully convinced. "You don't want to get your family back into the trouble your father had."

His expression tired like the time he had allotted for her nonsense had simply evaporated. "This is your only warning."

Amilia bowed her head. Respectfully in part, and also so he'd be encouraged to consider the matter finished. Daniel's nails dug into the railing with such force that he was leaving scratch marks in the wood. He didn't even notice the vice grip that was starting to make the bones in his hands ache until Lance put a reassuring hand on his shoulder.

"We need to get moving," Lance whispered.

"Yeah," Daniel said weakly. He took another look at Amilia, who was now moving towards her seat. He knew he needed to focus. He had done this long before Amilia and would continue long after her.

They ventured further, spotting a guard who was unfortunately—for the guard—stationed in the wrong direction. His job was to stop people from coming up from the first floor, not someone already upstairs.

Daniel seized the man from behind, grabbing him in a chokehold. The guard's strangled attempted for air proved useless. "Say your prayers," Daniel whispered, as he lowered the man to the ground. Fate could decide if he ever got back up again.

Their fellow thieves had moved silently through the crowd. From above they had blended in perfectly, but now that the duo was on the same floor, they recognized other uninvited faces. Their pockets must be nearly bursting at the seams now.

A surprised cry cut through the room. Everyone turned in rare union despite what group they belonged to. One of the thieves must have failed a check, and the quiet party now had a woman hugging her purse close. An annoyed knight had drawn his sword pointing it towards a young thief like he wanted the man's liver for dinner.

"You forgot my invite," Lance called out. Suddenly, everyone's attention was on him, and by his wicked grin he seemed to enjoy it. His hands were held out like he was the true threat in the room.

The guards snapped to attention in agreement, the humor just as unwelcome as their presence. The bold move gave the young thief enough time to run off. Lance waited for the right second then countered the first attack, slitting a guard's throat with an eerie smoothness as Daniel ran a dagger straight through the spine of another.

"Sometimes I fear you forget that we are thieves, and not musketeers," Daniel said, as he ended up back to back with Lance. There would have been enough time to counter if a wave of guards didn't ruin it. They had to keep them busy enough so the rest of the thieves could either run or draw their own weapons. Many did run. A handful of others were confident enough to join the brawl. Outing themselves as they downed the nearest knight.

"You know maybe this isn't our sort of party after all," Daniel yelled over the chaos. He turned, flicking two throwing knives at men who tried to flank him, and slid over a table taking advantage of the new ground he earned.

Lance didn't make it far as more men cut off his escape. Amilia's uncle, Dimitri, was in this new wave of more than just the armored guards now fighting to rid themselves of the party crashers. Lance twirled the sword around in his hand, a move that was nothing more than show. His movements were as fluid as water with every attack. A guard managed to get close to Lance, but instantly crumbled and fell back, holding his stomach as Lance returned a dagger back to his belt.

Daniel was helping usher anyone out that was trying to get away from the fight, whether thieves or just party goers. One of the knights decided that taking a swing at him would be more important. He dodged, and the man's fist hit the door with a thud that could break bones.

Getting back to Lance was key so sheer numbers didn't overwhelm him. Daniel jumped on a chair, tipping it forward to run over, and across, tables. The last of his throwing knives landed in someone's neck before his feet touched the ground again.

Both Lance and Daniel had been trying to ignore Dimitri, since he was obviously important to Amilia, but that consideration came back to bite them. He threw a punch to the jaw that was so unexpected, Daniel dropped his daggers in order to catch himself. Dimitri took the opportunity to kick Daniel when he was down, in a manner that felt all too personal. Daniel choked out a wheeze as momentum knocked him to his side.

If he was going to play rough, Daniel would have to play fair. He grabbed one of the daggers waiting on the ground and drove it into Dimirtri's foot. His cry of pain covered up Amilia's own scream as she stood and watched it all play out in front of her.

Daniel scrambled to grab the second dagger off the ground, and pulled himself back on his feet. He watched Dimitri cautiously until the sound of his own name drew his attention.

"Go." Daniel twitched this time at the sound of Lance's voice. "Go," he repeated. "I'll be right behind you."

With a nod, Daniel turned and bolted for the door again.

Lance blocked a sword with his arm. It wasn't the best plan, but it was that, or something far worse. The sword cut through his sleeve and into the base of his hand. His breath came out unevenly in an effort to cope with the sharp pain. A pool of blood gathered in the palm of Lance's injured hand, and he tucked his left arm into his side. Red droplets slipped between his fingers.

He was close to the exit, but became so outnumbered it really didn't matter if it was an inch or a mile. Pride might be the death of him if he decided to keep fighting, or be could hope to be taken prisoner.

The sword fell purposefully to the ground to signal his surrender. A tightness in Amilia's chest lessened as she swore she could hear it rattle on the floor. As Lance lifted his hands up, the cuff of one white sleeve was stained red.

Someone grabbed Amilia's shoulder, and she yelped. She spun around ready to fight, but found her escort there. "Run home," he said, looking past her for a second.

"But Celio," Amilia objected. She started to glance towards her uncle again, but he stopped her.

"No, go now," Celio insisted, "I'll go help my father."

LOADING...CHAPTER SIXTEEN

Owen hated leaving a mission like that, but Em had called saying she was having contractions, allotting no time for Daniel. Since Emily's husband was out of town, Owen and Neal were her support system. Owen lived too far away to help directly, his job was to simply show up at the hospital. He made it halfway there before Neal called saying it was a false alarm, leaving Owen to tell the taxi driver to turn around.

He pushed aside the annoyance of having the game interrupted. Not that he faulted her. The only blessing was that since he left the battle first he had been able to quit out without any penalty. It was late by time Owen got home again. He thought about logging back into the game, but it was all shut down, and that was for the best. He had to work tomorrow anyways.

The next day, after work, Daniel waited around the guild building. He had plans with Lance before training with Amilia later on, if he didn't give up and cancel completely. But he'd seen neither of them so far. It wasn't odd for him not to spot Amilia this early, but Lance should have met up with him some time ago. Being late was rare, but failing to show up altogether was unheard of.

112

Daniel tried to reassure himself that Lance had just lost track of the time. Unease settled into his chest, so he decided to do something more than wait around.

He found Gael in his office. "Sir, do you know where Lance is?" Daniel asked. If anyone would know, it would be their leader.

Gael looked up from his desk with a frown, offering Daniel a seat before he said anything else. Reluctantly, Daniel sat down. Gael got up, moving around his desk to lean against it. His hand rubbed over his mouth. "Neither Lance or you checked in after the mission last night. I was able to check on you, but Lance..."

"What?" Daniel felt the color drain out of his face. "Then, where is he?"

"We are trying to find that out now," Gael said. The tone was one Daniel has heard countless times. It was a political one, not one of concern.

"Well, look harder!"

"We are doing the best we can—"

"Like hell you are. Half of the thieves are just hanging around downstairs. A proper search party would have more looking. At very least you could have told me sooner, instead of having me figure it out a day later."

The two exchanged a few more choice words, but it ended up with Daniel storming out.

He searched the whole day for any sign of Lance's location. It was clear that the Knights had him, but *where* was still the question. Any stronghold he knew of wouldn't crumble from his efforts alone, and he didn't know anyone from the faction that would even confirm his guess.

It took a beat of his heart to realize that wasn't true.

He did know someone. Amilia.

Despite the anger and betrayal, he found himself on her doorstep. He bounced on his heels, hands balled into fists, and wondered if this was who he really should ask. His clear head had slipped away overnight, leaving him frantic and worn out.

Daniel knocked to no avail. He hissed between his teeth and glanced around. This was his only real lead. Going back now would only lose him more time. "Amilia, open up. I need your help," he called, loud enough to be heard through the door.

It took longer than it should have, but she came out. Scattered rays spilled around Daniel as he stood with his back to the sun. Five minutes ago, she would have ignored any problem the world tossed her way, but looking at Daniel now, she was unable to. "What's wrong?"

"I—I don't know where he is." Daniel's hands rose to the top of his head like there wasn't enough air in the world, but they didn't stay there long as they fluttered around. "I looked all over the city. I know it's a big city, but it isn't that big," he continued like a man who had lost his mind. "I think they killed him. I think the knights killed Lance. I need to find him."

"Just try to slow down. When do you think this all happened? And how?" she asked. If Daniel could have fought back the panic attack that was building, he would have caught the lie. She knew the answer to both of her questions. Deep down, she hoped the stories didn't match up. That Lance had escaped after her cousin told her to run.

"Lance was out on a mission last night. He hasn't been seen since. I think he was captured, or maybe killed. If the first is true, I don't have long until the second." Daniel took a big breath, as if he hadn't been breathing the whole time. It was a strain to settle down when everything in his head was screaming that time was running out. The fact that they had attacked a member of her family certainly wouldn't gain either of them any favors. Nor that fact that Amilia had said she wasn't really on their side. But who else did he have right now?

Fear was just making Daniel more confused. A spike of pain bolted through his head. He grumbled to himself and blinked hard as the color of the world seemed to fade. He looked around, as if to check his vision against things in the room.

"I...can't see blue." The comment was out of place, but the system made Daniel repeat words that were actually

Owen's. He reached up to the visor to check its placement, and Daniel mirrored.

"Hey, hey, it's okay," Amilia said softly. Daniel braced himself against the door frame, and she reached out to touch his hand. Everyone would likely blame that night on her, and helping him soon after wouldn't gain their trust. But she couldn't leave him like this. She bit her lip. "I'll help you. Just let me go gather my stuff."

Daniel nodded as she headed back in the house. It felt like a weight had been lifted off his chest once she agreed. Proper colors slowly ebbed back before his vision flashed solid white.

Owen and Daniel shared a gasp, with a stumble he found himself in Paris. Hard transitions were always the worst, but this was something else completely. Notre Dame stood proudly up ahead. He'd been here before. Daniel spun around, realizing he had lived this day before.

It had been years ago, back when Daniel was a new recruit. He was stunned at the cathedral and its ever watchful gargoyles. He had heard stories of how beautiful the church was inside, but maybe he should have been warned about how breathtaking it all was.

"*C'est un beau chose, n'est-elle pas?*" A man who spoke French stepped next to Daniel as he, too, glanced at the cathedral.

"Come again?"

Lance chuckled waving his hands in front of him. "*Excusez-moi*, I didn't know you were Spanish," he said, switching languages so Daniel could understand. Lance hadn't aged much over the years. The change in style, however, was notable. His ivory shirt had a large V cut into it, with baggy sleeves that were pulled tight around the cuffs. Black boots rose to just under the kneecap. To top it off, the sword on Lance's belt looked purely decorative.

Daniel didn't understand why he was reliving this day, but he had found him. Maybe he had to do something different this time, or—

"I said, it's a beautiful thing, isn't it?" Lance said, cutting Daniel's thought short as he remembered this. "The last time

I saw someone gawk like that, they were looking at a Da Vinci painting. I could show you around Paris. I have a feeling you'd get lost on your own."

Lance's bold grin was one Daniel learned to love. He hesitated at first. Sightseeing had never been the plan, but Lance served as a personal tour guide for the day. It took Daniel most of the day to figure out what Lance got out of it. Only later did he realized the man truly loved this city and showed it off to anyone who would listen.

The two stopped as the day wore on to get something to eat. Daniel's stomach had been uneasy with the fear he'd end up with something completely foreign, since Lance had to order because Daniel didn't know a lick of French himself at the time. The worry turned into laughter as Lance bit back a smirk.

"You should come back to Spain with me," Daniel blurted when food he knew arrived.

"What? Paris is my home! I don't think I could ever leave it," Lance dismissed with another laugh.

"It would only be fair," Daniel said. "I'm indebted to show you Spain. After tomorrow, I have to return."

They split up after dinner, and Daniel believed he'd never see the man again. How big of a deal could it be; they'd only known each other for a handful of hours. The following day had to be spent on the thieves' guild mission anyway.

Daniel walked up to a manor that looked to be asleep, as the morning air had yet to burn off. He sneaked around, making it inside as quietly. Daniel worked his way to a study, narrowing missing servants that roamed the house. His goal was to steal some info, nothing more.

It was going well until on his way out a guard spotted him.

"Stop right there!" the man yelled, and broke into a sprint after him. Daniel ran for it, but he picked up two more guards in the attempt to flee. Outrunning them didn't seem like was going to work, so he turned back to face the group. The first was easy to take down, but the other two were giving him trouble.

After a struggle, he managed to get it down to a one on one. Being winded and inexperienced wouldn't stop him; not when the stakes were life and death. The guard grabbed him by the collar and threw him down to the dirt.

Daniel reached for his weapon, which had also fallen. The guard blocked him, with a swipe of his sword, forcing Daniel to retract his hand if he wanted his fingers to come back whole. "*Voleur,*" the guard spit.

Daniel didn't know what the man said, but clearly it wasn't meant as a compliment. He looked up at the man, but the sun blocked his view completely. A shadow that seemed to signal his death. The wait dragged every heartbeat out as if to savor the remaining few.

When no blow came, Daniel opened his eyes. He saw a man standing in silhouette, and another shadow in a pile on the ground.

Lance leaned in, pulling Daniel back on his feet. "Looks like you need someone to have your back."

Speechless, Daniel's eyes fell to the man on the ground who had Lance's decorative sword in his chest.

"Daniel?"

He shook his head, as the voice didn't match what he expected. Daniel turned to the sound, and blinked hard as Amilia returned now dressed in her gear. "What?"

Her eyes narrowed a little, possibly wondering if he was all there. Daniel couldn't blame her. He stared feverishly at her as he felt like that memory had somehow been shared. "I said, you should lead the way."

"Right." Daniel shook his head. "Let's go."

Daniel headed out, pausing just outside the door. There weren't many more places he could check, leaving him with limited options. He wanted to simply ask her where Lance would be kept, but didn't want to scare his only help away. He grimaced and offered the last lead he had. "There is a herald down by the fish market that might know something. Worth a shot, I guess."

Amilia followed Daniel as they hurried towards the market. She couldn't help but glance at him every so often.

The company made him seem more collected, but she wondered if he'd unravel and take it out on the square preacher if the lead didn't go anywhere. What lengths would he go to reach his friend? Would he risk his own life? Maybe the thieves were just a group, or maybe they were a family. Would she do any less for her uncle or cousin?

When they reached the platform the herald used, Amilia found herself hoping this day would end well. Somewhere along the line she started to care for Lance enough to want him safe, for Daniel's sake at very least.

Amilia stepped forward, coming up to the platforms side and signaling that they urgently needed to talk to him. Hesitantly, the man agreed.

"We need information from you," Daniel said, "The Knights have taken one of our men, and rumor has it you know where he is." He tried to make everything sound as simple as he could. No reason to let this stranger know he'd walk through hell to get Lance back.

"If you want secrets," the herald grinned boldly, "it is going to cost you."

Daniel sighed, growing annoyed already. He knew that was going to happen. It was always about money to some people. Daniel pulled out a bag of coins to bribe the man with, didn't even care about paying more than the usual fee.

The herald's eyes widened at the payday and he stashed the pouch away, not wanting people to see him inspecting it. "The rumors are true. The thieves crashed a party. The knights weren't very happy about that. Most wanted to kill the man they captured, but others saw him as an opportunity to take the thieves down." The herald's eyes flickered over to Amilia. "No one can withstand torture forever you see. I've heard they are hiding him near the river."

"Where near the river?" Daniel's patience was gone, and it showed in the rough tone. He'd already checked that area, and a vague direction wasn't going to change anything.

"That's all I can give you. I don't want my own body being forfeit as punishment for telling secrets," the man said, keeping whatever information he had left.

The idea of Lance suffering longer because this little pissant didn't want to tell him the whole story was not going to fly with Daniel. He grabbed a fist full of the man's clothes, pulling him close so they were face to face. "Tell me, or we can see just how long *you* can withstand torture."

"I know how thieves work," the man said, barely keeping his voice even. "You don't harm innocents. You are honor bound."

Daniel moved his hand around like he was doing some sort of magic trick. However, the trick ended with a knife under the man's chin, the tip already lightly pressing into the skin.

"Do I need to repeat myself?" Daniel asked. The look on his face sent a chill down the man's spine.

"All right! At the dock. They use it for other things because they don't think anyone will pay attention to everyone coming and going. I don't know anything else besides that, I swear. Please, don't hurt me."

Now the man was afraid. He was an idiot for not being so in the first place. The herald might have spilled everything. Daniel believed that, but he hadn't backed down, undecided if he wanted to kill the sniveling informant for wasting time.

Amilia nervously glanced over at Daniel before speaking up. "I hope this taught you that next time you shouldn't play around. You'll never be this lucky again."

Daniel was the one with the choice, but she knew he'd regret it if he did kill him. It would be meaningless. There were far more productive ways to yield this anger.

They got there in little time. Amilia realized that she had been leading. Daniel made no comment on the fact. The building seemed small from the outside, but she knew the structure extended below the ground. She felt strange for knowing so much about it now. It should have made her feel confident, but it just brought uneasiness.

Amilia pulled her bow from her back, and prepared an arrow for the first guard she saw patrolling out of view from the others. Before the next guard came fully around now, she shot him down as well. No one was made alarmed, except maybe herself for how easy each shot was becoming.

It had been her hope to break off from Daniel once they found the building. That way she could avoid upsetting the knights, or her family, by directly helping Daniel again. But everything she saw, from his clenched jaw to coiled shoulders, made her fear he'd snap without help.

"I know what you want to do," Amilia said softly. "And I know that you will do anything right now. But Daniel, I need you to keep a level head about this. I've got your back no matter what."

Those had been the first—and only—words to cause a real change in his expression all day. Daniel remembered his own words when she was afraid of becoming a monster. Now they mirrored Lance's in ways, too. It didn't make sense that he should still trust her. Not after everything he heard her say to others, after everything he overheard.

But he did.

"I'm not so worried about getting in as I am getting back out," Daniel said. The two of them stared at the building Lance was being kept in. "I'll take the front, while you head around the back to see if there are other exits for us. Maybe if we are lucky, they won't realize we brought a war to their doorstep." Amilia tilted her head, thinking two people didn't make an army, but Daniel continued before she could reply. "Let's meet back up somewhere in the heart of the building."

It was once an option she wanted, but now agreeing made her nervous. Still, she ran around towards the back of the building while Daniel took the straightforward approach. The difficulty level didn't matter if he got results.

The first group of men Daniel found were having a get-together that would be their last. Daniel made his introduction by slitting the throat of one before his intrusion was even noticed. A free-for-all broke out. Daniel managed to hold off four men for a while, before a guard landed a hit and filled his mouth with a coppery taste of blood. The pain tipped Daniel's rage over the boiling point and fighting multiple targets became easier. He nailed one right in the chest with a dagger before spinning around to drop another seconds later.

Daniel turned to the sole survivor. The guard nearly jumped out of his shoes before he darted down the hallway.

Daniel followed behind in no real rush. Each step slowly gaining on the man. As smooth as a ghost, he grabbed the guard and snapped his neck.

The man fell, revealing Amilia as she came down the same hall. The zen-like calm Daniel gained made Amilia's heart pound like she'd been the one fighting. The hard truth was the thief could be a true predator when desired.

"I..." she stumbled around for words.

Daniel cocked his head to the side. "You got here fast."

Amilia shook her head, more at herself than his comment. "I think I know the way, or at least I have a feeling it's down this way." She led them down a flight of stairs, and stopped to wait for him a few steps past the landing.

When Daniel crossed the invisible line that separated the stairs from the rest of the room, he seemed to trigger a cutscene. The camera ripped away from him jarringly, like a moth pulling towards a flame.

"You need to start talking if you ever want to see sunlight again."

A knight stood in front of a man shackled. His hands and feet were weighed down with long chains, and the cuffs rubbed against a jagged wound that hadn't been left alone or cleaned enough to be healing. Lance lifted his hanging head. His eyes narrowed at the threat, or as well as he could with one nearly swollen shut.

"Who was with you at the meeting?" the knight pressed.

Lance stayed as silent as the grave he still hoped to avoid. The wrong word would lead them back to Amilia, then Daniel, and finally the rest of the guild. Giving up any of them simply wasn't an option.

"Fine, have it your way." The knight took a step closer, and leaned over one of the shackles. "I personally love getting to play with you thieving dogs." He dug a thumb into the old bandage on his prisoner's wrist.

Lance let out a strangled cry, his eyes prickling with tears. He hadn't wanted to give the man any satisfaction, but the noise was given by a part of him that was too weak to fight anymore.

"Ah, so you can make noise." The knight smiled. "Start answering and end this already." The suggestion almost sounded reasonable now. His hand hovered away, only promising relief if Lance cooperated. When Lance said nothing he was greeted with a sharp pain once again.

"All right!" Lance said, his voice breaking after just those two words. He took in a ragged breath. "I'll talk."

This answer was good enough to warrant his tormentor taking a step back and waiting for him to continue. Lance licked his cracked lips before he spoke. "Have you heard of the works of Shan Yu?" he asked.

The man's brow pulled together. "What are you talking about?"

Lance stared down at the cracked floorboards that had a concerning stain and wondered if someone had died in the very spot. Then he looked back up. "He said you can live your whole life with a man, but you don't truly know him until you threaten his life."

"Point?" Whatever leash he had given for Lance to go off on this tangent now reached its end.

"It's nice to meet you," Lance grinned, with a raw amusement.

The knight growled in annoyance. "Fine, be that way," He said, and moved over to a table, running a hand over several instruments before coming to a stop on his selection. "Maybe this little guy will scare you." He picked up an exceptionally wicked looking torture device.

Lance stared, his eyes widening instinctively with fear. It was a device that demanded a pound of flesh, and said something of the man who decided to wield it. Mostly that the wielder didn't desire to keep their prisoner for much longer.

The knight tightened the device as the six claws bit into Lance's bare stomach. It hadn't been pushed in far as it could have, but puncture wounds hurt regardless of their depth. Lance screamed, and yanked against the restraints to protect himself, but came up laughably short. Another, weaker noise echoed the first as the device was pulled back, each talon now dripped in blood.

"Do you have anything else to say?"

Lance broke out into a sweat, his breath crashed against his chest like a rocky shore. *"Nous protégeons notre propre,"* Lance breathed out in French, not caring if the man spoke it or not.

Since it wasn't what the man wanted to hear, he lined the device back up then dug into Lance's flesh deeper this time.

"Nous protégeons notre propre," Lance repeated. He turned the urge to scream into words, the words, into a mantra.

"First you won't talk, now you won't shut up," the man said, with a smug smile. "I guess we are making progress after all."

The sheer will to move seemed to pull the camera back and made Daniel stumble forward. His hand dragged against the wall to help steady himself. Amilia was instantly at his side, offering help that was ignored.

Daniel took a deep breath and lifted his head with a new fire behind his eyes. "I don't know why this keeps happening, but we need to move faster." The vision had shaken him to the bone, but it did help lead the way.

The knight left the room, closing the door to his dirty deeds behind him. It was a surprise to see the blue tint of a real player's name, and summoned a fury like nothing else could. It was one flick of the wrist to pull a knife, another to sink it into the man's heart.

Player kills were taboo in some areas, but nothing stopped them. He would have ripped the man's heart out after seeing the flash of color, unable to even focus to read the name. When the man coughed blood up in surprise, Daniel discarded him and moved into the room.

Lance was slumped in the chair as far as the bindings would allow. There was a large gory mess on his torso, and dried blood caked one of his hands.

Daniel's breath seized in his chest at the sight. He dropped to his knees to be on the same level as his friend. "Lance?" Daniel called, "Come on, you need to wake up so we can get you out of here."

He lifted a hand to gently tilt Lance's face up. "Wake up," Daniel repeated, louder this time.

Lance's eyes stirred under his eyelids before he found the strength to open them. His eyes tried to focus on Daniel, unsure if he was an illusion or not. They crossed briefly as he tried to look at the figure at the door. Somehow finding Amilia there convinced him that he wasn't dreaming after all.

"I didn't think..." Lance started, closing his mouth as if struggling to get the words out. "You were going to come."

"You should have known better."

Lance's mouth twitched enough to give a small smile.

"Is that man dead?" Daniel asked Amilia, as he worked on the locks.

"Yes," she said, "I'll keep an eye out for others."

Now that his own personal cavalry was here, Lance's eyes started to feel heavy again.

"Hey, none of that," Daniel said, making Lance wake with a start. It sent a shiver of guilt through Daniel. It wasn't Lance's fault. It would be hard for anyone to stay awake after their body was trashed by pain. Maybe if he just continued talking, it would be something for Lance to focus on. "I'm just glad you are alive. I really don't know what I would have done without you."

Lance winced as Daniel busted the cuffs at his hands free. "You sap."

"Pour vous, l'amour." Daniel smiled and carried on with picking the locks around Lance's ankles.

Lance opened his mouth to say something, but Amilia shifting nervously at the door caught the majority of his attention. His chest tightened for a whole new reason. "I didn't tell them anything," he blurted.

"I know." The comment was a throwaway one as far as Daniel was concerned. He freed Lance, and moved back up to his feet to offer a hand, but Lance just stared up at him.

"I'm serious," Lance said, "Not about Amilia, not about anything."

Daniel paused. Lance had literally sacrificed flesh and blood to protect not only him, but a girl Daniel didn't think Lance liked very much. He thought about repeating himself, but didn't. He leaned in to help Lance up. Daniel looped Lance's arm around his shoulders to help support him.

"Stay here a moment," Amilia said. She darted out of the room. Daniel twitched. He wanted to tell her not to run off, that even the idea of splitting up now felt beyond wrong. But he couldn't very well run after her right now.

They waited a moment in silence, before Daniel turned his head towards Lance. "I never doubted you, but thank you for not telling them anything," Daniel said, wanting to make sure he knew, really knew.

"Welcome." Lance's voice was starting to sound distant. He needed real help, more than just a rescue. Medicine, or maybe a doctor would have to be found. Daniel edged them towards the door, and Lance stared down at his tormentor. He grimaced in a fashion that made his cheekbones seem sharper than usual. "Good riddance."

"I'll make him pay," Daniel said, "I promise."

Lance nearly snorted. "I think you already did."

Daniel stared at the knight on the ground. He didn't look the part without any armor, but was still a member. The name Marc Bello appeared in blue. Name, time of death, and location would be enough for Owen to sort through the players and find who he really was. In game, he could restart or respawn after a penalty. But in the real world, would torture go over as well?

"Sorry, I'm back," Amilia said, as she jogged back. "And I have a way out." She lead the way, and the boys followed as they wove through corridors, some filled with bodies of those they had already killed.

Without further incident they made it outside, following the waterfront simply to put a greater distance between them and anyone else.

"We need to fall under the radar," Amilia said, "I'm not even sure for how long." She doubted the knights would rest until they had someone who was responsible for this. Luck had been a part of why they'd gotten this far, but it rarely lasted.

Lance's knees started buckled as the heat of the sun weighed on him. He would have fallen onto the soft sand if Daniel hadn't kept him standing. Daniel's voice seemed like it was far too loud when he said there was a safe house they could go to.

"I don't think he's going to be able to walk there, though," Daniel continued.

Lance opened his mouth to object, but shut it. It was true.

"I'll go get us horses," Daniel said. He carefully lifted Lance's arm off his shoulder, and Lance braced himself against a nearby wall. When Daniel ran off, he started to slide down. Amilia jumped to help him sit, quickly pulling her hands back as Lance shot her a look.

"Thank you for your help," Lance said.

Amilia blinked. She tilted her head, ready to ask what he meant before realizing she misjudged the look. He hadn't been angry, he was struggling to not slow them down. Maybe he wanted that ounce of dignity in being able to sit down by himself. "It's nothing," Amilia said softly.

Lance raised a brow. He could start a fight, but he was in no mood for it. "I guess you do like me after all." He grinned until a pain in his side made him reposition himself.

Amilia smiled. "You might be growing on me."

A smile returned briefly before he leaned his head back against the wall. Lance woke up to the sound of Daniel's voice. He wasn't sure how long he had been out of it. It didn't seem long, but still, enough for Daniel to return with two horses.

Amilia was already on the first. Lance gave Daniel a 'not going to happen' look as he helped him to his feet. It took further help to get on the horse. By the time Lance was up, his eyes were glossy, and a worrisome waver worked its way in his breathing.

Daniel pulled himself up on the horse afterward, serving as both a driver and something to lean against for support. The three rode for a while before they reached a safe house. It was the type of house that people in the city complained about not having. Somewhat tucked away, with enough room for a garden and a backyard. Of course, this was one held by the guild to hide and restock.

"Head inside and see what medical supplies we have," Daniel instructed Amilia.

She nodded and rushed in. When Daniel came in, Lance was in his arms. Amilia had cleared a long kitchen table, and gathered all the medical supplies she could find.

Daniel laid Lance down on the table. It would work for what they needed, despite Lance's legs hanging off the end.

Amilia pulled off some armor so she could help more freely. Her breath stuttered out as she lifted her arm. She glanced over to a patch of red on her sleeve. Any pain she felt had to be ignored for now.

"Are you injured anywhere we can't see? Broken ribs or fractures?" she asked Lance. If he was too severely injured, they'd have to find a real doctor.

"No, I'm fine." Lance tilted his head back trying to glimpse over at Amilia. He barely could see her over in the corner, getting a washcloth, by the sound of it. Simply passing out seemed favorable to being fussed over.

"Shut up, and tell her everything that hurts," Daniel said.

Lance sighed. "The bruises can be ignored. They pale in comparison to my side."

Amilia placed a rag on his forehead, and his whole body trembled. She hadn't been able to get cold water all the way out here, so the shiver suggested a stronger fever than she expected.

Daniel cleaned Lance's torso and pulled away the damaged clothes as best as he could. "You're going to need stitches," he said.

Next, he looked to Lance's wrist, which had a shoddy bandage that was rolling back and in desperate need of changing. "Amilia, can you fix that for me?" Daniel asked.

Being patched up wouldn't have been so bad if they both weren't touching things that hurt. The combined effect was threatening Lance's sanity. Overwhelmed, he stared up at the ceiling.

"You're gonna need to hold him down," Daniel said.

Lance looked over to him as nervousness made everything sharp again, but Daniel had a detached look on his face. He wasn't there for support right now; he was a man with a job that needed to be done. There was a reason doctors didn't operate on people they knew. Distancing yourself was hard.

Amilia nodded. "Here, bite onto this," she said, offering Lance a rag. Once in place, she put her forearms on his shoulders, distributing her weight so she had all the leverage she could get. "Ready when you are."

As the needle wove Lance's skin back together, nerve endings he would have sworn had died started chirping wildly like crickets that couldn't get enough attention. His fingers dug into the wooden table, splinters biting into his fingertips as he tried to hold still. Lance mumbled behind the cloth in his mouth. Whether words or a cry, the meaning was lost.

"Everything will be fine, I promise. You'll be better in no time," Amilia whispered softly. There wasn't much comfort to be had. His closest friend was unable to show support, and she wasn't in a position to really hold his hand. But she still tried.

Daniel paused to look over his handiwork. The black thread made it look like the legs of a spider. Without a word, he moved over to the basins to wash up. Daniel's reserve cracked before he dipped his hands in freshwater. His heart beat roughly, yearning for everything to be fine. He stood there, shoulders tight as he gripped at the edge of the table.

A quick glance at Lance showed that he had already passed out. Daniel's eyes continued over to Amilia.

"Your arm," he said. "Please don't pretend like we both don't know you hurt it."

"Oh." Amilia turned to look at the injury. An arrow had nicked it. The cut hardly seemed worthy of attention during the heat of everything else.

Daniel moved closer, meeting her brown eyes to check for any objections before he pulled up her sleeve. He reached over to grab the bandages, and mumbled an apology as he pressed it to her arm. Amilia's wince justified the comment after the fact.

"I could have taken care of it," she breathed, and watched his face instead of looking at her arm.

Daniel shrugged. It wasn't a far reach to want to take care of her. Helping was much easier than admitting guilt, or anger over letting this happen. "Done," he said. Amilia's eyes never left his as he finished, and now that he found them again his focus was completely shot. "Thank you for helping me...I don't know how to repay you."

"It's nothing really," Amilia said, and looked away towards Lance. "It was worth it. The Knights can be so horrible. Sometimes I don't—I can't even believe it. I thought the title meant nobility."

Daniel hummed an agreement. "It's not noble when you can buy it."

"Even stolen nobility looks good on you."

He smiled, and kissed Amilia on the forehead. She kept helping the thieves guild—no. She kept helping him. "Whatever it takes to keep one of our own safe."

//////////////

"What do you mean, it glitched?"

Owen glanced around the room that was decked out in pastel purple. What was once Emily's living room was now baby shower central. Katherine, one of Em's friends, had brought cookies cut in the shape of bottles and baby strollers. The frosting colors ranging from soft green to rubber duck yellow.

Maybe the setting is what made talking about this so hard. These were what Owen dubbed Emily's 'I'm a real adult' friends. Most were married and/or had kids of their own, a rare few were simply co-workers. Which left Owen and Neal as the only friends left over from before she was married. They were tucked by the food table, where bachelors not comfortable with babies always ended up.

"Well?" Neal asked. "Are you going to finish your story, or just stare at the finger sandwiches?"

Owen sighed. "When Lance was missing, I went to ask for help from Amilia. The game showed a flashback, and the headgear fucked up the colors. Blue looked gray, then when we got closer, my camera ripped away from me."

"You stopped seeing color when Lance was in trouble?" Neal asked.

131

"Well..." Owen had explained this twice already. His eyes narrowed slightly wondering if he was the one missing something instead of Neal. "Only blue."

Neal smirked to himself.

"What?"

"That sounds so romantic." Neal picked up a cupcake that was made to look like a rattle. He pulled out the stick that was tipped with a lifesaver. "You know, the colors leaving your life when someone you care about goes?"

Owen groaned loud enough that the whole room probably heard it. "That's too much. It's going to make me sick like the guess what smeared chocolate bar made the fake poopy diaper game. I'm never eating chocolate, or talking to you, again."

Neal laughed, but Owen broke off away from him instead of hearing any more. He was surrounded by other ladies, but ignored them to favor the arm of Em's recliner.

When the group discussions broke into side conversations, Emily looked up at Owen. "Was Neal picking on you?" Her smile lit up her otherwise tired expression.

"He's the worst," Owen said, without much feeling.

Emily patted his leg. "There, there."

Owen watched as Neal tried to flirt with a girl who had ventured over for a drink. It was a mockery, fit for a middle schooler. "I'm not sure why you even put up with him."

"Same reason I put up with you."

He looked back, gauging her comment before grinning. "Because, I'm so charming?"

"Bingo."

"Oh!" Katherine yelled from the small group sitting in on the couch. "We should start bingo."

Owen rolled his eyes, but no one seemed to notice.

"Alright, sounds fun," Emily said, before she glanced back up at Owen. "You should have invited Andreah. It could have been your baby shower gift to me."

"Oh yeah, *this* is something I wanted to invite her to." He glanced around the room. Within three seconds, he spotted the word *baby* four times. "It's totally her scene and everything."

Emily pursed her lips and shot him a look before she tried to get up. The simple task was getting harder and harder, now that it looked like she swallowed a watermelon.

"Help me up?"

Owen got up and offered his hand.

"Thanks," she smiled.

He mirrored the sweetness found there for a second before it faded. "I'm sorry Rick couldn't be here." His voice was a near whisper, and if they had stepped back, she wouldn't have heard.

Emily looked down for a second, before lifting her chin. "It's okay. It's what I signed up for, and he'll be home in a few months," she said. "Now if you excuse me, I have to go win bingo. The prize is extra shares in our office lotto."

"Maybe they will give you two cards, since you're playing for two."

"Oooh," Emily said, as she lingered between Owen and the group that gathered to play. "I should see if they would go for that."

Owen messed around on his phone as they played baby bingo. It was an odd sort of game. Instead of numbers, you marked down what gifts were given to the mother-to-be as she opened up presents. Emily had given Neal and Owen each a card to play for her, since she had to actively keep the game going. Every other gift or so Owen looked up to see what was opened and the marked it down.

"Bingo!" Katherine called at the second-to-last gift.

The cry was welcome, since boredom threatened to swallow Owen whole. He waited until Emily finished opening the last gifts before he decided to head home.

"Isn't this the cutest?" Emily asked as Owen came over to say goodbye. She held up a onesie Star Trek uniform complete with fake badge. "Rick's going to love it."

Owen chuckled. "That baby is going to be the cutest little one in the Alpha Quadrant."

"Hey! You got that right."

"I'll have you know..." Owen said, very seriously. He leaned in, and glanced if the others were listening in. "...That I've been studying up so your hubby and I will have something to talk about when he gets back."

Em's smile melted into one even sweeter as she brought the baby clothes to her chest. She knew Owen wouldn't like to be called out for the gesture, so she moved on. "Are you heading out?"

"Yeah, was planning on it." Owen bent down so he could give her a hug without making her get up again. He waved a goodbye to Neal, who nodded, as he was being talked up by one of the girls.

It was a bit of a walk back to his place, but Owen was in no hurry. About ten minutes in he decided to give Andreah a call. It rang for a while. He started to doubt she'd pick up.

"Hello?" Andreah said.

"Hey, beautiful." Owen thought he could hear her roll her eyes over the phone.

"You know you remind me of an old man when you actually call me, right?"

Owen scoffed, making a lady with a poodle look up at him as she sat outside on a bench. He didn't say anything, but turned his head enough so she could see the phone and connect the dots. "Maybe, I was worried about street harassment and wanted an excuse for strangers not to talk to me?"

"Does that actually happen to you?" Andreah laughed.

"No, I'm a guy, of course it doesn't."

Andreah laughed louder this time, less reserved since he had already made her grin once. "So, what are you doing?"

"Walking home from Em's." Owen was forced to stop at an intersection. The temptation to jaywalk was strong, but the half-second of thinking cost him the window of opportunity.

"Aww, I want to meet your friends."

"Really?" His head jerked with the surprise. He had only briefly met her friends, and meeting his felt like a step she wasn't into. "Well, it was a baby shower so..."

"Oh."

He would have shaken his head if he didn't want to book it across the crosswalk. This route was one he took fairly often, and if he moved fast enough there'd be no worry about catching the other lights. "So, what are you doing?"

"Just relaxing in bed, watching some TV."

"Yeah? What are you wearing?" The comment caught the attention of someone Owen was walking with. Their eyes went wide, and turned their head as if to gesture to one of their friends that this was actually happening.

Andreah took a few seconds too, likely deciding how she wanted to play this. "Well, I have thigh high boots and a fuzzy cat suit—"

"Stop. I'm sorry, stop," he said, now talking over her with a laugh. "I have to remember not to play chicken with you in public."

"Or ever. That was the shortest yet, I must be getting good. I was going to go with the skin of my enemies, but it seemed a bit...Hmm, I dunno, much?"

"You should have gone with a onesie," Owen suggested, if anyone was still listening they were lost now. "You know, because it would have been a throwback to the baby shower?"

"Oh, that would have been clever. I won all the same, though."

"You aren't even here, and you're trying to embarrass me."

"You get so cute when you are embarrassed, though. You just stare off like you can't believe this is happening, and the tips of your ears get all red," Andreah said with a renewed excitement.

"You need to stop." But she didn't. Owen had to avoid a car that decided to make an illegal turn into the crosswalk right that second. He might have flipped them off if Andreah wasn't more pressing. "I swear to god, I'm going to hang up if you continue."

Andreah chuckled. "Goodnight, Owen."

"Goodnight, brat."

When Owen got home, he should have cleaned up around his apartment, or tried to get a reasonable amount of sleep for once. Instead, he had a job to do, even if this one only paid in personal gratification. He told Lance he'd find the man who'd hurt him, and by god he would.

He dropped down into his computer chair and grabbed a pad of paper. Owen wrote down everything he currently knew. The character name of Marc Bello, the in-game time of death, and the city it happened in. From there Owen spent an hour or more scrolling through obituaries listed on the game's forums. These official lists were mostly ignored. A list of dead characters was about as interesting as a press release. Occasionally, a big name player died unexpectedly, and reporters could scoop the story this way.

For a bone digger, these ashes were a gold mine. If a player was trying to hide their username this is how they found it. It was paired along with time of death and location so that the system was able to keep the player's login, friends list, and cash items.

"Got you," Owen grinned. He highlighted the username of MarkLark. There was plenty of steps before he had a real name, but this was a start. The loose thread needed to find the man behind the torturer.

Frank's coffee barely touched his desk before one of his workers stormed into his office. "Owen?" he asked, blinking in surprise. He had barely gotten here himself. Half the lights were still off. "What are you doing here so early?"

"I have a story for you," Owen said. A manila folder was tucked against his chest as if it protected him against the morning cold. With quick steps, he dropped it on Frank's desk. Instead of flipping through the folder, Frank keep an eye on Owen as he spoke. "In game, I found a man that was torturing people. If the guy had just been an NPC, or a just an average person, we'd label them as an asshole, and that would be it. But this guy is a doctor. General practitioner Mark Byers."

Frank's lips parted as his head started to swirl with ideas of where this story could go, but he'd been in this business too long to get excited about possible headlines. "We can't just slam this guy for his choices. It will seem petty, and if we aren't careful, it will be downright libel."

"We don't have to actually accuse him or anything. Just state the facts of what he did and ask, just ask, a single question. Is it ethical for a doctor to play a torturer?" Owen pressed his hands together, it was all he could do to keep from pacing around Frank's office. The lack of sleep the night before meant he was running on momentum.

"How did you find this story?" Frank asked. He started to flip through the papers that proved the connection from Age of Shadows to a professional LinkedIn account. The doctor had made one mistake; he used the same username for multiple accounts.

"I, uh," Owen stammered. He never wanted this to be about him, but if the story couldn't be proven, Frank would instantly drop it. "It happened on a mission I was on."

Frank nodded, and looked through more of the papers that were on the doctor's practice. He lifted a skeptical eye back to Owen, who started nervously chewing on his lip. "Did you find this all legally?"

"Absolutely."

A grin crept across Frank's face as he slowly let himself buy into this story. It would make a killer editorial. "Write me up something and we'll run it in tomorrow's issue."

Owen felt breathless, and wanted to dart out of the room to get working on it. If he rode the high of a yes, he'd definitely be able to write up a draft before fatigue hit him.

"Do you want the byline?" Frank asked.

"All yours, boss."

"God, I should pay you more."

Owen chuckled. He didn't care about his name, or to personally gain from this. All he wanted was for that doctor to have real world consequences for the horrible things he did. The world would decide what they wanted to do with him after that. While more money was always nice, he just wanted to thank Frank for running the story. Instead, not wanting to look too eager, he bargained.

"The coffee in this building is awful," Owen said, "I'd call it even if you brought me the good stuff tomorrow."

When Daniel and Lance walked the guilds halls again, they were treated like ghosts. Their absence the past couple of days started rumors that they were dead. Everyone kept a careful distance. Well, almost everyone.

A young thief named Isidoro Martinez ran up. "I heard what you did," he said, with bright wide eyes that made him look too young for the guild. "Not everyone believed you guys were going to make it back. But I did." He grinned, like he won a bet with someone.

"Well, thank you," Lance said.

Isidoro nodded, and fell behind them as they marched over to Gael. Abel stood next to their headmaster. His tight expression made him look annoyed at their return.

"This is how legends are born," Gael said, his tone unreadable. "Your little mission was not very nice to Mr. Garcia. It was rash and put his cover at risk."

Daniel glanced over to Abel as he crossed his arms over his chest. Ah, so that's why he was so pissy. He must have been playing spy when they stormed the knight's building.

"Sir, if it wasn't for Daniel's quick action I don't think I'd—" Lance said.

Gael held up a finger interrupting him. "But I can't dispute Daniel's results."

"I would have found him," Abel grumbled. Daniel's stare didn't waver, and wouldn't until he knew if the man was going to make a bigger deal of it. Abel moved closer, and Isidoro took a nervous step back. A rookie move, not mirrored by Daniel or Lance as Abel stepped into their space.

"Welcome back," Abel said, as he walked past and out of the room.

With guild business cleared up, the duo headed to the archery field. Daniel's bow was down at his side as he sat on a tree stump that was doubling as a chair. After Lance nearly dying, Daniel wanted to make sure his friend didn't push himself too hard.

Lance pulled an arrow out of his quiver and lined up a shot. As he pulled the string back, a sharp twinge of pain ran through his hand, and up to his elbow. It completely ruined the shot, making the arrow fly a grand total of two feet. "This is pointless," Lance groaned.

Daniel stayed silent for the moment. More than Lance's body had taken a blow. His pride had also been beaten. "You have to give it time," Daniel said.

"I don't want to give it time!" Lance yelled. "I can't shoot an arrow; I can barely grip with my left hand. How am I supposed to do anything?"

In truth, no one expected Lance to do anything for a while, after what happened. Torture isn't the sort of thing you instantly bounce back from. The only person Lance was letting down was himself, and if he needed to scream until his throat was raw, Daniel would hear him out.

"You needn't worry so much," Daniel said. He brought his bow in front of him, resting his hands and head on it. "Even with a hand tied behind your back, you can give most people a run for their money."

Lance sighed. His eyes lowered to the grass before he finally was able to glance back up. As much as he wanted rage to fuel everything, he was tired.

"Come on," Daniel said, "We've been here for hours, let's go get food."

"Yeah, all right."

They walked to a small fruit market, and the change of scenery seemed to lighten the mood. "Look at the bright side of things, buddy," Daniel said. His grin suggested he was up to no good. "I'm just a better fighter than you now."

"Ha, very funny."

"No, no, really, hear me out," Daniel said. He purposely bumped into Lance as if to egg him on as he brainstormed more things to tease about.

Lance looked around as if searching for something to beat Daniel over the head with. "If you keep being mean, I'm going to tell your little girlfriend on you," he threatened.

"Please." Daniel's nose scrunched up at the very idea. There were so many things wrong with that statement. For one, he hadn't even seen Amilia since she left without a word once Lance was stable. "What are you going to do? Hunt her down just to tell her I am picking on you?"

"I don't need to hunt her down," Lance grinned. "Because she is right over there."

Daniel turned sharply towards where Lance was pointing. He hadn't believed it at first, but now his jaw dropped. Amilia had been missing for days, and now she was just casually walking about with a bag in one hand and a half-eaten pear in the other. He stared, thinking she might be a figment of their imagination.

He hung back for a moment. While her uncle hadn't been mortally wounded, he doubted stabbing a family member was a forgivable offense. Would she care now that someone else's life wasn't in danger?

Lance gave Daniel a literal push to go talk to her.

Daniel hesitated after the first forced step, then decided to ignore the politics of the situation and ventured the rest of the way. "Hello stranger," he said, playfully hoping to keep things light.

Amilia was caught mid-bite. She swallowed the bite nearly whole and wiped her mouth like she'd been indecent. "Hello," she mumbled before clearing her throat. "How's Lance?" Amilia glanced around for him, but in the bustle of the street only managed to have her bags bumped by others as they passed.

"He is doing pretty well. Full of complaints, but that's the nature of such things," Daniel said, trying to weave his words carefully. "Speaking of which, I—uh, heard a family member of yours fell ill. How are they?"

She bit her lip, wishing they didn't have a lie like this. But neither of them knew exactly what the other knew, and neither of them wanted to come out with it.

"Fine," she said. "Actually, I have to go. I'm sorry, but I'm glad Lance is feeling better." She shifted her bag over her shoulder before she tucked her head down and started walking. "See you another time, Daniel," Amilia quickly added, along with a silent prayer that he wouldn't follow her.

"Amilia, wait," Daniel called. It was no use. He sighed and let her walk away. Everything was always black or white between them. If they had a situation that brought something gray into the mix, she bolted.

Lance had moved closer as Amilia fled. "There is something wrong with that girl," he added. They could still see her in the crowd of people. "Well, go after her."

Daniel's frown was laced with a confused surprise. Encouragement was something he hadn't expected. But if she was playing both sides, maybe she did need help. That game could only be played for so long.

He ran to catch back up to Amilia. This time far less playfully. "Are you in some sort of trouble?" Daniel asked. "I might not know the whole story, but let me help. We said we were in this together, remember?"

Amilia stopped as he drew even with her. Her expression was pinched, as if he was just some guy bothering her on the street. "My problem isn't a part of whatever deal we have, Daniel."

"Why does it have to be?" His question was only met with a tired and bored attitude. It snapped his patience like a taut rubber band. "You know what? Fine. Do as you wish." The words bit down like they had little fangs of their own. He had the urge to wash his hands of this situation, possibly even her. "Maybe I'm tired of this, too."

He knew he was being just as childish as her now. But if they couldn't deal with this as adults, then maybe he would sink to the same level. This time Daniel walked away before she had the chance to.

"Things went well, I take it," Lance said. He had to fall into step with Daniel in a hurry, as Daniel seemed ready to book it right past him.

Daniel narrowed his eyes, but held his tongue.

"If I'm remembering correctly," Lance smiled mischievously, "you said you'd buy me lunch."

"Oh, did I now?" Daniel smiled, despite everything. "Did you also get a head injury you didn't tell me about?"

"Señor Ortiz," Lance said, sticking to his story. "You promised."

Lance's level of dedication to this free lunch made Daniel laugh a little. Daniel broke off from his friend, moving into a group of people who were walking. Carefully, he pickpocketed one of the citizens, carrying on like nothing had happened. Once the group passed, Daniel tossed Lance the coin pouch. "There. I paid for our lunch."

Upon catching the bag, Lance glanced at the man who had lost his money, still blissfully unaware. "Well technically..." He cut his own objection off with a shrug. "Close enough."

Owen had ignored this quest. He had forgotten about the bet he had made with Amilia for a while, and after that, well, he was afraid to complete it. Amilia had been acting flighty, and this mission felt like the only tie he had to her. But tonight, he finally felt ready to return to the archery range. Amilia was already there when he showed up. She shot Daniel a quick glance before focusing on her aim. If she could hit two moving targets on demand he'd promised to take her anywhere.

He gave it a moment, watching her arrow fly before she turned to let him speak with a raised brow. "I think I've given you more than enough time to practice. How about we finish the bet of ours?"

He couldn't read Amilia's expression until a slow smile built up, outweighing whatever else had been going on in her head. "Now works," Amilia said.

She looked at the field in front of her, then took her stance, and breathed in deeply. She poured her full concentration into the task at hand. A disc flew through the air, and she sprang into action. She tracked it for a moment before taking the shot, the string of her bow still vibrating as she spotted the second target. Panic graced her face as she quickly aimed again. But the disc hit the ground first, and broke on its own merit.

"Oh." Amilia stared at the pieces in disbelief. She hadn't really expected Daniel to take her to Santiago, but now that offer seemed even further in the past than it had only seconds ago. She forced a smile as she turned to Daniel.

"Well then, if your reward hasn't changed." She cleared her throat. "Is this still a case where the gentleman..."

Daniel stared, maybe in greater disbelief than even she felt. He'd never expected her to miss. Maybe if the challenge had been right away, but not now. Amilia set her bow on the ground, and seemed to steel herself, as if this kiss was just part of a mission.

"I—you've been doing great," Daniel said. He'd seen her hit moving targets when it mattered. It seemed unfair to fail her just because she didn't on his demand.

"Maybe," she said, "but you did win."

"I'll still take you to Santiago, if you wish."

The surprise hit her so hard that she didn't even move. It looked like she blinked, then froze for a few seconds. Amilia shook her head like she couldn't believe what she heard. "You'd really make that trek with me? After the cold shoulder I've been giving you lately? After...everything?"

"Yes," Daniel said. There was something about being pulled multiple directions, wordlessly even, that made him empathize, made him want to understand better. "It's obviously important to you."

Too overwhelmed for words, Amilia threw her arms around his neck to seize a hug. "Thank you so much, Daniel." A real smile came to her as she closed her eyes. There was a temptation in the pit of her stomach, and warmth she wished would wash over her completely.

Amilia rose onto the tips of her toes so her lips could reach his. They were past the point of second guessing this. Her lips raised enough to meet his, and every nerve felt alive and ready.

Daniel held perfectly still, afraid that the moment would be ruined if he so much as breathed. He had carefully kept his eyes open so he could be awake for this, until he lost himself to it as his hands reached up to touch the sides of her face.

Death in people's lives made them rash, and as a thief he knew that better than most, but this felt different. This felt like they finally stopped fighting each other.

After seconds locked between his lips, Amilia pulled away. Her only regret was that this moment had taken so long to arrive. Amilia waited for him to say or do something as she gazed up at him, but any words were lost, his mind trailing behind to relive the past few seconds before it clicked that he didn't have to. Daniel chuckled softly. She was right here; there was no need to wait any longer. His kiss found her quicker this time, as if drawn towards her by an invisible force.

Reluctantly, Daniel pulled away; taking a breath like it was the first. This was the last thing he had expected when he came out today. "I guess you don't owe me a kiss anymore."

Amilia laughed. She looked around to come up with a reply, but cleared her throat as she remembered others were also using the range. They all seemed too caught up in their own business to care, but Amilia still took a step back to be proper.

Daniel's eyes barely rose to see the others, and when he looked to Amilia again, he felt lighter.

Every day for the past week, when Owen got to the office there had been coffee waiting from the place down the street. He hadn't really expected Frank to do it once, let alone to keep it up. By the sixth day, he was starting to feel pretty spoiled.

The treatment, in no small part, had to do with the effect that one little question caused. A national paper had run their story. It even appeared on the front of their issue's gaming section.

And tonight, they'd celebrate. Owen had invited Andreah to tag along with him and a bunch of his friends at their favorite gaming bar, but hadn't gotten a text back to say whether or not she was actually coming. Between games, he'd glance towards the door as if he might catch her walking in. Otherwise, he gave his full attention racing his butt off against the rival racer and his friend, Seth.

"Shit, shit, shit," Owen said, as he cranked the wheel hard to get off the grass he had accidentally driven up on.

Seth laughed as he drove through a checkpoint, getting them an extra 30 seconds of playtime. "I thought you were good at video games."

"Cut me some slack." Owen righted his car and floored it to chase after him. "There are no driving tests in the 17th century."

"Or anywhere in the 1600's," Nicole chimed in. Owen stole a glance over at her as she perched over Seth's chair. Her bold black eye makeup made it impossible to miss the wink she gave Owen. "If you beat him by 20 seconds or more, I'll buy you a shot, Seth."

"Prepare to buy me a drink, then," he said. He switched gears with all the jerkiness the joystick allowed.

"And here I thought you were on my side!"

"Sorry, Owen," Nicole said. "Always side with the roommate."

Owen's car came to a stop as Seth crossed the finish line. He had caught up a lot, but not quite enough. His car halted agonizingly right before the checkered line. "Urg, I almost had you." He leaned into the wheel, and hung his head.

"Ruined my chance at free booze too," Seth said. He watched as the game counted down from 15 for more quarters. "Are we playing again?"

"Nah, I think food should be ready." Owen got up, and looked over to the table that Emily and Neal were holding down. It looked like they were just talking, and no food seemed to be waiting. "I'll go check." He got up, and took a few steps backwards. "Should I get us a pitcher?"

Nicole slid into his seat and lounged there. "This is why you are my favorite sore loser."

Owen rolled his eyes and headed back to the others. Charlie had been leaning against pillars that separated the arcade and the more restaurant-like section of the bar. There had been plenty of seats for them, but they didn't want to separate themselves too much from the group.

"They are talking about our game," Charlie said, and nodded towards the wall of TVs.

Owen turned. The little tag of #Rehashed appeared in the bottom of the screen as the TV played a clip of Age of Shadows. It was a particularly gruesome one. A player had cleaved through the shoulder armor of someone on the ground before running them through.

With a flashy intro, the show came back to a dressed up host and the ribbon graphic below that listed her name and handle. "Should in game choices have real world consequences?" Sarah asked. "That is what we were talking about before the ad break. We heard Aaron's opinion that no, a game is a different world, and therefore, has a different code of conduct. However, I disagree. Sure, some choices don't matter. If you have to kill a boss to get to the next level, that doesn't make you a murderer in person. But if you hang out in Age of Shadows spouting slurs, targeting gold farmers to 'let your rage out', and taking a sick pleasure in things you can't do in person, you clearly have issues. Realities in fiction matter. Maybe you should be exposed so people know the type of person they are dealing with. Recently we've seen the case of a doctor, who was torturing characters in game. Just because you can do something, doesn't mean you should. And those who report, protect, and heal the public should be held to a high ethical standard."

"That's my story," Owen said.

"What?" Charlie asked.

"That's my story," he repeated. "I gave my boss that story, and he published it, and now look. Sarah freaking Nett is talking about it."

"Tell us what you think using hashtag #Rehashed!" Sarah cheerfully reminded before they cut to more ads.

"Oh my god, dude," Charlie said. "This was the whole Lance thing, right?

Owen nodded.

"Oh my god!" they repeated. "I'm just going to hang out in Daniel's party all the time now. All the cool stuff happens to you."

Owen laughed. "Oh come on, don't fanby on me now. Friends sit at our table."

Once they neared the table, Charlie announced the news. "Guess who was on TV, again?"

"No." Neal's cry of disbelief made Emily fight back a laugh.

"It's true." Charlie took the seat on the other side of Emily, and saw that Seth and Nicole coming over to the table now too.

Owen didn't. Nicole grabbed Owen's shoulders from behind making him jump. "What's true?" she asked.

"I'm starting to think that Owen is becoming the most famous anonymous player. A story from his work was on #Rehashed."

"Don't be absurd," Owen said, and slid into the empty side of the booth. Cole slid in next to him, squeezed between him and Seth, who took the outside seat. Emily seemed to tune everyone out as she scrolled through her phone.

"Aw, I was hoping you were on the news for something illegal," Seth said. He leaned forward, scanning the table for food or drinks, but only Emily and Neal had anything. "I say we make you take a shot for everyone who talks about you while using that hashtag. Sounds like a fun game."

"I dunno," Owen laughed. "I guess, why not."

"The 'why' is, you don't want alcohol poisoning," Emily said. The group let out a collective 'what,' jumbled up in similar questions. "Here, look." She put her phone down in the middle of the table, and scrolled to show all of the messages. "There must be a hundred within the last five minutes, all about the story."

"Shots!" Nicole declared, and threw up her hand to call over a waitress.

"Cole, no, I don't want to finish a whole bottle myself."

"Do six," Seth suggested. He leaned forward to look around Nicole. "One for each of us."

"Yeah, that's not even with you drinking two in my honor," Emily added. Her grin widened as Owen shot her a look silently asking why she was doing this.

"Two," Owen countered.

"Five."

"Two."

"The board will compromise with four." Seth delegated like it was a serious court issue.

"Fine, but only if you guys pay for them." Everyone whipped out their wallets, and tossed bills towards him faster than patrons at a strip club with a hacked ATM. Owen stared at the pile of fives, and a single ten, with his hands above it all like he couldn't believe.

Nicole reached over and collected it into a neat pile. "Scoot," she told Seth. He did so she could get out. "I'll go order for us." When she came back had four shots, a pitcher of beer, and extra glasses for the rest of them.

Owen stared down at the shots that were placed in front of him, and glanced up at Emily who was giggling behind her water glass. One, two, three shots down without a problem. He paused as the fourth sat in his hand. "You had to get fireball, didn't you?" Owen shot Cole a look.

"I don't know what you are talking about," she said, and looked at her nails that were painted to match the purple dye in her hair.

"Don't you just love us?" Charlie asked.

Owen breathed out roughly. "Starting to wonder if that goes both ways."

Nicole patted Owen's leg encouragingly as he downed the last shot. "Atta boy," she smiled. "Come on, I want to see if I'm good enough to beat you at any of the arcade games yet."

"Alright. I'm too wired to sit anyways."

Seth scraped his short black hair back as he got out of the seat again to let people pass.

"Hmm," Nicole hummed and glanced over the arcade. "We already tested your skills in racing. Let's try an old school fighter game."

Owen studied the movement guide for a second, but any serious player would have considered their fighting technique as informed button mashing at best. While the game was closer to Owen's usual close quarter fighting, Nicole's moves were so unpredictable that it didn't really matter.

"Winner!" she shouted, and threw her hands in the air. "Next on #Rehashed, average college student turns professional."

"It's two out of three!" Owen objected. The game waited for them to make their next selection, but that didn't damper her celebration. "I demand a rematch right now. Right fucking now."

"Owen?" a new voice said.

He turned, and lit up. "Andreah!"

"Hi," she said, and glanced at Nicole. The two made an odd pair. Owen was unusually dressed up in a button-up and tie. While someone she didn't know sported bright colors in her hair, and wore muted clothes you might find in an art studio. "Who's your friend?"

"This is Nicole," he said, and she wiggled her fingers in hello. "Let me introduce you to everyone else."

"Are you drunk?" Andreah asked right off the bat.

"I may be slightly to pretty tipsy right now. I'm having, like, the best day ever though. Come on." Owen took her hand like she was kicking her feet on the matter. She followed, and looked over her shoulder to see Nicole beat up a character that was virtually a punching bag right now.

Owen let go of Andreah's hand as they stopped in front of their booth. "Everyone, this is my girlfriend, Andreah." He pointed to each person in order starting on the left. "This is Charlie, Emily, Neal. I know them via family, or the game. On the other side is Seth. I know him and Cole from elsewhere."

151

Andreah gave them a proper wave, but her attention lingered on Seth for a moment. He didn't look memorable in a hoodie and jeans. But he cocked his head as if he, too, thought she looked familiar. She broke the eye contact quickly to address everyone. "It's nice to meet you all."

"Oh food," Owen declared. He sat down and made Seth tuck in his feet so he didn't hog the whole side. The pizza they ordered was still steaming despite several pieces already being dished onto plates.

"It's nice to meet you," Emily said. "Help yourself, if you'd like."

"That's okay, thanks. If I would have known we were dressing up—" Andreah reached over to prod at Owen's tie. He half-heartedly leaned away. "I might have dressed up more myself."

"You look darling," Emily said, and turned sharply to Neal. "I do sound like a mother already."

"I told you," Neal said, around a mouthful of food.

Owen inhaled half the slice before he cleared his mouth so he could talk again. "And stop pestering me about the tie. I had to interview someone today, and I haven't gotten a chance to change yet."

Cole popped up between Seth and Owen, leaning against the back of the booth. "I won, by the way."

"Because you cheated."

"You forfeited."

That was true, so Owen decided not to counter it. Then Seth pulled out a lighter, which did warrant Owen's attention. "You can't smoke in here."

Seth opened his mouth to object, and then groaned at the fact that he had to get up again. Instead of making Owen and Andreah get up, he climbed over the back of the seat.

"Hey, come outside with me?" Seth asked Nicole, and the two of them headed outdoors.

"So, how did you two meet?" Charlie asked.

"Oh, uh." Andreah glanced over to Owen, curious if he was going to answer, but he seemed intent to finish off that slice. "I had to deliver a package to his office, and I guess we sort of hit it off."

"That's cute."

She wasn't sure if that's what she'd call it, but she wanted to be proper and agreed.

Neal cleared his plate and looked up to Andreah. "Before you came, we were talking about the racing games. They have the version that can connect four people at once. Did you want to join us?"

"I'm good." The trio across from her didn't seem too convinced. "Really, I had to bike over here, so just sitting sounds amazing right now."

"Fair enough." Neal waited for Charlie and Emily to get up.

They were still in the line of sight, but for the most part, the couple was left alone. Owen reached over to steal Em's water. There was still beer left, but he didn't want to have such a head start on everyone else. The food would help the most, but washing it down with anything else would be counterproductive.

"Alright, so go over the names again for me?" Andreah asked. Maybe this time, she could relax enough to remember them all. "Emily is the pregnant one, and the nerdy almost British-sounding one is Neal. And, who is the other guy?"

"The one with paint on his jeans?" Owen asked. "Seth."

"No, not him." Andreah shot a careful glance over her shoulder towards the door. "The other one."

Owen looked like he was confused. He glanced over to his friends. "Oh! Their name is Charlie."

Andreah slowly nodded.

Owen shot her a curious glance as he took another slice of pizza. "Is that a problem?"

"No, of course not." She shook her head.

"I know," Owen grinned between bites of cheesy heaven. "My friends are awesome. I'll give you a moment."

She grinned, and the tension drained out of her face. It made her look a bit tired, but far more comfortable. "I actually do have a problem."

"What?" He set his food down, stomach tightening.

"This fucking tie." Andreah reached, and started undoing it. "I can't take you seriously all dressed up like this."

"Geez, thanks." Owen leaned back in his seat as Andreah nearly attacked him to get it off. "What are you going to do? Undress me in the bar?"

"I just might," she said. It didn't take long to dismantle his professional appearance. The blue piece of fabric now sat around his neck.

"Did I mention I'm having the best night of my life?"

Andreah laughed, and wrapped her hands around the ends of the tie, and pulled him close enough to kiss. Owen let out a small moan of surprise. Somewhere in the back of his mind he knew this PDA was a bit much, but he couldn't find the care to stop.

A wolf whistle broke through the stray other noises of patrons, TVs, and cheers of people watching games. By the high tone of it, Owen assumed it was Nicole. One hand lifted from Andreah's hip and flipped Nicole off without breaking away from the kiss.

When he pulled away, he remained close. Their noses brushed against each other. Owen caught his breath first, and gave her one last quick peck.

It was a cold morning when Amilia found herself wandering through the streets. She tried to keep her steps even, but haste caused every third step to be quicker than the others. A horse whinnied, and she tensed as if the animal had set off an alarm. She'd need a horse of her own, and thought of stealing this very one. That's what thieves do, right? Following two sets of rules is what got her into this mess and confused every matter.

Her feet led her to Daniel's doorstep without any thought of her own, and now she stared at the building like it was a sign. A mixture of hope and nervousness stirred her stomach like a storm. She glanced back as the sun slowly stretched onto the morning street. Maybe she shouldn't, but felt no other choice than to knock on Daniel's door.

The door opened a moment later to a very confused Daniel. "Uh, come in," he mumbled, and stepped back for her. Amilia paced inside, turned sharply at the end of the living room like she was going to just as quick march out of the place. "What are you doing here?" he asked.

His words caused her to pause. She fought for control over the jumbled phrases her tongue wanted to spit out all at once. "Could I borrow a horse? Or maybe some supplies." She took a step towards his desk. "There was a map on your—"

Daniel stood in the way, coincidentally more than anything else. At the threat of bumping into him, she stopped short. "What's wrong?"

Her eyes lifted with the bright fear of a wild animal in them. "Don't you trust me?"

His lips parted ready to object, but none came. He trusted her when she likely didn't deserve it, and now, when she needed it, he couldn't. "No, not right now I don't," Daniel said. "Tell me what's wrong."

"I need you," Amilia said. The word struck a chord in Daniel, and he fell completely still. "To take me wherever," she continued. "Just drop me off somewhere. Surely you have enough supplies to spare."

"Amilia," Daniel said, adding weight to her name. "You have to tell me the whole truth."

"I can't stay for long. I need to go somewhere. The Knights. They...they're searching for me," she babbled all at once, "I need to get out of town."

He licked his lips as he thought about it. "Where did you want to go?"

"Santiago," Amilia said, with a confidence that had been missing before.

"I have no fidelity to the Knights, and you helped me save my friend. For that, I'd take you all the way to the new world." He already said he would take her to Santiago, and if she desired to leave this very second, so be it.

"I'll get your horse ready," Amilia said. She took a large step towards the door.

"Don't." He caught her hand before she dashed outside. "I'll do it. If you are wanted, it's not wise for you to be outside if we can avoid it."

"Thank you," she said softly. Her head wasn't clear, and she realized that maybe it hadn't been in a while. But together, maybe...

Daniel prepared a wagon that lived mostly unused in his backyard. It was tented with a dark brown fabric, and just big enough for three people if you didn't mind being packed together. There had been a time where he traveled a lot, even had trails to various cities set up, but now the wagon sat here waiting.

He frowned as he made preparations. It would take least a week to get to Santiago, and it wasn't like he could just go tell everyone that he was leaving town for a bit. "What did I just agree to?" he mumbled as he hitched a horse up.

Santiago wasn't the greatest distance he had traveled, but that was for official business. This? This was different. A proper trip took a lot of planning. Waypoint markers could be set up beforehand to make the trip faster. This felt more like running away into the remaining wisps of the night.

Daniel headed inside, stopping short as Amilia was standing in the exact same spot she had when he left. His chest ached at the sight of her so distraught. He stood there for seconds, almost afraid to disturb her when her mind was off somewhere else.

She slowly lifted her gaze to him and attempted a faint smile.

"It's okay," he said, as he moved closer to hug her. "We will get through this, alright? I haven't broken my promises yet, and I don't plan to, either."

Amilia tucked her head into his chest, nodding in his shoulder. The grief on her face slowly lessened. She opened her mouth, maybe to say her thanks, but closed it before any sound was made.

"Come on. Let's get going," Daniel said. He reached to pull his hood up. Anonymity was their weapon of choice right now. No blade would be as effective as simply never having to engage. Amilia pulled her own up, the fabric lifting from her shoulders like a great weight.

Daniel headed outside, making one last check before swinging up to the driver's seat, and pulled the reins closer. "It would be best if you hid in the back," he said. Amilia glanced over to it as she chewed on her lip. Daniel reconsidered. "But there is room next to me if you'd prefer."

The tightness in his shoulders vanished as Amilia moved to sit next to him. A shadow of a smile graced his face. If it was him, this was where he would have sat. Not the smartest move, but he'd rather have a heads up of what was coming than to be blind to his surroundings.

They successfully made it out of the city, but Amilia glanced back a few times. Part paranoia, part regret, maybe even part hope.

"I hope you are not getting homesick," Daniel said, the fifth time she looked back. "I believe you are stuck with me now."

Amilia shook her head, and quickly turned back to the road ahead of them. "I'm glad you came with me."

Most of their journey carried on simply; traveling, cooking, and sleeping while they got as many miles as they could under their wheels. As they passed the halfway point, Amilia took the map that had been resting on Daniel's lap. She wondered about what lay in the unmarked areas. The tales her family used to share about death, adventure, and near-magical things couldn't possibly be real.

"Daniel?"

The road ahead was clear, so he glanced over.

"Do you have any family within the guild? I mean, you could have been born into the lifestyle, or recruited," Amilia asked. How much did she even know about him? A huge failing if she had been a proper bard. She could imagine plenty of grand things, like being the bastard son of Spanish royalty. Or maybe the reverse, a man born on the streets and risen up through the gray of the world to make something of himself. But the truth was starting to matter more and more.

"I was always a part of this order," Daniel said. "I don't think it was what my father intended for me, but like father, like son. He wasn't very secretive about his business with the thieves. By not hiding things from me, he left me to decide if I wanted it in my life too."

"This trip," Daniel continued, and looked back to the road. "Santiago, that is. It means a lot to you, doesn't it?" He already knew the answer, even if she wouldn't admit the truth about it. What he didn't know was why this place had any meaning. "I'm glad you decided to do this with me instead of own your own."

"I've read a lot about the history of Spain's cities," Amilia said, "I've always enjoyed reading about Santiago. I've never really gotten to travel much before, to see things like a tourist. I've moved, but you miss a lot of things when you don't see where you're going as an adventure. You wouldn't imagine what we miss as everyday people in Siguenza. All because we've settled down, and stopped viewing it as new. Passing scholars, artists, and just people each day thinking the average is breathtaking. People rarely think about how important each thing is, or how important each person is."

Daniel stared at her for a moment in wonder. He never realized that bards could avoid your answer completely, and still tell you a story that was so full of the truth at the same time.

When the dark started to creep in, they decided it was best to rest for the night. Daniel let go of the reins as the horses stopped. The crisp air made him glad for the hood that shielded his ears.

Making a fire was the most compelling thought in his mind. Daniel carefully worked on guarding a young flame until it was large enough to survive on its own. The heat of it nipped at his fingertips and kissed away the cold.

Once Daniel had his fill of the fire, he moved back over to the wagon, and converted it to serve as a tent. Didn't take much, needing just two poles sticking into the ground. *"Mademoiselle,"* Daniel smiled, gesturing over their accommodations for the night.

"Thank you," Amilia smiled. She had tried to help set up the camp, but Daniel always seemed to handle things faster than she could. They wasted the rest of the night around the fire until Amilia retired to bed. After checking a few things, Daniel followed after a short time later, and found everything he needed for bed laid out and ready for him. He stole a small glance at Amilia, who was curled up on her side of the wagon, sleeping soundly already.

Owen expected a calm feeling to wash over him as they skipped ahead to the next day. Instead, the game continued to move in real time. He wondered if the headset had frozen all together. The usual peace of the day change was replaced with panic. Owen felt pins and needles behind his eyes. He gasped as his sight went black for a second before being replaced with the vision of Amilia near the water's edge. A waterfall rained down with a constant drumming before she stepped towards it. The world skipped ahead with jarring stitches. Amilia's arms trembled as she tried to push herself up off the ground. Now soaked down to the bone; her clothes and hair clung to her small frame. She blinked slowly as if her head had its own set of objections. The next time he saw her was when Amilia stumbled over to a horse.

A shadow of color moved down the side of her face. At first it was written off as water, but Amilia lifted a shivering hand to touch her cheek, and her fingers came back spotted with blood.

Another jarring stitch, and he saw Amilia now riding, or as well as she could as her body began to shut down. She had made it far enough that the falls no longer dotted the background. But it was still too far to make it back in her state. Amilia started to fall off her horse before Daniel woke up with a start. His heart pounded against his ribs. He might have been able to convince himself it was all a bad dream, but when he looked over to where Amilia was sleeping there was only a pile of blankets.

Maybe this nightmare wasn't over.

He climbed out of the wagon, and took a quick glance around their camp. One of the horses wasn't far, just a few paces from where he should have been at a new patch of grass. The second one was absent, likely still with Amilia.

Daniel closed his eyes, centering himself as he focused on the direction the vision showed him. He didn't have to ride far until he found Amilia, and the missing horse. The latter had been slowly making its way back to camp, while Amilia had been abandoned in the grass to freeze to death. Daniel dropped to her level as he scooped her up in his arms.

"Amilia, don't do this to me," he begged.

Panic slowed his mind, but the icy touch of her was enough to kick his brain back in gear. He moved as fast as he could back over to the fire. Very carefully he laid her down next to it.

The fire had gone down over time, so Daniel moved to feed it more wood. The fire greedily sparked back to life, making the area it touched warmer than the wagon had been.

"Please make it through this to be mad at me in the morning," Daniel said. He doubted that she could hear, which was the scariest thing out of everything. If she had been shivering, or at least awake, he would have found some hope lighting the way. Her soaked clothes would keep the cold in, so they'd have to go first. He pulled off what he could, and tore or cut away at the fabric if it proved too much of a hassle.

When she was down to her undergarments, he stripped off his own tunic just to give her something as he went to gather the blankets. Fear bit at his heels while he was away. Telling him he'd never move fast enough to save her. Once out of wet clothes, piled with blankets, and tucked safely close to the fire, the only remaining thing Daniel could do is cuddle up next to her to share his body heat.

He closed his eyes and pleaded silently. Instead of falling asleep, he stayed alert to the world. Listening for any snap of a twig, every rustling leaf, without a twitch, like a watchdog carved from stone. He'd lend her his heartbeat if he had too.

The next morning, Daniel woke to a small voice calling his name. He let out a sigh of relief before he managed to reply. "I'm here." There was so much more he wanted to ask, but it all fell away in simple gratitude that she woke up.

Amilia couldn't work up a smile, but Daniel's words did help. She turned back, pulling her fingers up out of the blankets to take stock of them. All were their proper color, and that brought a new relief that almost lulled her back asleep.

"I can't believe you are alive." Daniel's words were mumbled against her back, as his arms were tucked around her as if simply letting go would change it.

"Thanks to you," she said softly.

It was a sweet sound, too real for this to be a dream or another vision. If this would have been a Hollywood movie, they might have kissed. Had a crescendo of happiness and life play out of their lips. But instead, Daniel stayed exactly how he was until they had the strength to get up on their own.

It was later than Daniel would have liked to start the day, but it was of little concern, considering. Amilia sat up staring at the dying fire as Daniel packed up their camp. He looked over a few times. His concern didn't go unnoticed for long.

She smiled over at him, her serious expression shifting to a curious one.

"Where did you go last night?" Daniel asked. He hadn't wanted to push her first thing, but now she seemed well enough for a little prodding.

Amilia let out a heavy sigh, needing a moment to digest the question. "I don't know what I was looking for, exactly. I can't even really remember if I found anything last night, but I heard tale of something in this area. I thought I'd look without causing a detour. It was stupid of me." Her worn body made her look so tiny under the blanket around her shoulders, but also made the vague wording in the lie easier to spot. He wasn't sure for whose benefit these lies were for anymore.

Daniel lifted his eyes to the horizon, narrowing them slightly at what could be out there. "I should have a look around."

"Don't you think we better get going?" she said, her voice jumping up an octave. "We've lost enough time already."

He looked back down at her as he raised a brow. "We could afford to lose more. You can either go on, or wait for me to satisfy my own curiosity." It wasn't meant as a threat, just a matter of fact. Something had undeniably happened, and he wanted to know what.

Amilia got up on her feet, the blanket still carefully wrapped around her. They exchanged a glance. Neither of them was certain how this would play out. "May I change first?" she asked.

"By all means."

She tucked her head down and moved towards their supplies. The space in the back of the wagon still was enough for her to change into spare clothes. She took longer than needed before she came back out, but she needed the moment to ready herself to talk about things that even her uncle and cousin no longer wished to hear.

"As a child, I heard my father talk about one of his travels," Amilia said as she stepped out. Daniel paused in putting out the fire to turn and listen. "It was around these parts. At least that's what I believed when we stopped. He said that in a cave behind a waterfall, there was an artifact hidden. I didn't find anything besides freezing water. I slipped, and thus the real cause of the mess I've made."

"What was the artifact meant to do?"

Amilia's head cocked to the side at the question. "It doesn't do anything," she said, "It was just valuable."

Daniel nodded his head, and looked around in consideration. "I don't want you to leave this campsite for a second, for anything."

"Wait, what?" She stared with wide eyes as Daniel moved towards the horses. "I thought you said we'd go if I told you."

"I won't be long," Daniel said, as he swung up to the horse. He was off without any further objection. He rode fast, following the map he had and riding towards a speck of water it showed. The roar of the falls came early, and shattered his faith in the accuracy of his map.

Daniel got off his horse. The falls were a beautiful sight that sent worry into his bones. His steps were careful, not wanting to slip into the water himself as he tried to figure out the place's mysteries. Couldn't even imagine how little of it would have been visible at night. Daniel crouched down at the edge.

There was nothing besides the veil of water that fell like a sheet. Unwilling to give up, he edged as close as he could without fighting the force of the falls. Daniel reached his hand out, and it pressed up against an invisible barrier before it was even fully outstretched.

"It's like the edge of the world map," Owen said. In all of his hours logged into this open-world game, he'd never run into a barrier like this before. So few games had them anymore. Maybe Amilia needed to be here to trigger anything more, or maybe this was an incomplete section that hadn't been patched yet. Whatever the case may have been, one thing was for sure; this was already one hell of a trip.

It was now only a short trip to the beauty that was Santiago, and from this vantage point, the whole city was in view. Trees added scattered swatches of green and orange. A large cathedral defined the skyline with its sharp dark points. Despite the charm of the city, Daniel turned to Amilia, captivated by her breathless expression. "Just like you imagined?"

Amilia had been literally on the edge of her seat, waiting for the first glimpse of the city. She finally looked away to grin over at him. "Unbelievably so."

Their horses came to a stop outside a tavern, and Amilia immediately jumped down. She made a detour of ambushing Daniel with a hug before fluttering away towards the building. He chuckled, and followed her inside. Amilia asked the man at the counter for two rooms. The clerk looked at her, then, with a slight narrowing of his eyes, moved on to Daniel. The expression wasn't quite clear enough to say if he thought they were trouble or just secretly up to something sinful. But the exchange of coin silenced whatever objection was there.

Amilia turned to Daniel and held one of the keys out in front of him. "Your room is waiting for you, sir."

"Why thank you, *mademoiselle*." He pocketed the key and headed back out to pull the wagon and horses around to the stables. Afterwards, they returned to their rooms, which were separated by a measure of the hall.

The very first thing Daniel did was fall onto the bed, letting every inch relax into it.

The brief respite was interrupted by a knock on the door. He sat up as Amilia came in. "So, what's on our tourist to-do list?"

"There's the monastery, the cathedral, a museum or two, and even a library inside the University," she rattled on.

"Impressive list."

"And actually, if it's alright with you, I'd like to stop somewhere to get new clothes." Amilia nervously ran a hand through hair that she had barely touched up. "I didn't bring much to start with, and some of that was ruined."

"Of course," Daniel said. She had first come to him so upset, and he had thought the watery mishap days ago would have dampened her spirits further, but she seemed to find joy simply in being here. "We can even go right away."

As they walked down to the market, Daniel was surprised how many people carried on with bored expressions. It wasn't that they were unhappy, but what Amilia had said about seeing the same thing every day rang true.

A quaint shop with spools of rich fabric stretched out in its window caught Amilia's attention from around a corner. She let go of Daniel's arm as she took a few steps in that direction. "I won't drag you in, and I promise to be out as quick as possible."

He wouldn't have really minded, but let her go as she pleased. She was right in one respect, however; the wait wasn't long at all. His stare broke into a grin as she did a spin upon her return. The dress she loved enough to wear out of the store was bluish gray and flowed down to her ankles. The tint brought out the traces of green and gold in her eyes with ease. "You were right," Daniel said. "Everything in this city is beautiful." Her blush served as a new accent color.

They decided the cathedral would be their next stop, a joint choice that ended up surprising her. A thief wanting to visiting a church for fun was a rarity. Roman-Gothic spikes stretched upwards with crosses nested at the very top. The watchful clouds above cast a shadowy gray onto the stones. Amilia shared a smile with the statue of Saint James outside as they passed.

Their self-guided tour ended at the University's library, where some of the books lining the shelves seemed to predate the church's wisdom. Daniel tried not to get too wrapped up with a single text when everything begged for his attention.

When Amilia had her fill, she wrapped her arm around his so they wouldn't be captivated by the library's spell.

They wandered back into the street and decided to call it a day. As they moved through the crowd, someone bumped into Amilia. She glanced up to mumble an apology, but the face she saw caught her attention. "Sebastiano?"

The man's face lit up when he recognized who he had bumped into. "Ah, Amilia!" he said, "*Mi señora*, how are you? I haven't seen you in ages."

"I'm great, I'm just visiting town with my friend," she said. Her arm untangled from Daniel, to offer her hand in greeting to Seb.

He promptly placed a kiss there before giving Daniel a passing glance. "Just a friend?" His eyes lit up at the suggestion, and smiled as if he had said something more flirty. Amilia let out a nervous laugh and glanced towards Daniel. She seemed to pale at being put on the spot.

"If only that was all," Daniel mused to Seb's irritation. The comment soiled Seb's pretty smile, and was an opportunity Daniel took a step further. "It's nice to meet you," he said, and offered his hand. The silent start of a competition.

"Same here," Seb said with a forced smile as Daniel's sheer grip strength made him wince.

Amilia sighed, not attempting to hide it in the slightest. Daniel took back his hand and glanced over to see her up rub a hand against a fledgling headache. "If you'll excuse us," she said, "we were about to head back, but it was very nice seeing you again."

They hadn't even made it two steps before his voice halted them again. "Wait, we should catch up," Seb added. "We all missed you and your family. Are you free tonight?"

"Sure," Amilia agreed, without a second thought.

"I'm guessing you're staying at the inn across town, by the gates?" he asked. She nodded. "Then it'd be my pleasure to pick you up for dinner, *miquerida?*"

Daniel's neutral expression slipped at the term of endearment. It went unnoticed as Amilia agreed and curtsied a proper goodbye.

"I guess we won't have time for a meal ourselves," Amilia said, on their way back to the inn. "But now you are free to explore without me dragging you all over town."

"I'll likely just stay in."

Amilia dropped behind for a moment. Daniel let out a small sigh and turned around to face her. She looked intent on standing right there on that little patch of ground until he explained his tone.

"I just..." Daniel pressed his lips together. He didn't want to say anything. Nothing would come out right, and he knew that. "I don't like that guy."

"Why not?" Amilia's voice raised as she tried to conceal her outrage in the form of a question. "I've known him since I was a child."

Daniel glanced away and spotted a couple that was holding hands, so enraptured with each other that the dessert on their table was completely ignored. His eyes rolled back to find Amilia standing there waiting. "I don't know," he lied at first. "It's odd timing to just run into an old family friend like that after you wanted to flee town."

"I think you are just jealous."

"Jealous?" Daniel's expression pulled tight. "I'm not—"

"You can't even say it with a straight face," Amilia said, and pointed a finger at him. "Don't you believe in coincidence at all?"

"Not in this world," Daniel mumbled.

"Well, I'm going to enjoy myself tonight." She stepped away, headed towards the inn again.

"Good," Daniel grumbled. "Enjoy your date with a baby-faced creep." The words left a bad taste in his mouth. He hadn't said them very loud, but Amilia paused at the inn's doorway in shock.

"I will!" she said forcefully, and nearly whipped the door closed behind her.

Owen ripped off his headset in annoyance. They were both acting like children. All he wanted was a fun night running around a city he had largely ignored. Instead they were picking fights. He got up from the couch, abandoning the headset on the cushion for now. Owen hadn't logged out, but the game could run as he took a break. His character would just stand there like any other idle NPC might. At worst the game would consider him inactive after a while and bounce him to the nearest rest stop literal steps away.

He checked the refrigerator for anything good, but quickly closed it, not thrilled by the leftovers that were questionably old. Owen made himself some coffee, and sat up on the counter as he waited for it. A half-hearted vibration came from his pocket. He pulled his phone out as it reminded him of old notifications.

There wasn't anything to write home about. A few tweets from Emily, a stray text from Neal about the bullshit that was traffic. The usual, really. He finished half of his coffee and checked whatever else he could while he was at it.

Owen walked back into the living room, taking a large gulp of coffee before placing the mug down on the table. He ran a hand through his hair and pulled the headset back on.

As he expected, Daniel was now in his room. He found the book he had "borrowed" from the library sitting on the tiny desk. Daniel tried to focus on it, but kept thinking about how immature they had been about this whole thing. Why should he care what Amilia did? Just because someone rubbed him the wrong way didn't automatically make them a bad guy.

He had been jealous, and hadn't even realized it until he gave himself a moment to think. The self-confession at very least cleared his mind enough that he could properly read. The book retold the story of Perseus, Medusa, and a shield that rivaled the glory of the sun. Daniel read on, thinking this would be a proper prize to bring back to the guild.

"I had a wonderful time, Sebastiano." Amilia's voice, carrying in from the hallway.

Was the game still going on about that? Daniel shook his head, deciding he should stay out of it. He hoped the ambient sounds would die off, but that wish didn't align with Owen's settings.

"Me too, but the night is still young," Seb suggested.

"Pardon?"

Daniel tuned them out. It was their business, not his, but when a door slammed his stance on the matter changed in a heartbeat, and he quickly headed into the hallway.

Seb was dressed in his Sunday best, an odd contrast as he shamelessly banged against Amilia's closed door. "Open up!"

Without a word, Daniel walked over to a room service cart, grabbed a tray, and let the dishes underneath fall. Seb turned to address him, and Daniel swung the tray at his head. The force knocked Seb to the ground, and away from the door. Daniel tossed the tray away. It bounced twice before skidding to a stop upon hitting the base of a wall. Daniel picked the ass up off the floor by his lacy collar. "If I ever see you near Amilia without her say again, I will break both of your legs."

"You have no right to threaten me," Seb spat, and tried to pull out of Daniel's grip. When Seb found no success in doing so, he went on. "You will never reach the level of status and honor that my family and I have." He swung a punch and, in his half drunken stupor, missed without much effort on Daniel's part.

Daniel let go, and Seb staggered forward without the support. "Honor?" Daniel asked, and took a step back. "Doubt you know the meaning of it."

Seb tried to throw another punch, and Daniel returned the haphazard attack with an uppercut of his own. It bounced Seb back into Amilia's closed door. He looked ready to slide down it as Daniel grabbed a handful of fabric and pulled Seb down the hall.

Daniel pushed him out the front door, and the man fell towards the gutter barely able to catch himself in time. "Are we at an understanding about Amilia?"

"Do you think you are someone special to her?" Seb wiped his face, smearing dirt across his mouth on accident. "You know nothing."

"I know that gutter suits you," Daniel said. "That is enough."

He didn't waste any more time with the trash before he went to check on Amilia. Now that he was locked on the outside of the door, he worried about knocking. "Can I come in?" Daniel asked softly instead.

There was the hesitant sound of her slowly undoing the locks, and Daniel stepped into her room without a word. What could he even say about what happened? In the end, it might have been better that he had no words, since Amilia's stress refocused to a fury.

"Are you happy?" Her voice was hushed despite the anger guiding it. "You were right."

She tore out the pins in her hair and discarded them without care, littering the floor with the handful. Her fear twisted into anger and gained her some volume. "Is this all just a game to you? That if you saved the girl who 'didn't know better,' it would make you a hero?" Amilia asked, as she sat on the end of the bed. Defeated, she tugged her shoes off, and they fell to the floor with a heavier thud.

"How did I?" Daniel's question was so inelegant in comparison. He understood why she was upset, but was lost to where he personally fucked up.

"Please. Clearly you know better. Why should I even get a say anymore? Because seeing as you—*everyone* thinks they can judge, or control, what I do. My uncle, Sebastiano, all you men are all the same." The poison in her tone only seemed to get thicker as she went on.

172

"Dammit Amilia," he said softly. His brow was tight as he looked over her, more worried than anything else. "Do you think I tell you things because I'm trying to manipulate you? That I'm trying to pull your strings like you are a puppet?"

"And for the record..." Daniel continued. Amilia's cheeks felt like they were on fire, but she defiantly looked up at him with narrowed eyes. "No, I'm not happy. I'm sorry that your old friend was scum. I'm sorry that your life at home is awful. I'm sorry this happened."

He took a step closer, but quickly stopped as she fidgeted. Feeling trapped seemed to be a concern now, and in general. "Please just realize, none of this was your fault." he said, "And that when I tell you to do something it's because I genuinely care about you."

Amilia stared at him, jaw clenched as she listened. "How am I supposed to believe you when half the time we act like we can't care less about each other? How in the world am I supposed to believe you at all, Daniel? I know close to nothing about you, because you are always the guild's first," she said. "The only time you open up is when you get to act as the hero and save the dear damsel in distress.. It's been months, and there hasn't been a mention of me being accepted as part of your guild either. I know what I am to him." Amilia nodded her head towards the door as if the name was too much right now. "So, who am I to you? A girl you put up with for what benefit?"

The two just stared at each other as she finished, both looking a little surprised that she had said it. Amilia ended up looking away first.

"I..." Daniel started. She had asked him the same a while ago, and he still didn't know if he had the right answer. "Amilia."

Confused, she lifted her eyes to meet his.

"Amilia. That's who you are to me," Daniel clarified. "I'm sick of ifs and maybes. I'm sick of the world making it seem like we are so obvious. So, if you could just tell me what you feel, we can stop pretending with the rest."

"Please get out of my room," she whispered.

His mouth opened, more confused than he was a moment ago. Instead of pushing, Daniel willed himself to stay silent and returned to his room.

At least he could breathe in here. Their relationship, if that's what it could be called, was messy. He had been trying to keep it as simple as possible, but the game was forcing a rough inevitability.

Had he messed up somewhere? Or was this a trope that even Age of Shadows' system insisted on? Owen was ready to leave the game for the night when he heard Amilia's light voice.

"Daniel?" She gently pushed his door open and shifted her weight uncomfortably between her feet. "You wanted to know what I felt," she started, carefully building up to her point. "And, well, I'm sick of only causing damage. This has never been easy, but I promise not to run away from things again."

Daniel felt caught in the same sticky web of thoughts from before, making him unsure of what Amilia was doing. Even as she moved close, leaning into the chair he held perfectly still. Amilia's kiss made Daniel feel like he could breathe again. His hands flexed, and curled into themselves as the last line of resistance.

"Please, don't hate me," she whispered. Amilia pulled back enough to stare into his bright blue eyes. "Because that's the farthest from what I feel for you."

"I, uh," Daniel said. He was at a loss. What line hadn't been overused? What line could express that he was still worried? That he wanted to know if her fear was manifesting in a new way? "I could never hate you."

They kissed softly, as if every touch of their lips treated a part of their tired souls. Daniel refused to push an inch. They stood on such fragile ground as it was. "Amilia, I need this to be real, because I won't go back to our old dance."

"I feel safe with you," she said, "I feel like I belong."

Daniel smiled, despite the shake of his head. "This would never work in the real world," he commented to himself.

She lifted a hand to caress the side of his face, stubble feeling rough under her touch. "Good thing we aren't there."

The trip started to resemble a vacation, filled with the type of days that people lived for; careless, fun, free. Amilia lifted a trinket up into the light. It seemed to glow a warm orange as the sun ran through the glass sides. "Did you want to bring home a souvenir to add to your collection?" She turned the trinket lovingly in her hands. "If it was me I'd pick this one."

"It's nice," Daniel said, without much of a glance. Nothing seemed to catch his attention as much as the company he got to hoard to himself recently. "But I have everything I could want."

Amilia looked up, a light blush gracing her cheeks. They gave a polite thanks to the merchant for their time before they ventured further down the street.

Daniel's steps picked up as he veered off towards the mouth of a cross street. "Follow me."

"Why?"

"You'll see." Daniel picked up her hand and darted across the street. They found a good little hiding spot in a shaded path. Amilia stood close to the wall, carefully watching his face as he glanced to see if anyone else was coming.

"What is it?" she whispered.

"Nothing." Daniel looked back to her, grinning boldly. "I just wanted you alone for a moment."

"You rascal!" Amilia punched him in the arm for the ruse. He laughed and held his 'injured' arm. Amilia placed her arms around his neck. "As least you are my rascal."

"True," Daniel smiled. The agreement wasn't exactly the words he wanted to say, but they were easier to say. He thought about kissing her, but movement caught his attention. He looked up, and spotted a someone standing at the crossroads. "We need to go."

"Daniel," she laughed. "I'm not falling for that again."

"I'm being serious this time." Daniel didn't glance back as he took steps towards the stranger. The sun silhouetted where Seb stood for a moment until the hate in his eyes burned brighter. It was the look of a man who wanted blood. "You should run, Amilia."

"No," she said. Daniel looked back to her. She stood defiant. "I'm not going to be anyone's puppet anymore."

It hardly seemed like the right time for her to reclaim any loss of dignity, but if she believed it was, so be it. If Amilia refused to make a break for it he could at least take the focus off of her. "Come back for another beating, have you?" Daniel taunted. He strolled closer, and could now see men in armor waiting along the sides. Bringing friends, or more likely paying for friends, made things a bit harder.

"You have it all wrong." Seb grinned. Having men at his command boosted his sense of worth. "I've come for something, but it isn't that."

A snicker escaped Daniel. "I'm sorry, you aren't my type."

An expression of confusion shifted into horror as he realized what Daniel was suggesting. It would have made Daniel grin more, but Seb signaled his men to move closer first.

"Stop this." Amilia stepped forward, resting her disdain on Seb. Her hands balled up, but she stood firm. No one seemed to listen as they pushed passed her towards Daniel. Her fear spiked as one of the men decided to grab her arm.

"Now Amilia, show a little composure." Another voice called, one they've both heard before. Don Ambrogio stepped forward, looking at his nails before giving his full attention. It became clear that this was less about Seb's interests and more about Daniel and Lance crashing the knight's party. "After all, we don't want people to believe you actually want to defend the thief."

Daniel mumbled a curse and twirled a dagger around in his hand. The air chilled at the realization that this was the city that was founded by the knight order centuries ago. It was clear no one was taking him as a threat, and he hoped to change that. He expected them to pile onto him, but instead they glared and waited for the command.

"It's time to come back home." The comment seemed so much like an decree that another guard grabbed Amilia's arm as if they were ready to haul her back across Spain.

"Wait!" Daniel's booming voice caught their attention enough to warrant a pause. Amilia even pulled her arms free. The guards seemed content as long as she didn't take another step. His resolve wavered at the sight of her concerned expression. "It's me you want, right?" He looked back to the Don with his chin held high. "Just let her go home on her own, and I'll go with you without spilling any of your men's blood."

Seb uttered half a syllable in objection before Ambrogio cut him off with a quick gesture. He didn't say anything else, but pursed his lips in consideration.

"It's a win-win for you."

"You have a deal."

Daniel raised a brow. That had been surprisingly easy. Frankly, too fast for something else not to be going on.

"Don't do this," Amilia said. Originally, Daniel mistook the force in her voice as a reach for volume, but it was closer to annoyance. Whatever the knight's real plan was hardly mattered to Daniel if it brought her freedom.

Against his instincts, Daniel put the dagger away. He looked to Amilia, forgetting about the men. At first, there were no words to be found. His lips parted soundlessly for a second. "Be safe."

"I will take pleasure in killing you, Mr. Ortiz," Seb said.

Daniel barely glanced over to acknowledge the comment. His eyes found Amilia's again, searching, wanting, before he nodded that it was okay. She looked hesitant as she shifted her weight between her feet then bolted as quick as a bird.

The guards ushered Daniel towards their holding in the area. Another oversight that he would have normally investigated first if he hadn't literally run off with Amilia. Several times along the way, he thought of making a break for it, but as much as he hated the knights, they keep their word. Sebastiano might go back on his promises, but the Don had an honesty of sorts which should keep Amilia safe. It was hard to care about anything else.

The guards pulled Daniel down to his knees. They hit hard against the stone floor of a barracks a short ways from where he had been captured. With a glare, he looked around for their names, but they were just tools who didn't even warrant them.

Ambrogio came in and the others were waved out of the room. Seb followed soon after, and brought chains to bind Daniel's hands. He tried to watch the intricate lock that accompanied them, but was met with a slap that turned his head for the attempt.

"Where is it?" the Don ordered, like Daniel was one of his men that needed to report in.

"Where is what?" Daniel said through gritted teeth as he slowly turned his head back.

Ambrogio exhaled sharply like Daniel had just told a joke. "The stone aegis."

"I don't know what you are talking about. I didn't take—" The punch that came next from Sebastiano was hard enough that it sent an unnerving amount of feedback through the headset and cut Daniel's words off early. He wiggled his nose, worried for how it was fairing. It was clear Sebastiano was the one with a vendetta here, while the Don came purely for business. The difference in goals was something he could exploit. "You're right though," Daniel started, and glanced at the both of them in turn. "I did take something of yours. And do you know what I did with your precious Amilia?"

Daniel's expression rested on Seb as a near laugh escaped in his breath. "I took her to my bed," he finished. The words felt crude in his mouth. It wasn't how he'd like Amilia, or anyone, to hear him speak about her. It wasn't even completely true, but Seb's assumed ownership of Amilia stuck out like a knife in the man's back.

Seb's face filled with a rage that twitched its way through his features until he swung again.

This time the blow knocked Daniel off balance, and he landed on his forearms. "She's not your thing," Daniel said, staring at the floor as he spit out blood. "She's not a thing at all." He was forced up to his knees again, one of Seb's hands still gripping his collar as if he wanted a punching bag that didn't move so easily, but Daniel refused to stay silent. "If you were a man, I'd expose your abusive ass so fast."

Ambrogio held a hand to his mouth, and, at Daniel's words, he narrowed his eyes. "Sebastiano," he said, carefully without looking away from the thief. "Do you wish to tell me that you brought this person to my attention today for a personal benefit of yours?"

"No, of course not," Seb quickly replied. When the words weren't believed, he backpedaled further. "This is the same man who caused a scene at your party, who stole your hostage, killed your men."

When Ambrogio's eyes pulled away they turned sharply on Sebastiano. "You think I care about a few men? Especially ones who brought nothing except risk? I don't care what he did. I only care about what he can do for me. Which is apparently nothing, since the only reason he is out this far is for a girl."

"He was at the library!"

Daniel just stared wide-eyed at the scene. He should have taken the chance to work on the lock, but was too enthralled. What lie was told about him or Amilia? What the hell were they eager to beat a man over, if not pride?

"Guards!" The Don called. Daniel twitched at the boom of the man's voice, expecting another blow. Two men stepped in and waited for their orders. "Return Sebastiano to his family," Ambrogio continued, before he looked down at

Daniel. "Have someone...watch him until I decide what to do with him."

The guards positioned themselves outside of the room. It would have been more helpful if they had stayed. Keys could have been stolen off them. Daniel leaned back on his heels so he could pull himself to his feet. He looked around the room that was void of any furniture and a tiny window he'd never fit through.

It barely looked like the room was fully rendered, there was so little to work with. Daniel sighed heavily to himself and rattled the chains so the lock positioned itself between his hands. If he could pick the lock, that might be all the advantage he needed.

A song that didn't match the world started to play like a whisper. The music built until it was impossible to ignore. Owen, however, recognized it, and blindly felt around on the couch for his phone. He pushed the headset off one ear and answered the call.

"Hello?" Owen asked, as he watched Daniel try to work on the lock without much success.

"Hey," Frank said. "Are you coming into work today? You're sort of late and I have work for you to do."

Owen mentally cursed with enough annoyed focus on the word that Daniel spit out a cuss in Spanish. "Uh yeah." He cleared his throat. "I'm sorry, I'll be right there."

"See you soon."

The phone was tossed to the cushions, and the headset pushed back into place. He didn't want to log out right here. It wasn't the worst spot, since he wasn't at the mercy of anyone at the moment, but that didn't make it safe either.

There wasn't much choice. The real world called.

Getting ready turned out to be a mad dash of pulling on socks with an awkward hop, stealing a quick moment to push his hair into a uniform direction, and nearly missing the keys as he snatched them off the table. He dropped them into his pocket and mentally debated how to get to work. Lunch hour meant there'd be fewer taxis available, and if he was going to be any later than he already was, he'd rather have it be his doing. Walking seemed a bit of a stretch, but biking would be the perfect middle ground.

Owen booked it to work, weaving in between cars as if once again in an alley cat race. When he made it to his desk, he was completely out of breath. His lungs gulped in air for a moment before they realized that there was no rush anymore. Thankfully, Michael was off in his studio and therefore didn't have a snide comment ready.

Frank raised a brow as Owen sunk into his office chair. He glanced over his employee's face with a clear question on his mind, but didn't voice it. "I have these for you," he said, and placed a stack of papers on the desk.

The cover page had the logo of the city. Whatever this task was, it was for something official. Owen looked back up at his boss. "I'm sorry about being late."

"Mhm," Frank hummed, without much enthusiasm. "Just tell me if you find anything newsworthy in there."

Owen read about ten pages before he figured that there wasn't going to be anything interesting. The paperwork was a zoning bill and filled to the brim with repetitive information. The promise that someone messed up and accidentally zoned a strip club next to a school was his only real hope of a good story.

To distract himself before his brain went numb, he texted Andreah. By the end of the day she hadn't answered. Objectively it wasn't a big deal, but today was so off that the minor annoyance wedged itself under his skin.

He finished reading all of the documents; nothing interesting, like he'd thought. When Frank called it a night, Owen was still left with the notes from city council. While his tardiness was a fluke, it wasn't unusual for Owen to stay late if there was work left, so Frank waved his usual goodbye as he went home.

The building sat silently. The only sound came from Owen himself. There wasn't even the occasional shuffle from the night owl down the hall. Being stuck at the office tonight was daunting; he didn't want to be the only person here digging for a story that might not even exist.

Worry for Daniel and Amilia was all consuming. Anything could have happened while he was logged out. City council could wait. It was time to head home.

//////////////////////////

"Daniel darling, wake up." Amilia's voice formed before anything else in the darkness. "I'm here now."

In a blur, the world shifted until he felt he was sitting up. Daniel blinked roughly as Amilia's face swam in his vision. It took another second and the touch of her hand to convince him she was really there. "How did you—you shouldn't have come back."

"Can't the 'damsel' save someone every once in a while?" Her expression knitted together with annoyance, but it softened as she spotted the dried blood on his mouth and a bruise across his nose.

"That's not what I meant," Daniel said gently.

His tone caused Amilia to pause as she tried to read his expression. She shook her head, trying to clear the whole topic away. "No one has faith until you see them do wondrous things. The more downtrodden you are, the less everyone believes in you," Amilia said, with attention turned towards the lock.

Daniel just stared down at her while she fiddled with it, her hands and long hair covering what she was doing. "I'm sorry," he breathed out. For what, exactly, he wasn't sure. For her risking herself for him? For mistakenly treating her

183

differently? Because others did? Maybe for the pain he saw in her, but still didn't understand.

"You can't pick the lock," Daniel said, in poor replacement.

Amilia looked up from what she was doing with a rare smirk. "No one ever expects the lady to be a thief either." She lifted a ring of keys, and gave them a little shake.

"Bello." Daniel smiled. He watched her face she diligently worked her way through the keys. He felt the weight of the chains fall away, heard them clang against the ground before he looked down at his bare hands.

"Come on, let's go." Amilia moved towards the door ready to finish their daring rescue without any lost time.

"Wait," Daniel called. She stopped and curiously looked over. He pulled himself up to his feet, taking another second to stare at the chains before meeting her eyes. "I just...am having a hard time believing you are here. Already, I mean."

Amilia rolled her eyes. "It's been half a day. What did you think I was going to do? Sit around and do nothing while you took a nap?"

Daniel laughed, even though he was really laughing at himself. "You're remarkable."

"Yeah, I'm starting to see that." Amilia opened the door and looked both ways down the hallway. The guards were missing from the post, and the question of where they went was starting to press on Daniel.

Shock continued to weigh on him as they ventured into an empty hallway. "Amilia," Daniel said softly, as if the question was too much to bear. "How did you pull this off?"

"Hmm?" She was leaning against another door listening for the sounds of people inside. Amilia turned to Daniel as he waited for an answer. She looked away for a second. "I told them I didn't want to go home. That my place was with the knights. And once in, I lured the guards away from the door."

"You lied." Daniel wasn't sure if that was a question or a statement.

Amilia seemed to regard it as the latter, and smiled. "Bard training comes in handy for that." She wiped her hands on her dress, unsure which and what exit to use. "Are you good to fight?"

Daniel felt around for his weapons, which turned up missing. Figures. Something always happened if you don't rest safely. "It would be better if we could avoid a fight." He looked around the hall, spotting a large window that dropped a short distance to a lower level of the roof. "Are you up for running across buildings?"

She pressed her lips together considering it. "If you lead, I should be fine."

Daniel walked to the edge and glanced down to an angled side. He jumped down and slid to a lower level, running until his momentum ran out before he turned around to Amilia.

She had nervously stopped at the edge, staring at the jump like it was impossible.

"You got this," Daniel said.

Amilia looked up to the sky as if saying a prayer, then took the plunge. A roof tile gave way after she removed her foot from it. It followed her down to the next level, and shattered behind her.

Daniel smiled, as Amilia was too busy imagining if she had been that tile. He waited until she looked for further direction before running across the nearby roofs, gaining more distance between them and the knights.

They jumped down to the ground sooner than he would have liked, but the maze of streets was worth the risk. The crowd offered an opportunity to blend until the chance to steal horses presented itself. Then they rode until it grew dim, giving the horses and themselves a break.

Daniel ran a hand through his hair as he glanced back at the city. Its skyline was darkly set against the evening sky. "I wish I could have grabbed my weapons, or anything I left at the inn," Daniel said. His carriage was likely gone, if not seized, making the trip back likely slower and rougher.

"I managed to bring this," Amilia said. She pulled out the book he had lifted from the library from her bag. "Since everyone thought I was packing to go home, I had time to gather a few things. I would have taken more, but I worried it would give the ruse away."

Daniel took the book, and hugged it to his chest. Maybe it was just his desire to connect the pieces, form a theory that made the trouble all worthwhile, but this book was hope. "Thank you."

"You're..." Amilia started, but the words failed her. She sighed, despite the light smile on her face. "Something else. Just, please, never offer to do something like that again. I already owe you—"

"You don't owe me," Daniel interrupted.

Amilia sighed. Her hands moved to the reins as if she wanted to get moving again.

"I'd do it again," he continued, "For you, I mean. What is the point in fighting for a bigger cause if you can't protect the ones you care for?"

"Daniel," she said, nearing a whisper. The reins fell from her hands as she moved closer. Amilia stood toe to toe with him, her head down as she chewed on her lip. She must have figured something out, because when she looked up, her eyes were glossy. "I love you, so please."

His hand reached up, ready to wipe a tear away if needed, but paused at those words. "I, uh," he stumbled, stomach knotting with each utterance. Daniel wished he could pause time for a moment to digest this. Instead of standing there awkwardly, he pulled her into a hug. "I love you too." The words repeated back seemed so casual. "I think I always have."

Some moments in life just happen. A person thinks they can go back, pinpoint the first moment, but time jumbles itself up. It ties together in strange patterns, making it impossible to pull out a single moment without tugging on the whole thing.

"Let's go home," Daniel finished. "It's been a long vacation."

The TV prattled on as Owen laid on the couch half-watching. Between work and the game, he hadn't slept much over the past few days. His eyes were weighed down with hopes of sleep, but it hadn't quite found him yet. There had been a football game on, but he hadn't even noticed which teams were playing before he abandoned the channel surfing.

"It's these so-called bone diggers." The harsh words made Owen twitch in a half-formed dream. "Leeches. Spies. Privacy thieves is what they are. Are the actions of a man at home no longer safe?"

The man's tone stirred Owen from his attempt at sleep. He pulled his eyes open to see a balding white man with an old radio-style microphone in front of him. From the way he talked about games, he hardly seemed in favor.

"Join me anytime someone tries to take away your rights, anytime someone tries to pry into what you do behind closed doors. These bone diggers are a menace that someone needs to stop. "

Owen sat up, and hit the power button on the remote as fast as he could. Silence filled the room, and slowly built up an illusion of safety in his own home. He glanced around, feeling unsettled until he found his phone. Two text messages were waiting for him, both from Andreah. One was from a reply earlier today about coming over, and the newest one was asking if now was good. The time stamp showed that he missed that one by nearly an hour.

To Andreah:
Yeah, now's fine

Owen took a quick shower and was pulling on a hoodie with nothing underneath when he heard the buzz of a guest, and the intercom cracking Andreah's voice in a way it never did in person. A couple minutes later, he welcomed her inside.

"I was starting to wonder if I'd see you tonight at all." Andreah tossed her bag onto the couch before she slumped down in the seat herself. "I only have this movie for a day. You could have ruined all of my plans."

He rolled his eyes as he sat down close. "Oh man, I could have cost you a whole dollar for the rental."

"That's what I'm saying." Andreah ran her hand through the back of Owen's hair. He closed his eyes as her fingers ran from the base of one ear to the top of the other. "You aren't going to fall asleep on me, are you?"

While the smirk didn't make it to his lips, the humor was clear as he looked over. He reached his arm across the back of the couch. "Eh. Only if the movie is bad."

Andreah laughed as she reached over to grab her purse. "Fair enough." She pulled out the movie without any digging required and got up to put it in the player.

The movie wasn't the greatest, but wasn't so bad that it warranted falling asleep on. Andreah flipped through the menu looking for special features. "Stupid rental copies withholding the good stuff like commentary tracks and bloopers.

"Since when are director commentaries on par with gag reels?"

"Uh, since always?" Andreah tilted in her seat to shoot him a look before she stood up. "I like listening to the directors, or actors, talk shit on each other. Only then do I feel like I know the whole story." She waved a hand in a silent whatever. "Do you want a beer? Because I do."

"No, but help yourself." He watched as Andreah headed into the kitchen before noticing that his phone was blinking with a new alert. Such are the perils of silencing your device.

To Owen:
We could use your help for a raid. You busy?

Owen's eyes lifted from the phone just enough to watch Andreah as she sat down at his computer with an open beer bottle. She tapped on the keyboard to wake the computer up before glancing over to the movie's menu. "Alright, I'll admit, it didn't live up to the reviews."

"This is why I don't trust movie reviewers."

"Cut me some slack, it wasn't just some guy. Here, I'll show you." Andreah swirled the chair back to pull up the website.

"I believe you," Owen laughed. "I really do."

Andreah stuck her tongue out at him. Instead of pulling up the site mentioned, she made a detour to Twitter.

"Actually," Owen started, scratching the back of his head. "Charlie needs my help with a raid. It shouldn't take long. Do you mind?"

"Oh. Yeah, no, that's cool."

Owen's raised a brow. "You sure? I don't have to."

"I'm sure. Go ahead and help them. I shall watch and see if your skills are as great as you claim."

He got up to grab his headset off the side table, and paused before sitting down or putting it on. "Which screen did you want it to stream to?"

"The TV is fine," Andreah said. "That way if you suck I can still internet."

"Ye of little faith," he replied, without much care.

The raid had already started, which made joining a lot like stepping into a bar fight. It's hard to tell who started it, or even why. One just hoped to find their friends between the blows. Being a public event meant he could join the in-progress guild mission. The penalty was, he didn't have a chance to pick up new weapons after returning to the city.

Daniel took a quick step back, avoiding the point of a Spanish halberd. He looked over the shoulder of the soldier, seeing the main target with three other officers serving as a protective escort.

To the left, just over his shoulder, he found Lance. The guild was out-numbered, so if he was going to crash this raid, he should start it strong. Lance gripped the hilt of his sword, ready to draw it.

"Now," Daniel called, dropping down to one knee, and ducking his head.

Lance swiftly unsheathed his sword, and swung it through into a horizontal slash in one fluid motion. The Spanish officer blocked, catching the blade in the crook of his halberd. Daniel drew a knife off Lance's belt, and sunk it into the officer's gut. The officer fell back lifelessly onto the ground before breaking into polygons that dissolved into nothing.

Another officer broke off from Lucas, who had been fighting alongside them a short distance away. The officer readied their sword for a renewed assault. Being weaponless again wasn't the best fighting position, and Daniel stumbled back, falling on his ass as the knight's sword came down. He quickly spread his knees, watching as the blade crashed into cobblestone ground. Lance slashed a guard across the chest and clashed a sword against his. Daniel sprung up in the space Lance bought for him.

A knight's halberd passed just to Daniel's left, narrowly skimming over his arm. The near miss allowed him inside of the knight's defense, making it easy to grab the shaft of the halberd. Thrown off, the guard fought for control of it, but little did it matter as Daniel disarmed him. He swung it around, plunging the blade into the right side of the knight's abdomen before dragging it across to the left. The body did not even drop before breaking into shards of light.

Daniel looked to Lance, who was in the middle of combat against two swordsmen, then over at Lucas, who had been chasing down the main target as he tried to make an escape. There was no time to make a decision, so Daniel went with his instinct.

Lance delivered a kick to the gut of one of his foes before slashing at the other. Both backed away, one fatally into the range of Daniel's stolen weapon. Lance shifted his focus to the remaining swordsman, and waited for the chance to counter. The player lashed out with his sword. Lance dodged to his left, narrowly avoiding the blade. The guard tried to compensate with a slash. Lance took a cue from before and dropped down, letting the blade pass over, before running through with his dagger.

The player didn't seem ready to give up the ghost as his body lie with the hilt of the knife sticking out. "We need to get back to Lucas," Daniel ordered, and took the weapon for himself.

Lance nodded, and the two took off in that direction.

Lucas grappled with a man on the ground. The guard had knocked a bag of gold, gems, and things likely far more valuable out of their hand. The loot drop sat just out of reach of the fighting.

Daniel could have gone for the prize, but it seemed like a cruel thing to do when someone called him for help. Lucas managed to get on top of the guard and pinned one of his hands down, but the advantage was short lived before they had to roll off.

A blade came flying in, finding its mark in the guard's heart. Lucas looked over, finding Daniel standing there with a grin on his face and an arm still extended from throwing the knife.

More men joined the fray, and it wasn't clear from their armor if both sides had called for backup, or if vultures wanted to steal the prize at the finish line. Lucas scampered to they feet and grabbed the loot. They took a nervous step backward, and Daniel and Lance fell in as added protection.

"Who else is here?" Daniel asked.

"Abel is somewhere," Lucas said.

"Secure the intel," Lance added. "We got this."

A questioning look found Daniel, but when he didn't object, Lucas bolted as directed.

They returned to the fray, catching a guard down an alley who soon hit a dead end. The heavy armor he wore limited the options until only fighting back remained. After drawing a sword, he motioned for them to approach.

Lance went in for a strike, but the officer countered with his own attack, throwing Lance off balance. Daniel leaped forward attempting to keep the officer from taking advantage of Lance's stumble. The guard dodged back, avoiding the swipe of Daniel's knife.

Swifter than expected, the guard recovered and drove a knee into Daniel's gut. His body locked up as the air left his lungs. He retreated a few steps, bent over with his hands on his knees in an effort to stay standing.

Lance moved to Daniel, who was only letting exhausted breaths escape his lips.

"Hell of a welcome home, aye?" Lance said, grinning as he offered a hand to steady him.

Daniel lifted his head and found himself smiling as he righted himself. "I've had better."

"We could use Amilia right now," Lance said, readying himself for the remaining battle. An arrow came flying in and pierced the guard's shoulder. Staggered, the guard moved further away.

Lance turned, more startled by the help than pleased to see it. Abel stormed closer as he plucked another arrow from his quiver. Another arrow whizzed by the pair, this time diving into the officer's unprotected thigh. A third arrow punctured the right side of his chest in between the plates.

A smirk draped across Abel's face. "Where is the girlfriend?" he asked. The guard was trying to right himself but was coughing blood, giving time to taunt further. Abel turned to Lance, pretending he hadn't seen him. "Ah, brought the boyfriend today."

The silent glares both Daniel and Lance shot at him were ignored as Abel placed one hand on the guard's shoulder, finishing him and the public event.

Owen hadn't realized it until he took off his headset, but Andreah had gathered her things and was headed for the door. "Whoa, slow down, Hermes. Where are you going?"

Andreah opted for her phone rather than looking him in the eye. "Uh, I gotta go. Sorry," she said, tapping on the screen as if it was all right there.

"I thought, uh, you were going to stay the night?" Owen leaned against the wall near her, glancing down at her phone for a moment before looking at her face again.

"Well, there's the emergency," she said, locking her phone and stuffing it away. "One of the newbies ended up getting in a bad accident. I need to cover for 'em."

He could feel the tremble in her nervous lie, her mind too filled with whatever else to come up with a good excuse. But he couldn't bring himself to call her out on it. "Oh. Okay. Stay safe."

Andreah gave him a short nod, but before she could turn away Owen reached out to touch her hand. She rocked towards him for just a moment before grabbing the handle of the door again, and snapped out of it before anything else could be said.

The shock of it all rolled in when he heard the elevator ding down the hall. What happened? Did she get freaked out over something on her phone? Did he misread something? He should have asked her all these questions before she left, but the lump in his throat when she had avoided looking at him forced his silence. She obviously hadn't wanted him to ask, and he had nowhere to even begin to understand why.

"You're cheating." Amilia playfully accused as she handed Daniel her cards.

"Just because I'm a thief doesn't mean I'm dishonest," Daniel said as he shuffled the various suits of clubs, coins, cups, and swords. "Here, would you like to cut?"

Amilia smiled. Her hand hovered over the table as if to spoil his masterful plan. The second she committed to reaching down, Daniel pulled the deck back. "No, not that one," he teased.

Her laugh was echoed by the sound of a knock. That's when he knew this it was all over. No more hiding from the rest of the world and playing truc. He got up from the floor to answer the door and was met with a familiar face that surprised him far more than a stranger would have. "Ah, Lance," Daniel said. He blocked the door almost protectively with his body. "Hello."

"Ah, Daniel," Lance said, mocking his tone. Maybe not such a friendly face after all. "What were you thinking, running off with some girl for so long?"

"She isn't some girl."

Lance coughed out a laugh, and glanced away. "There were wanted posters for you all over town. You didn't even ask the guild for help. Didn't even tell me you were leaving. I was worried you were dead. Then, like smoke you appeared to do the guild's bidding."

The fact that Lance's voice wasn't raised made him feel so much worse. Pointing out that it had been Charlie's request, not the guild's, wouldn't make his friend feel any better.

"I'm sorry. I was in a rush."

"I don't want to hear excuses," Lance said, "You let her cloud your vision, and now you have to come with me."

"They sent you to get me?" Daniel swayed back before righting himself. "I'm not a wayward puppy."

"I volunteered," Lance corrected. "Believe me when I say I'm the one you wanted to show up." He paused, looking at Daniel with a funny little expression. "Why are you blocking the door?" Lance took a step forward to come in, and Daniel placed a hand against the doorway to block his path.

"*Que cachez-vous?*" Lance tilted his head to glance over Daniel's shoulder.

"I'm not hiding a thing," Daniel said purposely in Spanish.

The boys silently stared each other down for a moment before Lance broke the tension by pushing Daniel's arm away and walking inside. His steps ended abruptly when he spotted Amilia sitting on the couch. She lifted her head, and gave him a nervous smile. "My god," Lance said, "So, you're also alive."

"Daniel," Amilia said, hesitantly stealing a glance over to him. He had closed the door, and was awkwardly standing about until she called his name. Daniel sat down, and the simple touch of his hand seemed to reassure her.

Lance's lips parted at the gesture. It seemed like he wanted to ask something, but held a breath and let it pass. "If Daniel is going to play coy, maybe I can ask you," he said. "Why do they want you so bad? And how did you convince that bonehead to go with you?"

She stared at an empty space on the ground for a moment before she spoke. "I'm not sure. I guess they first wanted me for a helping you out, but when Sebastiano became involved, his money might have weighed in and made me more desired."

"That isn't—" Lance waved his hand. "That doesn't matter. No one seems to care whatever personal squabble is going on. All anyone seems to care about is a shield. Did you guys steal it?"

"No?" She didn't mean to seem unsure about it. But what could be so special about a shield?

Lance glanced from her to Daniel and back. Daniel's expression was slightly less confused, but it was clear neither of them really knew much about it. "You guys don't talk business much, do you?"

Daniel shrugged, and lifted a single hand up. He had been so busy with making sure they lived until the next day that the 'bigger picture' had fallen to the side of the road.

"What do you guys talk about?" Lance asked, completely derailed.

Daniel looked to Amilia. What *did* they talk about? While they traveled the only thing they could do was talk. "Uh, ourselves?"

Lance exhaled a small *huh* that summed up all his feelings. "That is so sweet I might vomit."

If the dozen of one-word texts weren't making it obvious that something was wrong, the fact Owen hadn't seen Andreah in over a week did. Not even for deliveries, since by the time he got downstairs she had already dropped the whatever off at the front desk. He leaned back in his desk chair at home, scrolling back and forth through his latest messages before deciding to make another attempt.

To Andreah:
So Michael totally got fired today. You should have seen it, this whole big scandal with this model. So much film everywhere.

It took a while, but he eventually got a reply.

To Owen:
Really? What happened?

To Andreah:
Nothing actually

This time the reply was almost immediate. Either she hadn't been up to anything or he had finally caught her full attention.

To Owen:
Wow...

He sighed, feeling things slip between his fingers once again.

To Andreah:
I'd really like to see you. I don't know how else to say that

He had a small feeling she would take her sweet time to reply, if at all. He put his head down, learning to accept defeat when the sudden noise of a new text gave him a start. Andreah invited him to come over to her place, which was a first. Any time he had asked about seeing it, she said her apartment was a mess and liked how quiet his was in comparison. She sent along the address before Owen assured he'd be there in no more than half an hour.

Owen decided to walk, using the time to think about everything; about what he would say, about what he did, which was still a matter of debate in his head. By time he made it to Andreah's apartment building, his thoughts were less clear than when he left.

The combination of being on a busier street, and on a lower floor, explained Andreah's comment about it being louder here. It wasn't obnoxiously so, actually endearing if you enjoyed the city. He exhaled sharply before he knocked on the door. There was no doubt Andreah would open up, but despite this, butterflies found their way into his stomach.

"Hey, come in," Andreah said in a single breath as she held the door open for him.

The plan was to open up into this big thing about how he didn't mean to offend her for whatever he did, and confess the accidental thoughtlessness, but the strange charm of her apartment silenced him. It was like a shrine to half-

197

completed to-do lists. Folded clothes were piled onto an armchair, and another, older pile on the couch had started to lean in towards the side. In the living room alone he spotted two empty coffee mugs. One on the main table, and another on a banister that separated them from the kitchen.

"Owen," Andreah said. He didn't turn towards her as he continued to glance around her place. "We need to talk."

Those four words, however, caught his attention. His arms fell to his sides as he focused in on her, wondering if anything good ever followed that statement. "About what?" She sunk to sit on the arm of the couch. Owen tried to give her a moment to speak, but they just stared at each other, both too afraid. "Is this about me playing while you were over?" Owen blurted out. "Because I asked you if it was okay."

"It's not that." Andreah started, "It's just, when I saw you with Lance, I realized..."

Owen's eyes narrowed slightly. "Realized what?"

"It's just that..." Andreah picked at an imaginary thread, before she met his worried and almost annoyed blue eyes. "I realized you play a lot. Far more than I imagined."

"Are you joking?" Owen glanced around the room, like he was looking for an exit this time, before settling back on Andreah with as much accusation as she gave. "You ignore me and then only invite me over for an intervention?"

Her head jerked to the side, before falling very still. "If it's not a problem..."

"It isn't!"

"Good," she said, her tone fully committed now. "Then it won't hurt to see others who do. We could go to one of those meetings."

"Like a zoo? Let's go watch the addicts be spooky animals?" Andreah was right about one thing. It was too loud in this apartment. Distant sirens and stray horns of annoyed drivers grinded against Owen's nerves.

"You know that's not what I meant."

"Whatever, I'm going home." Owen moved towards the door, but was quickly intercepted by Andreah jumping up off the couch.

"Please, don't go." Her breath seemed held captive in her chest, enough to give him pause. "Just...believe me when I say I'm worried about you."

Owen rubbed the back of his neck. He looked at her for a long moment, deciding if he wanted to challenge her further or just agree to be done with this conversation. "Fine."

Andreah lit up like she was given a second chance. "Really?"

He shook his head, wanting to back out of this whole situation, this whole day. Now he was the one who wanted to separate himself by sitting down. "I said fine."

"There is a group that meets a few blocks over."

Owen's jaw tightened at the mention. He knew that one, been there plenty of times for bone digging gigs. "But I'll only go if we can pretend like we don't know each other. Pretend we are meeting for the first time."

"What? No!" Andreah threw her hands in the air, confused as to where she lost her victory. "This isn't a game."

"Apparently everything is a game to me. Isn't that the problem?"

Andreah shook her head slowly like she wanted to cuss at him. "Fine," she said, with a bite as if it was some other four letter word. "You win."

"Sort of the point of games, right?" Owen moved past Andreah, being careful not to crowd her as he moved to the door. He paused with his hand on the door handle. "I'm going home. You can text me when you want to do this stupid thing."

It took two days, but that text came. He sat in a meeting watching a young woman with earrings longer than her short hair talk at the podium. "They told me success was just over the horizon," she said, pulling nervously on her collar before she went on. "As if the horizon wasn't an imaginary line that recedes as you approach it. But that's what is different in game, right? You can set a marker and reach it. You can chase, and catch, that horizon."

Owen was sitting in silence as he listened. He hadn't caught the name, but something about her made him smile. Maybe it was the near poetic way she tried to explain her problems. Movement caught Owen's eye, and he turned his head to see a brunette sit a few seats down. Lean, athletic build, and 100% gorgeous.

When the speaker stepped down, the seatmate glanced around before she leaned over on one of the chairs between them. "Are you going to speak tonight?"

"Why?"

He expected her to say something else, but they shared a glance that lingered far too long for strangers in a silent challenge. She edged forward on her seat as if she wanted to speak up, but in the end just listened.

Owen got up between speakers to get some coffee that tasted like it had been filtered through a sock. Why he had agreed to come was beyond him right now. He didn't see a problem, or have anything to share with the group. This game wasn't even fun, if she was only going to push for something he didn't understand.

She stood up and booked it out of the room. Owen raised a brow, and gave it a moment before he tossed his drink and followed her out. She turned, lit cigarette perched between her fingers. He might have said going outside to smoke was the polite thing to do, but that wasn't a word he'd ever used for her.

"Can I have one?" Owen asked.

She blew out smoke, looking as bored as he felt, before she held out the pack. Without word, he pulled one out, and handed it back in favor of his own lighter. What was meant to be fun got him thinking. Everyone was racing, all betting on what addiction would kill them first. Neither of them had money on lung cancer. Owen leaned against the wall and took a drag. He closed his eyes, enjoying it far more than the ten cent coffee.

"My name is Andreah," she said, her shoulder just turned enough to him. Andreah's tight expression made it look like she was pulling teeth, or maybe that hers had just been pulled.

"Owen."

"Is that a first or a last name, Owen?"

He cocked his head to the question. An amusement tugged at his face that he only barely could control. It was such a rare question, most assumed it was the first. "That would spoil the anonymity of this whole thing, don't you think?"

A smirk tinted that tough exterior. So she could still smile. Andreah shook her head like she didn't care, but the slight hitch in her shoulders suggested otherwise. "Maybe I just wanted to know what name I'd be screaming later."

Owen choked mid-drag like someone who had never smoked in their life. "Wow, what a cliché line."

"Are you telling me you aren't into it?"

"I didn't say that," Owen said. He looked up to the small patch of dark sky that wasn't hidden by tall buildings and street lights. Owen smiled to himself, and by time he shook his head he was laughing. "I can't believe we've slept together, and you don't even remember my full name."

"It isn't like we are Facebook official or anything." Andreah tried to defend, but lacked anything substantial since she should have known by now. "I bet you don't even know my full name either."

"Andreah Bourne," Owen said, "Birthday, August 30th. Your favorite thing to eat is a burger, the really fat and juicy sort."

"How do you know that?"

Owen put out his cigarette in the ashtray attached to the trash. He tried not to roll his eyes, but only managed to turn away before he did. "It's called listening, Andreah. Can we go? I think it's about to rain.

Sitting with the thieves gave Amilia hope. It didn't matter that it was a small group. Just being invited to a guild meeting showed she was accepted.

After going over old missions, Gael spoke about new business. "You might have noticed some...drama recently," he said. "In an effort to avoid favoritism, it's been decided Daniel will no longer be Miss Le Russo's mentor."

"That's ridiculous," Daniel said out of turn.

Gael shot him a patient look, telling him wordlessly not to interrupt again. "Trust is huge in our line of work," Gael continued. "Instead of pairing Miss Le'Russo with a stranger, Monsieur Tarlé will take over."

"What?" Lance blurted, "Me?"

"It avoids a conflict of interest, and you have already proven the ability to work together." His tone grew annoyed, as if tired of discussing the subject.

Amilia swallowed hard, mouth nearly too dry to do so. "I would be happy to work with Lance," she said. "Learning from multiple teachers is always prudent." The boys might be taken aback, but these sort of politics weren't new, or objectionable, to her.

Daniel, however, was so tense it radiated off of him. It wasn't that he didn't trust the replacement, more so the public slap on the hand. The surprise always hurt the most.

"It shall be done," Lance said, finding that edge of professionalism needed.

"Good. Meeting adjourned," Gael said. He gathered his papers from a small writing desk, and when he left to go back to his office Abel followed.

"Well, that was something," Lucas said. He glanced around to his friends who hung back in the library.

"Indeed." Lance broke into a wide grin. "What a most interesting turn of events. Just when I was starting to feel like the third wheel, too. I even know what my first official order is going to be."

"Oh?" Amilia asked.

Lance stood up and moved in front of Amilia. The amusement in his voice vanished to give an authoritative tone. "Make out with me."

Daniel's face went pale as Lucas started cracking up. Or at least, they laughed until Daniel shot him a look.

"*Quoi?*" Lance asked, unable to hide his enjoyment. "Is that not how you did it?"

"Not exactly," Daniel grumbled.

"Amilia." Lance gingerly drew one of her hands between his. "We need to address this underlying sexual tension between us. It must be assured that we won't be a distraction to each other."

She stood. Eliminating much of the space between them. She smiled faintly, examining his face for a moment as she tilted her chin up. "I'd rather quit," she whispered only inches from his mouth. After a glance to the others stepped away. "Now that we've addressed that, I hope to see you again soon for training."

Lance's eyes followed Amilia out, losing sight as she slipped into the hallway.

"Is your curiosity satisfied?" Daniel said, rougher than he intended.

"Yes, it's clear where we stand. But you, on the other hand..." Lance's words trailed off as their eyes met. His hands rose, fingers twitching over Daniel's biceps. "Have you been working out?"

"I hate you right now."

"Liar," Lance laughed, and Lucas cracked up again too.

Daniel looked over to Lucas again, but sighed this time. "You're right," he said, glancing back to Lance. "I'm sorry for my recent behavior."

The next day, when the sun rose, it threatened to bleach the city with its golden light. Lance waited, turning when he the heard footsteps of his new apprentice.

"Hey, frog," Amilia said, trying to cover her tiredness with an easy joke.

Lance tilted his head at the jab. Unsure how he felt about it. "Frog?" he repeated. "Does Daniel take such sass from you, *taureau?*"

"No, I save all my remarks for you. You should consider yourself honored." Amilia smiled a little nervously. The boldness on display died down as she shuffled her feet. Spanish she could do. French? Not so much. "What is tau— What did you call me?"

"Ah, maybe you shouldn't be so quick to call your peers names." Lance started walking, and Amilia followed, assuming she was meant to. "Would you like to go on an adventure?" He looked over to Amilia, who stared ahead in confusion. "Oh, you expected me to demand hurdles or push-ups. Maybe even pick-pocketing practice until you either get arrested or the sun goes down."

"Well, yeah, actually."

Lance let out a hum before he started walking again. "Maybe your Spanish blood isn't up for such an adventure."

Amilia stopped short. Upon her silent refusal to take another step, Lance turned around and waited with a stubbornness that rivaled hers.

"What is your problem?" she asked.

"You don't like me," Lance said. Amilia opened her mouth, but he raised a hand to stop her. "That wasn't a question. I don't know what your issue with me is. Maybe my untimely non-death got you in trouble, or maybe you think I'm stealing someone from you. Maybe you just think I'll let you get away with anything because of our shared fondness. Frankly, I don't care anymore. It is your defect, not mine."

"Lance, I—"

"I don't care to hear it." He interrupted. "I can fulfill my vow and train you the conventional way. But if you decide to show a little respect, and learn to trust me, we can explore places lost to mankind for hundreds of years."

Her cheeks burned with embarrassment. She'd been trying to just fit into the thief mold, just be one of them already, that forgot that Daniel and Lance hadn't ever demanded anything in the first place. "Let's go on an adventure."

Since Owen didn't have work today, or need to play mentor for anyone, his day was pretty open. The Saturday might have been spent with Andreah if she hadn't been so hot and cold lately. Instead, he decided to hang out with Charlie.

Owen was holding a table in a busy Starbucks cafe while Charlie was up at the counter retrieving their drinks. The time off should have thrilled Owen, but it didn't. Instead, it felt like everyone had everything handled without him.

"You need to learn to smile more," Charlie said. They leaned over the table, placing Owen's coffee down first before unwrapping a straw for their own frappuccino.

Owen pulled the lid off of the steaming drink. "I'm smiling now." And to his credit, he was.

"Good." Charlie's straw was in their drink for mere seconds before they pulled it out to get some whip cream. Once the drink was reassembled they went on. "Now, tell me why you weren't in the first place."

"I don't feel like the guild trusts me anymore," Owen sighed.

"As they shouldn't," Charlie said, as they took a sip.

Owen scoffed and sat up straight at the insult, but Charlie continued.

"Daniel is a man in love. Men in love should never be trusted. They are unpredictable. Their loyalties get pulled and stretched thin."

Owen took a drink, and instantly regretted it as it burned his tongue. Seemed this conversation was no safe harbor either. "So what? I just forget everything and go back to business? That will make everyone trust me again?"

"I didn't say that." Charlie's phone went off with a happy text tone, but they ignored it for the time being. "You know Lucas has your back. And I know you love the guild, but sometimes one needs more than an idea to fight for."

Charlie's phone went off again, and Owen watched as they checked their texts. A large crack ran through the back of the phone's blue case. "You're never going to replace that, are you?"

Charlie turned the phone over in their hands. "Sometimes you just want to hold onto things, no matter how broken they are. You know?"

Owen let out a little cough of a laugh at the answer. "I'm starting to."

"You should be flattered," Lance said, as he crouched down to pick at a lock. The worn door appeared to be the only thing still holding crumbling walls in place. "I generally don't bring people on these little adventures."

The ruins were untouched. After opening the door, his hands were covered in dust. A foyer extended only a few yards before the wood rotted away to a gaping hole in the ground. The shadows living inside seemed it suggest a passageway hidden below.

"Oh yes," Amilia said, giving the pit a wary look. "Very flattered that you brought me to a dark, wet cave. Let's hope there aren't any bears." More of the building existed beyond this, but the chasm hardly left any room to make it through. Definitely something she didn't want to test.

"Bears," Lance repeated in amusement. He moved to the edge, and kicked a colored tile down into the darkness. In no time, he heard the tile shatter against the ground. "Jump down."

"What?" Amilia's voice raised high enough that it echoed down the forgotten hall. "You've got to be kidding me."

"My darling Amilia, I would never jeopardize your safety. Come on, bull." Lance prodded at her with two fingers which mirrored horns.

Taureau. Bull. "That's what you called me before," Amilia said, as she resisted his nudging.

"Congratulations. You've learned your first French word," Lance said, sounding wholly uninterested for once. "Might I suggest you jump before I push you?"

Amilia shot him a dirty look and readied an insult. In the end, she kept it to herself. It did make them even. Which meant her biggest concern should be Lance poking her again. She breathed in, and stepped off.

The fall wasn't as far as she expected. She landed on her feet, but had too much momentum and fell forward on her hands. Her wrist took the majority of her weight, and she winced as she pulled herself up.

Lance jumped down a moment later, landing on the balls of his feet, and rolled forward. He popped back up with a grace that only added to Amilia's annoyance. "Ready to continue on?"

"I don't know how you expect me to explore if I get injured right away." Amilia held her wrist with a scowl on her face. "Unless I'm meant to stand here and glare for the rest of the day."

"Maybe your hate can light the way."

There was that tone again. It sounded like Lance, but the music in his voice was missing. Amilia frowned, feeling like a fire that was smothering the carefree air. "Could you..." she hesitated, "look at it for me?"

His eyes looked darker as they worked to capture rays of light from the broken floorboards above. His lips parted as if she were a curiosity. Amilia held out her wrist before he asked, and Lance moved closer. His cool fingers caressed her wrist. A touch that could have a much different meaning if it wasn't for his clinical expression. "I'm no doctor, but I think you've just pulled something. Likely because you were tense when you landed."

Lance's hands fell back to his side as he finished playing nurse. But his eyes never met hers, despite that fact that Amilia studied his face the whole time. "I'm sorry I snapped at you," she blurted. The confession was what caught his attention.

"If it makes you feel better, I broke my ankle the first time I went exploring."

Somehow it did, but she didn't voice it since it would have sounded cruel. Amilia followed behind him as he ventured farther into the tunnel. "Did Daniel have to carry you out?"

He chuckled. "No, this was long before I met Daniel."

Amilia nodded, trying to keep her manners about her. It was a pointless gesture, since Lance was walking in front of her. When her eyes adjusted to the low light, she noticed the floor had a shine to it. She crouched down so her fingers could touch the stone floor and they came back damp. "It's water."

"Begs the questions of where it's coming from."

"This isn't why we came down here?"

"No. Just imagine though, Lance Tarlé: Water Raider. What a dreadful title that would be." He thought she might take his joke as further argument, but instead Amilia laughed.

The deeper they went into the cave, the less it felt like a cave. The stones had telltale signs that humans had carved into them to make a path. The ground was too smooth. Amilia took a glance behind them. The tunnel wasn't getting tighter, but it felt like it.

They fell silent aside from the slight echo of their steps. When the emptiness was too much, he turned around. "You know, I don't understand the whole..."

Amilia's eyes darted around to the side walls which now appeared to have the same shine. She didn't even notice he had stopped until she had to pull up short or bump into him.

"Oh," he breathed. "You look like you need some fresh air."

"Yeah, I just...need to regroup a little."

"Try not to sweat it. I'm pretty sure the light up ahead signals that the tunnel will open up soon."

And it did, just not in the fashion he imagined. Lance's attention fell to the floor, and the odd way the stones swirled around in a pattern that made him think of the rings of a tree. "What a strange place."

Amilia, however, looked up. The sun peeked through the vaulted ceiling. The circular room seemed to spin dizzyingly. Amilia stepped back, and found the edge of a statue broken beyond recognition to sit on.

"Are you okay?"

She nodded, but it was one of the least believable things he had ever seen. "It's just..." She tried to answer, but her words seemed to lag on their way from her thoughts to her mouth. "I don't like bears much."

"I think I'm starting to understand your charm," Lance chuckled. "You can rest here. I'll scout ahead and find the best exit for you."

He stepped away to check a nearby hallway, but stopped as something scraped under his boot. Lance lifted a single foot to see an imperfect circle of gold shine up at him. He bent down to pick it up and realized it was a coin. An old one, at that. Lance flipped it between his fingers. The words appeared to be Greek, but he didn't have the slightest clue beyond that.

"Here," Lance said, returning to Amilia's side. "You can use this as a worry token."

"Thank you," she meekly replied. The coin sat in her palm and shimmered unnaturally in the low light. "Lance, wait. Why are you so nice to me?"

Lance raised a brow. "I thought that answer would be obvious."

The thought made her stomach double down on its nausea. She had rescued him from literal torture, and then what, ignored his concerns afterward? Amilia closed her eyes, and held tightly onto the coin. She thought he had left, but his voice drew her attention again.

"You have endeared yourself to Daniel," he said. "And me."

"Do you have your headset with you?" Owen asked.

"Yeah." Charlie followed Owen into his apartment, and closed the door before gesturing to their backpack.

"Sweet," Owen said in singsong as he sent off a text.

Charlie started unloading their backpack, then glanced up as Owen continued to text. "Something up?"

"Em's due date is soon, so we're all on alert if she needs anything." He looked up to find a questioning expression on his friend's face. "It's fine. I'm ready."

"Thinking he for Lucas today."

"Okay."

Charlie was one of those people who had a similar game boot up to Owen. For them, it started out in the chest, with a warmth that spread out to the palms of their hands and sparked to life like a flame. Catching the world before it rendered fully was rare, but to Charlie it looked like ribbons of bright color.

The game loaded into the safety of Daniel's home. Lucas glanced around Daniel's museum-quality inventory. He had some of the plot items, but most had been sold off afterwards.

Daniel walked into his room to equip his gear. He smiled over to Amilia's side of the bed, remembering the days when the bed didn't have sides.

"When did you get this?" Lucas called, from the other room.

"Get what?" Daniel asked, as he returned. Lucas held up a small coin that had a blocky gold shimmer as if the game glitched on the effects. "Why is it doing that?"

Lucas turned the coin over in his hand. "It looks like a quest item."

"It's not mine," Daniel said, holding his hand out. "I've been with you all day."

"Then whose is it?"

"Good question."

Daniel flipped the coin over in his hands. It should be nothing, but he didn't seem able to set it down. "What is," he started to ask, squinting at the coin. They looked like a random collection of letters. "A, N, T, omega sign? N, E—"

"Wait, wait, let me go ask the internet," Charlie said, while pulling off their headset. They moved over to sit at Owen's computer, pulling up a search engine. "Ok, tell me the other letters."

"I, N, O, C."

Charlie repeated the letters back as they hit the corresponding keys. "Um, let's see," they stalled as they scrolled down the first few entries.

Daniel looked up at Lucas, who stood there unnaturally still until the idle animation kicked in. Lucas cracked the knuckles of his left hand, then his right.

"It's an ancient Greek coin," Charlie said. "For Athena."

"Huh." However interesting, it didn't tell him much. When Charlie put on their headgear, Lucas' movements became fluid again. Transitioning without hiccup instead of cycling between animations.

"What are you looking for?" Lucas asked.

212

Daniel had moved over to his desk, checking on the maps spread out over it. "Amilia," he said. Her little marker was nowhere to be found. Wherever did she go? He would have sworn she'd be back by now.

"You are so smitten, it's bordering on obsessed." Lucas raised his hands surrendering when Daniel shot him a silent threat. "Sorry. Who was she last with?"

"Lance."

Lucas walked around so he could see the map as well. "I don't see him right now either."

Amilia perked up when they made it out to fresh air. She smiled up at the sun like a daisy after days of clouds. But far too soon, that grin wilted. "Could I ask you something? Maybe for a favor?"

Lance had been keeping an eye on the guards patrolling the area. So far, they stayed out of the small courtyard he and Amilia had found. Once he felt sure the guards wouldn't bother them, he pulled himself up to sit on the carved stone banister. "Of course. What's on your mind?"

She leaned back against the stone as well, unable to meet his gaze. The words had to be gathered up within wisps of courage. "If something were to happen, I mean to me. Or if I need to go about something on my own, I need you to promise me that you'll keep Daniel from getting involved. And I won't stand for you doing anything on his behalf, either. I don't think either of us could convince him not to help, so this might be a difficult request. But, if the need ever arises, I know we both want him safe."

Lance's lips parted to object, but now her request seemed to be gushing out.

"You know he'd risk everything, he has before." She glanced towards the ground. "With the lives we lead, there is bound to be trouble, and I couldn't live with myself if something happened to him."

"Amilia, I..." He didn't want to refuse such a favor, but it was a lot to ask to go behind Daniel's back.

"And, you can never tell him I asked you for this. He would never trust either of us again," Amilia added.

"All right." Lance might have caved, but was quick to clarify. "I will keep him safe." It wasn't exactly what she had asked, but it was the most he'd agree to with the limited information. The request was one of a lover begging for protection against the foolish things that lovers did for each other. Being in love could be as dangerous as any blade.

He'd come out to have fun while he taught Amilia, but the day filled with gloom all the same. "Whatever is going on," Lance said, "just remember, we are here for you."

"I know." She smiled weakly before trying to wave the whole thing off as she pulled on a bigger smile. "Enough of that. I feel like we still have a couple more hours of adventure we can squeeze into this day."

Mirth that normally found Lance with ease took its time to return. "Actually, we can stop messing around and do something official for the guild instead. But we should have more than two people for it. Let's regroup and find Daniel first."

Amilia wasn't convinced that Lance wasn't just dragging her back to spill everything. But if today taught her anything, it was she had to learn to trust him.

Lucas looked up when the two just walked into Daniel's place without a knock. "Ah, the trio is back together, I see."

"Well, if it isn't my favorite Rivera son," Lance said.

"Today it is, indeed."

"You are my favorite Rivera son, daughter, or offspring any day."

Lucas smiled at his word choice. "Flatterer."

"Shall I flatter Amilia instead?" Lance wavered in his stance to look towards Amilia. She barely contained a jump at the sound of her name. Whatever compliment he was going to pay was lost to the incredulous expression he gave instead.

"I see you haven't broken his spirit," Daniel said, broadening the smile he'd had ever since Amilia had walked in. "I assume he is treating you the same?"

Amilia eyed Lance as he silently urged her to speak. When she realized he had brought her in earnest, she smiled. "Better than ever," she said, finally turning to Daniel. "I hear that there is a mission to be had? I'd hate for anyone to suggest you've become a slacker who stands around all day."

"Oh no, now there are two of them sassing," Lucas teased, before looking down at the quest map. "We could do some good old espionage. Steal intelligence, sneak out, get rewarded."

"Sounds great," Daniel said.

"What should I do?" She glanced from one thief to another. Lance seemed impressed. Despite her panic earlier, she still had the urge to prove herself.

"Step one," Lance said. "Tag along with a group of thieves. Step two, do not die. Step three—"

"Profit!" Lucas chimed in.

Daniel moved towards the door, making a detour to give Amilia kiss on the forehead. The gesture threw her off. A blush raced to her face. How was he able to balance his focus like that? One minute thinking about the mission and the next showing fondness.

Amilia followed behind the boys. The only thing keeping her nerves at bay was the bow on her back. Lucas took point as they traveled to a small fort on the edge of town. Its walls were so tall that they were able to stare up at it nearly the whole way there.

"I'm going to go scout ahead," Lucas said, and without another word, sprinted ahead. The trio waited, tucked into the shadows of the nearest building for his return. Lucas returned moments later. "It's pretty fortified, but there seems to be gaps in their patrols. If we can distract the first guard, the others shouldn't notice."

Daniel leaned out of the shadows, peering past Lucas to a lone guard who was blocking the door inside. "We got this," he said. Without a glance to anyone else, he started to walk towards the guard. After a few steps, Lance started following. Daniel walked past the guard, just on the edge of a restricted zone, and dropped his coin purse a few steps away from the guard's feet.

The man stepped a few precious feet forward and turned away from watching the cross-traffic to pick up the money. A second after he stood up, Lance reached up from behind and caught him in a choke hold.

Daniel turned back around as the man let out a muffled cry. He ignored the plea and searched the guard's pockets as Lance held him still, retrieving not only his money but a key.

"What I wouldn't give for an extra pair of hands," Lucas said.

Amilia glanced over at him. When she looked back, Lance had hidden the guard somewhere, and Daniel was opening the door. "Go, now," Lucas prompted, and Amilia sprinted to the door.

In quick succession, they all raced inside. Daniel came up last and closed the door behind them. Stealth was more efficient than swords, if less flashy. The few times they did run into guards, Daniel would set them up and Lance would knock them out. Perfect, wordless teamwork.

Several hallways and a few looted rooms later, they came to another area at the end of the hall and ducked in. Inside, a single Knight sat at a desk. At the sight of four thieves, he rushed to his feet. Lucas dispatched the guard with a throwing knife, and he slumped back down before ever reaching a weapon.

"I thought we weren't killing people today," Daniel said, more curious than anything.

"I didn't want the alarm tripped at the last second."

"Good throw," Lance added as he moved around the desk. Maps and designs for things he didn't quite know what to make of lined the walls. He searched for letters that would talk about troop movements, and correspondence between factions that weren't officially aligned with the knights.

Amilia and Lucas checked the room for anything else of value while Daniel watched the door.

"Daniel," Lance called as he held a letter up.

Daniel didn't understand why Lance couldn't just share with everyone, but moved away from the door and took the letter. The neutral expression on his face turn to a frown as he reached the bottom of the page.

She had to know. There was no other reasonable explanation. "This is your family's crest," Daniel said, lifting his eyes up to Amilia.

Both she and Lucas turned at his voice, but Amilia was the only one to speak. "That can't be."

Daniel held the letter out, but Amilia didn't reach for it. Lucas shot her a curious glance before taking a long stride and taking it himself. Amilia's family connection to the bards was known. Even played to their advantage, at times. Since then, Amilia had been proving herself to their cause.

The boy is of no concern. The memory burned hot and fresh in Daniel's mind. The two stared at each other, their expressions painted with unsaid words.

"All this means is that her family has talked to the knights recently," Lucas said, trying to break the tension.

"Her uncle is more than just a paid hand, he's practically one of them." Lance's face twitched at the memory of it. "I have the scars to prove it."

"My uncle's actions are not my own," Amilia said. "I've been with you, or Lance, since we got back in town. Neither the knights nor my family came to look for me in that time. I'm not going to act on some letter that I don't know the story behind. I won't risk my family, or the thieves guild, like that."

"You guys could call it a day," Lance offered. "We'll go deliver the papers."

It took Lucas a second to realize that "we" Lance included him this time. "Oh," he said in surprise. "Yes, why not. My house is in that direction anyways."

Lance looked over to Amilia with his own silent plea for them to talk before they split up.

Daniel found it strange to return home with just Amilia, but not unwelcome. She took her time washing herself up before she came over to sit on the settee with him. Amilia sat close enough that her hand almost absentmindedly reached for his. "I know you're worried," she said. Daniel looked up unable to deny it. "But know my world is perfect when I'm with you." She leaned forward and kissed him, letting their lips stay tenderly locked for a long moment.

Daniel smiled at her sweet comment, nuzzling his nose against her as the kiss finally ended. "Then you'll just have to stay forever, love."

"Amilia?" he called, but only silence greeted him. Something was wrong. A fear he didn't understand knotted in his stomach.

Daniel searched his home without any luck. Amilia must have left. But where to? He nearly tripped over himself in his haste to get dressed. After yesterday, he couldn't just write this off. Maybe she had gone to the guild to look into the letter. Wherever she went, he needed to know she was safe.

He went straight for the guild hall, but once there, he realized the place was nearly empty. It was early, long before people usually met. A few people were around, but Amilia wasn't one of them. Maybe he could just snag the letter from yesterday and reread it for clues. He could break into the room where the eldest members keep such things.

Just as Daniel was plotting to bust the lock, Lance neared. "Is everything alright?"

"I need another look at that letter. If you help, together we can make quick work of it," Daniel said.

Lance's worry strengthened as he watched Daniel's restless motions. "Why do you need it now? What's wrong?"

"Amilia. She left without saying where she was going, and I have a bad feeling about it. I need the letter to see if it would have made her go look for her uncle." Daniel knew he sounded frantic by the look Lance was giving him.

"I still have the letter. I kept it so I could look into it myself." Lance retrieved it from his pocket. Daniel reached for it, but Lance pulled it back. "If I give you this, I'm going with you. I didn't hide it from the guild to be cute, I did it to protect Amilia. And you. You get reckless when you are scared."

"I'm focused." His friend didn't look convinced, but tipped the letter forward all the same. Daniel nabbed it out of Lance's hand. "And I wouldn't be scared if people started telling me things." He kept his eyes on Lance for a second longer before unfolding the letter. The first time he had only skimmed it, too drawn down to crest at the bottom. Now, he took his time with the scripted words. It slammed Dimitri for not watching his charge better. Even accused him of interfering with their plans. It didn't name Amilia, but together they ruined the knight's missions several times. The dinner, rescuing Lance, fleeing town, then fleeing yet again.

"The gallows." When Daniel read over the words his chest seized. It had been a vague, meaningless, threat without context. Now that Amilia was missing it held a suffocating weight.

If something were to happen, something to me.

"*Merde*," Lance swore. They'd been fools. "Let's go."

It started to rain as they hit the streets again. The light drizzle was as persistent as Daniel's dread. They climbed up rooftops so they could run over streets that would soon fill. Looming over the gallows as a reminder of who controlled life and death within the city's walls was the knights' headquarters.

They stormed the complex. Two men trying to change the tide, stealing lives at the edge of their blades and staining their path red. They tore through the halls. Guards readied their swords for the onslaught. Daniel sunk his dagger in the gap in the guard's armor. Such a small target between chest and spaulder that allowed him to slash down further.

As Daniel slammed the first man down, another guard tripped over his fallen comrade. A helmet might have saved him from Lance's quick sword.

They made it up two floors before every guard in the building became dedicated to stopping them. It was impossible to go about this with any haste. "Go," Lance ordered during a lull between waves. "I'll catch up."

Daniel bounced on the balls of his feet, torn between protecting Lance and sprinting to make up time. He followed Lance's order and ran up the side of a wall to avoid the slash of a knight who was in his way.

There had only been one direction that guards were flowing from, one door that he was placing all his hopes on. Daniel lifted his knee to his chest and busted the door open with a kick.

"Stop!" It was Amilia's voice that stayed his hand. Daniel froze. She stood as stunned as he was. The men surrounding her twitched forward, like attack dogs waiting on Don Ambrogio's command.

The only one physically restrained was Celio. His hands were bound with cloth and he shot a glare towards the thief that planned to save them. Daniel looked to Amilia and her somber expression.

"Why don't you do that now, Miss Le'Russo?" Ambrogio said, clearly part of a conversation that Daniel had missed. "Your antics as lovers have cost me my last man."

Amilia just stared as Daniel dripped both rainwater and blood. His chest pounded in a fashion that made him worry he'd been injured. "I don't understand," he said, far the speech he would have rather had in the moment.

Her eyes fell to the floor, unable to return his gaze. "I told you not to come."

"Like hell you did!" Daniel's volume made her words sound like a whisper. His head felt hazy. Nothing made sense anymore. Daniel stepped closer, not even looking to see if the guards took it as a hostile act. "Don't give me that," he said, with a bewildered look on his face. "You should have known better."

Lance slid into the building, expecting it clear from the type of guards he was fleeing from. "You got to be kidding me," he mumbled, and raised his hands, hoping they wouldn't just drop him on sight.

"You thieves are like cockroaches," Ambrogio spat. "How many orders does it take to kill you?"

Amilia glanced at Lance before turning to the Don. "We can settle this without them being further involved." Ambrogio tightened his lips into a thin line, but otherwise didn't acknowledge her.

"Let her go," Daniel said.

His demand was met with a laugh. It was the short, curt sound of an aristocrat and general. He looked ready to order an end to it all when Amilia's outburst stayed his hand once again.

"I am where I should be. You however, should leave." She glanced at Lance for a second. "He was right all along. That you refused to see it is on you." She blinked hard, stiffening, then turned her back on the both of them. A poor attempt at hiding her fear. She had felt so strong up until this point.

"Your traitor has asked you to leave," Ambrigio said in a tired tone. "If you don't take this opportunity, I'll consider her concessions void."

Sweat made it feel like Lance's sword was going to slip from his fingers. He wanted to shake the feeling away, and adjust his grip, but either could be seen as an act of aggression. "We really should go," he whispered, "We can try to find another way."

"No." Daniel shot a look over his shoulder to Lance before glancing around the whole room again in a dizzying swirl. "No, I refuse." If he could only offer something better than her, maybe they could trade instead. It was clear Ambrigio wanted Daniel and Lance dead, but they seemed to hold no value either way. The shield, however, and its location, had been demanded before. If he had it now... "I know where the stone aegis is. I'll lead you right to it."

Ambrigo pinched the bridge of his nose. He waved a hand, and a knight roughly pulled Celio to his feet. Another grabbed Amilia's arm and pulled her without resistance towards a distant door. "Lies will get you nowhere, boy. I have what I want, and someone to pay for my not having it sooner."

Daniel jumped forward and pulled a dagger from his belt, the movement useless as Lance pulled him back.

"Our business here is done," Lance announced. "We will go in peace."

For a moment, Lance was certain Daniel was going to kill everyone in the room to get to Amilia. But they were far outnumbered. It took several tugs, and encouragements in French, before Lance was able to get Daniel to back down.

Lance nearly pushed Daniel onto the safety the street offered. The only thing Daniel felt in his bones was hate. He glared at Lance as if he was to blame, wishing he had the right curse words.

"Just, stop it." Lance groaned. "You don't even care if she is a knight, do you?"

"No."

The anger in his voice suggested it was a lie, but Lance didn't call him out on it. "She made her choice, Daniel. There is nothing you can do about it."

It didn't appear that Daniel was listening anymore. He looked up at the building for another way in, or anything else that could to steal the upper hand back. Lance had all but given up. He watched with his arms folded over his chest.

"I will not let her be their sacrificial lamb," Daniel said without turning back. He reached up to an awning to see if it could hold his weight. When it didn't wiggle, he pulled himself up, groaning at the odd angle.

Lance sighed and started to climb as well. Each window they tested proved locked, or rather, not designed to be opened. The height of the room gave them a clear advantage to see everything over the gallows. "What is your plan?"

Daniel shot him a sideways look, but said nothing.

"You don't have a plan."

"I have a plan," Daniel corrected. "I just don't know how to *execute* said plan."

"So, you don't have a plan," Lance sighed.

They watched for a short time, looking for anything that could be used. Anything that could be exploited, stolen, or outright killed so they could meet their goals. While everyone said they hated death, a lynching somehow always drew a crowd. The street started to fill with NPCs and curious players.

An executioner readied the gallows with a single noose while a town herald spoke over a murmuring crowd. "By the wishes of the crown, we gather here to end a sinful soul. On counts of treason against the crown and church, and illegal acts of thievery against the Knights of the Order of the Golden Fleece we sentence Amilia Le'Russo to death by hanging."

"Why is this happening?" Daniel whispered to himself. He stared down at his hands, flexing his fingers in front of him as if confused whether he still had control or not. "I need to do something."

"But what?" Lance asked.

Ambrogio stepped out, followed by Amilia, and two guards that were making sure she stayed in line as they walked up the few steps towards the gathered officials.

"I don't know. Anything." He needed to be down there right this second if he had a chance to stop any of this. Climbing down was an option, but it would waste time. He took a few steps back, then ran towards the edge of the roof, and jumped.

The air whispered by.

Daniel landed in a crouch. The fall ripped the breath out of his lungs, and his vision blinked out between the seconds. The world seemed to crack more than any bone, held together by will and programming, as Daniel lifted his head. He shoved his way through the crowd towards the gallows.

He yelled her name, and Amilia twitched as if waking up to look down at him. Her once warm brown eyes had gone dark, with only a glimmer of life left while they stared at each other. A rope was placed around her neck like jewelry.

"You don't need to do this," he begged, prayed, at the foot of her.

"Any last words?" A hood covered the executioner's face in shadows. The sound alone enough to steal Amilia's attention away. She shook her head and closed her eyes instead of looking back at Daniel. With a pull of a lever, the wood under her disappeared.

He wanted to fall to his knees and scream. There only one thing stopping him: The game didn't let him. It didn't register Owen's want as something Daniel would do here. Daniel let out a whimper of a sound. Lance didn't even realize he was still breathing until he finally caught up and saw the short, trembling gasp.

"Okay dear, take me with you," Daniel breathed like before.

Daniel voice echoed in her head, or rather Andreah's head. She pulled off her headset, setting it in front of her as she stared ahead in an attempt to distance herself from that world. She had to do that—they both did.

"How's the bone digging?"

Andreah blinked as she looked up, as lost as if another language had been spoken.

"I said, how's the bone digging going?" Abigail repeated slower this time, confused herself now. "You've been working on that case for a long time. Our boss is going to kill you if you lead him on with this story any lo—Are you okay? You don't look so well."

Abigail reached out to Andreah's forehead to check her temperature. Andreah swatted Abby's hand away. "I'm fine. I'm fine. I just need some air." As quick as that, she was out the door.

Andreah stretched her neck out as the cool air hit her like water in the face. "Okay, dear take me with you," she said to herself. Daniel's voice was clear in her head. She shouldn't know these things, but she did.

She had no right, but she was worried about Owen, and Daniel. Would Lance keep his promise? There was no way to find out now. She literally killed off her connection to them. Owen, however…she could reach out to him. It was the only thing she was sure of as she whipped out her phone.

But that faith slipped as she stared down. The last text Owen sent was a little <3 in reply to something stupid. The first time, the text had made her smile. Now it made her feel like a tool. Texting now would only make covering everything up harder anyway. As far as she was supposed to know, it was just a normal day for him. Muscles tightened with her conviction. What was done was done.

Ah, the price he would pay for that traitor's kiss and his lost love. Amilia's family home was silent enough for ghosts. Daniel found a chair that he figured to be Dimitri's, considering the fine detailing. He pulled out his weapons and placed them down before sitting. This wasn't about revenge.

Dimitri walked into his house without much wait, but came to a short stop inside when he found Daniel. He glanced at the weapons spread across the desk before speaking. "What do you want, boy?"

"Daniel," he corrected with an extra harshness. After everything, the man could at least call him by his name. "Where is she?" Daniel asked. "I want to be at the funeral."

Dimitri cocked his head in confusion before annoyance won out. Celio stepped in, nearly bumping into his father before he saw the scene he walked into.

"Don't tell me you don't have the stomach for such a simple request," Daniel added.

Celio drew a sword, but his father blocked his path with his arm. "Leave it," Dimitri demanded. "He just came to ask about your cousin's funeral."

227

"You don't belong at her funeral. It was you that dragged her into the mess, and it's your fault she's gone," Celio said.

"We appreciate the sentiment, *Daniel*," Dimitri said. He paused for a second with the practice of a salesman. "But you are not a friend of the family, nor are you her husband. In the wake of losing yet another lady of the family, you have no right to be here. Amilia would have wanted it this way."

"I belong with Amilia," Daniel said. The words made him feel rather silly. She wasn't a claim to be fought over. "It wasn't me who caused her to run away. So don't you dare tell me what she would and wouldn't have wanted." He tried not to make things personal, but it was proving impossible. "What sort of beast would deny such a request? Once—just once—will you allow me to mourn my dead?"

"I lost control of her when she met you. I lost a girl that was like my daughter," Dimitri said, also losing his calm. "You've known her for a matter of months. So don't tell me you belong with Amilia, and don't call her one of your dead. She isn't yours to mourn, not when she denied you at her last moment." He stepped out from the doorway now, waving a hand to get Celio to step back too. "Now, I think it's time for you to leave."

Daniel grabbed one of the throwing knives off the table. His fingers tightened so hard around the handle that his knuckles turned white. Despite the anger, Dimitri shook him up so much he looked down, as if reprimanded by his own father. "It would seem that way."

He took a moment to gather his weapons, putting everything back in its proper place. As Daniel walked to the door, he paused and turned to Dimitri again. "Pray we never meet again, for if we do I'll take your last heir as well." A bitter part of him wanted to do it now, but someone who Amilia loved should be around to go to her funeral. Even if it wasn't him.

Daniel walked out of their house with a confident stride. But once he was far enough away, that waned until he needed to brace himself on a nearby wall. Days ago, Amilia was in his arms, and now she had been ripped away by design. Had everything been a trick, or was it as simple as trading her life for her families? He walked on, until he found himself climbing up the stairs to her other home. This place was as neutral as Amilia got, away from her family, and away from him.

Being inside somehow made him feel better and worse at the same time. He curled up on the bed he once woke up on. "Please come back," he whispered. Returning from the dead, however, would take no less than a miracle. Daniel repeated the words over and over until they spilled out of Owen's mouth too.

"I can't do this." Owen ripped off the headgear. If it was all just a game, why did it matter so much? His hands soon ran through his hair in frustration. He didn't have time for this. Owen checked his phone, and realized he *literally* didn't have time for this. He had to go to work. Owen wasn't even sure he had slept last night, but it wasn't like he could call in citing that his favorite character had died.

No matter how much you loved a job, some part of it was always torture. Today it was the combo of dyslexia and spell checking for his boss. Owen squinted at the text on the page. It wasn't hard to read per se, more that after reading the article over a couple of times he started to question if dreadfully common words were actually spelled that way. He had confirmed it was right three times already, but it still looked wrong.

Owen lifted his eyes off the paper and exhaled. Maybe a quick breather would help. Breathe in. Breathe out. He glanced towards the glass door, imagining the lobby between this office and the others on the floor. He imagined somewhere open and free of words that made him doubt he passed a single spelling test in his life.

A woman passed by, her dress a rich green and not of their time. Chestnut curls bounced on her shoulders as she walked. "Amilia," Owen whispered. Within a second he was up, and pushing the door open to catch her. A step outside their office, he stopped cold. Wait. That was impossible. Owen spun around the lobby trying to figure out what he saw that made him ever think it was Amilia in the first place.

"Hey stranger."

"Oh, it's you."

"Who did you expect, silly?" Andreah asked. Her hands were holding onto the straps of her backpack. Owen narrowed his eyes, like this wasn't quite right either. He looked past her for someone else. Andreah looked over her shoulder in confusion. "What?"

"Nothing." Owen shook his head, and looked at Andreah without actually focusing on her for a second. "What are you doing up here? I thought you liked dropping packages downstairs."

"I just wanted to see you. Okay, fine, and the lawyers on this floor tip friggin' well if I come upstairs to drop off their paperwork. But seeing you is a pretty nice bonus." Andreah leaned in as if preparing for a kiss, but when Owen didn't seem to get the hint, she fell back onto her heels. "Why don't you come over tonight? I'll cook something."

"I'm not hungry."

"Uh, that's why I said tonight?"

"I'm sorry. I'm in a weird head space right now." He took another breath, and started the conversation over. "That sounds great, but I made plans tonight. Rain check?"

Andreah nodded along, but couldn't work up another smile. "No, it's fine. I should have asked sooner."

Owen gave her a peck of a kiss that caused her sure footing to waver. "I should get back to work, I sort-of stormed out without telling anyone." He took a backward steps towards their office. "You, me, dinner another night."

"Well, if you insist."

A smile graced his face before he headed back.

Logging on to Age of Shadows felt excruciatingly harder each time. Daniel's emptiness was contagious. Even worse was the sense of red hot grief that boiled in both of them. He must have messed up somewhere. This was on him, and it was driving him mad that he didn't know where the mistake was made. But the game went on.

Daniel sat in the thieves' bureau, looking out into the courtyard. This was where he belonged, he told himself, married to duty, honor, and the tenants they wrote. His fingers traced along his lips, obsessed with other thoughts.

He felt someone put their hand on his shoulder as they walked around. Startled, he turned to see Lucas walk around and take a seat near him. "I'm sorry about what happened."

While it was nice, the thoughts didn't settle.

"Lance told us everything," Lucas continued, "We all lose people, but what happened was regrettable. You still have us though. We are a fellowship until the end."

"Thanks." Daniel's eyes lifted with Lucas as he stood, and were silently drawn to where he glanced. Lance was off down the hall talking to Abel. Maybe he should just thank God that Abel hadn't come over to rub everything in his face. Daniel's brow knitted together. Maybe Lance didn't tell them everything. Certainly why Amilia was put to death, and that her uncle was one of the knights would be included. But other key parts, like finding Amilia first and her refusal to return, could have been left out.

When they were called to gather in the main assembly, Daniel rubbed his eyes before joining the others. Not even a hint of a single tear would do around them. The slight delay made him the last one to fall into place, but it didn't seem to matter.

"The Knights can take someone from us at any minute," Gael said, surely referring to what happened with Amilia. "Which is why we must stay vigilant, but we also must remember we are in another war. Not just as thieves, but as Spanish citizens. I'm going to send four of you to go steal an important message coming from officials outside the city."

"Four of us, Master?" Lucas asked.

"Seguridad en los numeros," Daniel said, despite the question not being for him.

Gael nodded. "*Sí.* I want the four of you to go." He waved his hands towards Abel, Lucas, Lance, and Daniel, who were loosely grouped together.

"Awh, but I wanted to go!" Isidoro whined.

"Maybe next time," Lucas said, poking at him like he was their collective little brother.

"Now go get ready," Gael said, and dismissed everyone but Daniel. "Are you with us right now, son?"

"Of course," Daniel said, but this didn't seem to be convincing enough, so he continued. "I'm a thief first and foremost."

Gael still wasn't convinced, but he really didn't have time to spare because of the British. "Go catch up with the others, Ortiz."

During the mission, Abel tried to take the lead despite them all being in equal rank. "We will cut across the bridge, and split up to cover more ground. We can intercept the messenger, then reconvene at dusk."

"The bridge has too many people," Lance said. "We should go up further and loop back around."

"Let's just do what Abel says. It's going to be faster anyway," Daniel said, and ran ahead with bridge plan.

Lance's jaw dropped. Since when did Daniel agree with Abel over him? The only vote left was Lucas. He shrugged as if to tell Lance 'guess we are stuck now' before running ahead as well.

Abel smirked, proud of the unusual support he got from Daniel. Now alone with Lance he taunted him. "You can go around if you want to, but I would have thought your frog legs would have preferred the path over water."

Lance glared, not willing to back down. It was pointless to get into with Abel. He didn't pick fights for a reason, he just enjoyed being an ass. Lance mumbled in French that it would've been better if Abel had died instead before taking the same path as everyone.

Just like Lance pointed out, there were too many men stationed. Their group quickly became stuck behind cover. Any chance of taking out the guards was ruined by the foot traffic. The thunk of an arrow hitting their cover caused Daniel to do something about it. "Do you want me to go out there? I could be a distraction, while you three crawl around the side." he asked Abel.

"Go ahead," Abel grinned.

The interaction made Lance sick as Daniel ran out from the cover. Abel always enjoyed sending people into danger. Anything to avoid him risking his own life. The only thing that could have made him happier was if he was behind a desk somewhere moving Daniel like a pawn.

Abel and Lucas ran to the sides, and climbed down on the bridge. Lance stayed behind, stealing a glance at Daniel, wondering if he should help. Daniel seemed to be doing fine on his own. He threw two knives in separate men, and left them there to suffer as he moved onto to the next target. Gael shouldn't have let Daniel come, he wasn't even fighting like himself. With a sigh, Lance decided to climb around the side with the others, doubting they'd be able to fight together with their usual grace. Daniel was no longer himself, and the lack of remorse hinted that this was only the beginning of his bloodlust.

The others secured the letter they were assigned to steal, and Daniel broke off from the fight at their signal. The lot made camp in the forest for the night. A fire provided warmth and light in the gloomy evening. Lucas and Abel sat on one side playing marbles. Abel was clearly losing, and made Lucas snicker every time he complained about it.

Daniel was hardly paying attention to them, or Lance, who he sat next to. Instead, he stared ahead to the forest as if expecting someone else to show. Lance watched the others play, not feeling enough mirth to join in, when there was a sudden weight on his shoulder. He turned his head to see Daniel resting his head. It seemed doubtful that he'd fall asleep so suddenly, but the hood covered all the evidence either way.

Owen pulled his headset off with one quick motion, letting it clatter against his desk. The piece of tech was worthless at the moment, and only served to annoy him further. He put his head down, waiting for his headache to dull before he sat up again. If losing your companion NPC was normal, this must mean it happened to someone else, right? He pulled up the AoS community boards, checked the keywords of companion death, and NPC death. There was a shit load of questions about how to get them, what they could do once found, and one person—who everyone thought was trolling—claiming they lost one after an argument. He thought of writing a new post, but groaned at the idea of twenty people asking him his username. Especially after seeing a sponsored article about if role playing would become the next big thing.

The faint pulse from his phone caught his attention, and he scrolled over the collection of texts and missed calls all from Neal and Emily. Owen sat forward quickly, cursing under his breath as he called Neal back.

"Where the hell have you been?" Neal scolded even before a hello. "Emily went into labor two hours ago."

"I'm sorry, my phone was on silent." It was the truth, even if he knew better than to have done it. "You're at Memorial, right?"

"Yeah. Hurry up and get over here," Neal ordered before hanging up.

Owen dashed downstairs and hailed a cab. He probably shouldn't have run the whole way from the cab to Em's room, but in his haste, any 'no running in the hallway' rules were ignored. When he saw Neal, he slowed his pace to calmly stop in front of him. "What's going on? Is she still in there?"

"Yeah, I just came out to wait for you. She's fine. They aren't sure how much longer until the baby actually comes. The doctor is expecting any minute. Which could be..." Neal tossed his hand in the air. "Who knows."

Owen's hands nervously rested on top of his head, like he was the one who needed measured breaths. "Right, can I go in?"

"The doctor was being an ass about some policy I think they made up. Anyways, they weren't going to let any non-family in until Em blurted a lie that I was the father." Owen shook his head, mishearing that at first, and stared wordlessly on as Neal went on. "Anyways, I have to get back in there. I'll come back out when I can."

Neal went back in, leaving Owen awkwardly standing in the hallway. He glanced around, wondering if he should find a waiting room, before he decided to just camp outside. Being crouched out front made him feel like an ass, and each text or missed call notification he cleared seemed to prove it.

Owen rested his head on his knees and waited. Sometime later—an hour at least—a doctor and their staff came out of the room. A nurse gave him a funny look, but said nothing. He scrambled to his feet, wanting to rush into the room. Should he? Shouldn't he?

Another doctor stepped out, and after seeing Owen's face light up, realized he must have been waiting. "You can go in."

"Thank you," Owen mumbled, and squeezed past.

Emily was sitting up in the bed. In a cream blanket, he spotted a small hand holding Em's pinky. In a close to silent room, he heard the tiny breathes from the baby. Owen's eyes finally tore from the child when he got closer.

"Took you long enough," Emily said, smiling despite—or maybe because of—what obviously just happened. She looked tired, and her cheeks were bright red under the ugly hospital lights, but seemed to glow all the same.

Owen smiled faintly before looking back down at the baby. "I'm sorry."

"It's okay, you're still ahead of Rick by weeks," she joked, and looked back to her child. "I went with the name Rachel."

Owen blinked, trying to refocus too. What did you even say to someone who just gave birth and was being unjustly nice to you? Emily's light tone didn't fix the feeling that he let her down for not being here sooner. "Such a cute baby, Em."

"Yeah." Emily smiled. "I know I'm biased, but I think so too."

Owen pulled a chair closer to the bed, both wanting to hold the tiny bundle and never wanting to be allowed to touch.

"Em said that I get to be the godfather," Neal said.

Owen turned in the chair towards him. Neal had been standing in the corner, certainly not far away enough to be forgotten about. But Owen had, for a moment. He laughed, and shook his head as he glanced towards Emily. "You know what they say about early birds."

"Well actually," she started, but the baby made a strange noise. It was actually a very normal sounding noise, but today, any noise warranted attention. Em chuckled softly, trying not to disturb the bundle resting on her chest. "Godparents aren't a Jewish tradition. So, if I'm going to have them, might have well break a few other norms too."

Owen started to get a sneaking suspicion that they were up to something. Neal chuckled, and sat on a counter he likely wouldn't been allowed to if the doctors were still around. "She wants us to both be godfathers."

"Two fathers?" Owen glanced at them both still expecting a punchline. When none came, he grinned along with the rest of them. "How progressive of you. What will your mother say?"

Emily pursed her lips thinking about. She looked down at the baby as if a suggestion would be volunteered. "Likely, 'oh gosh look at my adorable grandchild," she said picking up a baby voice, "I could eat 'em up.'"

"Do you want to come with me?" Abel asked, clearly looking for a volunteer on his solo mission. Why risk yourself when you could risk others?

"Busy today, sorry," Daniel said.

"Your loss." Abel shrugged before leaving to do his own work. Since Daniel had been all business as of late, they'd been getting along better than ever. It was easy to make friends when you did their work.

Daniel watched Abel carry on down the road that would lead to the thieves guild. That's the direction he should go, and yet...he glanced down another way, a path that would take him where he really desired.

He was like the ocean, a force that could be guided until it swells and becomes uncontrollable. Inside the training hall of a very different faction, Daniel walked onto a mezzanine.

"Knights, hear me," Daniel called, as he stepped up onto the railing. He stood gathering as much attention as possible. "I warn thee well. No bloodier spirit between heaven and hell. I'll give you a choice, unlike what I was given. Talk to me, or talk to your god."

Once he jumped down, he was met with a wave untalkative folks. Blood spilled over his sword as he dispatched them all with a cold urgency. Except for one, who ran.

Daniel's boots scraped against the floor as he came to a stop. The man hadn't gone far. He ended up stuck, huddled in a corner. "Please, I'll tell you anything," the guard pleaded.

"I'm looking for your leader, Ambrogio Spinola," Daniel said dryly. "Tell me where he is and I'll let you leave."

The look the man gave Daniel was similar to the look he'd seen Lance give him before. One that silently asked *still? This is still your main concern?* Despite the look, the man answered. "Most rumors claim he left with his men on a boat, but I heard whispers that he is visiting with the Archbishop. That's all I know."

"I'm a man of my word. Begone."

The guard looked up, blinking at the choice he didn't think he'd actually be given.

Daniel carried on without a glance back. Moving deeper into this labyrinth to areas his original warning likely wasn't ever heard. Based on how quick some of the men attacked, it didn't seem like they wanted to talk anyway.

They were all faceless people until one spoke. Daniel wouldn't have recognized the executioner if the man hadn't. "I remember you," he said. The man paced in a half circle around Daniel with his ax resting against his shoulder. "It was a shame I couldn't chop that pretty little girl's head off. Maybe I can get yours instead."

The man swung the ax high and wide, managing to cut off Daniel's reply. The thief ducked and moved in close with his dagger. The executioner caught Daniel's arm as he continued to push for the kill before he was shoved to the ground.

This time, the executioner swung towards the floor. Daniel rolled away and sprung back up to his feet as the ax wedged itself into the wood paneling. A thief's speed compared to the powerful, but slow, swings turned out to be the man's downfall. Daniel caught him square in the chest with his dagger.

The man wheezed unable to breathe with metal in his lung. His weapon dropped as Daniel helped him to the ground. Any final words the NPC had were lost through the hole in his chest.

"I hope you were able to bully your last victim, or *follada* your wife. Whatever it takes for you to feel better about yourself. As you lay here, ask yourself, was killing her worth it?" Daniel stood up from the warm body of the man he just killed. His head was dizzy with anger. Hunting him down had helped, but it wasn't enough. It wouldn't be until he held everyone accountable.

Exploring the base only provided one more man for his folly. He was tucked close to the wall, not out of fear, but to work on a series of pulleys. When the bloodstained thief walked in, the man dropped his tools in fright.

"Tell me where your boss is," Daniel ordered.

"Excuse me, *señor?*"

Daniel let out a small growl and grabbed the man by the collar. "Don Ambrogio? The man you work for? Where is he?"

The man let out a laugh from fear. "I don't know. I'm not told such things."

Daniel silently judged if he was telling the truth. The man stared back, growing fearful at the harsh glint he witnessed in Daniel. He noticed the eyes of a killer a few seconds before Daniel's words confirmed it.

"I don't suffer the useless."

With a flick of Daniel's wrist, the man eyes went wide. He stumbled and grabbed Daniel's shoulder for support. Blood spilled over Daniel's blade, his hand, everywhere.

This was wrong. He had crossed a line killing him, brought harm to someone who didn't deserve wrath. And realized it all too late. "I...I'm sorry," Daniel said near whisper, looking as confused at the man whose blood he now wore. A long forgotten feeling washed over him, one that he had not known in many years after a kill. Guilt.

There was a choking sound before the light left the man's eyes. Carefully, Daniel laid him down, brushing a clean hand over the man's eyelids. His own eyes started to well up as he sat there on the dusty floor. Daniel wondered if he would ever get the will to stand again, but fear was quick to remedy this.

Daniel fled, realizing that there'd be no protection under the sun after this. Where could he even go? Any mercy the guild had for him would evaporate with this news.

A group of girls walked by, their dresses a riot of color that sparked an idea. There might be someone who would still help.

Lily was outside tending a small garden. "Hello there, dear," she said, momentarily distracted by the flowers. "Daniel? *Mi dios*, what happened?" He didn't look like much to fear, all dirtied and shaken.

"I'm not sure where else to turn right now."

Lily looked at him with uncertainty on her face. Hiding people that made themselves targets only brought trouble down on her girls. Yet, friendship wasn't meaningless. "Come quick, before anyone sees you."

After getting changed into clean clothes, Daniel ended up telling Lily everything. About traveling to Santiago with Amilia, about saving each other in more ways than the usual, and about the troubles they faced on their way home. As he got closer to the end, his words slowed. It was hard to say, even to himself, let alone honestly with someone else.

"Wow. That is an impressive story my friend," Lily said, and dipped a rag into a bowl. She allowed herself a moment to soak in more than just the water. Lily took Daniel's hand and gently scrubbed the blood off his knuckles. He didn't resist. After running off hate and pain for days, he was on empty, and couldn't fight the kindness he didn't deserve. "I might not know a lot of things," Lily continued, "But I know people. We have our reasons for doing the things we do. And I can tell you this, it's not all that usual to love someone and not want them around."

Daniel looked at her, trying to see if she knew something he didn't. Her eyes didn't hold guilt. Maybe just a story he didn't know. She moved up from his hands, cleaning various other scratches that littered his skin. When Lily first saw Daniel, she thought he was on the edge of death. After inspection, it became clear. The real wound was somewhere that couldn't be cleaned with water. "Let it go, love. Even if you figure it out, it won't make you feel better."

Lily dabbed a fresh cloth on his lip, and he cringed at the sharp pain. "You are going to be lucky if this doesn't scar," Lily mused, changing the subject before she did more harm than good. She got up, glancing at him as if she wanted to say something more.

He felt a kiss, not on his lips, but on his forehead. She started to pull away before Daniel caught her hand. "Thank you," he said and let go, hoping those two words could explain everything he meant.

She smiled. "I need to check on other things now. I wouldn't suggest roaming the house, but you may if you wish."

As always when one of them is lost, Lance came around a few days later. However, he was stuck outside, as Lily refused to let him in. "If you don't have business here, then leave!"

"Fine, how about you and I go a round?" Lance's rough tone made it hard to pinpoint it as a threat or not. "Afterward, I'll tear through the rest of the place."

"Oh, so you do have business for us?" Lily said, with false sweetness. She reached up to touch a curl by his ear, but Lance slapped her hand away before she got there.

"Stop messing around. I know Daniel is in there. You are his only friend left in town, and the only one with enough power to hide him. I hear you officially run this house now. Was this your first act of business? Hiding a fugitive?"

"Is that what he is to you?"

"You know better than that," Lance growled. He wasn't getting anywhere, so he took a deep breath and tried a new way. "He isn't himself. You must know this."

Lily paused, but only for a second. "I don't know where he is. If we hear anything, we'll let you know."

Lance balled his fists, resisted the urge to just force her out of the way. "If I get proof, expect me on your doorstep."

"I await that surely joyous day," Lily said, with the same mixed tone.

Lance had been right about almost everything. Lily's new job title wasn't official, but it might as well be. The lady of the house was almost always doing other things across Spain. Something Lily didn't understand. The people here were her family, why would anyone want to leave them? Lily swore to protect everyone here, and that included Daniel now. She headed back inside and grabbed some food as she went up to Daniel's room.

She sighed at the state of things. Plates of food from the day before sat untouched. A rat would have nibbled more away. "Man can't live off wine until kingdom come. You need to eat something."

Daniel looked up from the book in his hand. A small stack was piled next to where he sat. Lily held out a glass of wine, knowing far too well that men could actually live off the stuff. For a little while, at least. She placed the fresh meal down by the old one. "You know, if food isn't doing the trick, maybe I could help in other ways."

Daniel didn't flinch as he stared up at her, wearing the expression of a wounded animal who wanted to be left alone.

"Fine then," she said, a bit more annoyed than she meant. Lily gathered up the old plates, finding another in a different corner of the room. She was a bit louder then she needed to be, but the action was completely ignored. It seemed like he wanted to shut her out, too. Lily thought about storming out, but stopped at the door. "You know, there are people still around who love you," Lily said. This finally got his attention even though he looked confused. "Lance stopped by."

Time passed, although it was harder to track how much, before Lily and Lance found themselves outside debating the merit of his visit once again.

"I know Daniel is here, Lil."

She crossed her arms over her chest. "I don't know what you are talking about."

"Rumor has it there is a man staying here. Who doesn't partake in any of the girls. So unless you have opened up to service new clientele, he is here."

"Why? Are you interested?" Her eyebrows rose with her joke. Lance, however, was not amused, and stared until she became serious again. "Fine! Fine, I can't get through to him anyways. Maybe you will have more luck. I'll bring you to him."

Lance followed her upstairs, spotting one of the courtesans on his way up. She likely didn't have a clue what was actually going on. From the context clues, she would have thought something suggestive.

Daniel looked up, expecting Lily again, but found Lance in the doorway. "I'm not very good at hiding, am I?" he asked, and closed his book.

"No, not from me." Lance quickly glanced around the room, but the most notable thing was Daniel. He would have sworn his friend was thinner than the last time they laid eyes on each other. "You look...well."

Daniel sat back in the chair, doubting that was the word Lance really wanted to use. Lance pulled over a chair and sat down. "Your father and I, we've been making sure you still had a place to come back to."

"Come back?" What did he have to return to? Amilia had been able to open him up a bit. Now that she was gone, he'd shut down. An over correction he didn't want to fix. He didn't want to go back. It was too much responsibility.

"When you are ready," Lance added. "We don't have to talk about this right now."

"How is he?" Daniel asked. "My father."

"He's well. That man is strong as a bull," Lance smiled. "We been working together a lot lately, hunting down the aegis."

Daniel's jaw started to drop before he reeled back his reaction. He didn't like the idea of his retired father working again. But what say did he have when he wanted no part of it himself?

"We are making a lot of progress thanks to the book you found."

"That's...good," Daniel said, but didn't sound like he meant it. The whole thing made him feel uncomfortable in his own skin.

Lance didn't push. Talking about something related to Amilia would have been hard to handle on a good day. Many now believed the aegis was part of what got Amilia killed. There were even whispers that she was still alive. No one seriously believed the ghost stories, and he definitely wasn't going to tell Daniel about them. There'd be no better way to mess with his head.

Lance simply changed the subject. Talked about lighter things. A copy of Don Quixote was sitting nearby, so Lance mentioned letters with his friend Chloe who was reading Shakespeare. Citing that while the stories weren't translated from English yet, she claimed they were quite good.

A comfortable silence fell between them. Lance didn't think he was going to get anything more out of Daniel today. Which was fine. Daniel was alive, and having him of sound mind was a huge plus. Lance had feared when he found Daniel he'd have to pick him off the floor. One could work with this.

"I just..." Daniel said, to Lance's surprise, "...can't believe someone who I've known for so little nested so deep in my head. How did I let this happen?"

So, he *did* want to talk about it. "The thing about you is that you always know what you want, and waste very little time getting it. Hell, you asked me to move to Spain the first day I met you. It is not a surprise that when you fell for Amilia, you became swept up in it." Daniel shifted uncomfortably in his seat, but Lance continued. "Sometimes life just carries us places like that. Now, I'm asking you to please come home."

One modern torture was watching someone progress in a meaningful way. At least Facebook allowed people to be mad about it in the privacy of their own home. What's worse is seeing the world change while being absolutely hung up on something else. Things that shouldn't have mattered did, and pixels cut as sharp as anything else.

When Owen wasn't working, he helped Em and her new child. He'd even fallen asleep with the baby on his chest once, since any minute the real world could spare was given to the virtual one.

Daniel was so close to finding something, a clue from the book he'd found in Santiago, about magic that shouldn't exist. If he could give Amilia's death meaning, then he could carry on himself.

Missions were filled with guessing and level grinding. Upon Daniel's return to the guild, he was placed at the helm of things. It took some haggling from his father and Lance, but dedicating himself fully eliminated any doubt of Daniel's commitment. All his time was spent making plans, deciding who would be best for the mission, and securing a ship. A few clues suggested it was here in Spain. However, Daniel personally believed that the stone aegis was in the Canary

Islands. It was someplace new, and the promise of adventure raised his spirits.

The thieves guild was abuzz with a possibility of a shield that held powers that didn't exist anywhere else in the world. Only a few didn't buy into the rumors, believing it was nothing more than misread patch notes. Isidoro was part of this group, but his disbelief was for personal reasons. His rank wasn't high enough to join the party, and therefore didn't want it to be true. But that didn't mean he wasn't going to go quietly. "Please," he begged, "Please, please. Another hand never hurts."

Daniel completely ignored him, as he did most things that didn't help forward the mission. Lance filled in for his recent lack of social skills. "Try not to take it so hard," he said, "A party of five would be too many. Lucas, Abel, Daniel, and I are a proven combination that gets results."

As the day wore on, everyone headed home. "Hey, wait up," Lance called, running to catch up with Daniel on his way out. "So, I was thinking we should get some dinner." A man passed between the two, parting them briefly. "On me. Well, technically him." Lance smirked, and held up the stolen coin pouch.

Daniel stopped only after the act of thievery. "Can you go a single day without messing around?"

"I—uh," Lance stumbled to say anything at first. It wasn't like his friend to be so humorless. "But we always get free dinner like this."

"We have money," Daniel said, and started walking again. "There is no reason for the added bullshit."

"But..." Lance frowned, feeling daft that he wasn't catching on yet. "It's more fun this way."

Daniel spun around like he had enough. "Grow up. You can't act like a child on this mission."

Lance's footsteps came to a dead stop. He stared as Daniel pulled down on his tunic as if it, too, annoyed him. Lance knew better than most that Daniel had been acting different for a while now. But he had hoped, if given enough time... "Finding the damned thing isn't going to bring her back," Lance said. "Even if you do find it, then what? What are you going to do, without your prized Amilia, and without your beloved mission?"

With a growl, Daniel moved closer into Lance's face. "Don't you ever talk to me that way again."

"Or what?" Lance dared. Daniel was right about one thing, this was bullshit. "I'm done here."

They continued to work together, but not with the same smoothness as before. Their friendship was turning into a formality. When the morning of the mission came, there was a knock on Daniel's door. Lance stepped inside, but seemed far too uncomfortable to come in further.

Daniel looked up and instantly saw something was wrong. Lance was dressed in the same clothes he had met the man in. A style that hinted at money, instead of the light armor of a thief. "Why are you dressed like that?"

"There's trouble back home," Lance said. He had been meeting Daniel in the eye, but the floor seemed far easier now. "I've been putting it off because of...what happened. I didn't want to leave if you needed me, but now it's clear I'm needed elsewhere more."

Daniel's expression flickered over melancholy, but he seemed to crush the emotion. "Fine," he said, biting down on the word. "I have other people who value the mission."

Lance looked up with a slight nod. He took a shaky breath, like the room lacked enough air for the both of them. "Goodbye, Daniel."

Daniel thought about stopping him. Not letting things end this way. But in the end, he let Lance walk out. It was clear he lost both of his companions now. Daniel looked down at his plans, feeling as if they weren't enough for him anymore.

No. This was the stuff of legends. It was all that mattered right now. What he needed to matter right now.

Daniel headed to the guild and found a young thief preparing the horses with a disheartened expression. Helping out without being part of the real action sucked. But it wouldn't today. "Isidoro," Daniel called, "You can come with us."

"Really?" He dropped the reins in surprise. "I'm so happy I could hug you!"

Daniel smiled. "Getting ready will suffice."

It was a long mission to get to the southern town of Cadiz. From there, they boarded a ship to take them the last leg of the trip. The open sea was more turbulent than expected, but the bad weather was just barely holding back. Isidoro's stomach was holding up equally well. He leaned over the edge of the boat, trying his best not to lose it.

"Still glad you came?" Daniel asked as he rubbed Isidoro's back. The kid was going to risk falling overboard, if he wasn't careful.

"Yeah," Isidoro said, before a wave made him stick his head back over the side. He flashed a weak smile as he slumped down against the side. "On second thought."

"Try not to worry, I'm sure you'll get the hang of it soon enough."

Their next port was in La Palma, located on the middle island. "The shield is close," Daniel said, moments after landing on dry land. "I can feel it."

"Right." Abel shook head, thinking that Daniel had gotten a little too much sea air. "Which way, then?"

They followed a passage along the cliffs that helped shape the shoreline. The four of them traveled until they made it to a waterfall. A beautiful thing that showcased shades of green they hadn't seen in a few days. Abel and Isidoro looked around for a suspected hidden entrance, but Daniel's mind went elsewhere. Hadn't he seen another waterfall like this before?

"Found it!" Isidoro yelled.

Lucas took a few steps, but stopped when he noticed Daniel wasn't following. "What's wrong?" He glanced towards the waterfall, not understanding why Daniel looked so bewildered.

"This is somehow familiar," Daniel said.

"Have you been here before?"

"No."

"Hmm, must be *deja vu*," Lucas smiled. "Come on, o' fearless leader."

Daniel joined up with the rest of them at the mouth of a cave that had been hidden behind the falls. They soon realized that calling this a cave would be an insult to the work put into it. Stone statues lined the halls, forever standing guard over the place. The farther in they went, the more impressive it became. Everything was carved from same the piece of stone that seemed to defy time.

"Wow," Lucas mused.

Something had to be here. Why else would someone spend countless hours working on this place? Lucas stopped to look at one of the statues that lined the hallway. "These statues are so well done. They look—"

"Real," Daniel interrupted, before he strolled on. The hallway opened up to a large round room, and on a pedestal sat a stone shield that looked far too heavy to carry. On the shield was a face in pain, with snakes twisting as if they shared the woman's troubles. The story of Athena's shield having Medusa's head was literal?

"You have come far for what you seek," a disembodied voice said. The game displayed the text in English, but it artifacted with extra symbols as if unsure of what language to use. "The stone-hearted one may touch."

Daniel glanced back at the others, who looked equally as lost and amazed as he felt. Well, this was his mission and his responsibility. Why shouldn't he be the one to take the plunge? Despite previous bluster, his fingers hesitated to reach out and touch it.

The tips grazed the surface before he placed his palm down. The shield glowed bright and Daniel averted his eyes for a second. The snakes in the stone surface seemed to move. Just for a split second that made him want to jump back. But something greater pulled at him, as if digging for something hidden within his bones.

Lines of white flickered in everyone's vision, getting a chorus of complaints. The light pooled at Daniel's feet, then radiated out in a circle before flooding the whole room. Everything in reach turned to stone. Freezing looks of fear and attempts to flee solid.

The rings pulled back in with a blinding light that couldn't be seen with any of their stone eyes. Owen's headset flashed a warning before blacking out for a second. He felt like he had dropped to his knees when his vision came back.

Daniel was on his hands and knees, panting, as the shield laid toppled nearby. He tried to lift a finger, doubting that he could at first. Once that checked out, he slowly started to stand, and turned towards the others. Whatever was left of his heart shattered right then. Isidoro, Lucas, and Abel were still frozen in stone. The statues. That's why they looked so real.

He walked as if in a dream towards them. Lucas was the closest. His eyes had a divot where the iris was. Daniel glanced over to Isidoro and Abel, who also were masterpieces of themselves. "I'm so sorry." Daniel's words were so soft he wondered if he even had said them out loud.

Maybe if he put the shield back they'd be returned as well. Daniel turned to pick it up, but noticed a ghostly white bit of cloth in the corner of his eye. He rose to take in a translucent image of Athena. Robe, hem, and all.

"You shouldn't be here," she warned. "This was not meant to be part of your story."

Daniel coughed out a laugh despite himself. "Well, it seems it is now."

She seemed to smile. "You are correct. You resembled another."

Riddles were not desired right now. No matter what prize or favor it could provide. "Why did you do this to them?" Without breaking eye contact, he gestured back towards the others.

Athena seemed to blink an acknowledgment, but carried on. "Like Jason before you, you also seek treasures from the fables. There are many pieces not yet ready for this world. You desire the Argonauts' piece, but what you found cannot grant you the same wish. If you decide to leave the shield, I can try to give you something else."

What did one ask a Goddess upon meeting her?

Daniel thought about what he wanted. What he had really and truly wanted this whole time. He wanted Amilia back. He wanted Lance with him again. Wanted his friends to be okay, and wanted this device never to fall into the wrong hands. It was literally a game changer. "I just," Daniel sighed. "I want everything to be how it needs to be."

"A noble request," Athena said, and glanced towards the shield on the floor.

Daniel looked back down at it too. Fear darted across his chest realizing that she wanted him to pick it up again. Touching the cursed thing as the last thing he wanted now, but if there was no other way....

He picked up the shield with both of his hands, the weight somehow manageable at the moment. It took control again, pulling at his mind, what he had been, what he was, what he might yet be. His vision skipped like a stone, and saw flashes of Amilia, Lance, home. Images fleeting so fast it was impossible to hold onto any of them. Every cell was pulled upon, making him wonder if there would be any survivors from this mission.

Daniel heard his name being shouted over the roar of the falls. No, he heard Owen's name being called.

Owen flinched as he woke, staring at the edge of the water that made him wonder where he was. The picture shook as he realized his headset was being pulled at, a small gasp escaping his lips as he sat up on the couch. He reached up to pull off the headgear, but it seemed too light and lifted off without much effort. Owen blinked up at a startled Charlie standing over him, with their hands frozen in the air.

"Christ, man. Are you okay?" Charlie asked, quickly setting the headgear down to turn back.

"Lucas," Owen said sounding lost. "Are they—"

"They're dead." Charlie kneeled down to be more on Owen's level.

The change of heights allowed Owen to spot Neal standing by the door. Spare keys in hand, expression shifting to concern as Owen made eye contact. "I need to get to Paris," Owen mumbled like he was half asleep.

This time, Charlie touched his arm. "Owen, I've been worried about you all day. You know you aren't meant to fall asleep with that shit on. Do you know where you are?"

Owen shook his head, not as an answer, but to separate himself from the fog he felt. "Yeah, sorry. I didn't mean to scare you." He glanced up as Neal moved closer. "Either of you."

"You hadn't until I got here," Neal said, as a wrinkle ran between his brow.

Despite not drinking last night, a hangover-like headache had settled in. Owen got up, glancing at them both before walking to the kitchen. He felt their eyes follow him before looking at one another. Whatever the fuck happened last night, Owen didn't want to talk about it. He picked up an empty glass, and filled it with water as someone stepped into the kitchen with him.

"What happened last night? I texted you."

Owen shifted, taking a drink as he pulled out his phone. He found a few from Charlie, most notably an open-ended 'WTF', and a text from Andreah he had never gotten around to. "Huh." Owen looked back to Charlie who skeptically stared. "It was nice of you to check on me, but I'm fine."

"That doesn't exactly answer my question."

He evaded it for a moment longer, watching as Neal picked up the headset like a broken toy. "I'm not even sure," Owen said. "We found something, but I don't think we were ever meant too. The quest was just *soo* long. I must've fallen asleep."

Charlie nodded, but they didn't look completely convinced. "I was dropped into the End Game screen. Is Daniel okay?"

"He's alive." Owen could remember the drumming sound of the falls. The sound numbed his senses more than easing him asleep like he suggested to Charlie and Neal. He didn't recall leaving the cave, just Daniel soaked at the water's edge.

"Well, that's not nothing."

"Shit, Lucas," Owen nearly repeated from before. It suddenly clicked that he was standing across someone he got killed the night before. Charlie had put in so much time in that character. "I'm so sorry. The whole mission was my idea. I can't even—"

"Stop."

Owen instantly did, swallowed roughly, and waited to be reprimanded.

"It's fine. I mean, I was thinking about playing a girl next anyways. The game's whole forced gender binary thing throws me off."

Did Charlie really not blame him for anything? Owen studied their expression, wondering if they were lying just because they were worried. "Well, I'll miss my favorite Rivera descendant all the same."

Charlie smiled. "Me too."

Neal slipped into view, but still kept an observational distance. Before he could speak, Owen's phone started ringing. It was still in his hand, so he swiped to answer it. If Owen wanted his friends to leave him be, it was best to pretend everything was normal. "Hello?"

"Hi, this is Paul. I wanted to check on the progress about my stolen account?"

Right. The bone digger job that Owen keep forgetting about. Jobs about cash trades gone bad never paid well. Clients already felt ripped off, so they didn't want to pay extra for revenge, names, or whatever else. Owen glanced over to the random magnets on his fridge. "Oh, yeah. I have a lead. But I also have people over right now, can I call you back?"

Owen wasn't even sure how many lies that made today. Or if that even counted as a lie. His guess was the guy's character had been killed off after all the items got willed over to a new character. It was a simple matter of checking the kill list and going from there. The lie of it was this wasn't a new lead, he said he'd do it days ago. After a meaningless pleasantry, they hung up.

"Sorry, I forgot about this job. You guys can hang out if you want, but..."

Charlie wasn't buying it, but Owen not opening up lately was par for the course. They had pestered Neal to let them check in, but didn't want to push further. "Just, give us a call sometime? We could get out of the house, like old times?"

Owen walked to his desk, turning in his chair to look at them both, and tried to ignore what Charlie meant. "Yeah, the moment I get this done."

Neal had something to say this time. "We now know your phone still works, so answer us when we text you."

"I promise I will not miss another friend-going-into-labor moment."

Neal nodded, before patting Charlie on the back. "Come on, let's leave him to it then."

Owen turned back to his computer and started scrolling the kill list. He didn't fully pay attention until he heard the door close a moment later. It was nice, what they were trying to do. Owen just didn't want them to do anything in the first place. Didn't they ever just want to be left alone?

The character name he was supposed to look up was Amir-something, so it shouldn't be hard to find. Even the mention of death reminded him of the flashes of Amilia last night. It wasn't the job, but he had the urge to check back.

Just when he thought he was wasting time, his eyes skipped right to it. Amilia's name. He rubbed his eyes in disbelief. Since when did they include NPCs on the player death list? The single line of text listed Amilia's full name, time, location of her death, and a user name of Xinshi. That wasn't his username. If a player was listed at all, it should be his name.

"The fuck's going on here," Owen mumbled. He googled the name first, and several cities with the name popped up. Then he checked the wiki and forums. Still nothing meaningful. His fingers tapped on the keyboard trying to think how else he could check this username.

Two things were known. One, the name didn't show up on the forums or any other character listing. That made it really unlikely it was just a listing error of some other active player. Two, that name seemed Chinese. Since the languages weren't close, Owen started to play around with the different versions of the vowels. A little digging, and several websites later he found a few translations.

"No way." Owen got up, grabbed his jacket, leaving the translation on his screen as he ran downstairs. Xinshǐ: courier, messenger.

The trip there was a blur. He hardly remembered getting in the taxi, or coming up the elevator until he was standing outside of Andreah's door. When he was just about to knock, a wave of doubt hit. Maybe this was a coincidence. Maybe this all meant nothing.

No. Owen knocked on the door. This meant something.

With no answer, he tried again, hoping she'd magically appear. Nothing. He wanted answers, and he wasn't about to wait for them. The logical thing was to call her, but Owen found himself eyeing a hide-a-key lock box on an A/C unit hanging outside her apartment. He wondered if it would be difficult to crack, but once he entered the four numbers of her birth year, he realized Andreah was making this entirely too easy for anyone that knew her.

A spare key fell into his hand and he let himself in. The same empty coffee cups were scattered about. What was once cute now brought a bitter taste to his mouth, like he took an ashy last sip. He needed proof. A break in and accusations would only get him thrown out, and maybe arrested. Owen glanced around the room he'd only seen once before. He spotted a tablet on the coffee table, and instantly moved towards it.

He scrolled through a page of apps until he found Age of Shadows. As the app loaded, his chest pulled tight, hoping that it would say anything else besides Xinshi. But there it was. Six little letters that made him reel back in need of a seat.

He sat there, wondering if he should just leave, but couldn't bring himself to get up. He should just leave, forget about Andreah, and about all this. But the urge to run didn't overpower the need to know more. An hour passed before he heard a key slip into the unlocked door. She grumbled, blaming herself for forgetting to lock up. He wasn't sure if he should stand and announce himself, and only managed to lean forward by time she came in. The couch made a small creak, which caught Andreah's attention.

She glanced up and jumped. Her hand automatically reached for something nearby to defend herself. But when she realized it was Owen, she came up with nothing. "What the fuck? What are you doing here?"

He wondered if he wanted to get defensive, or get right to the point. "I needed to know something."

"Yeah, well, I need to know a lot of things too. But I don't creep into your apartment and sit on your couch till you come home. How did you even get in?"

"Not using your birthday for a password is, like, 101." Owen shook his head and finally stood up.

Andreah slowly put her bag down. "I kept forgetting any other code for it." She didn't step further into the room, nervous over whatever picture she had painted about this current situation.

Owen picked up the tablet, holding it out to her as it displayed the login screen for AoS. "Amilia. What do you have to do with her?"

"What?" she asked, a little too quickly.

"The system shows that Amilia is an NPC. Then why does the game also tie her to you?" He asked, slower this time.

"Look, I didn't mean—"

"What did you do?"

That cracked the mask she was hiding behind. She finally came inside fully, leaning against her desk rather than standing near him. Andreah hardly looked at him as she spoke. "I've just been, you know, following you throughout the game."

"How long?"

"Almost the whole time with Amilia."

Owen exhaled. He paled and needed to sit down again. All his questions felt pointless under the weight of one. "Why?"

"If I figured out who scored two NPCs, who was behind Daniel, it meant a big payday for me."

"You out-bone-diggered me."

That got Andreah's attention in a whole new way. She knew she was playing a player, but not one who also made money questionably. "I didn't mean it like that."

"Then what did you mean it like?" Owen's tone gained an edge of anger, and his jaw set tightly after the last word.

"Look, the moment I realized you play Daniel, I stopped. I didn't sell your name. I started closing up my part in her story."

"Your part?" Owen said, like it was the most ridiculous thing. She didn't counter before he went on. "You got her killed. Why couldn't you have left her alone? Why didn't you just fucking leave *me* alone?"

She stepped towards him, not quite getting in his face, but a challenge of some sort. "I needed to change things for the job. If I had left her after that, you would have noticed it. I just—I had to end the story."

"You should have left her alone." Now Owen's fingers curled into fists at his sides. "Here I was thinking I failed. That it was my fault Amilia died, but it was *you.* And you didn't even tell me. You knew you hacked my game, and you just pretended it was nothing."

"How was I supposed to tell you if I never even see you anymore? Don't you think I would have tried again eventually?"

"Eventually," Owen scoffed. How polite. This was the cruelest prank ever, and it was still somehow his fault. He wanted to rage, but was far too taken back to do much more than sit. So far he covered the when and why, which left... "How did you end up doing it, anyways?"

She pressed her lips together before answering. "Drew modded it so I could play an existing NPC. I've spoofed other accounts for some low-level prizes before, but then you ended up with two NPCs and I thought that trick could be my in."

Owen was paying attention, though he no longer looked like it. On some level he was listening, on another level, he was thinking back. Drew was that programmer he met on their second date. Her friend, Abigail, had even mentioned a story. "Fuck," he breathed and closed his eyes. *He* was the story. It had all been right fucking there. When she stopped, he looked over at her again. "You're not a bone digger, you're an asshole."

"Amilia is this important? You break into my apartment after obsessing over her like—I can't even compare. Now you're just going to what? Break up with me?"

"Yes." Owen stood up as if accepting the challenge. He glanced over her face as he moved closer. The distance that was once so comfortable now filled every fiber with annoyance. "I don't trust you, and I frankly don't think I can stand the betrayal I feel looking at you. You've messed up enough, and I'm not going to stick around to see what else happens." He stepped around her, reaching the door handle before she caught his arm.

"Owen, stop. Please, I'm sorry."

He pulled his arm away like a stranger had grabbed him. "Don't touch me. What part of this are you not getting?"

When she didn't answer, he pulled the door open. Her hand caught it before he managed to go anywhere. In the moment before she could speak, something else clicked. "Is this why you wanted me to go to those meetings? Oh God, how early did you know it was me?"

"I thought if I could hear you mention them first, that I'd be able to bring it up."

Owen narrowed his eyes. He glanced back into the living room before looking at her with an unwavering expression. "The first time you invited me over was because you were—" He paused to bring his hands up to do air quotes. "'Worried about me.' That's when you figured it out, wasn't it?"

"You played in front of me. I promise, before then I had no idea."

"So yes. What am I supposed to say, Andreah? Thank you for not stabbing me in the back with a bigger knife? Thank you for knowingly invading my privacy and fooling me for two-thirds of our relationship?" Owen pressed his lips together to give an unforgiving little smile. "Oh." He reached into his pocket, and pulled her spare key out. "Let's not rely on dumb luck next time, hmm?"

Her face was red with frustration over his taunts. "I was going to tell you. I was scared of telling you upfront, and I tried looking for a way to make it easier, but I screwed up. What do you want me to do now? What should I say? You can throw everything in my face all night, but none of this is going to make you feel better. So do or say what you will already, for fucks sake."

"That's the best thing you've said all night." Owen wiggled the key on its cheap wire keychain until she held out her palm. "I think I will."

"I can't fix my mistakes, Owen. But you have to believe that I never did this to hurt you. It wasn't supposed to be you. And when it turned out to be, all I knew to do was kill the project. I didn't know Daniel's pain would become yours. But if you could just, for a moment, understand that—"

"This story, these characters matter to me. What exactly am I to understand?" Owen had already taken a few steps down the hall before turning. Andreah had stopped just outside her door. "Understand that you tried to take the easy way out, and now it's making you look bad?"

"I didn't want you to ever find out. We're different. You liked what you knew about me, what you saw. But I'm not some sort of manic pixie dream girl."

"When did I ever?" The half-formed question was a clear sign that Owen was thrown for a second. "All I ever wanted from you was to talk to me."

"We're too casual for that, Owen. I'm full of half-truths. You know what I want you to know. Like with everyone else. But that's my mistake, among many, because you're the wrong person to do that with." She didn't give him any time to question her. "Whether I told that to you today, or a month ago, it wouldn't change the fact I accidentally found my way into cyberstalking you. If you really are a bone digger, you know it isn't as clear-cut as it seems."

Owen sighed, feeling defeated on too many levels at once. "What do you want then, Andreah?"

"Can't you just, like..." she paused, swaying between him and the door. "Stay, and we can try to talk it out?"

He glanced around the hallway, feeling exposed like a raw nerve. Being one of those couples who fought in the hallway was another thing he never meant to do. But he couldn't deny that some part of him did want to stay. "Alright. I mean, it's a fair enough trade for you excusing the whole B & E thing."

The nervous lift of his tone made the joke clear and Andreah smiled as he walked back inside. "Technically, I didn't see anything broken."

Owen coughed out a laugh, shaking his head at himself, this...everything, maybe. "Well, I'm considerate like that."

She ducked into her kitchen. "Do you want coffee?" she asked. Owen followed her, because he felt like he should, and offered a small "Sure" in reply. She grabbed two mugs and made a quick pot before finally turning back to him. When she handed off the warm mug, she smiled softly while lingering close.

His gaze instantly fell to the cup of coffee that warmed his fingers so well he was afraid to take a sip. Any other time he would have been content being this close, but not today.

"Creamer?"

"Huh?" He looked up to see her standing with a bottle of creamer in her hand. "No, thank you."

She set it down, and made herself comfortable on the counter for a moment before taking a sip. "I don't know how you can drink it black always. I need a little flavor sometimes, y'know?"

"Andreah."

She blinked. "It's your coffee. I was just suggesting a little extra sweetness in your life."

"Andreah," he repeated louder this time. She paused, and he took an extra second to gather his words. "I knew you were a liar, but I didn't *see* it until now. You were right. About everything. We were too casual to withstand this much. And I can't do this. I need to go."

She watched silently as he put down his mug. Didn't even budge as he made way for the door. It was remarkable he had even tried to stay, so she wouldn't stop him this time.

He wasn't sure he preferred this, either, as he headed down the hall and out the building. He wondered if he should have said goodbye, but it was too late now.

Spending time with Lance was the silver lining of many dull missions. Everything felt easier when he was around. The only problem was that Daniel and Lance still weren't talking.

Instead of sneaking around like a thief, Lance got to enjoy the golden Paris sunlight as he ran errands for his father. But trouble was lurking right around the corner.

A crossbow bolt flew straight into the heart of a man who stepped onto the street. Lance stepped back. The guard hadn't even gotten a chance to take a breath after spotting him.

"Tarlè," the shooter called from behind.

Lance turned towards the voice, confusion only deepened when he saw Daniel standing there. "I'm assuming that was your work, Ortiz. Nice trick," he said, before glancing back at the would-be attacker. "How did you know he'd be there?"

"I have much to tell you," Daniel said. The foresight was wearing off, but it had given him exactly what he had asked for, the chance to make everything how it needed to be. There was another advantage of not wanting to return home to Spain right away. Time. He had a chance to explain the near-magical things that happened to him, and apologize for pushing Lance away while chasing ghosts. The tear in their

263

friendship wasn't instantly fixed, but it wasn't an uphill battle, either.

Days later, Lance sat in front of a fire being lulled to sleep as its warmth protected him from the cold outside. He'd been staying with his family, and this spot in a distant wing made him feel more at home than anywhere else. When his eyes started to grow heavy, there was a knock on the door. Lance must have been asleep for some time, since when he woke, only the deep orange coals of the fire remained.

Lance rubbed his eyes as he got up to answer the door. Who would stop by this late? Let alone detour to his small section of the house. Soon he had his answer. "Daniel," Lance said. He noticed that his friend's eyes looked glossy. "What are you doing here?"

"Can I come in?"

His words seemed a bit slurred, but Lance let him in regardless. Better to have Daniel here instead of wandering the streets on the way to the inn. Lance closed the door, ready to stay something else, but Daniel wasn't there. He must have gone straight to the bedroom.

Lance rocked on his feet to check if Daniel wandered towards the main house, but it didn't appear anyone went in that direction. That simply left one place for him to be. Lance walked back to see Daniel lying down on the bed, curious if he had already passed out.

For a moment, Lance didn't know what he wanted to do. He held a hand out as if to ask *why*. The chair where he had been napping would have been the proper place for a guest. "Alright then," he mumbled to himself, and settled down on the other side of the bed. "Can you at least tell me why you are in my bed?"

Daniel wiggled, and flipped over so they were face to face. His eyes never left Lance, who was having some trouble maintaining eye contact. There was so much pain there. Lance felt like he could see a crack in those sky-blue eyes that ran straight down to the soul. "I don't want to be alone," Daniel said at last.

That answer was so raw it sent a pain into Lance's chest. "It's okay, you're not alone." He'd known that Daniel hadn't been fully himself since Amilia was killed in front of him.

Something inside broke that day. Lance missed her too, but was nowhere near as shaken up about it as Daniel. Seemed fitting, since the only way Lance could imagine what his friend was going through was to picture Daniel's death. The fact that other members had been taken from them would bring a whole new heartache that mirrored the first.

Lance pulled a blanket over them both so they could stay warm. When he settled back down, he ended up tucked closer. "You never are alone," he said, placing his hand against Daniel's chest holding onto a tiny bit of cloth between his fingers.

Daniel looked as if he was thinking. "I miss us, too," Daniel said after a long silence. He didn't even miss a particular moment, just all of it, any of it.

The words sounded as sweet as a bird's song. Time and again, Daniel chose her instead, a choice Lance understood. He'd made his own choices too. There had been discussions about his legacy that happened so long ago they seemed written in stone. Still, Lance smiled and closed his eyes, content with just those few words.

As soft as a feather, Lance felt a kiss high on his cheek causing his eyes to flutter open. He searched Daniel's face trying to read it. He was tempted to ask why again, but he knew. It was an attempt to feel whole again. Daniel caught Lance's lips, kissing him before either of them ruined the moment.

The taste of bittersweet wine was still there, so sharp that Lance wondered if he could get intoxicated as well. If not from the feeling alone. "I've missed this," Lance admitted before drinking down another kiss.

There was so little sweetness to be had, but Lance ventured further to create some. "What can I do for you?"

"You are going to call me a sap again," he said softly.

"If I recall," Lance whispered back, "You said you were for me."

Daniel nodded slightly, an agreement that this close, said magnitudes. "I was scared."

"Like now?" Daniel looked away, and confirmed Lance's question. "I get scared too sometimes, so try me."

"I feel shaky. Could you—hold me?"

Lance didn't even take a second before lifting his arm and leaning back so Daniel could rest on his chest. Once he was settled, Lance wrapped both arms around him.

They knew they couldn't stay like this forever. Both of them wanted things the other couldn't provide in the long run. But for now, in this moment, it was enough to feel at peace. It was a bit of sweetness the world didn't seem to give on its own. When the morning came, they faced it together in one sense or another. Daniel knew there were plenty more bridges that had to be rebuilt. He'd spent far too many days trying to hide in the past.

The journey back to Spain was one Daniel dreaded, but didn't try to delay it any longer than he had already. He needed to face the reality of everything. Lance returned with him as support when Daniel made his first appearance at the guild.

"Ortiz, where have you been? Where is everyone else?" Gael asked, as he turned away from some newer recruits. He glanced between Daniel and Lance before realizing this shouldn't be discussed in public. "Come, not here."

Once they were closed off in a more private room, Daniel opened up about the events, struggling at first before it all spilled out without censor. Lance stayed at his place near the door, wishing he could help steady Daniel's voice.

"What of the artifact?" Gael asked.

"I...didn't bring it. It's a danger, and I was too weak to protect it on the return."

Gael's lips tightened as he considered if this was true. He stood before speaking. "I will send a group to scout that area. That should keep other visitors away until we can figure out how to collect it without losing anyone else."

Daniel didn't agree with the idea, but he kept silent.

"For now, just rest and return tomorrow for some further questions before any missions."

Daniel nodded before being excused.

Owen excused himself as well. He leaned back into his chair, exhaling as he roughly brushed his fingers through his hair. Working at the newspaper seemed to lose its spark. Owen felt sluggish and wondered if anyone noticed he was getting by doing the bare minimum. The only upside was that Michael steered clear of him now that he seemed more zombie than human. Owen placed a cigarette between his lips and headed downstairs after his shift. Without being hard pressed for answers in AoS, or having a story to be passionate about at work, things were a bit colorless. His complete disinterest with life made him realize how easy it was to blend in with the background noise of New York. The realization was unsettling enough for him to consider a small idea.

"Hello, my name is Owen, and my best friend is a fictional bisexual French man." His fingers gripped at the faux wooden podium in a confusing mixture of feelings and fear of the waxy top coat wedging itself under his nail. "Normally, that's fine. But uh, god, I didn't think I'd ever be up here talking to, well—" Owen cut himself off to gesture to the group sitting in folding chairs. "You all. But my ex-girlfriend left a giant fucking crater in both my lives. And I just really wish he was here. That...that we could get a drink, and talk as I walk down the same street I take to get home from work every day. Just talk, you know? Have someone who understands without being so involved in my day to day life. Playing feels like opening a wound, and not playing is slightly more tolerable. But *dieu tout-puissant* I miss him. You are all here because you want to play the game, but know you shouldn't." A bitter laugh broke up his words. "I'm here because of the reverse. So, uh I'm going to step down now." Owen dragged a hand across his brow before he committed to giving up the soap box.

Manners would have dictated that he listen to others speak, but he was in no mood for it. He headed straight outside, nearly forgetting his jacket on his chair. His hands anxiously pulled out a pack of cigarettes, idly remembering the cashier's expression when he bought them. Since when did people judge so harshly for smoking?

Someone else stepped out of the meeting. Owen assumed it was an older guy by the paint-speckled work boots he spotted, but he didn't bother to confirm until the man spoke. "What are you, like 24, 25?"

"Something like that."

"Yeah, that's what I thought." The man nodded to himself before continuing. "I know what it's like to lose someone at that age. When fiction mimics a reality, it hurts just as much. If you want, we can talk over drinks, or something."

"Look," Owen said, exhaling heavily. "I came out here to smoke, not try to find a replacement."

The man grumbled something that Owen thought was about people his age, but the gravel in the man's voice made it too hard to tell. The guy dug for his car keys and headed for the parking garage. Owen raised a brow, surprised the guy had a car. Maybe if he had been nicer he wouldn't have needed a taxi later. But then again, nice wasn't on his agenda tonight, or at least not until this cigarette burned down some.

Owen was dangerously drunk; not a danger to himself, but of the bartender cutting him off. He played with the empty shot glass, completely losing count of how many had come before it. The TV in the corner of the room was annoyingly replaying—for the third time—an ambush interview with an fnVR rep, citing that they always had an eye on players worthy of official sponsorship. The guy didn't want to talk. Owen could sympathize.

"Buy you a drink?"

He turned to the unfamiliar voice, finding a gentleman leaning into the bar next to him. Or, at least that's the best word he had for the man who was dressed in a well-fitted suit at this hour. His eyes had the same sly amusement that Lance carried. "Unless you were waiting for someone else?" he added. Owen had been staring without realizing it.

"No." The glass fumbled as he drew his hands back. "I'd love a drink, but it depends."

"On what?" The man pushed up his rimmed frames. He didn't have freckles like Lance, but the glasses still brought his features together in the same endearing way. And thinking of Lance again, made this feel possible, and maybe even something to revel in.

269

Owen bit his bottom lip, slowly dragging it past his teeth. "How well you kiss."

The man didn't shy away, despite a quick glance around the room. He leaned in, and Owen grabbed his tie pulling him roughly closer. The man placed his hands along Owen's jaw, pulling gently with a shared want that incited a soft moan to rumble underneath his fingertips.

Owen's heart beat unevenly in his chest, and he only realized his fingers were still wrapped around the stranger's tie when he glanced down.

"Did I pass?" The man asked, certain of his success. A hint of red now graced his cheeks and added color to the slight curl of his black hair. It was an attractive look on him.

Owen nodded. "What's your name?" he asked far out of order.

"Does it matter?"

"God no, unless you plan on staying here longer."

Owen woke up to the smell of coffee. It was great for a moment before the smell seemed to die. He pushed himself up to a sitting position, eyes barely open. His hand reached towards the nightstand, but fell, touching nothing but air. Owen opened his eyes more to see why the nightstand had moved, but ended up staring at a sleek glass set. Those weren't his...and neither was that headboard, or those lamps.

Panic made him nearly lose his stomach, but in a bedroom that wasn't his, where would the bathroom, or even a trash can, be hiding? Owen squeezed his eyes shut with enough force that they hurt and tried to remember to breathe.

"You're up," announced a somehow familiar voice. Owen jumped up so fast that his vision dimmed around the edges for a second. This time at least, the nightstands were there to help support him.

"Jumpy little guy, aren't you?" The man took a sip of his coffee, and it clicked. The guy from the bar last night. Lane? Levi? Leo? Fuck, it was an L something. The name search was abandoned when a second thing in his head clicked. The guy was shirtless and in boxers.

Owen glanced at himself. Shirt on, but uselessly and completely unbuttoned. His jeans were on, but also undone. "Oh god," he breathed, and stumbled to sit on the bed again.

"Hey, hey, it's okay, Alex." The man neared, setting his coffee down on a dresser.

"You know my name?" Owen blinked a few times completely dumbfounded. He never told anyone his first name.

"Yeah," he said softly. He sighed then pursed his lips. "You don't know where you are, do you?"

"I don't even remember your name," Owen mumbled as he stared ahead at a patch of wall.

"It's Luke." If he sounded offended, Owen was too busy feeling like shit to notice. "If it makes you feel better, nothing really happened last night. After the bar, we made out in the taxi, and then we stumbled into my bedroom, before I realized that you were way too wasted to be fooling around. So, I let you sleep it off here."

"Oh." Owen lifted his head up to see more of Luke again besides his feet. Owen ran a hand through his bedhead. "Thank you."

"Let me, uh, go get you a glass of water," Luke said, before retreating from the room.

Owen closed his eyes and tried to remember last night. The kiss that sold him was clear, but everything else was a mess. He couldn't even remember the last time he had been blackout drunk. Years ago at least.

Luke came back, and this time Owen didn't jump. He took a sip of the water offered before setting it down. "I gotta go to the bathroom," Owen said, finding little point in feigning dignity now.

"First door on the left." Luke watched his guest like he was the strangest thing, and Owen didn't object because, well, he felt it.

"Thanks." Owen got up, steady this time, and headed to the bathroom. His hand found the light switch, but he instantly flipped it back off with a cringe. He could see well enough to take a whiz. After washing his hands, he pooled the water to splash over his face. It did nothing for his appearance, but it made him feel better for a split second. Owen pushed now-damp stray bangs back and actually felt sorry for Luke. He wasn't a pretty sight; pale, with bloodshot eyes.

"Are you okay?" Luke asked, when he came back into the bedroom.

Owen took a few more gulps of water. "Yeah...look, Luke, um, I'm sorry about everything. This wasn't what you were looking for. My girlfriend and I recently broke up, and I've been a mess over some other things. And—what?"

Luke seemed lost, like he was the one who woke up in a stranger's place. "Girlfriend?"

"Yeah...but like I said, we broke up so? Oh!" Owen's voice spiked a bit too high for his ears. "You thought I was gay. Sorry again, I guess? Look, uh, I should go."

Owen stood up, fighting off any feeling his hangover was going to throw at him. He checked his wallet to make sure he could get home before glancing around for his leather jacket.

"The rest of your stuff is in the living room," Luke said.

"Thank you." The words had started to lose their meaning. Owen headed for the living room without help. He was shrugging his jacket on when Luke came in. The couch he found it on looked like it cost more than what Owen's rent.

"Are you sure you are going to be okay? You could stay until you're not hungover."

Crawling back into bed, even a stranger's, sounded so good. "Luke, um." He was trying to say his name enough that he wouldn't ever forget it again. But couldn't quite manage to look him in the eyes again. "You're a dynamite kisser, and maybe if I didn't make this the most awkward moment of my life it could have been a thing. But all I really want right now is to get in a taxi and go home."

"Are you sure? You don't even know what part of town you're in."

"Honestly, I would rather pass out on the subway right now than be here." He winced. That sounded harsh.

Owen checked for a reassuring rattle of his keys as he moved to the front door. He fumbled with the lock for a second before getting it. "Um, thank you again, and your place is really nice by the way." Owen paused at the door deciding if that's all he wanted to say. With a nod, he made a beeline to the elevator.

The ride down felt like it took forever under the bright elevator lights, but once he was on street level, he missed that little silent box. The city was too awake, too full of everything. At the first trash can he saw, he stopped and emptied his stomach.

Owen wiped his mouth and resisted the urge to collapse. The nearest taxi ignored him, likely a witness to his horrid display, but he was able to hail another and tune out the world on the ride home.

The next day, Emily invited Neal and Owen out. He wasn't going to agree, but Emily insisted, citing that this was her first night out without the baby.

With a lethal amount of mirth, Emily sat down at their usual booth near the bar, not caring for a second that the waitress forgot to wipe it. Wordlessly, she pulled out a napkin and wet it down with the water provided.

It wasn't long before the waitress came back and awkwardly took over. She pulled on a brighter smile. "What can I get you, tonight?"

"We are going to share the house pizza," Neal said, "And can I get a rum and coke."

The waitress nodded and glanced over to Emily, who ordered a lemon drop, and finally over to Owen.

"Nothing for me, thanks," he said.

"Not even a beer?" Emily asked, "It's on me."

"I'm sure."

The waitress left, but the comment about not wanting to drink tonight lead to another, and another, until Owen just backed up far enough to tell them everything he hadn't.

From Amilia's death, to the break-up with Andreah, and how he still felt a bit hungover after the night with Luke.

"Geez, and I thought the baby poop made my month pretty shitty," Emily said.

Owen hadn't realized how long he had been taking until he noticed that drink Emily was babying as half gone. Neal, however, was still stuck on something Owen said earlier.

"Are you having a gay crisis?" Neal asked.

"Are you kidding me? I'm not having a 'gay crisis' for god's sake. If I find someone attractive, something might happen. In my case, it's called bisexual." Owen paused, not meaning to say that out loud. But then again, he'd accidentally committed himself by mentioning Luke in the first place. He exhaled sharply before continuing. "Just lay the fuck off. I don't have the patience right now."

Owen pushed up to his feet, grabbing the smallest bill out of his wallet to cover his share. It was more than double what he owed for a pizza that hadn't come yet. He didn't care. All these tiny comments were getting to him. Owen grabbed his coat and stormed out.

Emily stared wide-eyed at the empty seat across from her. Slowly, she turned to Neal, who looked baffled. "You should go talk to him."

"Maybe he needs space, or got a taxi already," he nervously countered.

"Go," Emily said, and gave him a little push.

He gave her a quick glance before bolting for the door. "Owen, wait," Neal called, hoping his voice would carry.

But it didn't need too. Owen was standing outside with his back to the door as he fidgeted with something in his hands.

"I'm sorry," Neal blurted. "I didn't mean to offend you. You just—I'm so bad at this. What I really mean is that it was stupid of me to assume."

"It's fine." Owen turned to waved the comment off with a lit cigarette in his hand. "I've known. I just always—tried to just ignore it. But then in game, I see and *feel* what these bi characters do and I...relate. They make it seem okay." Owen took a long drag like he was done with this conversation. "Bet that all sounds pretty stupid, huh?"

"No, it doesn't." Neal bounced on his heels, but not because he wasn't taking the subject seriously. He had run out into the cold without his jacket. "I'm really glad you found someone who let you not to ignore a piece of yourself."

The annoying buzz of a phone against the nightstand was the first thing that had roused Owen from sleep. He rolled over and checked the time. Two in the afternoon. Finally, he checked what number was calling. Maybe it was a job, but who would call on a Saturday afternoon? He had his times listed as only weekdays. Either way, he answered by the last ring. "Hello?"

The person on the other line took a moment, probably because of the groggy sound of Owen's voice. "Hello, is this Alexander Owen?" He gave the peppy girl a small 'mhm' in reply. "Well, this is a representative for functionVR, creators of Age of Shadow. We came across your account and there seems to be some suspicious activity for the past few months. We were wondering if you could come to our offices on 3rd Avenue so we could nail down a record of what occurred."

"Suspicious activity?" Owen repeated, and found amusement in hearing it again. "What type of 'suspicious activity?" Every time he said it, it just sounded funnier than the first. Did they mean the dual NPCs, the bone digging, or the situations he kept glitching into?

"We don't think it's a problem anymore, and you're certainly not in trouble. We did, however, lock your account

276

just to make sure the issue is cleared up. If there's any information you can give us, I'm sure we can get your account up and running again soon. Would today work for you?"

Owen let out a long sigh. Why couldn't they do their job without forcing him to travel across town just to get his account back? He rolled off the bed and onto his feet. "Yeah, sure. I can be there in an hour."

He expected the New York fnVR headquarters to be full of people. Especially if it was routine to call people down to their office every time someone had an account issue. When he got off the elevator on the right floor, a receptionist covered the mouthpiece of her mic and greeted him. Owen nodded a hello and glanced around to an empty lobby.

Well, empty besides a stupid cut-out of a professional player.

There wasn't much to hold this attention, so he stared at the cardboard version of the riotously bright player who took advantage of modern hair colors. Curious of who it was, he moved closer, and noticed the back had an Age of Shadow character. Rather clever actually. Adding to Owen's mild amusement was how decked out the avatar was in unnecessary items.

His train of thought was interrupted as a guy who looked around his age came out of one of the glass doors holding a tablet. "Alexander?"

"Owen. But yeah."

"Hello, I am Chris." He offered his hand, which Owen shook. "It's nice to meet you, and thank you for taking the time. If you'll follow me."

If given a second before Chris had started walking, Owen would have commented that he was more blackmailed than invited. He seemed to be the no-nonsense type, so Owen just followed silently behind.

He was led into a small conference room, and sat down before a couple others came into the room. A blonde girl with thick rimmed glasses smiled pleasantly as she passed. She didn't introduce herself as she went to sit at the furthest edge of the table. Two men sat across from Owen, and the entire situation started to make him feel uneasy.

"This is my partner, Jorge. Sorry to keep you waiting, but we may as well get rolling into things right away." Owen didn't object, so Chris went on. "We noticed a few hiccups in your story data. First off, we noticed you recently found an area that was still under development. Could you tell us if you, or anyone on your team perhaps, used any scripts, or brute force into that area of the game?"

Owen blinked, glancing from Jorge to Chris before shaking his head. "No, we just picked up on some hints that there was an artifact in that area, and tried to find it."

They both nodded, eerily, and at the same time as if taking mental notes. Jorge was the one to speak this time. "Did you come across any glitches before or after that?"

"No, not really," Owen said, matter-of-fact despite the lie. There had been several things that shouldn't have happened, like headaches, colors outright vanishing, and the invisible wall.

"Hm. Well, you see, we've backtracked the trouble to the start of your companion, Amilia. That is where the code starts to have issues, and after some key choices, you seemed to trigger her endgame rather quick."

Owen could smell the bullshit, but he didn't say anything about it. He'd let them believe what they wanted, at least until he knew what they wanted. The tone of blame skewed his expression to one of little patience. "And?"

"Well, we were hoping we could compensate for the problem our system caused by rewriting some of Amilia's story. And since this would be an all new, original story for just you, we were hoping you could return the favor."

"You want to retcon Amilia?" Owen glanced at the developers like he misheard. Jorge leaned forward in his chair as if ready to further explain, but Chris seemed silently amused by Owen's word choice. "And pay me for it?"

Owen didn't know a single person who wouldn't want to bring their favorite character back from the dead. But, the writers didn't just find fans on their own and offer to make the trouble up to them. What should have been a miracle, felt like a crossroads deal.

"In turn," Jorge said, "We'd like to contract to stream your gameplay. We're hoping your style of play will further promote the roleplaying aspect of Age of Shadows. We even assigned a brand new writer to Amilia to handle the conversion, and should help minimize any further glitches."

"Since when do NPCs, or any characters, have writers?" Jorge was ready to answer, but Owen kept talking, not allowing for any excuses. "I'm going to politely ask you to cut the crap. Because you aren't really making sense unless you are trying to give me a weird Make-A-Wish, or frankly have never played your own game."

The room settled for a moment, as if silently testing who would answer that dare. "Who'd even 'write' Amilia, anyways?"

Jorge placed his hands against the glass table, palms down as if to try and level with him. "This is something that—"

"Seriously?" Chris cut his co-worker off before Owen could roll his eyes. "Just be real with him."

They exchanged a glance, silently debating something before Jorge sighed. "We like Daniel. From what we can tell, we'd like you. We want to buy the story so far, and have you officially continue it for us. Months ago, when you first picked up your second companion it caused a stir. People realized that maybe they were ignoring some of the game's features."

"Why is Amilia part of this?" Owen didn't mean to sound ungrateful, but he really didn't understand.

The woman on the end pushed her glasses up. "We noticed your play style is different without her. Your login time and perceived enjoyment is all over the place now. We thought it would fix the problem."

Owen narrowed his eyes, not because she was full of crap, but because it seemed like she was the only one here that understood. Money was nice, but if he had wanted it, or the fame, he could have cashed that news story in already.

"Was I wrong?"

If they could ignore questions, then Owen figured he could too. "Who would 'write' Amilia?" he repeated, letting the weight of his glare sit with Jorge. He almost spilled the beans before, but he didn't have to in the end. "You mean play. I play as Daniel, and you want someone to play as Amilia."

"That's right," Jorge said.

Well, too bad. Someone already 'played' Amilia, and talking to her wasn't on the to-do list.

"And, we'd like to introduce the right person for the job," he continued. "Carmen, will you?"

The blonde left the room, and through the frosted glass Owen watched her walk down the hall. Carmen soon returned with three people following her. They paused for a moment at the door before Carmen opened it. He caught a quick glance at two security guards before his eyes fell directly on the third person of the group.

"Owen, this is Andreah. She's familiar with Amilia, and we're hoping the two of you will work well together."

Andreah entered the room with her head down, and seemed to think about sitting before opting to stand to the left of Chris. "Nice to meet you, Owen."

"Are you shitting me?" If one could go into shock without any trauma, he was certain his expression reached that level. "You are going to let the person who hacked my game keep doing it?"

"Uh," Jorge stalled, and looked over to Chris who just stared. Carmen looked at the table like something important was written there.

"You weren't going to tell me."

"We, um."

Owen leaned back in his seat, and it creaked with the shifting of weight. "I can't trust anyone in this fucking room," he said, more to himself than anyone else.

Andreah ran her hand through her hair, and paced slowly behind Chris and Jorge. "They didn't know, Owen."

"What didn't we know?" Jorge turned in his chair to look at her, obvious in his expression that he didn't like her much even before this.

"That he knew I modded the game."

Chris nudged Jorge before getting up. "I think we need a moment to speak about this, please excuse us." He motioned to the security guards to stay put at the door before leaving as Carmen trailed behind.

Andreah watched them leave before taking Jorge's seat. She slid down, before finally settling. He stared at her, too focused on her face to notice the lazy attitude.

"What's going on here?" Owen asked, his muscles as rigid as his voice.

Her eyes were closed, as if she was ready to take a nap. She looked exhausted, so it seemed fitting almost. Her eyebrows pulled together as if to acknowledge the question. "I didn't tell them about you. Or us. So way to blow that up."

"You are like a stray cat who refuses to leave me alone. Was this your idea, or did you get caught?"

She opened her eyes, lips pursing at his words. "Don't be so self-absorbed. This is still on you. We wouldn't be here if you didn't look for unfinished DLC like an obsessive fanboy."

Owen faked a laugh, and flipped her off as the trio of developers came back in. Security shuffled at the door to make room for them to pass. Jorge glossed over the loss of his seat even though his growing annoyance was clear. But Owen wondered something else. Why was fnVR security here?

Chris seated himself in his old seat, next to Andreah. "Won't this be interesting," he said, noting Owen's previous gesture.

"Trust me, it'll get better," Andreah commented, sitting up and setting her elbows on the table.

"Now son, you should just—" Chris started.

"I should just do a cash buy," Owen said, without much thought. The idea of selling Daniel made his stomach sour, but he didn't care for this situation either.

"You could," Andreah agreed, which wasn't what he expected.

Jorge sat down in a free seat, raising a hand to stop Chris' likely objection that cash buys weren't officially allowed. "You are a part of Daniel, we'd like to keep it that way."

His eyes rested on his ex. Despite her bored expression, her knee bounced under the table. She stared back at him for a moment before reaching for a pen, and messed with the click release on it. "What would you do, Andreah?"

She didn't look up, but she pursed her lips while she gave it a quick thought. "I'd tell me to go to hell."

Her comment made everyone tense. Everyone except Owen. He smiled, and shook his head. "Well, I guess," he said, and licked his lips. He didn't even know what he wanted to do, and looked to the others in the room. While bone digging wasn't illegal, the bullshit Andreah pulled definitely was. Drew had helped her go beyond modding into the world of outright hacking. Hell would be a good place for her, but not jail. And that's exactly where she'd go if he didn't make a deal. It might count as payback, but it was an added chaos he didn't desire. "You can at least show me the contract you want me to sign."

Signing the contract was pretty straight forward. The mess came when everyone fought over the carcass of what was once his private gaming life. It was agreed upon that they'd stream older footage in the style of an episodic recap.

Exclusive scenes with Amilia were to be divided at Andreah's discretion. Who quickly passed it along to Abigail, who passed it along to her boss. It was eerily close what would have happened to the information if Andreah had finished her bone digging job in the first place. At least instead of pieces being torn off like hungry vultures, they stuck to news of the matter rather than sensationalism. Owen wasn't sure how Andreah convinced them to let that happen. Maybe she annoyed everyone into submission.

But it didn't end there. When Owen's boss heard that Abigail's "tacky TMZ wannabe" site was going to scoop a story another big fuss was made. Everyone in the know wanted full claim on the story. Owen sat silently, headache growing as they fought over *his* story. Kids with a piñata would have been more reasonable. Once boundaries were drawn across character lines everyone seemed content, for the moment at least.

One perk Owen didn't expect was that their little operation was given an office. They were told they could use it however they wished as long as the gaming area stayed consistent for streams. There was already a couch with a laptop lying on the cushion. He wondered whose for only a moment before Andreah walked in with a coffee in hand, and sat down.

Her pressed white blouse was the second surprise of the day. She had left the top buttons open just enough to show off cleavage. Which reminded him he shouldn't be standing gawking at everything. His eyes dropped, catching fitted slacks paired with heels before he cleared his throat. "You look nice. I don't think I ever seen you dressed up like this before," Owen commented, or complimented. He wasn't sure which he was going for.

"Well, I'm single now."

"Right, cameras and all." Owen pushed past the patch of carpet he had been camping out on. There was no literal dividers between the lounge are and streaming area, but you could see where the out of frame area started from the paint and decor.

"Why can't someone else edit this crap? I'll be the producer-director that yells when they cut something important," Andreah complained, gesturing with her cup at the screen in front of her.

"Well, if you need a break I can take over," Owen offered. He leaned into the stations set up for them to play. Shiny new headgear sat waiting with large but remarkably thin screens in front of them to help record every detail. "As long as you don't yell at me."

Owen looped back around to check out a private little office off the main room, and came back to the heels discarded in front of Andreah. "It's a bullshit double standard, huh?" he asked. Andreah glanced up, not realizing that his conversation as had circled back around to her outfit. "It's a gaming company. Guys can wear whatever they want as long as they don't look homeless. But all the ladies, you all have to look professional all the times."

"That isn't exclusive to the workplace."

Owen nodded to himself. Wouldn't argue with that one. His attention soon waned again. The only real desk in the place was in the private corner office, which had a mini fridge where one might expect a filing cabinet. "This is weird, right?" he asked, and glanced back to Andreah. A short while ago, he didn't want, or even expect, to see her again. And now? Now, they were co-workers. Their stories were literally interwoven again.

Andreah watched the screen for a second before she placed the laptop over to the side. "Yeah. If you want to back out I won't blame you."

"No." Owen couldn't hold her gaze. He looked down to his own sneakers, and the new patch of carpet he'd been hovering over. Was that a stain? What was this room used for before? He exhaled shakily, and crossed his arms over his chest like there was a sudden draft. "I mean, I don't know. If I'm going to play anyways might as well get paid, and help at the same time."

Andreah was silent for a few moments longer than he expected, which made him glance up again. She watched him with a small smile, and Owen sensed she wanted to say something more, but settled with something easier. "Thank you for doing this for me."

Owen shifted his weight, and uncrossed his arms. "I'm doing it for Amilia." That wasn't the complete truth, but again, it was easier.

Her smile disappeared into a tight frown. She tried to cover it by taking a sip of her coffee, offering him only the smallest of nods before she returned to work.

They both ignored the silence of the room, with just the two of them awkwardly trying to get along. It worked, and then it didn't. But this time, Owen knew he was the one to suck the vibrancy out of the room. "I should run a mission."

It was a good thing that he wasn't looking for approval, since Andreah didn't even blink as he went to do a test run. The headgear was lighter, but to be fair, his whole head felt lighter. The newness of everything wasn't a comfort. Andreah sitting so close in this world wasn't doing him any favors either.

When Owen connected, it felt both unreal, and the only right thing in the room. His eyes scanned around, almost expecting to see her. Of course, she wasn't there. That would be even sillier than this rabbit hole he'd fallen into. Amilia wasn't going to magically pop up because Andreah was physically near him.

There was one familiar comfort—Lance. He stood in front of a carriage, rocking back and forth on his heel, idly waiting as a mission trigger point. Daniel approached his friend without much enthusiasm, despite this being the better part of his day. "Where are we being sent?"

Lance pulled out a letter from his breast pocket. The creases were deep from many refolds. "To London," Lance said, and offered the letter to Daniel. "I took the liberty to gather our things since we have to be there before the end of August."

The letter cited the guild wanting extra protection for the treaty that was going to be signed between Spain and Britain. Daniel frowned as he folded the letter back up. This sounded like a job for the knights. Why send two thieves as extra guards?

"Let me guess," Lance said. "You are happy to visit London, but why us?"

"Exactly." Daniel messed up, he didn't understand why he was now the golden boy. "Honestly, the guild mustn't want us around."

"I don't know about that," Lance said, as if to reassure as he got into the carriage. "Surely, they've missed my face."

Before Daniel thought of anything clever to reply, their bags began to rustle. They both sat for a second eyeing the pile that was stacked along one row of seats. "I think you packed a stowaway."

Lance raised a brow, and stood as much as his height allowed in the carriage. He lifted a blanket revealing bright blonde hair that fell around a young woman's face as she looked up at Lance. *"Que faites-vous, Chloe?"*

"Who?"

"Daniel, meet my friend Chloe." Lance offered his hand out so she didn't have to dig herself out of the pile. When he spoke again, the game switched the native language back to French. It had been so long since Daniel heard people speak fluently that he had to focus to understand. "I told you that you couldn't come with us."

"Should we turn around?" Daniel asked.

Chloe glanced over at Daniel, not understanding his Spanish, then she looked back to Lance with a real urgency that sharpened her brown eyes. "Please let me go with you."

Lance opened his mouth to object again, but ended up just sighing. "She does know English better than we do," he said, now supporting their stow away.

More than her face, or even her name, that clue connected the dots. She was the woman well read in Shakespeare that Lance mentioned before. "Fine."

"Thank you, thank you, I could just hug you!" Chloe's excitement made her French faster, and Daniel sighed at both the volume and struggle to remember the correct words. "But I'll resist." She pulled her hands to her chest, and sat down next to Lance after he scooted closer to Daniel to make room.

She only added to his annoyance, but Lance was smiling. He watched Chloe like she was a fluttering bird he wanted to playfully paw at. Being part of a trio wasn't something Daniel felt ready for, but if she made Lance happy, he'd learn to deal with it.

As they traveled to England, Lance told the story of how he knew Chloe. Their affluent parents encouraged her to write, and when Lance went back to visit his father, they met. Lance expected Chloe to be shocked when she realized he wasn't the proper son his parents wanted, but she was curious about his real life in Spain. Chloe pushed to hear more stories, citing that she'd only heard of such tales in the books brought back for her.

Such lively company made the chore of traveling by carriage easier. They traveled as far as horses would take them, then needed a boat for the final leg. Daniel's hands started to quake before he realized why he was nervous. The ship reminded him of the one he took to the Canary Islands.

"It's beautiful."

Daniel turned to look at Chloe as she lit up with excitement. It was strange to see someone else so excited about something that was making him doubt not only his sea legs, but himself.

"Don't you agree, *monsieur* Ortiz?" Chloe asked.

"It's Daniel."

Chloe smiled. She'd known that of course, and simply had been trying to endear herself to him the whole way here. "I've never been on the water before. Is it fun?"

Daniel glanced away and towards the ship. He wasn't sure how to even answer that right now. "It can be."

"Well, then I'm glad I get to travel in such good company," she said, and managed to get Daniel to faintly smile. "That always makes things better."

"It does."

Once they boarded and took off, Chloe's excitement evaporated. Turns out Chloe wasn't a fan of boats after all. Seasickness was a factor she hadn't even considered. After turning green at the gills, Chloe rested her head in Lance's lap. He ran his fingers through her hair while softly singing a French lullaby. "*L'était une petite poule grise. Qu'allait pondre dans l'église.*"

Daniel silently watched. He'd never heard Lance sing in French before and the beauty of it made him not even care what the words meant for a verse or two. When words like hen and eggs repeated he figured they didn't matter anyways.

What warmed his heart one minute made it hurt the next. He was reminded of Isidoro being sick, and Amilia on days when the only way he could help was to simply be around. When land appeared on the horizon, he was more than happy to call it a day.

Owen slipped the headset off, glad that—other than the introduction of a new character—there wasn't too much to pull from this. He stretched back in his chair and folded his arms behind his head before glancing around. This space here was definitely an upgrade from his desk at NY Today, and hopefully, there would come a point where he liked his co-worker at least as much as his other ones.

Andreah crossed her legs onto what now seemed to be her couch. A slight wiggle of her toes appeared as she typed away.

"What are you up to?" Owen asked, curious about what had gained so much of her attention.

"Writing."

"What are you writing about?" Owen swiveled his chair to face her more.

"I can't just tell you all the secrets. Or else they won't need me here after all."

"Well, do I at least get to know what you're doing *eventually?*"

"Even I don't know what they will highlight from the game. They could end up bringing in Amilia's evil twin sister for all we know, and then I'll have to write about that load of shit."

Owen chuckled as he stood up, and checked his pockets. He wondered for a moment if inviting Andreah on a break was the right thing to do, but he opted not to. He took the elevator down to the main lobby of the building to a cafeteria with a small patio in the back of the building. He noticed some people that worked at fnVR eating together, maybe talking about some work in progress. It dawned on him why they were given their own workplace now. There had been enough leaks already. The last thing anyone needed was further spoilers coming out. Owen wavered as he stared up at a backlit menu, debating on the various sandwiches and soups before settling on a vice for lunch instead.

He walked out to the boxed-in patio before pulling out his pack of cigarettes, lighting one, and bringing a long puff of smoke into his lungs. The small area didn't have much. Some water-damaged patio furniture and potted plants, but it was still something to look at when you needed a break from staring at a screen all day.

Owen's phone gave an unusual chime, it was a theme to something he couldn't ever remember. The only thing that stuck in his head about it was that Cole changed her text tone to custom ringtone one night.

To Owen:
What's up rock star enjoying your first day?

He breathed in smoke, holding it until he almost coughed. That was a loaded questioned.

To Nicole:
It's alright

Since any ashtrays out here had either been swiped or removed to discourage smoking, Owen carefully put his cigarette out when he heard his phone go off in a rapid succession.

To Owen:
yeah being famous must blow
come hang out with us tomorrow I promise no one will
know you there~

While the tilde symbol held no official meaning, in this context he read the text in her sing-song voice reserved for when she wanted something. Owen headed back inside, ignoring the text for a moment. He hadn't seen Cole in a while, but he also had been planning on spending his free time at home. He had almost walked all the way back up when he decided to text back.

To Nicole:
ok, but I won't be free until six

When he rounded the corner into their office again, Andreah was hunched over her computer. Instead of typing, her hands were at the sides of her face, eyes closed as she looked frustrated. She flinched when she heard Owen's feet drag as he paused. She exhaled fully and tried to recollect herself in a manner that would look less disordered.

"Everything okay?" Owen asked, taking slow steps into the room, but stopped before he had to decide where to be.

"Yeah," she said, but the low dismal sound of her voice wasn't convincing. She made a face acknowledging the lie they both know she told. "I just can't figure this out. It's just so...complicated? I have a mental block and just—" She cut herself short, closing her eyes to take in another deep breath.

"Is there anything I can help with?" Owen took a spot on the far arm of the couch, closest he'd been yet, but still out of reach.

"No. It's fine. I just feel like I'm buying time, but..." If she hadn't ended the sentence with that last word, Owen would have thought she was done. Instead he waited. "This isn't going to work out. I shouldn't have tried to do this. I should have just lawyered up."

"Why didn't you just spill everything to try and save your ass? You could have bargained with that, maybe."

"What do you mean?"

"I don't know." Owen moved up on the arm of the couch, and pretended it was the furniture's fault for his discomfort. "Sell me out, like you intended to." He didn't mean to sound harsh, but it was the truth regardless.

"I was trying something new and decided to respect your privacy."

"Oh." He heard Nicole's newest text, but couldn't tear his eyes off Andreah to check it.

"Yeah," she said, and closed up her laptop.

"Thank you," he said, despite his tight confused expression.

She barely nodded as she tipped over her heels to slip them back on and left without saying anything else.

For all his twitching before, he was now still as he stared at the glass doors that connected them to the rest of fnVR. Why would she do that? The only thing he knew was that he wasn't going to chase after Andreah. If anything, he had learned she could handle herself just fine.

Cole's text said they'd pick him up at eight pm. So, around seven the following night Owen killed time by putting on Age of Shadows arena streams and pretended to pay attention. A larger question than why a knight was wearing such impractical armor was what Cole meant by 'picking him up.' He couldn't even remember the last time he just didn't meet someone somewhere.

There was a knock on his door exactly five minutes before Nicole said she'd arrive. Both she and Seth were always surprisingly punctual. It was a feat that always impressed Owen. He assumed they were trained by going to classes. That perfect attendance must have leaked into the rest of their life.

Owen opened the door to Cole and was instantly drawn to her pink and blue hair. Even if he had thought it looked ridiculous, the soft pastels drew attention all the same. No roots showed, so it must be new. "Your hair is actually too cute for words."

"Aww, you are so sweet." Cole's smile grew. "Are you ready to go?"

He patted his pants pockets, feeling his phone in one but the keys were missing from the other. He went back to grab them off the table. "Ready," Owen said as he locked the door. "Where exactly are we going?"

"To an open mic." Nicole took slow steps backwards until Owen caught up, and then looped her arm in his.

"Like a comedy show?"

"No, more like a poetry slam."

Owen paused in his steps, and Cole had to give him a little pull. "Don't be a sour puss. You already agreed to come with us."

"True." His mood lightened, but he didn't look all that convinced as they took the elevator down. Soon after that, it didn't matter since a far more curious sight waited for him. Seth was illegally parked in a newer style VW bug. "Who's car is that?"

"Mine." Nicole beamed. She opened the passenger door, and folded the seat forward. "My dad got it for my birthday."

"Hey," Seth said, leaning forward to see Owen.

"Hi," he said, and got in the back. "Wait, wasn't your birthday like nine months ago."

She didn't answer right away, too focused on watching Seth pull her new toy out on the road. "Yeah, he tends to add a grand for every month he misses."

"Wish my dad did that."

Cole glanced back at him with a small flash of a smile. "I'd complain about him being a shit parent, but it's hard to complain in this beauty."

"Well, you are going to find a reason to complain if you don't remind me how to get to that cafe," Seth interjected.

"Oh." Cole wiggled in the seat to pull out her phone that had been sticking halfway out of her tight jeans. She hummed to herself while checking the directions. "Take the next right."

"Alright," Seth said, and changed lanes like a taxi driver. "Before I forget, can you remind me of my MPRE study group on Tuesday later?"

"At four, right?"

"Yeah—What are you smiling at?" Seth accusingly glanced back at Owen who only laughed.

"You take knowing the law so you can break it to such an extreme," Owen said. He leaned over in his seat so he would be more in the middle. "If you ever get caught you can represent yourself, and be halfway decent at it."

"More like three-quarters of the way decent, but he'd still have a fool for a client," Cole corrected.

"Studying is very important for us lowlifes who don't have daddy's money," Seth started, and Cole stuck out her tongue without even looking up from her phone. "Or have a sweet deal playing video games."

"Urg." Owen leaned back into his seat. "I don't even want to talk about it. Do you ever think something is going to be fucking awesome, and then it's just hell?"

"Yep," Seth said, as he made another turn. "Took E without prepping once, was god awful."

Owen laughed, and shook his head. "Thank you, that was a beautiful and moving comparison."

"Not a problem."

Parking was less of a worry then Owen would have figured. Seth found a paid parking garage so the walk to the cafe in question wasn't too far. Only a block or so.

The Common Grounds logo on the tinted window hid any indication of how packed the place would be. They bottled up together just inside the door, and looked into the full room. Chairs and tables sat in front of the stage, and farther back couches served as not only more seats, but a divider from the rest of the store.

"Oh, I see a spot!" Nicole took off and headed towards the back. She asked a couple if they could scoot to one side of the couch. Without a word they moved over, but she didn't sit down right away. Maybe because it only looked like enough room for two. Unless one of them was planning to stand, this spot wasn't really workable. Owen's thoughts must have been written on his face because Nicole's bright expression dimmed. "*Sit.*"

Owen sat down first, and Seth took the sliver of space left next to the arm. Just what he thought—not enough. Cole sat down on the arm and draped her legs over Seth's lap so they weren't in the way of anyone. Owen glanced down at her galaxy converses. Oh, that did work.

"We'll get started in ten," a woman at the mic announced, flashing her hands to show ten minutes like one might for kindergartners.

"So, when is the big fictional reveal?" Seth asked, while Cole watched the speaker step down.

"Couple weeks," Owen said, "They are doing some publicity before the launch party. fnVR is going to tie it in with a historical world event to really stir up some attention."

"That's awesome."

"It's alright."

Seth pressed his lips together, and glanced away as someone walked too close on their way to get to the rest of the cafe. "You love Age of Shadows, why aren't you excited?"

"I have to work with my ex."

"Andreah?"

Owen nodded.

"That bites."

"Hey, I'm getting coffee," Cole interrupted, "Do either of you want anything?"

"Coffee sounds great," Owen said, as Cole swung her legs to the floor.

"Can you get me a smoothie?" Seth asked.

"You have no respect for the name of this fine establishment," she teased, before walking off to place their orders. There didn't seem to be a line, but it took so long to get back with the drinks that the event was introduced, and the first poet went up. It was an older woman who read an erotic poem to a room full of twenties-somethings. Strange, but any objections were made in hushed tones.

Nicole handed a Styrofoam cup to Owen, keeping the other in her hand since there was no patch of table anywhere for them. "Hold on, I have to go back for the damn smoothie," she whispered, so she wouldn't talk over the emcee. When she came back for the second time her lips were over the bright orange straw that was stuck in a pink smoothie. "Mmm, this is so fucking good."

"No trades," Seth said, smiling as he held his hand out.

She handed it off and carefully sat down on the arm of the couch again, this time letting her legs hang over the other side. A band got up to play and a few in the crowd sprung to their feet. What started as a cheer soon turned into full fan mode as mid-song they stood on chairs to get a better photo. The whole audience wasn't excited, but the front row was hyped as fuck.

"Thank you, Stage Against The Machine," the emcee chuckled to herself getting the pun, before introducing the next person up to the mic.

Owen's coffee finally felt cool enough between his hands to try a drink. He took a small sip, and instantly his expression went askew.

"How is it?" Cole asked, speaking softly as someone read a poem off their phone.

"Bitter."

"I meant the coffee, not you."

Owen opened his mouth to object, but glanced over to the poet realizing now wasn't the time to disagree. By time there was a break where he could talk without being rude, it felt too out of the blue to bring it up again.

A new girl stepped up, hands nervously adjusting the mic. She looked just barely old enough to be allowed in a place that served alcohol. The overhead light harshly showed that her long hair had been dyed several times. Nothing too out there as she stuck to close shades of brown and red.

"I fall to my hands and knees, eyes lifting to the skies to let out a howl," she started reading, eyes never glancing up to the crowd. "A prayer to the moon for a change in the tides. I don't know if my constant companion can hear me, but it is always there even in the light.

"The constellations above hold stories and promises of those guided before. Such visions light years away now as I fear that their brightness has already died. Their light now a siren that calls people to the darkness."

"Hey man," someone close-by said. Owen glanced over to a guy in a beanie, but the stranger's attention was solely on Seth. "Do you have anything?"

"Pick yourself up, fall back down, pick yourself up, fall back down." The words from the microphone easily carried louder than the misplaced question.

"Do I look like I do?" Seth said. Cole slid down fully into his lap, currently looking over her shoulder to the stranger. Seth however, didn't stand out in any notable way. "You know I don't deal here."

"A timer that ticks as it counts off each hit the drugged masses can take." Owen glanced over at the speaker, her words a world apart and yet... "This land is filled with its own loops. Eat, work, sleep. The world's cycle moves so much slower than the gears in my head. With no tangible prize besides making our hearts beat faster."

"Right, sorry," the guy said with a little nod, anxiously rubbing a hand over his forearm. After a slight hesitation he wandered off.

"I fuck'n tell ya," Seth mumbled to himself.

Owen leaned forward in his seat watching silently. He didn't see where the guy went, but he did spot someone smoking outside. "I'm going to go smoke," he declared, and headed outside catching the end of the poem on the way.

"Tragic tales, and noble narratives of past successes and failures, that we hope will entitle us to the same divine right. My name is Andromeda, chained to these rocks as the tides ebb and flow."

An act or so later, Cole came out too. "I have a question for you," she said, sidestepping around the man watching the door.

"Shoot."

"When did you start smoking again?" Nicole leaned against a patch of wall away from the window next to him.

Owen carefully watched her as he exhaled a plume of cigarette smoke. "Recently," he said. She raised a brow, but didn't any say anything more. "Should I share?"

"Nah, that shit will kill you."

He grinned.

"What?"

Owen took a final drag before knocking the ashes off. Carefully, he tapped the lit end against his finger to put it out. It wasn't an instant thing, but it worked, and he didn't burn himself. "Should I go back to smoking what you guys do?"

"Um, yeah," Nicole continued as Owen brushed his finger clean. "Weed is a bronchodilator. Tobacco only hecks up the works."

"Is that true?"

"You are a researcher, look it up."

Owen broke into a smile. "Putting your classes to good use?"

"Nah, I watch a lot of documentaries. All my textbooks are outdated, they still think Christopher Columbus was a cool dude." Nicole reached her hand out for his, leaning on one foot to suggest they go back inside. He took her hand and headed to the door without any resistance, except a minor detour to throw away his cigarette.

After two weeks of endless arguing over the recap episodes, Daniel's story was about to hit the internet. It also marked Owen's first night of live streaming. An unnerving task, as if his past life would be on display. Everything would be out in public, every personal moment, every stupid thing that was said. He was a bone digger, for fuck's sake. He needed privacy to expose secrets, but now his own game experiences were out there for everyone else to judge.

Tonight fnVR was hosting a party, mostly for press, to introduce Owen and Andreah as their newest sponsored players. So much hype and money was put into this warm welcome. A far warmer welcome than begrudgingly signing contracts.

Owen felt like making a run for it until he spotted Neal and Charlie. Their presence anchored him, and at times gave the appearance that he was socializing.

"I got completely rekted this morning while playing," Neal said, "by a dude I don't even remember starting problems with. He sure was pissed at me, though."

"That is why we stick to the tenets," Charlie chuckled, trying not to be too amused with another Neal death story. "Killing rashly is practically asking for it to come back around."

Their conversations were short lived, since Owen couldn't go long without being interrupted by other party goers. Then there was the press.

Oh god, the press. He had evaded them for so long when first getting two NPCs. And if he stayed close enough to the office he could duck in and continue avoiding them. That is, until they started camping outside.

The only person he hadn't caught sight of was Andreah. Curiosity mixed with an acceptance of his fate resulted in him touring around the room. Thankfully, a popular player in the area, SniperV, showed up and shifted everyone's attention. Owen had been curious of the man behind the avatar, who drew attention towards himself like a neon light in a crowd of moths. His volume, style, and attitude all suggested a star. Or more that he was going to ride his privilege up to the top, and everyone else seemed vaguely okay with as long as he was entertaining. Within fifteen minutes, Owen heard the origin story about the username three times. It wasn't even a good story. He'd been a sniper and the fifth member on a professional FPS clan back in the day. Yet everyone seemed to love it.

Owen separated himself from the crowd as much as he could. Even if it meant walking over to the dreaded gaming area. Here only Carmen buzzed around as she finished setting everything up. This spot wasn't much better. He could see both the party goers and a media line with other sponsored celebrities whose interviews were being streamed.

He was still wandering around the room, hoping to get lost more than anything else, when he noticed someone that looked like Andreah. If anyone had been fighting for his attention, he would have missed the woman in a long shimmery black and gold dress with a low cut back. It was by far the fanciest thing he'd seen Andreah in. Even her hair was styled to a new extreme, emphasized by the fact she had shaved one side of her head.

Every day he was looking at a different version of her. His heart ached for the bike messenger in reflector yellow.

Andreah was tucked away with a beer in hand, talking to a girl he recognized as Abigail. Her name was easy to remembered since his secrets had been meant for her. Owen approached slowly, like he was a crasher to his own party.

Andreah turned to look at him with a huge, bright smile. "Hey! How's it going?"

It was a change from their new usual of 'exes who were both too stubborn to quit their jobs.' But to be expected in this setting, really. They couldn't appear dysfunctional on day one. "It's uh, pretty okay. How about you?" Owen looked over at Abigail, who offered a softer smile, and gave her a nod hello. "It's nice to see you again."

Andreah lifted her drink up, sloshing what was left of it around in the bottle. "It's good so far."

He glanced at Abigail again, taking a breath to gauge the moment before proceeding. "I've been meaning to talk about something. Do you have a second?"

Abigail cleared her throat, giving her friend a look to make sure it was okay. "I'll get us some more drinks."

"Thanks, Abby," Andreah said, before looking at Owen. "What's up?"

"Um, I know we haven't really talked about anything of real importance in like weeks." Owen ran his hand through his hair, certainly messing up the carefully sculpted shape they wanted for photos. "Sometimes I feel like I was pushed into this, that I have no privacy anymore, but then I remember you tried to protect that at the end. And I guess, I just wanted you to know that I meant to thank you."

She gave him a small nod before taking an abrupt chug of her drink. "I get it." She considered leaving it at that at first, but she decided to go on. "Look, we don't need to repair things. You don't have to learn to bear my existence. And you don't have to thank me for being a decent person when I end up being one. Because I don't need the validation."

She lifted the bottle again to her lips, so Owen figured he had a chance to speak. "I never meant to—"

"I was more than okay with how things ended. You don't need to treat me any differently just because we're stuck working together now." Her eyes hadn't moved from his the entire time. "I don't have the time or energy to focus on more than our work, so let's just focus on that. Not trying to be friends again."

"Right." Funny, how quick and easy the word came, when it wasn't right at all.

"How are my two stars?" Chris called from steps away as he walked over. He didn't wait to for an answer, or even to take a second to notice the awkwardness that was ready to smother the whole area. "We're ready to do the interviews, please come with me."

Andreah abandoned her drink on the table she was leaning against, and was the first to follow after Chris. Owen lagged, needing a moment to recover. No one seemed to notice as they reached the staged-off area. Andreah paused, then turned to Abby to ask how she looked. Or at least that's what he gathered as she messed with her hair and tugged on her dress.

He got lost in the bursts of gold on the long dress, fireworks of glitter pulling his attention away from the person who putting a mic on him. Carmen patted him on the shoulder once finished. "Alright, all set. Do you need anything?"

"Uh, water. Please?"

She nodded and swiftly grabbed a nearby bottle, handing it off. He took a few sips before turning to look for his own friends. He spotted Charlie and Neal off behind the imaginary 'employees only' line. They must have seen him head towards the stage. His fingers rose to mess with his tie, wishing they let him keep his jacket so he had somewhere to put his hands besides the pockets of his slacks.

Andreah fell into place next to him as they waited for the previous interview to end. Despite their proximity, the two virtually looked through each other. When called to go on stage, Owen and Andreah stepped off at the same time, nearly bumping into each other. He ended up letting her take point.

"I'd like to welcome Alexander Owen and Andreah Bourne, the players behind Daniel and Amilia." The speaker, Noah, was instantly recognizable to anyone who watched gaming events. He never streamed, instead opted to make his own news channel that garnered a ton of attention from the community. If there was a conference that had to do with MMO or PC gaming, he was there as an honored guest. Made sense, since the guy had the charisma of a used car salesman that you couldn't help but trust.

Noah came over to their side of the stage and offered a hand to Andreah, assisting her with the walk over to the seats as Owen helped himself. There was another woman on stage. She had bright pink hair, but Owen didn't know her despite what seemed like a clue. Maybe a blogger?

Andreah gave the camera a wave and winning smile as the clapping and cheers erupted from the crowd. It was a loud reminder that Owen needed to wear a smile as well.

"So, hello! How have you been enjoying the night so far?" Noah asked.

Andreah gave a glance over to Owen, offering the chance to respond first. He'd rather let her, but since everyone was waiting, he spoke. "It's really been something else. Everyone is so excited to see the story."

"Oh, we definitely are," the woman a few seats down chimed in. Owen took a second to glance at the playback monitors and saw her name was Zoey. "We'll jump right into the questions, since right after we're done you'll be playing Age of Shadows for us. The biggest thing about you is that you have two companions. So many people try to get one, and even that doesn't always work out. How did you manage it?"

"It was kind of dumb luck. No one even knew you could have two. Amilia just sort of fell into my lap, and I was lucky enough that she decided to stick around."

"Man, I wish you didn't make it sound so easy," Noah said, with a breathless laugh. "Why did you end up keeping it such a huge secret? You could have had, like, ten sponsorships by now."

Owen fidgeted; maybe for a little too long, since Andreah ended up answering for him. "Lance and Amilia are two very important characters to Daniel, and Owen. He didn't want to make the game something more than the experience."

"Spoken like a true roleplayer," Noah commented. "I hear we won't be seeing Amilia tonight. You're the player behind Amilia though, correct?"

"In part," Andreah said. "Amilia is a special case. All non-player characters are pre-programmed to, well, act human. She existed before me, but I definitely took a shine to her. And now Amilia is mapped to me like any other player character would be."

"Funny how that happened," Owen added, grinning the brightest he had since coming on the stage. Andreah laughed like it was an inside joke.

Zoey leaned forward, clearly knowing she missed something, and looked over to Noah in case he understood. "What do you mean?"

"Hmm?" Owen turned to look at her as innocent as an angel might. "Nothing. I love your hair by the way. My friend has the same color. It looks just as stunning on you."

"Oh." Zoey's blush added a bit more pink to her face and a hand reached up to her hair. "Thank you."

"Alright, lady killer, next question," Noah said, "Roleplaying has never been as big as competitive matches on Age of Shadows, how do you feel about taking it mainstream?"

"It's pretty exciting. There's so much story everyone at fnVR puts into the game and it's a shame so many people pass over it," Andreah fawned.

"I used to think roleplaying was a dirty word to some gamers. It'd be nice to not have to hear another 'one v. one me bro' for a while," Owen joked. It was unlike him to make those kinds of comments, but he slowly felt himself slipping into the shoes he needed to fill.

"So Amilia is special, but what about other players? Could they ever get NPCs that become tailored to them?" Zoey asked.

"Lance, for example," Noah quickly added. The name caught Owen's attention, and he glanced over to Carmen who flipped through her clipboard as if that was not agreed upon.

"There are no plans to make that a feature," Andreah said without losing a beat. "Age of Shadows is still quite proud of their current system."

"Alright, last question before we let you play, and show us what we've all been waiting for," Zoey said, determined to get the last one in. "What is it like collaborating together on such an expansive story?"

Andreah simply turned to Owen, waiting for him to answer. It was like she wanted to test if there were any more smart comments he might still have in him. And he stared back as if daring her, too.

"It's a hell of a ride," he said to Andreah, before looking back at the reporters and checking if that answer was acceptable. Andreah smiled as she moved her hand to gently pat his back. All of it was one giant show, but the touch was too far. Owen ground down his complaint between his teeth. There was no room to complain right now.

"Thank you so much for your time. Now we'll take a short break as Owen gets ready, but stay tuned for an exclusive sneak peek of the Treaty of London. Sure to change things up for every player."

Andreah waved again, and Owen forced a smile before the red light on the cameras switch off. She was up first as Owen watched the monitors for a moment longer until they switched to a logo of Age of Shadows.

"It's so nice to meet both of you." The smile Andreah plastered on for the two reporters was too big.

"Do you have Twitter, or anything else I can add you on? I'd definitely love to stay in contact, if that's okay," Zoey said.

"Oh, yeah. I'll give you whatever you'd like," Andreah said. "And definitely follow back."

Owen watched their exchange with disdain until he realized Carmen was trying to get his attention. He held his hands up, feeling like he should help her take off the mic, but she did it so fast all he could do was stand still. "Thanks," he mumbled.

Once he stepped off the stage, he was free of obligations. At least for three minutes or so. He found Charlie leaning against a patch of wall. Neal wasn't in sight, but Owen assumed he was trying to meet new people. There wasn't much room, but what Charlie had, they shared.

"This is your big night, and frankly it's fucking awesome in here," Charlie said, but Owen didn't see it. He glanced around the room, to all the sponsored gear they brought in, then to multiple stations they set up in what had been a shared study only days before. The people were electric and the tech was alive. It really was something. "So, why do you look like someone ran over your pet."

"I don't."

Charlie raised a brow, and Owen instantly shut up. Since his friend wasn't going to give him room to lie, he might as well go with the truth.

"I don't think I am the person they think I am. Or the person I need to be to pull this off. I can't just pull on whatever mask I need so people only see what they want. I only have one mask. It's Daniel. I don't think he's the straight white hero they are looking for."

Charlie tilted their head, and swayed to look over at the fnVR executives. "Would that be a problem?"

"I have no clue." He and Charlie had been standing close, close enough to talk to each other in hushed voices that wouldn't carry in a room so filled with noise.

"Hmm." Charlie squished up their face as if trying to figure the answer out by simply miming their curiosity. "Lance, right?"

"What?"

"Daniel loves Lance, right?"

Owen glanced around like he was being watched, then remembered he actually was, and tried to casually look ahead again. "Did Neal tell you that?"

Charlie rolled their eyes. They made no rush to finish before speaking. "I'm asexual, not blind."

"What?" Owen shook his head. Blurting disbelief in such a distasteful way was starting to sound rude. "I didn't know that."

"Should you have?"

Owen was so dumbfounded that he couldn't even manage to get a syllable out. Charlie laughed. "My point is, it doesn't

306

matter. If you want you can tell everyone you can. If you aren't comfortable telling people, you don't have to. Visibility is important, but so are you. Being open about it is one of the few choices you have in the matter."

"What would you do?"

Charlie put their drink down, and raised both their hands up to give the bird. "Screw heteronormativity, is what I always say."

"I've never heard you say that," Owen laughed.

"Oh," Charlie grinned, and picked up their drink again. They looked a little disappointed it was empty, but that was the only thing not going for them tonight. "That's because I normally assume straight people are around."

"Yeah, show me your O-face!" SniperV yelled loud enough from a group of arena fighters that both Owen and Charlie looked over. That group was clearly only here because it was the place to be tonight.

"Like that guy." Charlie whistled their disappointment. "Embarrassing."

Owen laughed again, and Charlie swung their free arm over Owen's shoulder. "You got nothing to be embarrassed about. Least of all anyone's sexuality," Charlie said. "Now go knock them dead."

"Thanks." After talking to Andreah, he felt a little stupid for saying the word again to anyone.

"What are friends for? Oh!" Charlie suddenly pulled their arm back, and dug out their phone. "Emily wanted me to record a first-hand account of everything since she had to stay home with the baby."

"Why didn't she get Neal to do it?"

Charlie held their phone out and looked at Owen through it. "She thought he'd be too distracted. Now say hi."

"Love you, Em," he said, and blew a kiss.

For a second, Owen had forgotten there was any other camera besides Charlie's. But the flashes of much larger cameras and shouts from reporters asking who he was talking to made quick work to remind him.

"See, nothing to worry about," Charlie said, having to raise their voice now to be heard. "The camera loves you."

"Owen, are you ready?" Carmen was suddenly at his elbow, all too ready and eager to usher him over to play. He nodded, and found even newer headgear waiting for him. The most notable difference was the visor wasn't tinted. Likely a marketing effect to make him more personable.

Everything in his life and the game had been different lately, but at least this headgear booted the same way. First in the hand, then stretching out in his fingers. Lights outlining London appeared on top of the real world until it was all fully rendered within seconds.

Meeting the King was by far the loftiest thing a thief without noble blood could ever expect. Daniel stared at the guards that protected the Somerset House with Lance and Chloe at his side. This day had massive importance, not only for him, but for several countries. Treaties would be signed today.

Everyone was a little nervous. There was a current in the air. Within the last year, Britain crowned a new King, and everyone wondered how well he could handle it. No one said so, of course.

The trio walked around the building at a safe distance, trying to find the best way in. One entrance had a single guard posted, and looked like their best opportunity. "How do you want to go about this?" Daniel asked, and glanced over to Lance.

"Leave it to me, boys." Chloe grinned, and strolled up to the man protecting the door. "Hello," she said in English. The guard blinked wordlessly at her, and she did a small curtsy. She leaned in like she had a secret. Her eyes flickered to the building behind them, and flush of red rose on his cheeks.

The boys were too far away to hear everything, but when Chloe and the guard went inside they turned to look at each other. "What did she tell him?"

Lance looked equally as surprised. "I don't think I want to know."

Not more than a minute later, Chloe popped back up by the doorway and waved them in. The boys sprinted in, not wanting to be caught by anyone else. Once inside, the guard was notably absent.

"What happened to him?" Daniel asked.

"Oh, I locked him in the closet," she said simply, before glancing down the hall. "I think we should go that way." She ran now to the nearest corner and paused to peek around it. Lance grinned, and took a step to follow, but Daniel tugged on his arm to hold him back.

"You are going to get her killed."

"What?" Lance asked. "Did you miss how helpful she just was?"

"Send her away."

"No." His brows knitted together, oblivious to the problem. "What do you want me to do, ship her back home?"

"Yes, actually."

Lance sighed. He looked away to see if Chloe was still waiting for them, and feared she wouldn't wait long enough for him to say what he needed to. "It's fine. You can't live life like everyone is going to die or betray you."

The color drained out of Daniel's face.

"I'm sorry, but it's true," Lance said. "Come on, *amant,* if you can't trust yourself, trust me." Lance gave him a careful look as he slowly stepped away and headed towards Chloe.

Daniel swore his ears were ringing, but he couldn't stand around and be shocked. If he wanted everything to go smoothly he had to carry on. He had to trust Lance, and despite trusting him the most, it still was hard to do. After cursing under his breath, he followed.

Despite his having no direct or indirect control over Chloe, she listened to his orders quite well. The only time she disobeyed was to hide when needed. They blended in with various guests, and Chloe stayed close, keeping an ear open.

"The King should be coming this way soon," a noblewoman said, looking to impress the others of equal status around. Daniel signaled for Lance to break off so they could check it out. The only slight hiccup was Chloe's second of confusion before she took a quick double step to follow. Days ago, that would have annoyed Daniel. Now it only made him smile. Despite his best efforts, Chloe was growing on him.

Since their duty wasn't to harm the King once he was in line of sight, they kept a respectable distance. They held back, claiming a bench for themselves. A man caught Daniel's attention as he nervously glanced back every few steps.

"I think we have an intruder," Daniel said.

When the King turned a corner, the man broke rank completely. They had to act fast. Daniel's eyes darted around trying to think of the best way, which seemed up and over a tall wall of an enclosed garden. "I'll go up, you go around," Daniel ordered, and was up and over in the time it took to give the command.

The intruder they had been following pulled out a dagger and took careful steps to sneak up on the King. Lance was almost in position to interrupt, but Daniel jumped down in-between the would-be killer and royal.

King James stumbled back, filled with panic as a bunch of foreigners seemed to appear from thin air and started to spill blood just as fast. Daniel's hands were covered in it as he stepped away from a man he just killed.

"We are here to help," Lance said, and brought his hands up to try to defuse the situation. But the words weren't understood.

Chloe rushed in last. She needed to catch her breath, but didn't have the time. "Your highness, these are the men sent from Spain. To protect you and this treaty." Her English was certainly something he could understand. "They mean you no harm."

The King's personal guards rushed in far too late to be of use. Chloe let out a small nervous sound as the guards pointed their swords at the lot of them.

"At ease," the King said, taking a good look at the trio that saved his life seconds before he knew it was in danger.

He gave a curt nod towards the man on the ground. "You are unusual delegates, but thank you. It seems our countries still may come to an agreement after all."

In the days after the launch party, everything boiled down to waiting. The 'leave' Owen was given from NY Today had come and gone, and now he was left to juggle both. Days were spent at the newspaper and afterward he headed to fnVR. Thanks to them, he didn't need the extra money, from either the paper or bone digging gigs, but he refused to drop the ball on either. Nor was he was the only one holding on to their old job. By the look of Andreah's riding outfit, she had gone back to her day job, too.

Their office phone rarely rang. If it did, it was usually Jorge. Andreah always answered like it was a mini-game to persistently to annoy the man. When it rang today, Owen continued to ignore it.

"Insert Credits? Yeah, I've heard of your place," Andreah said, as she twirled the coiled phone cord in her hand. "Tonight? Uh, I'm not sure. Let me check." Owen had already looked up at her when she moved the receiver away from her face. "There's a happy hour going on at an arcade bar on West 24th. They're wondering if we'd like to attend as honored guests."

Owen held out his hand for the phone, which meant Andreah had to pick up the base and carry it over to him.

Once he was on the line, he cleared his throat. "Hello, this is Owen."

"Hey, Owen! Nice to talk to you. We were wondering if you'd like to come by tonight to our arcade. We've been playing the live streams of Daniel's story and would love to have both you and Andreah attend as a surprise. Your night will be on us."

Owen was pretty sure he'd heard of the place before, but hadn't ever had the chance to stop by. "Sure, why not. What time should we be there?"

"Nine should be good. We're so excited to have you."

"No problem, see you then." Owen handed the phone back to Andreah, who returned the entire assembly back to the desk it belonged on. She mumbled something that sounded like a curse as she walked over to her bag.

"What's that?" he asked, his eyes following her.

"Nothing. I was just hoping I could depend on you to keep this a boring night, as usual."

Owen ignored the backhanded insult for the sake of not ruining the entire conversation. "You could just not go if you don't want to."

"And let it look like I'm the boring one? Nah son." She pulled a skirt and crop top out of her bag. The wrinkles hinted it had been in there all week in case of situations like this. "I wonder if anyone has an iron." When they shared a cab to the arcade, splitting the fare so evenly it was almost suspicious. Owen even held the door for her as they walked in. The atmosphere wasn't anything like a surprise party, which was a relief to them both. That didn't mean they were anonymous however. A girl, who looked just old enough to serve the drinks, bounced over to them so fast that she must have been waiting. "Hey! Owen and Andreah, right?" Andreah nodded with an awkward smile as she clutched her purse. "Awesome, well, I'm Jamie. We reserved a table for you. Carl is over at the bar. Let him know you arrived so he can get your drinks going, and if you need any tokens. You're welcome to help yourself to all our games." She walked them over to their booth. The seats had high enough backs someone could stand on the seat and still not match their height.

"Thanks," Owen said, and glanced at the table that had a large screen with game systems hooked up somewhere. The only way he could tell was the controllers sitting there. He made a hum of approval towards Andreah before leading them to the bar.

"Hi! I'm the guy who called you," said who Owen guessed was Carl. "Where's Andreah?"

Owen thought she was following. He glanced away from the white countertop that was currently glowing blue. She had somehow disappeared into thin air. "She's here, just...not here."

"Well, alright," he chuckled. "What can I get you two?"

"Uh, a Dos Equis for Andreah, and you can just surprise me."

Once he got the drinks, he turned to look at the number of people he'd have to mingle with the rest of the night. It was busy, with a solid mass of people both hanging out by a DJ and moving around the maze of arcade games. Everyone seemed to be enjoying themselves. There didn't seem to be a need to put on a show. He smiled to himself. This was doable.

Even better, he spotted Andreah by an old school Asteroids game. She was watching the current player like a hawk, already wanting to jump on. It was an odd change, since she hadn't seemed up for going out before.

"Here," Owen said once he reached her, and handed over her beer.

She looked at the beer, at him, then back at the beer. "Oh. Thanks," she said softly, blinking a few times before reaching out to take it. Owen couldn't make sense of her confusion for a second. Without thinking, he had remembered her favorite beer and brought it to her without being asked.

He narrowed his eyes at the awkwardness before just sidestepping the whole situation to find his own retro love. It took a little bit of wandering before he found it. But there it was. The black-lit beauty that is a 1982 Tron game. No one was occupying it at the moment, so the temptation was all too easily indulged. He retrieved a few quarters from his pocket and dropped them into the machine. The click of the coins traveling before the game musically registered the credit was a welcome and nearly forgotten sound. He wore an even smile as he abandoned his drink at his feet and played.

After many, many rounds, someone called next game. His demise came from clearing too many grid bugs and running out of time. Unable to play again, he decided to walk around and see the rest of the place. If he wasn't there more or less alone, he would have sat down to enjoy the view rather than searching for new entertainment.

Over the loud music, a good Bastille song at that, he could hear Andreah's voice before he caught sight of her.

"No, that's completely the wrong tactic. You two need to keep up with each other. You can't just jump around all willy nilly. You need to find the sweet spot where nothing hits you."

"If you think you know so much," some guy said, after she berated his Contra gameplay, "prove it."

"I don't have a second player I can trust."

Owen lingered around them for a moment longer before deciding to step forward. "I'll play."

Andreah looked over her shoulder, raising her eyebrows as if to ask 'seriously?' Owen nodded as he looked at his new opponents.

"Fine. Challengers go first," Andreah said, as she stepped to the side.

"So, I'm guessing you'll take Lance?" Andreah quipped after the other team started to play. A mere coincidence of character names was apparently hilarious to her.

"So, I'm guessing your sense of humor is rusty?" Owen countered. A player two joke was such a low bar.

She lifted her chin. "You liked it once upon a time."

"I trusted you once upon a time."

Their opponents snickered, making it easier for Andreah to keep the offense from showing as she straightened her posture. "Look, if you're going to—"

"I just want to play," Owen cut her off. He didn't want this to become something else, especially here and now. Andreah seemed to agree. She settled for crossing her arms and watching the game.

Once they finished, Andreah clapped at the men's somewhat valiant efforts. They messed up during the fire pipes by rushing around too much. By their sour looks as Owen and Andreah took their places, they knew it too.

Owen was uncertain if they would fare any better. "We could really use the Konami Code right now," he said, despite picking up a gun that sprayed multiple bullets at once.

"It's okay. We got this."

He stole a glance over at her, wasting a second with a surprise that turned into renewed confidence that was better than any power up. *"Plus ça change."*

Andreah dared to look away from the screen, a dangerous move since there were turrets shooting at them. Owen didn't have to look away to feel her question. "The more things change," he said, jumping up to a higher level of the map, "the more they stay the same."

Her attention snapped back to the game as she escaped the part of their world where his words existed. If he had looked at her, he would have seen the warm pink that brushed her cheeks.

"Y'all are gonna lose if you keep talking to each other," one of the guys piped up over their shoulders.

"Yeah, Owen. You're gonna make us lose," Andreah said sarcastically. They were actually doing very well so far, despite what the guy thought.

"Maybe I will," Owen said, before reaching over to jerk her joystick around.

"Hey! The hell, man." Andreah recovered quickly enough to avoid death, her hip bumping into Owen as a weak attempt to push him away. "If you throw this game, you're dead."

"Okay, okay." Owen said with a smile. "Just keeping things fun."

"Focus," Andreah said, before she picked up the flamethrower by accident. No one should actually ever want the thing. It had no distance.

They made it safely past where their opponents died, and could have called it good. But from the look on Andreah's face, she was in it to go beyond winning it. She wanted to make it to the end. It was amazing watching the predictive nature of her play style. Owen guessed that she had played enough times to know what part of the screen the next enemies were coming from. She shot there before they even appeared.

They made it to the mouth of the final area, quite literally since they faced a toothed maw that released small enemies. Andreah looked ready to break off the buttons with her urgency. Owen grinned a little at her competitive flare, wondering why she wasn't a PvP player on AoS with that kind of energy.

When they stepped away, the credits started scrolling and Andreah was beaming. "Fuck yeah!"

Their competition shared a grumble, and fled before Andreah could trash talk them. With no one besides Owen to gloat to, she threw her arms around him.

He took a step back in surprise as she seemingly came out of nowhere, since he'd been staring at the screen in disbelief. It was impossible not to laugh at it all and give her a celebratory hug back. "I thought this game would have a kill screen."

The comment sobered Andreah's excitement slightly as she stepped away. "You never beat it before?"

"I always die right after the pixeled wannabe jock throws shit at me."

Andreah stared, wide-eyed at him. Long enough that it started to make him nervous. "You little devil!" She tapped him on the arm. "Look at you, hotshot."

Owen laughed again. "I guess we make a good team."

Some parkour was just practice. You had to train and work towards being able to control your movements. But some moves were also a matter of commitment. The gym's fourteen-foot warped wall was one such feat. Charlie ran up three-quarters of the wall in only two steps before jumping to reach the ledge above. Once on top, they moved back to make room on the platform. "Tonight's a big night for the stream, isn't it?"

"Yep," Owen said, without paying too much attention. But it was still somehow too much of his focus. He ran up the wall, but even three steps didn't give him enough boost before he had to bail and slide back down. Owen bounced on his feet to shake off the attempt, and glanced up to Charlie. "There's going to be a guest NPC and everything."

"London is treating you well I see."

Owen ran up the wall again, with solid footing this time, and within seconds was above it all with Charlie. London was alright, but he really didn't want to talk about it. "How's Spain?"

"Pretty good," Charlie said, "Luca is fun to play. She's a different class, but I doubt that's why people treat her differently than Lucas."

"What do you mean?"

Charlie scrunched up their nose debating if they wanted to explain this. "People hit on Luca more," they said, hoping that would explain everything.

Owen took a second. The game's population was mostly female, so you'd think that would prevent some things—like female passing characters being aggressively hit on—but apparently not. Another problem was that Owen didn't know what to say about it. That never happened with Daniel. "No romance for the thieves guild newest, I take it?"

"None for me, nor Luca," Charlie said. "Gotta try to cosmically balance out Daniel's all-consuming romantic attraction."

"How sweet of you." Owen slid down the warped wall again, and got up with a few quick steps.

Charlie sat down on the ledge. "Where are you going?"

"It's past five. I'm gonna be late to fnVR if I don't head over now."

"Oh." Charlie glanced about the gym, wondering if they wanted to hang out here or call it as well. "You should have done a flip and made it interesting for me."

Owen turned around to face Charlie, and placed a hand over his heart. "I'll try to do one tonight, and you'll know that flip was for you."

"Get out of here." Charlie gestured towards the door and laughed. "Happy streaming."

A single taxi ride over and Owen was greeted with a definite "you're late" from Andreah. She didn't have to stream tonight, but she did have to be here. Maybe even more to her annoyance was he wasn't late. There was still another two minutes before he had to log in.

"Oh really, Miss Bourne," Owen said, mirroring the same inflection Jorge had when he said it. It pissed her off every time, and he noticed. "Thank you for the update."

Andreah grabbed her soda, only to frown when it was nearly empty. "Fuck you, Owen."

He gestured up to the headset that was already on. "I'm sorry, can't right now. I don't want to be late."

God dammit, walked into that one. Despite herself, Andreah grinned over at him, thankful he couldn't see.

The fact that Daniel seemed stuck in London for a while was much to the chagrin of Spanish players. Suddenly the game was being promoted, and suddenly events were no longer on their turf. It was a valid concern, but for Owen it was a nice change of pace. It was easier to play without Amilia in a city that didn't remind him that she was missing. When Daniel, Lance, and Chloe got a place together in Britain, some feared the move would be permanent.

A uniquely British attraction was the Globe Theatre, where it cost only a penny to go in and see a play. Chloe was the only proper one of the trio, while Daniel and Lance took the less conventional approach and climbed the building.

The building had a circular roof that lined the edges, but otherwise was open to the air. Daniel slid down the inner slope of the roof, grabbing the ledge, and dropped onto the top floor. Definitely more fun than paying at the box office. He heard someone else land, and grinned at what surely had to be Lance.

There were people on the stage, but the lack of costume suggested they were just practicing. Daniel explored for the simple pleasure of looking around until a yell shattered his pleasure.

"Thief!" The cry came from below, and Daniel rushed to the railing to see what was going on. The yell came from a gentleman with a high collar and a neatly trimmed beard. The boys exchanged looks before springing into action. Lance ran across the top level, while Daniel climbed down the banister before jumping to the ground.

The thief in question was getting close to the door. The man's tunic bore no guild or country markings, meaning he was simply stealing. Daniel stood up, and threw a knife that implanted itself into the door as the man reached for it.

"Your naïveté at stealing shows," Lance said, as the bandit jumped back. Papers were clutched in the his hands.

Any tighter and they'd be crushed. Nervous eyes darted up to see Lance perched above like a gargoyle.

When the man didn't budge, Daniel walked over and grabbed the papers out of his hands. "Be gone," Daniel said, waving his free hand. The man stumbled towards the door, spending too much time watching Lance twirl a knife in his hands.

"Thank the heavens you saved my newest creation!" Chloe was standing next to the man who spoke, likely trying to put him at ease. He looked eternally grateful as he went on. "I don't know what I'd do if I lost Othello before I even finished it."

"You're Shakespeare," Daniel blurted. He looked down at the pages of the play and quickly moved to give them back.

"I see my reputation precedes me," the playwright said, and smiled down the pages as he tenderly smoothed them out. "It hasn't even been performed yet. Without you, it might have never be shown to the King."

Owen played for few more hours, and when he logged out he found Andreah sitting across from him with a headset on. He walked over to stand behind her to watch. It was clear he missed a bit, probably several scenes that explained what happened to Amilia, but what he did see made him uneasy.

Amilia looked like she could disappear. The corset she wore looked like the only bones that held her together. Her starved body was in stark contrast to the expensive clothes she was adorned in. Owen immediately recognized the area she was in, though. The dark London streets gave Amilia a quiet place to walk as she was escorted by an older man. Amilia looked sick at his mere touch, but didn't cower. Her strength was lost, replaced with a hollowed expression that was as significant as any change in her.

They moved into a building, and the man removed his coat the moment they entered, obviously feeling at home. Amilia drifted in, but stopped short of the bedroom. "I'm going to change for bed."

"Very well," the man agreed, as if to give her permission. Once Amilia closed the door, he seemed to contemplate something as he poured himself some wine. "You were quiet at dinner. A terrible guest, really. It's very rude to ignore the hostess the way you did."

Amilia stayed silent in her room. The NPC lagged outside the door for a moment before taking the liberty to enter without an announcement. Amilia flinched as she pulled on her nightgown quicker. "My apologies, Señor Viktor."

"Are you not thankful for all that I am doing for you?" he asked, advancing toward her. He stood before her, looming in a way that Amilia had grown too familiar with. She shook her head, whispering small words to assure him the opposite. The hand that wasn't holding the wine glass raised to brush her cheek before moving back quickly to hold the nape of her neck, and pulled her hair roughly. "Start acting like it, my dear."

Andreah just barely waited till the game saved to close down and remove her headgear. It nearly clattered off the desk before Owen reached over and caught it.

"Can you not fucking stand right behind me? I don't do that to you." Andreah snapped. She looked flushed, with glossy eyes that she blinked hard to hide.

Owen kept an even tone as he took a few steps back to give her room. "What happened? Why would the game do that?"

"The fuck if I know." Andreah pulled her hands through her hair, leaning forward into her chair as she looked ready to pull her knees up and hug them.

"Did you plan for that?"

"No," Andreah answered after a long breath, still not lifting her head to look at him.

Owen stepped forward, but stopped so he didn't disturb her personal space again. "What happened, what's different?"

Andreah sighed again before getting up to pace around the room. "Amilia was supposed to go to 'the new world', and lead the Knights on a wild goose chase after faking her execution. She tricked them into thinking she knew where the shield was, and was supposed to lead them on until she and Celio could get away. Another boat was coming that would offer them safe passage back to Europe. But there is

322

only colonialism and the death that follows right now. No one lasted the hands of their would-be protection besides Amilia. The only option was to beg this man to take her back to Europe. He only agreed to...to practically own her. It just fucking destroys everything Amilia could hold onto."

"This is bullshit." Without another word, he bolted out of the door like a man on a mission.

"What? Owen! Wait—"

He paused a step out of their door and glanced over the other fnVR workers before heading to where Jorge's office was. The secretary of the week was guarding his door, but even her objections didn't stop him from storming in. Jorge's chair was turned away from Owen as he barged into the office.

"I need to talk to you," he demanded.

Jorge swiveled his chair around and gestured with great annoyance towards the phone held up to his ear. The curled cord stretched across the desk. *Oh.* Owen had missed that. He bit his tongue and waited. And waited. Jorge said nothing to him.

When the chair started to turn towards the window again, Owen took a step forward and hung the call up for him. That got Jorge's instant attention, and anger. "I said," Owen repeated, "I need to talk to you."

"And you didn't think that other people have the same need?"

"No."

Jorge hung up the phone that was now giving him a dial tone. "What do you want?" he asked with a heavy sigh.

"What are you doing to Amilia's story?"

"She has to travel back to Spain, obviously, if you want her back in your game."

"This is the last time I'm going to ask. What are *you* doing to Andreah's game?"

Jorge sat forward in his desk, hands folded on top. "Amilia wasn't testing as well as other characters. People didn't trust her. It was decided we'd make her more sympathetic."

"By abusing her?" Owen accused, his voice raising when no one seemed to see the problem right away. "People don't give a shit about abuse victims. If they didn't like her before, they will just blame this on her too."

Jorge's turned his palms up, as if to show that this wasn't in them. "Age of Shadows prides itself on being a 'choose your own.' If people perceive it that way, that's the way they see it. There is nothing shown on—"

"That's a cop out, and you fucking know it." Owen likely should have given Jorge a moment to reply, but he didn't. "Is this meant to be for my benefit in some sick way?"

"We'd never intentionally write such things into the storyline. However, the game allows such drama. If players choose to—"

"Amilia and Andreah didn't pick this."

Jorge balled his hands up. "Surely, you aren't going to accuse me of hurting a fictional character's feelings," he laughed.

"You're upsetting Andreah, isn't that good enough?"

"She's a big girl, she can handle it. Obviously has handled herself fine so far. Furthermore, she's under contract, an employee, and how am I to know what offends her?"

Owen gritted his teeth, wishing he could do more than hang up Jorge's call. "If I see anything like a kick the dog trope again, even as a 'joke', I'm walking."

Jorge narrowed his eyes, done with the fury that had whirled into his office uninvited. "Do I need to remind you are also under contract?"

Owen held his hands up, pulling his wrists together. "Maybe next time you should handcuff me instead." It didn't matter if the asshole believed him, it was a credible threat so he turned around and left the room.

But it wasn't long before Owen stopped again. Andreah and Jorge's secretary were both staring in from the open door. He exchanged a glance with Andreah before stepping past her, and headed back to their joint office.

Andreah closed the door behind them before collapsing onto the couch. She closed her eyes for a long time, and when she opened them again, ended up staring at Owen. He wasn't sure why. Maybe she was looking for something to say.

"What?" Owen pressed finally.

Andreah shook her head. "I'm going home," she said, as she got up and started gathering her things.

"Does it bother you, or not? Because before I went in there it seemed like it did, but now I can feel your disapproval."

She shoved her laptop into her backpack. "I'm in no position to say anything anymore. And maybe you shouldn't care so much."

"I'll care about what I want to," Owen countered without a second thought. "You telling me what to care about, or not, isn't going to change that. Things like that are harmful."

Andreah glanced down for a moment before looking at him. "Well, wait until you've actually been handcuffed, and we'll see how loudly you'll speak up for the smaller things like this."

"You used to have the guts to tear this building down if things didn't suit you. And this isn't small, I saw what it did to you. What it's doing to Amilia."

Andreah turned for the door. Her hair hid whatever expression she had on her face. "It's interesting that you only notice the pain when it's hurting Amilia. What it could do to others."

"That's not true."

Whether she believed it or not, she didn't wait a moment longer before walking out. Her steps were loud against the wood floors as she walked to the elevators, the silence they left behind even louder.

Andreah and Owen fell into whatever was their natural way of working the next few days. Owen arrived a little early for once, and oddly enough, so had Andreah. She was settled and already one empty coffee mug into the evening. Her job at the courier service must have been letting her off early.

Andreah looked up at Owen as he walked in. "Jorge is looking for you."

"Oh yeah?" Owen said, as he dropped his bag onto the chair.

Andreah nodded. "He told me to call his secretary when you arrived. But I'm not *your* secretary, so he can honestly go fuck himself."

Owen couldn't help but grin at her.

"Well, now that you're here, I'm going to go hide, and act like I had no idea you ever arrived." She picked up her laptop before opening the door to the small private office they rarely used. It was mostly reserved for when one of them didn't want the company of the other. She stopped herself from fully closing the door enough to look back at him. "If you want, I'll share, so you can safely avoid Jorge until you need to stream."

326

The room barely passed as a supply closet. Andreah sat on the desk while Owen leaned against the door. Andreah ignored her responsibilities for a while longer and messed around on her phone. Owen was about to say something, until he heard someone enter the other room. He moved away from the door and towards the desk, hoping whoever it was wouldn't check their refuge. Someone mumbled to themselves about needing to find Owen. Jorge. A few seconds passed before Owen heard him finally shuffle out again.

Owen turned back to look at Andreah who had her phone camera pointed at the door. "What are you doing?" he asked.

"I was hoping if he caught us I could catch all the different colors his face turned." Now that the opportunity had passed, she put her phone down. "It's safe now. He's too lazy to check again, I think. Do you want to go back out?"

"I don't trust he won't come back."

Andreah smiled softly, leaning back with her palms against the desk. "Look at us slacking off together."

"Yeah, look at us..." Owen's words slipped out so softly that they gave a chill to the air.

Andreah glanced away as the sense washed over her. Owen could tell she had some comment tucked up her sleeve. She sat up, and crossed her arms over her chest. "I wanted to talk about the other day. What I suggested before I left wasn't true, I shouldn't have said it."

Owen almost wanted to mimic her body language, but instead he stood awkwardly in front of her. "It's okay. It's just...we're on the same team. I will stand up for what's right, and I didn't understand why you weren't. And I probably should have asked what you wanted to do about it." He fiddled with his jacket, not completely sure he was saying the right thing. Andreah simply nodded, before averting her eyes to the floor. Somehow, Owen found some more to say.

"When we broke up, I didn't originally miss you as much as I thought I would." Owen knew his words sounded harsh and abrupt, but carefully tried to hold Andreah's attention. "I was too hurt, too angry, too...everything. But now, there's no avoiding you anymore, and I don't think I want to, either." Owen shook his head, and looked away himself. "I guess, what I'm trying to say is, I'm sorry I said things before I didn't mean either. I don't even know how you feel anymore."

A beat passed before Andreah glanced back up. "I feel cowardly, and nervous," she confessed. The tension she felt for weeks melted, and instead of pushing him away, her fingers reached out to touch him. Her eyes fell to her hands as if to silently question what they were doing as Owen edged closer. "I didn't want you to care, Owen." Andreah paused again, her lungs pulling in a wavering breath. "And I didn't want to care."

What had started as slacking off was now something so much more important.

"Are you nervous right now?" Owen whispered.

"Terrified." Her eyes danced around his face before falling on his lips.

"Me too." Owen didn't let a second longer pass as he reached up to Andreah's face, feeling the softness of her cheek before indulging in the velvet warmth of her lips. He could feel the stiffness up her jaw disappear as she leaned into him, her hand tightening on his arm as if to steady herself back into his world, and him in hers. He broke off the kiss, and leaned his head against her forehead. "You should have let me hate you," he whispered with his eyes closed.

"That's okay," Andreah smiled, and leaned back on the desk again. "I haven't decided if I hate you yet, either."

Owen's smile grew. "Fair enough."

"You know, there is a bit of time left before you have to stream."

He raised a brow at a vague suggestion before someone shouted his name. His real, first, name. The sound of it alone made Owen pale, and he turned towards the door.

"Oh wow," Andreah said, more amused than worried. "Jorge must be really pissed at you if he's calling you Alexander."

"That's not Jorge." Owen said. He walked out of their office and into the main room barely lifting his eyes off the ground.

Andreah followed and stopped short when it was indeed not Jorge at all. It was someone she'd never seen before. Without her heels, his statue was even more daunting. It wasn't that he was even that tall, but he carried himself like he was the biggest man in a march of giants.

"There you are," the man said, ignoring Andreah's presence. "I've been waiting in the office for you since four."

Owen slowly lifted his head to give the man a bored expression that caused crinkles around his eyes to form. It aged him in a way that added a familiarity between the two. "Maybe you should have called first."

"Maybe if you didn't give excuses when I did."

"'I'm busy with work' isn't an excuse."

"Alex, you are playing video games." He said the words with such disdain it almost sounded like he was selling knockoffs.

"I'm sorry," Andreah interrupted. "Who are you?"

"Walter Owen," he said, finally addressing Andreah and held his hand out to shake her hand. The handshake was firm, like he lived by the theory you could judge someone by it.

"Owen?" She glanced between the men and the familiarity she noticed before now made sense. They were related. Meeting your boyfriend's parents was always weird. But meeting your ex's parents was weirder.

"I don't have time for this right now. I'm going to be late for the stream. I'll stop by after work tomorrow, okay?"

"Which work?"

Owen stared at his father for a moment. Whenever his dad replied too fast, there was always attitude to the comment. But children can rarely point out such a thing. "We're doing a historical tie-in, so I'll be there after *both*."

"Does he give you this sass too?" Walter asked Andreah.

Owen threw his hands in the air muttering something to himself as he took a step away from it all.

"Oh, I don't know. It grows on you," she smiled.

329

Her charm had some effect, since Walter gave a little *hmm* before turning back to his son who was now leaning against the gaming stations. "Do you know where I'm staying?"

"At Rick and Emily's," Owen said. "Like always."

"I'll let you play your game," Walter said, turning back to Andreah as Owen was left to roll his eyes in peace. "Nice meeting you, miss."

"Same to you." Andreah whistled as Walter left the room. "So that's your—"

"Let's not talk about this," he said, soon realizing he sounded short with her. "Please."

She crossed her arms over her chest and held her tongue from any protest. "Well, since you said please."

The next day of work went slow. It shouldn't have been a bad day, The Gunpowder Plot mission was tonight, but the weight of meeting his dad later just dragged his mood down. Of course, the fact that he had to check over a sports article wasn't helping either. Crediting a layup or a three-pointer to the wrong player would greatly change the story.

Frank came out of his office glancing over at Owen before Michael, who was just waiting with his gear assembled. "Can you run downstairs and pick up whatever they have for us?"

"There is a package?" Owen interrupted.

"Yeah, the front desk just called."

Why wouldn't Andreah just run it up? They kissed yesterday, surely that meant they were close enough again that she could spend an extra minute in the elevator. Maybe the business with his dad was too awkward? "I'll go get it," Owen blurted.

Michael glanced over to Frank who just shrugged and returned to his office.

The lobby was surprisingly lacking Andreah. He stared at her would-be co-worker before the messenger realized he was being watched and looked up. "NYC Today?" the bike messenger asked.

"Uh, yeah."

The guy shrugged off a backpack identical to Andreah's, pulled out a package, and tucked it under his arm as he took out the tablet for Owen. Owen felt weird about it. Like this stranger was wearing Andreah's stuff. "Sign here."

Owen took the tablet, staring down at the pen like there was something wrong with it. "I thought, uh..." He picked up the pen before looking up. "A girl named Andreah did deliveries?"

"She doesn't work for us anymore."

"What? Why not?"

The man sighed, and dropped whatever professional script he was meant to follow. "Look dude, I don't know. She was let go. Something about scheduling issues."

Owen looked down at the unsigned square where his signature should go. "Oh, thanks for letting me know." He shook his head and signed.

"Yep." It was a bored reply and a tired exchange of the package for the tablet.

Even after the messenger left, Owen was dumbfounded that Andreah didn't tell him.

A letter came one late October day in 1605. It had passed from Lord Monteagle to the King's spymaster, Robert Cecil, until it finally made it to the home shared by Daniel, Lance, and Chloe.

"My Lord, out of the love I bear to some of your friends, I have a care of your preservation. Therefore I would advise you, as you tender your life, to devise some escape, to shift your attendance at this parliament," Daniel read aloud.

Whispers of treachery were in the air, but this was the first concrete sign of it. Yet the warning almost seemed out of place. "Is this a setup?" Lance asked.

"I'm not sure," Daniel said, glancing up from the letter. "Let's go find out."

Robert Cecil was found on his way to a meeting. Instead of being panicked at the arrival of two thieves, he welcomed them. After all, why wouldn't he, as the head of the British guild. Having the ear of Kings and Queens was a rare position for someone of their guild, but it served them well. "Walk with me, boys."

"Sir, we had a concern," Daniel said.

"About the letter," Lance finished for him.

"Of course you do," Cecil said humorlessly. "Gael warned me about you. He said you liked to bend the rules, turn them into your favor instead of being limited by them."

Daniel looked away, thinking about what happened brought him no joy. It's the reason why he stayed away from the ghost town that was once his home. Despite his discomfort, Cecil went on.

"I think we have something in common. We both know the tenets are not as rigid as Gael believes they are. You also know of the King's reluctance to kick out the church's Knights. It's a violent world we live in. I merely plan to fight fire with fire."

"Preying off someone's fear that way makes you no better than those you seek to stop," Lance said. It was a horrifying suggestion that left no room for morality, just results.

Despite Cecil's age and smaller stature, Lance ended up on the ground when his elder threw a punch. Whether it was strength or surprise that caught Lance off guard, Daniel froze.

"I didn't think he would understand," Cecil said, looking at his fist that now hurt. Politics were his normal battleground, but it seemed the man had more in him than many gave him credit for. "But you, Ortiz, you understand the good that could come out of my plan."

Daniel broke eye contact with Cecil to look down at Lance. "The letter is a ploy. Allowing you to protect the few you desire, while sacrificing others like Guy Fawkes. In an attempt to force the King's hand against the rest of the Knights."

"Very astute of you," Cecil smiled as he spoke. "I knew you would understand. Now you can help me by—"

"No."

"What?"

"I said no," Daniel repeated. He reached down to help pick up Lance, whose eyes finally stopped watering. "I didn't mean to twist anything before, and I won't willingly do it again. Even if it helps, at what cost? Truth is all we have in the world."

"Is that what you tell yourself at night, *dago*?" Cecil hissed. "I serve king and country. If you don't approve maybe you should return to yours." Daniel had been treated as an equal until it had no longer benefited Cecil, then he was Spanish once again.

"You're right," Daniel said. He looked over to Lance, who glared as though he was the one insulted. "This mess is yours, and yours alone."

Maybe they should have gone directly back to Spain, but they decided to stay. Lance wanted to kill the bastard before he could do anything else, but Daniel convinced him to hold off, saying that his life wouldn't fix this problem. Hate didn't end with murder.

They waited and watched until the eve of November fourth, since the letter warned of the very next day. Gunpowder had been stockpiled underneath parliament a few barrels at a time. By their best guess, thirty-four now waited for a single spark.

They had a choice: walk the cellars with Fawkes, follow the spymaster's wishes, or make their own path.

"Ready?" Daniel asked.

"For King and country," Lance smirked.

If one thing living in London made clear, it was they weren't English. While King James was not their sovereign, his death could reignite the Anglo-Spanish War that had only ended months ago.

While the King's men feverishly searched, Daniel and Lance remained close as his guards. It was a quiet night away from parliament, and no fire would end up changing that. From the moment that letter was penned, the plot was doomed.

Fawkes was captured that night, and after days of torture, other plotters were arrested. They were all pawns, like so many people before them that hoped, and prayed, they were doing the right thing. Only to have their belief used against them. A traitor's death was not a beautiful one.

In December, whispers suggested that Lord Monteagle had started to clean up loose ends. The writer of the letter was believed to be his brother-in-law, Francis Tresham. He had been already rotting with the other plotters, and soon was found dead in his cell.

Or at least, that was the story being told. Others believed it was Cecil who poisoned him. Only one clear thing was for certain, staying in England was dangerous. It was only a matter of time before they became witnesses that had to be "taken care of."

Despite the sunshine playing house granted, simply watching the world turn was taxing. More so somehow than actually living it. Daniel sat at their dining table along with Chloe and Lance as his food remained untouched. "We should go home," he said.

Lance looked up from his meal, more curious than anything else. "Don't you think we should do something about Cecil? Expose what really happened?"

"No," Daniel tried to smile, but only had his own worn faith to hold onto. "Everything is how it needs to be."

"I heard a poem," Chloe said. "The King's misuser, the Parliament's abuser, hath left his plotting and is now rotting."

"Where did you hear that?"

"On the street." She placed a hand on Daniel's as if to suggest he had more than he thought. "I know it isn't exactly what you wanted, but it's a ray of truth."

"It's enough to light the day." Daniel glanced from Chloe to Lance across the table before leaning back in the chair. "I'm starting to feel there is nothing more in London for us. It might be shameful to say, but we should go back."

"Shame be to him who thinks ill of it," Lance said. "It is our choice, not theirs. Is it not?"

The corner of Daniel's mouth curled up in a smile, a small gesture that Chloe made bigger. "To Spain then."

Homecoming meant dealing with the ghosts of the past. Sometimes they remained hushed whispers in the corner of your mind. Sometimes they sneak in a window.

A man three times Chloe's age appeared in Lance's kitchen. She jumped at the sight of him, but his weapon silenced her from calling out to the boys in the living room.

The man brought a finger to his lips in a promise to leave her be if she remained quiet.

His sudden presence didn't scare Lance as much as the direction he had come from. "Señor Garcia," Lance said, glancing past the musket to the kitchen for a moment. "To what do I owe the visit?"

"You boys killed my son." With the accusation thrown into the air, he lifted his gun. It wavered between them as if unsure of who he was most upset with.

Daniel wrinkled his nose as if something distasteful was said. It was true; well, partially so. *"We* didn't, it was m—"

"The artifact," Lance interrupted, and shot Daniel a harsh look.

"Don't split hairs," Garcia snapped. "On the ground. Both of you."

Without hesitation, Daniel got down on his knees. "I'm sorry about Abel."

Garcia looked like he was going to lose it all together, so Lance kneeled as well. Garcia's finger was a twitch away from the trigger, only a hair's width keeping the bullet secure. "He never liked you," he scolded, "You know that, right?"

Daniel's jaw set before he looked down, like a child who couldn't meet the eyes of a disappointed parent. "I do."

"Tell me where the artifact is now so I can bring it back. A simple task you were too weak to do yourself."

"He doesn't know where the device is," Lance interjected.

His voice alone made Garcia re-pick his target. "Yes, you do. You both do. Things just don't vanish into thin air."

"What you want isn't here. It isn't anywhere," Lance continued, despite the glare from Daniel telling him to be silent.

The man considered this for a moment before looking back over to Daniel. He recognized that pained look that only knowing too much bestowed. "If you don't tell me, I will kill you, boy."

"Then do it," Daniel said. "There are people I care for on the other side."

"Again with that traitor and whore?"

"You shouldn't speak ill of the dead, *monsieur*," Chloe said, revealing herself after a slow creep behind the assailant. She pressed the tip of a sword against his back. "Unless you want me to ring you through, you'll leave my friend and my fiancé in peace."

Daniel turned to Lance, suddenly more interested in what Chloe said than the weapon still pointed at him. "Fiancé?" he mouthed to Lance, who simply grinned with downright pride.

"What happened to do no harm to your own, gilipolls?" Chloe asked.

"You mean *gilipollas*, my dear," Lance corrected, amused.

"More death isn't going to bring back your son. End this before you break your heart with bloodied hands," she added.

Garcia looked over his shoulder to Chloe. His hate and rage exhaling with a breath that showed his age once again. "Missing someone can do horrible things to you."

"I know." Daniel slowly stood up, with his hands out in front of him. "I miss Abel too."

"As does the world," Lance added, as he too dared to move to his feet. "We are not your enemies."

Garcia wrung his hands. "Maybe you are right, and this was the foolish errand of an old man." No one moved, not even when he took the first step towards the front door he completely ignored originally. "Tell none of this. I wish to retire with some honor intact."

"Of course." Daniel watched him leave, knowing in his heart that he missed another fight. Whatever other options might have been available, he didn't want them. Too much guild blood had been spilled already. But that left something else important unanswered. "Do you two have something to tell me?"

"We were thinking about it," Chloe said, albeit nervously. "I guess it just slipped out."

"Oh," Daniel said. "Don't worry about it. This is finally some good news."

Chloe looked at the sword she had stolen for a moment before handing it off to Lance. "Then why do you look so sad, *mon cher*?"

"I'm not," Daniel quickly countered. He looked to Lance to vouch for him again, but he must have used them all up. The lie he had ready, that he wasn't jealous or fearful that he'd get left behind, failed him. He just couldn't do it; a new truth had to be found. "It's just, I shouldn't have told you where I thought aegis went. I put both of you at risk." If their idealized futures matched up, he shouldn't be the one putting that in jeopardy.

Lance stepped in front of Daniel, making sure he had his complete attention. "It is an honor that you trust me enough to tell me these things, not a burden. You aren't a burden. I know you saw some things, that changed you in a way I can't understand. But I'm here for you." Lance put a hand on Daniel's shoulder and glanced over to Chloe, who was smiling. "*We* are here for you. Always."

Daniel exhaled, feeling his guilt settle in his chest. "I'd hug you, but I saw how protective your betrothed is."

"She is something, isn't she?" he laughed. "Her Spanish insults need some work, though."

"Being bilingual isn't enough these days," Chloe said. Her mock annoyance was clear.

Having to pay for a taxi to get here was an insult to future injury. The injury came when Emily opened the door and looked taken back to see Owen standing there. "Hey," she said, and moved away from the door to let him in. "Something up? You don't usually just stop by randomly."

Owen tilted his head and glanced over to his father, who was lounging on the couch. "You didn't tell her I was coming over?"

Walter tossed the magazine in his hand onto the coffee table. "I didn't think you'd show up."

"The fuck, Dad." He shook his head, and turned to Emily. "I'm sorry, I should have texted you."

"No worries," she smiled. "I'm going to check on dinner. You two play nice." Her glance hovered on Owen, in support rather than accusation.

Owen wavered on his feet. He wanted to follow her, but instead swayed towards Walter. He brought his hands up and, uncertain what to do with them, tapped them against each other. "So, what brings you to town?"

Walter gave him a measured look before shifting through the magazines again. Baby Talk, Parenting, Wired, Parents. None held his attention. "Have you talked to your brother?"

"Is that why you're here?"

"I do live here."

"In New York state," Owen corrected. "Not city."

"Would you just answer the question?"

"No, Dad. He doesn't keep in touch." Owen said. He tried to hold his tongue, but after the first word he was a goner. "Not even with me."

"Is that attitude I hear?"

Cussing didn't bother him, but talking back was a no-no. It didn't matter if you were thirteen or thirty, that gruff parent voice always sounded the same. Over the years, Owen had worked out the exact inflection to shut his Dad down. "No sir."

Walter stared for a second, a harsh glance, like he knew what his son was doing. Whether it was years in the service or something else, Owen was never sure, but when Walter looked away, he knew it had worked again.

"Hey Owen." Rick stepped into the room with an instruction sheet in his hand. He hadn't even realized he'd caught both their attention until he looked up. "Uh, Colonel Owen. Sorry. I was hoping I could enlist your help."

Owen smirked to himself about the word choice, but didn't breathe a sound. If he did, the two of them would stay.

"Sure, it's no problem, Berkley." Walter got up and followed Rick into the baby's room.

Owen was left alone in the living room, which, if he had to pick, was one of the better choices. They'd be back. For now, he was free.

When he heard footsteps, Owen glanced up, and was relieved to find Emily. "Have you come to save me?"

"Actually," Em stretched the word out in a fashion Owen knew was trouble. "I'm inviting you to stay for dinner."

"Fantastic," Owen said, with a mock smile. "What are the GI Joe buddies doing, anyways?"

Emily shot him a look that actually made him feel like shit. "Rick promised when he got back he'd take care of everything so I could have a break. But he needed help with this dinosaur thing we bought." With a slight shrug, she headed back into the kitchen.

Dinner was delayed fifteen minutes, but soon enough they gathered around the dining room table. "You'll have to forgive me," Em said, "I haven't had to cook for anyone besides myself in a while, so I might be rusty."

"I would have taken care of it," Rick reminded.

"We would have ended up with pizza that way," she laughed. "Plus, I wanted to sit down properly with everyone while I could."

If by proper she meant awkward, then Owen thought she was nailing it. The others didn't seem to mind, so he did what he normally in times like this and remained seen, not heard. Rick and Walter exchanged stories, which they never did while actually deployed. A quirk that eluded Owen, since telephones existed. Rick texted Emily enough so it wasn't like they weren't able to be social.

"I've seen this graduation class," Rick said. "Definitely some winners."

"We'll see if they don't run after my speech."

"Your speeches are great."

Owen's eyes widened as he listened. Those speeches were dry as hell, but at least he knew the 'why' of his dad's visit now.

The dinner was interrupted by the shrill cry of the baby, and the echo of a chair being pushed out. "I'll get it," Emily said, and her chair added to the chorus.

"You don't have to get up," Rick said.

"Rachel is likely hungry, and you sadly can't help me with that." She glanced over to Walter and Owen. "If you'll excuse me."

The silence didn't last a second after the baby stopped crying. "You know, when I heard you were playing video games for a living, I wasn't the least bit surprised," Walter said, clearly disappointed.

Owen looked up from the green beans he had pushed from one side of the plate to the other. "They say the newspaper biz isn't what it used to be."

"When are you going to start taking life seriously? I saw some of one stream. You didn't even really do anything. You passed on the action in order to play house."

There was a lull as Owen stared at the napkin holder. He debated pointing out that he let actual 17th century history run its course instead of injecting himself as the hero.

"Why play war when I could *play war,* am I right?" Owen glanced over to Rick as if asking him, and he just stared in horror. Owen smirked.

"I didn't raise you to be so disrespectful."

Owen carefully put down his fork, then slowly looked up to meet his dad's militant gaze. "You didn't raise me to be a lot of things that I just am."

"Grow up."

"Whatever *viejo.*"

Walter narrowed his eyes. "What did you just call me?"

Owen leaned forward putting his elbows on the table. "If you want to know, learn Spanish. It's the second most spoken language in the country. Or is that not American enough for you?"

"Good God," Emily interrupted. Her words had as much weight as her presence did in the room. "I could hear you bickering from down the hall."

"Sorry," Owen said, as he pulled his hands back properly to his lap.

Emily pressed her lips into a thin line as he glanced to her husband, and sat down. "I've seen him play, he literally draws crowds. Just because it isn't what you saw for him doesn't mean it's without merit."

Walter let out a curt laugh. "Every time I talk to you, you hide behind someone's skirts."

"Wow. That didn't sound sexist or anything," Owen scuffed. "And Emily is wearing pants."

"Now you're just being ridiculous."

"Good." Owen dared further. "If I'm unfit for duty, may I be dismissed, sir?"

"Dismissed." He replied out of a mixture of habit and annoyance.

The baby started to cry again at his tone, and three chairs pulled out. "I got it." Rick was quick to offer, and Owen was equally as fast in making his exit.

He was four steps out of Em's door when relief hit him. It was a gulp a freedom soon replaced with a sense of isolation. Sitting alone all night after a failed dinner seemed daunting. Neal was out of the question. He cracked like an egg when it came to the Colonel. Charlie was his best shot, but by time Owen made it home, they still hadn't texted back. Which left an option he could, and likely should, have done earlier.

To Andreah:
Sorry for the late text but I forgot to remind you that they wanted us to come in early tomorrow for an interview

To Owen:
k thanks

The reply had come so fast that he stared down at the screen, fighting himself for a moment. Owen wrote and deleted several texts before committing to one.

To Andreah:
can I see you tonight?

There was a long break between the texts, but when he was about to give up, a text came in.

To Owen:
I'm at a party come if you want

That wasn't quite what he was looking for but it would work. He ended up at a club that looked like an abandoned apartment building that had been retrofitted for the kind of crowd he saw pouring out of it. They weren't overdressed tourists, though a few had a certain New Jersey look. The bottom floor was a large open room, and the balconies looking over appeared to hold more private areas. The music boomed, vibrating the windows with every beat. Andreah ending up here made a lot of sense. It was hard to think of anything beyond the bass.

It didn't take long to find her, and when he caught her eye, she swayed over to him.

"Hey there," Andreah smiled, lacing her fingers into his. Owen looked her over before holding the look in her eyes. There was an unabashed carelessness for personal space.

"Hi," Owen said, with an amused confusion. "How long have you been here?"

Andreah shrugged. "Hell if I know. What time is it?"

"Uh, around 12," Owen said. Andreah nodded, her eyes lingering away, not really caring about the answer. "Do you think we can go talk somewhere for a little bit?"

Andreah looked back at him instantly. "I know the best place to be alone." She quickly moved through the people while pulling him along, and climbed a set of stairs with grace. They were down a small hallway when she snuck a peek back at him. Like it was a secret, she knocked on a door once, and when no one answered, she let herself in.

The room was long and filled with mirrors along parallel walls. It was reminiscent of backstage dressing rooms he saw in movies. Tonight must have been an off night. No one was here.

"Do you come here often?"

He meant it in earnest, but Andreah smirked like it was the most cliché pick up line. "Next you're going to invite me to 'Netflix and chill'. I mean who asks someone at midnight if they can talk?"

"To be fair, my text was definitely before midnight." Owen glanced around the empty room before running a hand through his hair. "And I did want to talk."

"Okay, let's talk." Andreah said, pulling him over to a chair that was close by. He sat, but glanced around wondering if he should first grab her another chair that was further down. His attention was immediately pulled back to her when, once discarding her jacket, she sat on his lap and wrapped her arms around his neck. Oh.

Owen leaned back just enough to blink up at her. "I, uh, was disappointed when I found out a different messenger now does deliveries for the office."

"Aw, I missed you too." Andreah brushed her thumb against his cheek before leaning down into a kiss. Owen didn't object, indulging in the moment. This was where they left off before, and by her persistence it seemed Andreah didn't like having to wait so long. Her hands made a mess of his hair. Owen's found their way around her waist, squeezing her closer for a moment as he got caught up in the whirlwind. It elicited a small sound from her, which would otherwise encourage him if he hadn't realized how quickly things were beginning to move.

He managed to break the kiss enough to pull himself from the spell. "Andreah, wait." He shifted back just enough so she couldn't lean back in. After getting a better look, he noticed something was off. Her focus was just off kilter. Her small giggle confirmed the hunch. "Are you...high?"

"Ding ding," Andreah perked up. "The winner gets to choose his prize."

"Get up."

"What?"

"Get up."

Slowly, as if she had to concentrate this time, Andreah got up and took a few steps back. Any thought that he'd instruct her further soon vanished with a frown. "You know, I thought you'd be a lot cooler with friends like Seth."

"What? No, I don't care about that. I just—fuck. I just wanted to talk to someone without bullshit pretense." Andreah just blinked, like she either didn't get his problem or was bored. It gave him a second to connect all the dots. He wished he could be mad, but this was what her former co-worker had meant. "I always feel like I'm this close to understanding you, and then I miss the obvious."

"I'm too high for this," she said, too on the nose for Owen at first. "I wish I could be here for you, but I don't think I'm the right person to make you feel better right now."

"Right, of course. I didn't mean to pull you away from your fun." He stopped short, realizing he was filling his disappointment with near meaningless words. "We should head back down."

"Alrighty."

She reminded him of someone who popped their gum during conversations. That mixture of listening and not listening. By the time they stepped off the last stair, she was gone. It was only seconds before she wove herself back into the crowd.

What good was a den of vices if you didn't want to break a few laws or self-righteously scoff at it? Owen already felt like a fool, and going home now would truly be admitting defeat. So he wandered around trying to get a feel for the place. He convinced himself to stay for at least a few songs that turned into more. He enjoyed the beat. When boredom threatened to sink in, he headed toward the balcony to smoke.

"Hey, I know you," a voice said. It took a second for his eyes to adjust to dim lights that didn't flash in rhythm to something else. But sure enough, the voice did know him. Against the back wall of the patio was Seth. He looked a bit disheveled at the moment, but it might have just been the ripped jeans.

Owen pulled himself up on the railing next to Seth. This wasn't the most interesting spot, but was more peaceful than anywhere else. More so than where Andreah took him. That was too far removed. Here was more party adjacent, one could see the liveliness without actually being a strong part of it. Any surprise he felt over seeing Seth was dampened by Andreah mentioning him earlier. "Not dealing tonight?"

"Nah, not feeling it." Seth's arms were braced against the railing like he wanted to pull himself up and take a seat as well, but never did.

"You aren't high or anything, are you?"

"No, I don't normally get a high during flare-ups."

The amount of candidness gave Owen pause. "Feeling that bad?"

"Honestly?" Seth looked over with an eyebrow raised. People who knew he was chronically ill asked how he was all the time, but they rarely seemed to care about the details. It was more of a mindless to-do list item for most.

"Yeah." Owen had seen Nicole check in on him before. He'd give a mumbled 'fine' and without another word she'd find a seat in some crowded space only to give it up to him. But they had never talked about it personally. "Honestly."

"I've compared it to a night and day before, but it's more a night vs. twilight feeling. You'll be feeling fine one minute then..." Seth shook his head and fixed his focus on the party goers. His eyes held a wanderlust of the people themselves mixed with an exhaustion from their movements. "When it's really bad, I don't have it in me to test my luck with the cops. All I can do is exist until it gets better. When I am feeling better, I'm a bit more daring. I feel like I have a chance to defend myself. I'm given the chance to worry about trying to pay bills again."

"What a privilege," Owen said, sarcastically.

"Fucked up, but true." Seth lifted a red solo cup that was surprisingly filled with water. "So, what's the matter with you?"

"It's just..." Owen hadn't ever told Seth about his messed up family. The only thing Seth knew was snide comments he made when Nicole complained about hers. So he opted for a more recent wound to lick. "I don't understand why Andreah was let go for this 'scheduling' when I feel like things should be going better for her."

"Mmm, I think you are oversimplifying the matter," Seth said. "Some people do drugs to lose themselves; others, like me, do them to feel human again."

"Which of the two is Andreah? Right now?"

Seth looked like he was trying to figure it out then pursed his lips and shook his head. "She's an addict, I'm not sure it matters." Owen glanced over, thinking that sounded a bit harsh, but Seth went on. "It is what it is."

Champagne was gathered as people prepared for New Year festivities, but Lance's focus was on the guild's newest member. "What do you know about Rivera?" Lance asked.

Daniel narrowed his eyes, ready to comment 'plenty, and so do you' before he glanced over to where Lance was looking and saw the problem. Ah, Luca. The tiny new thief recruit that filled him with hope that things were going to be normal again. "They are a cousin of Lucas. I've heard the Riveras didn't want to lose ties with the guild. You should go talk with them."

Lance lifted a brow at Daniel's last word. He considered it for a second before stepping off to greet them. Luca looked over from the event board, growing curious at Lance's uncertainty. "Hello, my name is Lance Tarlé. I know it's been a little while since your family's loss, but I wanted to say it was an honor to know such a good person as Lucas."

Luca smiled at Lance's word choice. Charlie hadn't wanted much to change with this new character, and it seemed they were granted that wish here. "I was told much about you," they said. "In part that you were very understanding, and that ease was most appreciated. It is my hope we'd might also have a similar fluid friendship."

"Of course," Lance said, catching the meaning. "If I could only be so lucky with another of the Rivera kin. Maybe we could see you tonight during the festival."

Daniel watched them contently for a moment. Even stalling what he had willingly planned to do today. Coming home meant confronting the past, before he could celebrate the future. It was a big day that Daniel planned to quietly spend.

The real show tonight was with someone else, and started long before this day. London built itself around Amilia, and stitched itself together with the cold of winter. Amilia locked the door to the bedroom before pulling out a box from under the bed. The collection didn't show a hint of dust as she removed its contents. Where many would store treasures, Amilia had a shirt fit for a male, trousers, and work boots that barely fit her small feet. She took in a large breath, and wrapped a scarf around her as she looked in the mirror. Her shaky hands braided her hair.

She was alone for the day, given whatever freedom her bitterly betrothed Viktor allowed. She pulled the braid forward, admiring the one thing that hadn't changed much over the years. Amilia retrieved something else and, with the mirror's help, put scissors to the bottom of her hairline. Curls bounced free once the braid fell away with a few rough snips. She ran her thin fingers through what was left, any thread of remaining length was cut. With a little more refinery, she would have looked just like Celio in his youth.

She then stripped away at the clothes she had been ordered to wear as someone else's accessory. When she looked back into the mirror, she didn't know the person in the reflection. Her lack of makeup showcased dark circles under her eyes, and would further help her pass for a homeless boy.

The coins she had managed to pull together were just enough to make a small rattle as she hurried over to the window to escape into the city. Amilia ran across the rooftops, feeling something build up in her chest, a well-deserved freedom. She looked like a bird, cageless at last.

London was pieced into different lands over time and distance until the landscape settled as Amilia looked up at the Spanish sun. Its rays beamed down on the valley ahead.

At first, she hadn't cared where she'd end up as long as it was far away from England. But when a merchant mentioned he was going to Siguenza, she decided it would be best to return and clear out what was left of her old life. She hoped to sell off whatever belongings were left at her family's properties.

Ivan, the old man who offered her travel on his carriage, knew she wasn't the homeless child she had been trying to come across as. The trip was too long for her casual disguise to last, but he never questioned it. Ivan even helped in the ruse by calling her son in public. Even going as far as claiming her as his nephew who was lending a hand around suspicious strangers.

Once they reached Siguenza, he refused the coins she promised, citing his opinion that she helped enough. When Amilia reached her house, she didn't have the energy to do much other than curl up in her aged bedroom. The dust and spiderwebs crawled far further than she had imaged. Everything was still, as if waiting for someone's return. Only the spiders preyed on her absence. As Amilia fell asleep she made simple plans for the rest of her life.

Later, a coat was pulled over her wrinkled clothes as she headed downstairs. Teacups and silverware were plucked from the kitchen. The tour around the rest of her home was spent mentally dividing things into sell or ignore. Sentimental value would never translate into worth for anyone else. Her bag had no room for such things. What had been would never come back, so she shouldn't mourn it any longer.

There was a single item that her heart did want to find; the mask. She searched the house, but still hadn't found it. The room felt a little colder as she came downstairs again, but she didn't give it much thought over her disappointment. At least, not until she heard the weight of footsteps in the small room. With her back turned she pulled up her hood to conceal herself.

"I don't know why you are here, but you won't find anything you are looking for," a male voice warned and moved further into the room. "If you want to make it past this eve, tell me who you are."

Amilia's eyes closed the second she recognized Daniel's voice. Her hands trembled as she now regretted staying the night. She tried to disguise her voice. "You don't want to know."

Daniel pulled a sword. The metal helped close the space between them. The tip of the blade pointed at the bag across her shoulder. "Well, you're obviously a thief."

"At times." Amilia lowered her head, resisting the urge to look back. She slowly set down the bag. "We can both just walk away from this." Tearing down whatever he had built after losing her wasn't the intent. He deserved to continue his life as he wished, without more of her interference.

"Not until you tell me why you are stealing from the dead," Daniel pressed.

In her frustration, Amilia found herself wanting to question him. She swallowed hard before stiffening up. "I am where I should be. You, however, should leave."

She couldn't see his reaction, but she could hear it. His breath caught in his chest causing an eerie silence. "I know you," he said, despite the uncertainty there. "Turn around."

Daniel was skilled years ago. She could only imagine how much better his tracking was now. Which left her with only one civil option. Amilia turned around, lowering her hood before finally looking at him. "I never meant for this..."

Daniel was here and it meant something terrible. That she haunted him all the time. That he hadn't moved on as she had convinced herself. Her heart sank. She had told herself plenty of times that she didn't want him to be waiting for her as if she had never been dead.

It was unclear if Daniel was listening as he held still beside the roaming of his eyes. All the changes she had made to her hair and clothes, all the wear that added to the thinning of her face, caused him doubt. He lowered the sword as he stared for a moment longer. "How are you alive?"

"The hanging," she paused, reminding herself to breathe. "It was staged. I had to make a choice for my family, for you. It was either that or the chaos of watching everyone die." She blinked hard after realizing her words. Her family *had* died. She might have admitted the folly if Daniel didn't speak first.

"I watched you die." He wasn't so much questioning her as hearing himself say it out loud. It had been the truth, but now it wasn't. Nothing felt real or true right now. "I watched everyone die in front of me, and yet somehow you are here."

Amilia blinked. Who had he meant?

"I can leave," she found herself saying the words almost feverishly. "I can leave, and never come back this time. I won't presume to force my way back into your life. That's not why I'm here, Daniel. I promise."

"Then why are you?"

Amilia glanced back at her bag of things she deemed valuable in some way. Had she honestly come back because she needed money? She had the skills to steal whatever she needed to survive. This was a want. "I guess I wanted to see home once more; I wanted to see if things were..." She shook her head feeling rather foolish about the whole thing now. "Still carrying on."

"The world still turns."

"Why are—" Amilia started to ask, but his sober tone made her hesitate. "Why are you here?"

"Oh." Daniel exhaled, as if he realized that her being alive made him the intruder. "I uh, I used to come here after you...left. It was a way to see if I was getting over things, and a way to hold on. I haven't been in town for a while, and I thought this time I could visit without it feeling like it was a crypt."

"You're here because of me?" Amilia heard him, but almost didn't believe what she heard.

Daniel looked away, his breath wavering before he looked at Amilia again. Here. In front of him. Whole. "I guess I am."

Amilia started shaking her head. Everything was wrong. "I didn't mean for this. I didn't mean for any of this," she mumbled near incoherently as her eyes started to well up. She didn't know why she was feeling everything at once now. "I know I have no right to demand anything from you, and I didn't want to see you, but I'm just so happy that I am."

Out of pure instinct, Daniel took a step forward to comfort her, but stopped short when she flinched at his movement. Their world had aged two years, which was such a long time to just fall into each other's arm like idealized star-crossed lovers. "I don't know what to say. I'm glad you're alive."

He held his hand out, and Amilia had to blink a few times to clear her eyes. It was an invitation for something, but she could only guess what. Her hand fluttered up like a cautious bird before coming to rest in his hand. A smile graced Daniel's face, and he moved his hand slowly to test if Amilia's fingers fit between his like he remembered. If he had closed his eyes, it would have felt like years ago, but today looked much different.

"Why aren't you mad at me? I lied, I—" Amilia had trouble finishing that thought, even though Daniel knew what was coming next. "I know I hurt you. I could hear it in your voice that day."

Daniel wondered if they had haunted each other over countless miles of ocean. "I thought if I just showed that I didn't care about the truth, it would allow you to be free. All the signs were there, but love made me blind. Not acknowledging what was going on, and only offering platitudes was shallow comfort." Daniel slowly pulled his hand back, his fingers tensed before both hands fidgeted to rest on top of his head. He breathed in as if they had been running. "I know that now. I'll never agree with what you did, but I wish I had told you how I really felt about it all."

"Which was?"

His hands fell unceremoniously to his sides.

"I'm the one who owes you the truth," Amilia added before he misunderstood. "I've missed you with every cell in my body every minute of every day. I have no clue what to do about that now, but I'd like to find out."

Daniel smiled. "That sounds like a New Year's resolution if I've ever heard one."

Owen stood with Andreah for a while as a party went on around them. They were newer on the scene, but had gathered enough attention on the stream to officially be included where the 'big leagues' partied. Owen recognized more and more people every time he went to these things. The easiest to spot was Elliot. He was the real life version of the cardboard cut-out Owen saw in the fnVR lobby. The tuff of brown hair on top of a pastel purple undercut must make it nearly impossible for the graphics department to match him to his avatar. The host of #Rehashed was also here. Owen recognized her voice before he found the group she was standing in.

Instinctively, Owen felt like he should listen from having the show on almost daily. It didn't take long before Andreah shifted away like someone who wanted to flip the channel. "I'm gonna go get a drink, do you want something?" she asked.

Owen shook his head. "No, thanks though."

Andreah turned on her heel and left as Owen watched her for as long as he could. They still hadn't really talked about things or established what their relationship was now. He figured she didn't feel obligated to hang around him all night, and wandered around until someone ended up inviting him over.

"Hi, I'm Asha. I'm a streamer too, and one of Tiansheng's friends." Owen only knew the second name because that was the username of the item hoarder who constantly bested him on the leaderboards. When the small Latina girl saw the name register with him, she perked up. "I've been hoping to run into you. We all would love to chat with you a bit."

Owen wasn't sure who she meant by 'we' but with a shrug, he agreed.

She brought Owen over to a corner that was roped off, even though he didn't quite know why. It wasn't on a higher platform, nor did it appear to be an official VIP section. More like they had just claimed this area and someone let them.

With a username like Tianshena, he assumed the player had an Asian background. Only one person of three fit that bill. Asha soon confirmed his guess with a proper introduction.

"You're that role-player, right?" Tianshena asked, as he sat forward to grab a finger sandwich off the table.

"Yeah." If Owen sounded unsure, it was because the question sounded like a judgment. Perhaps Tianshena was one of those people who 'didn't play for the story.'

"That's pretty cool," replied the other man on the couch. Owen hadn't recognized him until he spoke. This was Hank, the co-host of The Rundown. "We caught your last stream."

That refocused Owen's attention. As much as he wanted to say Daniel was his, and that he didn't care if anyone else knew his story, he still did. He wanted people to care.

"Yeah, but didn't you want more that night?" Hank said. "I would have taken her right then."

"Excuse me?" Owen asked, being formal instead of cursing.

Tianshena slapped his friend on the arm. "He can't do that sort of thing now that she's not an NPC."

Owen blinked hard. "I think you misunderstand. Amilia isn't there to fulfill my, or Daniel's, desires. She's a person. She should have a say in the matter. NPC or not. You can't just discard that because you think your male entitlement is worth more."

Tianshena was taken back enough that he sat up. No one moved, except for Asha who shifted uncomfortably on her heels. "What is this PC bullshit?" Hank blurted.

Tiansheng fixed his eyes on Asha. "You've never complained, so why do you look so uncomfortable?"

"Well...I mean, I don't disagree with what Owen is—"

"Oh, is he your knight in shining armor now?"

"Thief, actually." Owen corrected. He surprised himself. Months ago, he would have said nothing. He actually clearly remembered his co-worker harassing a model, and not saying anything. "Why don't you listen to her? I mean, you could at least let her finish her fucking sentence."

If Asha were any more surprised, her jaw might have dropped to the floor. Owen glanced over. "I'm sorry, you were saying?"

"I, um." Asha shook her head with a quick jerk. "You covered it."

"Boys," a new voice called. The tone was that of a schoolyard teacher. Chris stepped forward, having no trouble crossing the velvet rope as one of the game's developers. "Is there a problem?"

No one spoke, so he went on. "Actually, I'm glad to have caught you. You wouldn't know anything about the price fixing on those ranked items, would you?"

It was a threat that made Tianshena keep his mouth shut while Hank just rolled his eyes. He reported on Age of Shadows, and drama would only boost his ratings no matter the outcome.

"Owen." Chris finally turned to him. "Could you come with me? There are some people I want to introduce you to."

"Yeah, sure."

Chris excused himself from the trio and walked back into the party, and Owen followed. He was about to say thanks when Chris spoke again. "Could you please not harass people that aren't under fnVR contracts? You have a reunion panel tomorrow and I don't want it sidetracked with drama."

"Could you give me a copy of that list?"

Chris cracked a smile and stopped walking. "Please behave."

Owen nodded, and wondered if the scolding was going to go further or not. His boss's attention was soon pulled elsewhere. Owen looked over his shoulder to see where it went and found Sarah again. The expression on Chris's face softened and Owen almost laughed to himself. "I'll let you go."

Behaving, as it turns out, is easy if you simply don't talk to anyone. After playing at this for a while, he began to wonder where Andreah had ended up. It was hours into the party and he hadn't run into her again. The first place he checked was the entrance where all the smokers gathered before heading back inside. Andreah was nowhere, but he took a moment to light his own cigarette.

Once he adjusted to the outside world, he realized there was a blonde girl almost screaming at the bouncer that kept the uninvited out. When he recognized Abigail, he bumped past the person next to him as he moved over to her.

"—she's in there and I can't get a hold of her again. I told her I couldn't make it tonight, and that's why I don't have an invite. But she needs—" Abigail had barely any air in her lungs left before she saw Owen approaching. "Owen! Please get this guy to let me in."

He glanced at the scene in confusion. "What's going on?"

"I will tell you inside, I just need to get to Andreah, please."

Owen looked at the bouncer. "She's with me."

The guy didn't put up a fight. "Fine, go in."

Abigail grabbed his hand and pulled him inside. She glanced around in a panic. "Where are the bathrooms?"

"Uh, somewhere on that wall." Owen pointed, and grew more confused. "Please tell me what's going on."

"Andreah called me almost an hour ago from the bathroom. She said she may have taken too much and is freaking out. She never freaks out." Abigail explained, sort of, before bumping her way through the crowd until they reached the hallway that led to the bathrooms. There was a line that Abigail completely ignored, gaining her some disgusted looks. Owen lagged for a moment before following her in.

One girl at the mirror saw him and quickly left, but Owen's focus went to the row of closed bathroom doors. Abigail was already at the third one down, knocking and calling for Andreah. One door got no response. Abigail glanced down at the handle. It was a simple latch. She pulled a bobby pin from her pocket before sticking it between the door and side to pop the lock. Andreah was sitting with her back against the wall, looking over at them with lazy eyes. She rolled her head back as Owen instinctively rushed to her, with Abigail on her other side.

"Babe, do you need to throw up? How much did you take?" Abigail started, ready with a quiz to figure out how to help. Owen was too much in shock to do much other then check her forehead for a fever. She looked like she was burning up.

Andreah breathed heavily before licking her lips. "Already have. I just...Everything feels too much and I want to sleep."

"You shouldn't sleep here," Abigail said, before looking at Owen. "We need to get her out of here."

"Okay." He leaned down and pulled Andreah into his arms as gently as he could.

"Stay here," Abigail said, at the mouth of the bathroom.

Owen nodded, ready to follow any order she gave right now. He looked down at Andreah, who didn't seem to acknowledge she was in his arms. She'd turned in a bit, fingers pulling on a seam of his shirt, but there seemed to be a disconnect.

Abigail popped back in, wasting no more time. "Okay, I know the best way out of here."

He followed behind Abigail, who led them to a back exit, rushed down an alley, and just about jumped in front of a cab to get them out of there. They squeezed Andreah between them, but ended up with Andreah's head on Owen's lap. She was clearly conscious as she crossed her arms over her chest like she was hugging herself.

"Please, Andreah. Stay awake," Abigail begged. "Owen, can you try?" she said, before turning to tell the driver where to go.

Owen nodded and pursed his lips together. "Andreah," he said weakly, and brushed her hair out of her face. In that second he realized he had been in the same building, yet she had called Abigail for help instead. How disconnected had they become? Andreah barely stirred. He kept trying. "You know that guy who is on The Rundown? You wouldn't imagine how much of a dick he is," Owen began, finding it the only thing he could think to bring up. "If you were there I would have felt bad for the sucker. You probably would have punched him in the throat."

Andreah actually managed a smile, which Owen mirrored. While brushing her hair back, he discovered a small tattoo behind her ear. A tiny heart that he hadn't remembered seeing before. "When did you get this?" he asked even though he knew she wouldn't respond. "I would've sworn you didn't have this one before."

Abigail was staring at him from across the cab. "It's not new."

"Huh," Owen hummed before looking back at Andreah as her breath started racing again. "Anyways." He went on to tell her about how he should have known the person in first forever would be an ass, and by time he finished, Abigail had a new story ready to keep Andreah's focus.

When they finally got to Andreah's place, he carried her up then let Abigail take control of the situation. She made Andreah drink some water, and together they went off to the bathroom. Owen didn't feel comfortable leaving yet, so he ended up sitting on the couch. Once Abigail pulled a slightly more sober Andreah out of the bathroom fitted in pajamas, he helped guide her to the bedroom.

"I can stay with her for the night," Owen offered before Abigail said anything.

She gave him a suspicious look while he was focused on Andreah. Something must have clicked before her expression softened and she gave a slow nod. "Okay. I'll check in the morning, and please call me if you need. I'm only fifteen minutes away so I can be back for anything."

"Okay. I'll update you if something happens."

"Owen?" Andreah called loudly despite the crack in her voice.

"Go. I'll let myself out," Abigail said, even though she paused for a moment to watch him walk back to the side of the bed.

Andreah's eyes were searching for him till he came into view. A hand moved out from the sheets and curled around the pillow next to her. Owen tugged his shoes off, since he was planning to stay, and sat in a small chair near her bed.

"No," she whispered, and patted the bed. "Here." Owen paused, but soon caved. He would have sat on the bed, if she didn't fumble with the sheets, making her intent clear. "I'm sorry."

"Don't be," Owen whispered. "Wasn't a good party anyway."

Andreah blinked a few times before her hand moved to find his under the sheets. Owen wasn't sure what to say, or how to say anything even if he could think of something. She just seemed pleased with the small contact they had. Andreah licked her lips before speaking again. "May I kiss you?"

Owen took a few seconds to watch her carefully before offering a nod. She closed her eyes slowly before willing herself closer to him as Owen met her halfway. The warmth from her cheeks reminded him of a strong drink, and ranked up there as one of his favorite parts. She was bright and harsh like the sun, filled with fire that threatened to burn everything away. Owen was trying to hold his ground, but as Andreah shifted a hand over his chest, he held her a little closer.

She broke the kiss and smiled. "Thank you."

"You should get some sleep now," Owen suggested.

She nodded, but didn't close her eyes.

"I'll stay here all night, so you don't have to worry, okay?"

Andreah summoned a little more energy to tuck herself into his chest. Somehow they'd never been this close.

Andreah wasn't sure how long she slept, but by the light that had snuck its way past her curtains, she guessed it was afternoon. Oversleeping wasn't her biggest surprise. No, that could be explained by overdoing it last night, and not setting an alarm clock. It was a fact that Owen was still in bed, lying with an arm over his eyes.

Andreah called his name, and his arm moved back, fingers lingering over his eyes before he turned to look over. The slow ease suggested he'd been awake, or near enough. She simply stared for a second longer until Owen elegantly broke the silence. "What?"

She shook her head, burying her nose into the pillow. Her eyes flickered back up a second later. "Hi."

"Hey," Owen grinned. "Feeling better?"

"Yeah." Andreah sat up as if to test her statement. When that went well, she swung her feet over the bed. Seeming pleased, she glanced over to Owen again. "Thank you, again."

Owen propped himself on up his elbows. "Not a problem. Don't give me too much credit, I didn't do all that much. You seemed to have it once we got you home."

362

Andreah's face tightened around her nose, reminiscent of a rabbit. She wasn't sure why he was downplaying things, or if he really didn't feel troubled. "Well, anyways. I'm going to take a shower. I don't think I'll be fully human until I do."

"Wait," Owen called. "What happened last night?"

She swayed on her feet as if she didn't understand the question fully. "I overdid it. Thought that was painfully obvious."

Owen waited. Giving her time to confess more details she didn't want to give. The silence stretched out to an impolite length. "Right. I'm just glad you feel better."

Andreah went off to the bathroom. By the time Owen got up, he could hear the shower running. He glanced at the door and the line of light from under it. Why were some drug users annoyingly boastful about what they took while others skipped over it entirely?

Another curiosity was how plain her bedroom was. It was awfully simple compared to the mess of her living room. The fanciest thing about it was a swoop chair with her jacket from last night over the back. He didn't want to be nosy, but not knowing what drug she was using was dangerous if a situation like this came up again. He picked the jacket up and checked the various pockets. There were two in front, one across the bust, and in another, tucked inside, his fingers caught something plastic.

He pulled out a tiny zip lock bag with several pastel pills, and placed the jacket back down to get a closer look. Ecstasy. Now that connected the dots of her party behavior.

The door creaked, and Owen tucked his hands behind him. Andreah stood at the bathroom doorway, dry, and wearing nothing but a towel.

"Did you want to take a shower with me?" she asked.

His surprise shifted into a sly smile. "I'm going to pass. I was told that sort of nonsense past 12 only meant one thing."

"I meant AM," Andreah laughed.

"Plus, did you forget there's that reunion panel today?

"Oh shit," Andreah said, as glanced across the room to the alarm clock. "I'll hurry. Then we can swing by your place if you want to change before heading to fnVR."

They got to the office a little late, but it didn't matter because a large enough buffer was built into the schedule. Owen was going through the footage that was cut for time or content to prepare. He didn't want to accidentally reference a scene or tell an inside joke that, to the audience who didn't watch live, didn't exist. His feet were up on the desk, blocking a bottom corner of the screen.

He'd watched himself play before, but had always been around others at the time. It always made it too awkward to actually pay attention. Being alone and watching was jarring. It was, and wasn't, him.

"Wait a minute." Owen said, and swung his feet off the desk to lean in. "Why isn't this included?"

Owen replayed a deleted scene from before his reunion with Amilia. He thought it happened while he was in Paris, but he couldn't remember for sure. No matter where it happened, he considered it important.

"I love her like I love you," Daniel said. He held Lance's unwavering glance, and had for the whole conversation. "After I felt something for you, I thought everything I knew was wrong. That love would never be this all-consuming thing I was lead to believe it was. And that was fine. That was wonderful, freeing even. I was able to be honest, and open for once. But this...I don't have words for." Daniel sighed, and leaned his head on Lance's shoulder. "This hurts."

Lance turned to kiss the top of Daniel's head. "I know it does, and that's a part of life."

"*C'est la vie*," Daniel said.

Lance smiled. Daniel didn't see it, but he could hear it in the way Lance exhaled. "Somehow when you say it always sounds so—" He lifted a hand, trying to think of the word. "'Oh well' sounding. *C'est la vie*. That's life. The enjoyment, and the pain. It's all a part of living. You don't have to pretend it doesn't feel the way it feels."

Daniel lifted his head and caught a kiss like one might a cold. Effortlessly and with a shiver. "Thank you, amant."

"For what?"

"Being you."

Owen stared at the screen with his jaw hanging. Why did they cut this? Was that...not okay?

"Well, at least you don't have to worry about your mom showing up," Andreah said, from her spot across the room.

"What?" It took Owen a moment to realize that hadn't been the rudest comment ever, and notice a newspaper in her hands. Someone thought it would be interesting to interview his father. It wasn't. Owen's face scrunched up. "My mom isn't dead."

"Oh, I, I thought..." Andreah stammered, before shaking her head. "Never mind. I'm a mess still, and that was so out of line."

"Thought what?" Owen prompted, when she didn't fill in the blank, he did. "That because Daniel's mother died, mine did too? The real world isn't so simple, and there are plenty of ways to lose someone."

Chris walked in with a pile of wires and mics that drew Owen's attention far more. "Whatever, I have more important things to talk about," he said, and was out if his seat before she had the chance to say anything.

"Hi, I had a question," Owen said.

"I'm doing this because Carmen is out of the office," Chris said, while sorting the wires.

Owen laughed a little, bridging the awkwardness like it was a scripted joke. "That wasn't my question. There was a Daniel and Lance scene that was cut. Why?"

"The test group reported it took away from the moment between Daniel and Amilia. I believe they cited it being too close and distracted from the 'end game'." Chris turned to Owen, with a ready mic, but stopped wiring at his paled expression. "Is something wrong?"

"No," Owen said, a bit too fast for his liking. "That's fine, thank you."

Chris finished up and went over to Andreah. Her expression stayed with Owen. She wished to go over and comfort him, but was stuck as fnVR got them ready.

They sat in front of the cameras, and an aid touched up Andreah's hair that had been braided to one side. Owen again caught a glimpse of the little heart behind her ear. She glanced over to Owen, giving him a slight smile before adjusting the mic they'd given her.

Since there was no one physically interviewing them, they got to skip the intros. Instead they watched a small screen of the live broadcast studio as they went into the details. On cue, they smiled and said hi before falling right into questions.

"Through all the drama and loss, it seems we've come full circle with Amilia. What does her homecoming really mean to Daniel?" the man asked, who's name Owen had already forgotten. Andreah looked at Owen waiting for him to lead.

"It's a second chance for her to lead the life she might have wanted before," he explained. "She's no longer held down by her family or any rules."

"But what about between Daniel and her?" the interviewer insisted.

Owen shifted, thinking of the rude comments made by the guy yesterday. Andreah picked up on it.

"They both have a lot to rebuild. And I think they both want to help each other through that process. It's going to take time, but there is love still there." Andreah said, finally giving them something of the reply they wanted.

"Are you concerned that Amilia coming back is going to strain Daniel's and Lance's relationship again?"

"No. I'm not concerned with that," Owen answered, leaving no room for anyone else to answer for him this time.

The interviewer looked down at their papers before trying again with the same question. "Because Lance has been there for Daniel this entire time and has always disliked Amilia. How will her being back be okay with Lance?"

"Lance knows how much Amilia means to Daniel," Andreah said, "They both matter. And I know that Lance is just as understanding as Daniel is."

Owen leaned forward ready to pick up right after her. "You need to understand, first off, that Lance and Amilia are not pitted against each other. Sure, Lance doesn't support some of her choices. But that's because he cares for both of their safety. It's not like he's going to be annoyed she's alive. That would be fucked up," Owen said without pause. He noticed their handlers tense.

"Alright, so, was Chloe added to avoid a love triangle?" the interviewer went on, despite the obvious annoyance Owen was feeling.

"Chloe wasn't *added*, and Dance doesn't work in a traditional sense for different reasons. No one came between them." Owen answered, without second thought.

"Dance? Is that your, like, ship name for them?" The reporter asked. Owen paused at the question, unsure if this was some trap he was going to fall into. "What's the ship name for Daniel and Amilia?"

"Um," Owen glanced at a cup of water on the table that he didn't notice until now. "I've never thought of one."

"That's because they're so cute, they don't need one," Andreah said, playing to the reporters. She glanced over at Owen with a camera ready smile. "Right?"

"Right," Owen repeated. Only able to keep his tone neutral by looking back at her.

"Everyone's excited that Amilia has come back. Definitely no one more so than myself," Andreah added.

"Just in time to defend her relationship with Daniel, too," the reporter joked.

Andreah opened her mouth, but Owen was quicker. "Seriously? That's fucking rich," Owen interrupted. "You make it sound like I'm just making things up. You could look up my first year of play that apparently fnVR doesn't want to reference. I'll tell you a story; Daniel wakes up in a familiar bed he never slept in before. He feels awkward, but currently no one is sharing it with him, so had some space to collect his thoughts. Daniel wandered out to the kitchen where he spots Lance making tea. Nervous, and desperate to say something, Daniel asks what last night makes them. He says, "Well, the technical word for it is *amant*." Daniel by this point knows a handful of French words, but not that one. Now, I was a great researcher. Do your job as reporters and look it up."

Owen gave the stunned newscaster a second, which was used to sit stunned as Owen's fingers impatiently thumped against the table. "I would have had the answer by now. It's French for lover. If you are curious how the scene ended. Daniel, and I, actually, stood there blushing as Lance handed Daniel the cup of tea. I hate that word in English because I don't know how people mean it, but I grew to love the way that word sounds when he says it. If you think for a second that the present takes away from that, or that the past takes away from the present with Amilia, you're dead fucking wrong. Look, I'm sorry if this isn't what you wanted, but it's my story. Stuff I needed to be reminded of. These characters did that for me and I won't have you boil that down into...shipping discourse." Owen ripped the mic that was nested along his collar. "You know what? Fuck this. Interview over."

Andreah ended up wide eyed as she watched Owen leave. She swallowed hard before looking back at the camera. The interviewer also took a few seconds before recovering as well. "Okay, so maybe we can expand on some more questions."

"I...don't think this interview is going to go any further. I'm sorry," Andreah interrupted, before getting up from her seat right as the feed cut. She walked off to find Owen. She had her mic half removed before finding him in the makeshift green room. Andreah took a moment before fully entering the room. "Owen, are you okay?"

"No. Nothing is okay right now." He snapped, rolling his hands up into fists.

Andreah couldn't find words for a while until finally something clicked. "You're bisexual, aren't you?"

"Wow, you think?"

"Please hate me for the things I meant to do, and not the ones I didn't," she pleaded, which threw Owen off.

He closed his eyes before standing up straight, breathing in deeply as he looked at her. "I don't hate you, but I do hate the fact that I'm in love with you right now."

Andreah's jaw moved like she was looking for a quick response, but nothing came out. Her eyes bounced between trying to meet his and avoiding his gaze all at the same time. She was so obviously thrown that Owen wasn't sure she'd be able to talk.

"We need you to come back and close this up for us," Chris called from behind the closed door. This seemed to kick her into gear, even though it was the opposite of what Owen needed right now.

"I need to go," Andreah said.

"Some things never change."

"Really, are you going to be okay?"

"Just go," Owen sighed. "Or stay. Just don't linger."

Owen could hear her even though she had left. He couldn't tell what was going on exactly, but by her tone, she could have been telling off the interviewer. Chris' voice followed hers and was trying to keep his tone even. After a few moments, Owen turned to see her coming back into the room. She took her time to calmly close the door before turning towards him. In only a few paces, she closed the gap.

His eyes were closed by time he was pushed against the wall. Hands hovering, fingers flexing, before they settled to rest on her lower back. Her kisses were short, and almost sloppy in their transitions from one to another. Each brought a desperate urgency that couldn't wait.

"I wanted to do that earlier. I should have." Andreah's eyes remained transfixed on his lips, as if debating if she'd silence herself by kissing again. Instead, they flickered up to meet his. "I'm sorry if I ever made you feel like being you wasn't okay. You're a goddamn car wreck of everything that is right in the world. And I love it."

"I...uh." Owen's hands pulled tighter around her like it was all he could do to hang on for the moment. "Don't know what to say to that."

"I think you said your piece."

Owen pulled his hands up to nurse a headache that threatened to come back at the mention of that interview. "I clearly need to stop."

"No, it was good," she reassured. Owen raised a brow in disbelief. She capitulated.

"Okay, maybe not corporate good. But I told Chris he could shove that bullshit." She breathed in before resting her forehead against his. "I'm sorry you were put through that."

"I'm sorry your moment was stepped on."

She shrugged. "I like this moment better."

"You got this," Daniel whispered to Amilia, who was doubled over in a breathless panic. The first time it happened Daniel wasn't sure what to do. To be honest, he didn't do anything of real help for the first month. But as time went on, he found that holding her hand, and reminding her to how to breathe evenly, was all he could really do. It was a simple thing that ended up working after other simple things didn't.

Shortly after Amilia's return, they had to pick things up and travel to France for Lance's wedding. Daniel offered to support her staying home if needed, but Amilia assured him that it would be fine. Now he wasn't so sure, even though where she was hardly seemed to matter.

She clutched her stomach as she stood. Her breathing still mimicked a stone skipping across water. Daniel watched silently before opening up his arms, an invitation Amilia sometimes took. Today, the hug was welcomed. "Thank you," she managed.

She didn't have to explain how or why the tension of the wedding, stress of traveling, or having to meet so many new people had gotten to her for him to understand. "Is there anything else I can do?" he offered.

Amilia shook her head. "No. I'm okay," she said, convincing herself.

Daniel was just glad he was around to help. "I love you," he reminded.

"And I love you," Amilia whispered back. "You should go help Lance get ready."

"You sure?"

"Yeah, I'm fine now."

Daniel kissed her hand before he left. She was due somewhere else too, and after taking a centering breath, she headed out of their room to find Chloe.

"Sorry I'm late," Amilia said, as she squeezed into the room that Chloe was getting ready in.

"It's okay, dear," Chloe said, turning back as far as she could as Lily fastened her corset. "Somebody thought they could squeeze the truth about how I met Lance out of me."

"I've seen the lives those boys lead." Lily grinned as she finished up with an extra little tug. "And here you tell me this causal story about the power of chance."

Amilia nervously turned her hands over each other. Chloe had been more than sweet, but Lily hadn't warmed up since her return. "I actually haven't heard that story."

"It's nothing real exciting, you know nobles and their politics," Chloe said. She reached a hand up to work on her hair. Lily shooed her hand away, and after a half-second pout, Chloe went on. "Our families do business together, and some time ago there was a health scare with Lance's father. During that time, Lance came back home, and that's when we met."

Lily gave a glance to Amilia, who was still standing by the door. It was meant to silently ask 'can you believe that?' Which Amilia did, so she just pulled on a quick smile.

"Lance's stories are so full of adventure." The admiration was clear in Chloe's voice as she spoke. "Most soldiers only tell tales of their own glory, but not Lance. It was from his stories that I first heard of you. I think he even included the painful stories, the ones where things weren't so perfect, so I wouldn't fall for the grandeur of it all.

"When Daniel came to visit, I did not know if I would never see Lance again. But, I knew one thing. I wanted to be a part of those stories, good or bad. I have no craft like either of you, so hid in their carriage as they traveled to London. Or tried. I swore Daniel was going to throw me out on the street for hiding away."

"But why so soon?" Lily said, as she placed a final pin into Chloe's blonde locks.

"Oh please," Chloe said. It was the roughest tone Amilia ever heard from her, and while still kinder than most people's default, it made Amilia's heart race a little faster, as if she was the target. "I've written to him for almost a year before meeting, and we were in England for quite some time," Chloe continued. "And while playing house there was fun, Lance has always wanted to start his own family and I couldn't be more excited."

Amilia couldn't remember Lance talking about kids. She racked her brain for him mentioning it, only to realize she had missed it. Who knew what else. It proved one really doesn't know a couple by their outward appearance. This thought added to the painful combination of London and marriage, and caused Amilia to stare off. She noticed someone move closer, but jumped after the fact. When Amilia's attention was dropped back into the present, she was confused of where she was.

Chloe mistakenly took this as a sign she was a bad host. "I'm so sorry, listen to me babble on." She was now close enough to hold both her hands out to Amilia. It took a second, but Amilia took her friend's hands. "I just wanted to say, thank you so much for coming. I know we aren't the closest, but it means a lot that you're here. Both Lance and Daniel told me so much about you, and I never thought I'd get to meet you. Oh, look at me babbling again." Chloe sniffled hard, eyes welling.

Amilia could see Lily's tight expression from over Chloe's shoulder, but she willed herself to focus on the bride. "I'm glad to be here, too," Amilia said, and gave her a little squeeze before letting go. Chloe shined brighter than the summer sun, full of joy and hope for her future. "You make a beautiful bride."

"Prêt, ma chèrie?" Chloe's mother peeked in from the open door. She, too, was short, and held herself with a quieter charm then her daughter. Amilia wasn't sure what she said but contextually she figured *prêt* meant ready.

As they all funneled out of the room, Amilia separated from the bride to find Daniel. He was seated right behind Lance's family, with whom she had barely become familiar. She took in a deep breath before braving the crowd to reach him. Once Daniel saw her, he stood to help her sit and gave her as much space as she needed.

"You look gorgeous," he said, smiling from ear to ear. Amilia mirrored him with lively excitement. He looked dashing as well, suited in what men with money usually preferred to wear. For a moment, she reminisced over her father and how he dressed when she was young.

"Should I give introductions while we wait here?" Daniel asked.

Any plan that didn't involve being paraded around, Amilia liked. She scooted a little closer so he could whisper. "I'm sure you could guess, but the stout fellow across the way is Chloe's father. The Carré family does a lot of trade with England, but their main interests are in this state. Simply home, I guess."

"Any gossip I should know?"

Daniel had a sly smile that boarded on nervous. "Yeah," he went on as his volume dropped further. "If this wedding had happened not even a year ago, I wouldn't have been allowed to sit on this side."

"Why?" Amilia mouthed.

"I'm never...." Daniel frowned. "Quite what anyone's family expects. Blamed as a distraction it seems. I'm certain the guild was no help with that."

Amilia placed her hand on his arm, a small reassurance that seemed to brighten his expression. "I've never met your family," she said, not really a question or a statement. Amilia knew his father was still around, but it was a clear contrast between them. She had been all about family. He, on the other hand, had always been about faction. Which happened to sometimes include friends and family.

"I should introduce you to my father," Daniel said. His attention was divided as Lance stepped out, looking far more prim and proper than usual. The livery collar he wore even made him look princely. Lance also had the right amount of nervousness as he ran his hands down his tunic.

Daniel looked back at Amilia, smile growing. "I think he'd love to meet you."

The idea made Amilia nervous, even though it was something she wanted. But that was another day. All she had to do was enjoy today. Daniel looked around to do a quick head count, trying to gauge how much longer it would be, and before he finished, Chloe stepped out.

Children who sat in the back rows stepped in front, dragging white ribbons with them. While Amilia had already seen the wedding dress, *oh*s and *ah*s escaped from those who had not. Her rare white dress kissed the floor as she walked, and her hands had lace delicately dripping off.

Her father brought over a small pair of ornate scissors to cut the ribbons that blocked the bride's path to the groom. While it was customary watch the bride, Daniel looked back to Lance. He stood, with his lips slightly parted and a clear look of love on his face. Daniel had always worried his friend would marry for an heir, but not now, or ever again.

Chloe cut the ribbons, and handed the scissors back to her grinning father. When she moved to stand next to Lance, he nervously smiled towards her family, then the priest, until finally back to Chloe. "The Anne of Brittany would not outshine you today." He whispered, since it was out of turn.

The ceremony was in French, and when it got to the vows Daniel leaned in again. He started translating as quietly as he could. "I, Chloe Carré, take you, Lance Tarlé, to be my husband. You are the only man I know that can be a force of nature without losing his humor, and spirit to it. I look forward to every day we spend together, and cherish every laugh we share. You told me your stories, and I want to be a part of them forevermore."

Amilia recognized a line from earlier. Chloe's vows must have been in her head for days. Lance started speaking and Daniel let him get a little ahead. "I, Lance Tarlé, take you, Chloe Carré, to be my wife. Never have I met a person more charming, sweet, and loving. Your laugh is a sound I'd cross oceans to hear. From the moment you tagged along with me, I knew I would be lost without you, and it would be an honor to be wed to you."

Lance stopped talking, but Daniel continued adding a line of his own. Even after priest started to talk and the translation became even more out of sync. "I saw the world from a young age, but I didn't feel much of its beauty until I found you," Daniel said, as he now looked over at Amilia.

She had been watching the wedding, but ended up looking at Daniel, confused. When it dawned on her, she felt a small pain in her heart. Her lips spread into a smile as she leaned into his shoulder. It took what felt like the entire ceremony for the smile to subside.

The wedding shifted into the reception. Lance and Chloe stood on opposite sides of the croquembouche cake, leaning over it to kiss. Chloe had to stand on her very tiptoes to reach. Daniel and Amilia were seated by the bride and groom as the toast got underway.

"It pleases me to no end that our paths have brought us here. All together, and now we get to celebrate you two becoming family." Daniel lifted his glass as he finished his speech. "To friends in love."

Before they were free to mingle, pieces of bread were placed in the bottom of the newlyweds' drink. Tradition claimed whoever hit the bottom first would rule the household. They raced, but it wasn't long before an excited noise came from Chloe signaling she won. Lance sighed, putting his glass down that was awfully light itself before laughing.

"We didn't get to dance at the wedding," Amilia said when Daniel entered the room. He smiled as he lifted the livery collar from his shoulders and placed the chain on the dresser. She'd only retired to the room fifteen minutes ago and had settled into the plush bed.

"You are right," Daniel said, with a light smile. He moved over closer and held out his hand. "I think we deserve a dance."

Amilia smiled, and noticed her cheeks felt a little sore. She shook her head as Daniel sat down on the bed and watched her expression. His own made her smile even bigger. "The only thing I want is for you to stay with me," she said, and rubbed her thumb against the slight stubble on his cheek. "Weddings make me think of happily ever afters. Kids, and everything else it can mean."

Daniel closed his eyes, chin lifting ever so at her touch. After taking a breath, he opened his eyes to meet hers. He guided Amilia's hand to his lips and kissed her fingertips. "I spent nearly two years of my life without you. I know what it is like. I want you, and whatever that means or doesn't mean."

"But—"

"And I will always choose you," Daniel continued. "If you are the sea, and I am the shore, I will take everything that the tide brings in."

"Are you a poet, my love?" she asked. Daniel was always the light that would shine brightest, the fire that would burn through the shadows and be the truth in the ashes. Maybe he made her a poet, too.

"For you, I try."

Amilia pressed her forehead against his, taking a gentle moment before meeting his lips. Daniel had learned to be delicate, but not tense, whenever they kissed. That balance made her feel the most comfortable. His hands hovered before resting on her waist, which received an automatic shiver. "Sorry," he whispered before moving them away.

"No," Amilia said, and reached for them. "I'm just...cold."

Daniel apprehensively looked her over as she placed his hands back. Once there, her hands moved up to his shoulders. Daniel couldn't help but freeze as he let her do as she wanted, and received a series of kisses that felt like pleas.

"Amilia..." he mumbled, bewildered by her.

"Just stay here," she said softly. Daniel nodded, and followed her next order, which was 'kiss me.' His hesitation melted away quicker than he expected.

She had only brushed her fingers through his hair with love or adoration in the past months. But this time, they tangled and knotted around the strands. He broke the kiss to be able to look at her. Her jaw was tight before opening her eyes, her body tensing up like his did. "I want you," she repeated his words, "and whatever that means."

Daniel tenderly touched her face, and she instinctively turned her cheek against his palm. "As you wish, *mon amour.*" he whispered, and gave her the choice of when their lips would meet again.

"Great, good place to end today," Carmen interrupted.

If taking a cold shower does the trick, then her voice was an ice bucket dumped over their heads. Owen clenched his jaw and pulled off the headgear. He stared at his hands for a second before looking up in a silent search for Andreah.

She held his glance before pressing her lips into a thin line. "Wouldn't want to break TOS," Andreah said, with a veiled tone.

"Oh please," Carmen said, "No one enforces that. It just had to be there."

"Unless someone pisses off fnVR," Owen added.

Carmen's weight swayed towards him with a grin. "Exactly."

Owen smiled, but it was a practiced one he learned that signaled someone to move on. If fnVR dictated a stop for any reason, from pacing to viewership of another stream, they put an end to their playing. With the stream over, Carmen left, surely to be hyper-efficient somewhere else.

"Heading home?" Andreah asked, as she looped her purse over her shoulder.

"Yeah, I don't have anything else planned."

Andreah paused for a second. "I'll ride downstairs with you."

They moved through the lobby, only glancing at each other to be mindful of where the other was walking. Andreah pressed the down button and waited.

"So, uh," Owen started, which got Andreah's attention. Her expression could have been paired with an animated '?' above her head. The elevator dinged before he began again.

He licked his lips as they stepped in, waiting for the doors to close before looking at her. "Did fnVR plan that?" he asked, as casually as possible.

Andreah smirked a little before looking down at her hands, inspecting her nails. "No, I wouldn't trust them to make it right."

Owen's eyes lingered on her lips for a few moments longer than he meant to. "Good. I'd trust you more."

That earned a curious look. "With what, exactly?" she asked, the blush on her cheeks deceiving her confidence.

Owen smiled at her before looking away and shaking his head. He felt her eyes still on him as he looked at the screen to see they were about to stop at the bottom floor. When he finally glanced back, she was now focused on the screen too. But noted her grip on the elevator's railing. She let go as the elevator dinged and opened to let them out.

"I'll see you later," Andreah said, and pulled out the key to her bike lock.

"Later."

Owen muttered under his breath. A lid kept catching the top shelf of the dishwasher, and he had to wiggle it around so it was flat enough. He kept telling himself he needed to get around to the dishes all week, but now here he was, with a shit ton too many. He was about to tackle the pans that needed to be hand washed when he heard a knock at the front door. He walked through the living room. Whoever it was knocked again before he made it to the other side.

At his door was Andreah. She tried to brush off the water that had stuck on her raincoat. She blinked up at him, but didn't say anything.

"Uhm, hi," Owen managed, further inspecting how wet her hair was. "Did you walk here?"

"Biked," she responded without a beat. She glanced over him now too. "Were you sleeping?"

Despite what his pajamas bottoms seemed to suggest, he shook his head. "Is everything okay?"

"Yes," she answered, then shifted. "Can I come in?"

"Sure." Owen stepped aside to give her space and closed the door once she was in.

She paced away a short distance, feeling more embarrassed than anything else. "I don't know how to eloquently say this." She turned back to look at him. "I wanted to kiss you in the elevator. Actually, I wanted to stop the elevator and spend a good hour in there. And I haven't thought about anything else all day."

"Wow." Owen's footsteps slowed to a stop a few feet from her, wondering what the right words were. "I don't know what to say."

"Is there anything you want to say?"

"I don't think so," he said. Andreah covered what he also felt pretty well.

She stepped forward and stood up on her tiptoes to give him a more polite kiss then he was expecting. His hands moved to wrap around her before realizing her jacket was still soaked from the rain. He quickly moved for the front zipper, and she let it slip onto the floor. Andreah pulled her arms around his shoulders, pressing against him while playfully biting his bottom lip.

Owen pushed her against the door, roughly pulling his hand through her hair. Hers were cool against his feverish skin. Only when Andreah pushed forward did he slow enough to savor the feeling, to really believe this was real.

Andreah willed him eventually to move more into the living room. Her breath was heavy against Owen's skin as they stumbled around. He braced himself against the arm of the couch as his foot accidentally caught the rug.

"Careful, you're going to break something," Andreah teased, taking the moment to pull off her shirt.

"Then we should get you to the bed where it's safe," Owen countered. He closed the space between them and easily lifted her into his arms, as she wrapped her legs around his waist with a laugh.

They both let out a huff as they crashed into the pillows. Andreah smiled brightly at him as they adjusted to the soft bed. He gave her a few quick kisses before moving down her neck, and pulling at her bra with impatient want.

It felt like the first time again, yet he knew all the right moves. Where to kiss, where to hold her, how gentle or how rough he should be. Andreah fell into the same rhythm, knowing exactly what made him desire more. The notion that everything between them wasn't right until they were in bed together felt wrong. Yet, having the same touch that once cut so deep into his soul now soothe was the closest he came to a symmetrical perfection. Being with Andreah, as more than just business partners, more than what they once were, was everything he never realized he wanted.

Andreah thought as she pulled the sheets tightly around them that being in Owen's bed was the only place she wanted to be from now on. Not just for things like this. But other stuff, like being *real* naughty and eating dinner in it while watching that movie collection she hadn't gotten around to investigating. "Tell me something I don't know about you," she asked, after lying in silence for a short time.

Owen chuckled, making her adjust at the rough exhale. "Isn't this a little backward?"

"So?" she seemed to dare. "Talk to me."

"Okay." It felt like the silliest thing, but it made him smile in an unstoppable way. "Um, I'm a middle child." Andreah smirked, but buried her nose into his chest. "What?" Owen laughed again. "Why is that funny?"

"Explains so much," she teased.

"I'm going to bop you with a pillow if you don't behave."

Andreah tucked in closer, and felt a small laugh vibrate through his ribs. "No, no, I'll be good I swear. Okay, I have a real question."

"Shoot."

"If you hate your family so much, why do you go by your last name? I'd think it would be a constant reminder."

"It is, and I don't hate them." Owen waved his free hand in the air. "But there is a power in taking what you're called and twisting it around in your favor. In hearing it said in that fashion, it reiterates the meaning you want."

"Huh," She let out a little hum as she thought. "I guess to be fair it should be my turn. I should make it good like...saying my favorite color is red."

"No way," Owen said, with utter disbelief. "Me too!"

She sat up, narrowing her eyes slightly. "I can't tell if you're shitting me or not."

"Guess you'll never know until we get to that one."

"Well fiiine," she said, extending the word. "I'll just stay here until you tell me."

"Good," he said softly.

Andreah echoed him even softer as she settled down again and closed her eyes, falling asleep with an ease that made him jealous. Even though he didn't even want to fall asleep, really. Lying here with Andreah curled so close, and the light thumping of bass coming in from the open window, promised to keep him perfectly content. It didn't even matter what song it was. It was enough that it was steady, like a heartbeat.

Most debauchery-filled nights made for blurred mornings, but today was too bright, too clear. It provided no distractions to the fact that Andreah wasn't here. Owen sat up in bed, tempted to call her name to be sure. But it was too quiet. He fell back in bed, feeling foolish that he'd ever thought she would be here. Declarations of love and passion do not make a commitment.

He needed to talk to someone. Anyone who wouldn't judge whatever this on again off again thing was. Unfortunately, only one place came to mind.

"I don't even know if I belong in these meetings anymore. I'm not anonymous. You can practically watch my lives unfold on TV in front of you. You can witness my past life, and watch as I try to not feel too much in this one." Owen tapped his fingers on the meeting hall's podium. "Maybe I shouldn't be here, and I guess my point is, I miss being anonymous. There is a certain freedom in being unknown."

The room was silent as Owen stepped down. He walked over to the snack table and thought about walking right past, but stopped. A shorter girl with her hood up came to the table, and he took a step over to give her room. Instead of focusing on the cookies, her attention was undivided on

384

him. Or rather, nervously not on him in a way that made the void's meaning clear. "I um," she said with a false start. "I wanted to tell you that Daniel helped me. I know you miss what you had, but thank you. Daniel's refusal to give up helped me do the same."

Owen opened his mouth, but found his tongue tied. What could he even say to that? What sounded sincere enough?

"You don't have to say anything," she said, with a quick jitter of her hands. "I just wanted you to know. I should sit back down."

He wordlessly watched as she did just that. The support held for a time. Until he got home, looked around, and felt alone again. How many half fixes and momentary reprieves would it take to feel okay again?

It was just another day indistinguishable from the rest. With a sigh, Owen grabbed his laundry basket and started the long trek to the laundry room downstairs. He mindlessly tossed shirts and socks in, only pausing to check the pockets before throwing it all in.

Usually nothing was there, and at most a few coins were found. But this time, he pulled out Andreah's stash. It had been a while since he'd accidentally lifted the bag of ecstasy off her. Owen stared in disbelief before hiding it in his jeans and glancing around. It wasn't like he could just toss it in the trash down here. Who knows who could find it?

As soon as the washer was loaded, he booked it upstairs. He paced through his apartment stopping in his bedroom and pulling the drugs back out. What should he do with them?

He stared down and decided to take a seat at the foot of a chair. The unmade bed across from him was now an echo of the night before. Owen pulled out a pill and placed it between his lips. It rested there for a thoughtful second before he grabbed a water bottle off the side table. If he could only catch that content feeling again, the whole day would go by so much easier.

But like the best-laid plans of mice and men, his, too, went awry. Fifteen minutes later, Owen pulled a hand to his chest. He thought he could push past the tightness until it settled into nausea that signaled only two things: dehydration or too high of a dose.

He could try to help one of those. Owen's fingers felt cold as he reached for the water bottle. The plan was to ride it out on the bed, but the floor seemed just as good right now. He felt tired, but knew he wouldn't be able to sleep and decided to hum the only song he could think of to help him get through it.

Minutes passed, maybe hours, Owen couldn't tell, before he heard his front door open.

"Owen?" Andreah called. "I found your spare keys before I left, I hope that's..." Owen's attention drifted in and out while she rambled. "...some tasty pho from that place..." His eyes fluttered open to look around for her before closing them again.

"—ere are you?" He heard his bedroom door creak, signaling that she was close now.

Andreah's hand on his shoulder was the clearest feeling that followed. He moved his jaw uncomfortably before speaking. "Where did you go?"

"I had to help Abby with a story, I thought I told you."

"No."

The short answer gave her pause. "I'm sorry. I swore I did." Owen nodded slightly, and went back to whispering something. It was clearly words, but they were so foreign and woven together she couldn't tell which. "Owen, baby," Andreah said, "What are you saying?"

He raised his voice so she could hear. *"La petite poule grise."*

"Lance's song?" Owen let out a small sound in agreement. She must have moved away for a moment because he felt her come back. "How much did you take? Do you need anything?"

"No...I know what's wrong. Just let me pretend to try to sleep."

Andreah pulled him up by his arm, and he leaned in making it easy to support him enough to get him onto the bed. "Okay, then you're not a complete idiot." She gave him a small kiss on his forehead, her breath smelling of chocolate and coffee. "I'll be right here 'til you're over the hill."

Owen was disappointed the kiss wasn't on the lips. That is, until he felt fingers brush his hair and made being awake bearable.

The diner's brew the next morning didn't smell as sweet. Andreah's eyes were as black as her coffee as she rubbed away the fatigue. Owen felt the need to apologize, but Andreah waved him away each time. The next topic led to her taking many frequent sips from her mug and messed with the silverware. "You had a bad roll last night, and this morning you want to get back together?"

"Yes."

"Why?"

Owen sighed. "I did it because I knew I didn't have...*this* in real life. And I desperately wanted that loved up feeling. And I know that sounds like I'm putting it on you, and I'm not. It's on me, and if you say no, I will responsibly take care of myself. But I don't know why we need to fight this. If you love me too, why aren't we together?"

Andreah stared down at waffles, already topped with syrup but otherwise untouched.

"Come on," Owen smiled. "Don't you want to date a bisexual with an addictive personality? We share one story, why can't we share this one too?"

"God, you're so—" Andreah shook her head and grinned. "I love you."

"So, that's a yes?"

"Yes."

Owen leaned over the small table and Andreah mirrored him. "Can I kiss you?" he asked, already feeling her breath unevenly on his lips. It was a closeness where centimeters meant as much as miles.

"Yeah," she breathed, and sweetly kissed him. "I forget how scary and weird it is from the other side. We both really need to watch the drugs."

"Can't really disagree with that."

"Just do this one little thing for me?" The plea was clear in Owen's tone.

"It's kind of illegal." Andreah turned forward in her chair and pretended to pay attention to the memo fnVR sent out. She had got in the habit of reading them and she'd be damned if she missed the one that was finally important.

"Oh please, like you've never broke laws during the alley cat races."

"That's different."

Owen edged closer, eating up more of her desk as he sat down. He leaned in like he was going to reveal the truly illegal part of his plan. "Is it the height? The Empire State Building isn't *that* tall for parkour."

"Are you kidding me? It's—" Andreah stopped as Owen turned his head into his shoulder to stifle a laugh. "You are joking. God damn it, why did I believe you for a second!"

"I admire the trust you have in me," Owen beamed.

Andreah bit her lip as she grinned. One day everything is wrong, then when you least expect it, it's another day, and it's okay. Despite this insight, Andreah made a face. "Ew, gross."

"How are my stars?" Chris announced, "I have news."

"Is it in the memo?" Owen leaned forward to skim something about the lunch room. Not likely.

"No." Chris's brow furrowed as if insulted that he'd come here for that. "We set up a Big Bad for you guys."

Owen scoffed as he got up from Andreah's area and moved over to his streaming space. The game was solid, and it was tiresome the way fnVR had to keep messing with it.

"The last big event wasn't that long ago," Andreah said. "Shouldn't we pace ourselves?"

"The wedding was not planned. Therefore, we could not market it properly, and thus ratings were lost. Furthermore, the arena streams kick our ass because of the action. Our target demo isn't going to tune in for an NPC's wedding."

"Pretty sure you are underestimating everyone's love for Lance," Owen countered.

"Plus," Andreah added. "They say sex sells."

"Touché."

Chris stared at them silently, wondering if they were done. He considered them insufferable when they worked together. Before he ran off to get someone who'd be less civil, Andreah spoke up. "Who is the target?"

"Don Ambrogio Spinola."

Andreah paled at Chris' choice. It didn't matter how many missions ago it was, one does not forget the name of the man who ordered their hanging. Fictional or not. Thinking back that far made her worry that the pain would tint what was going on now. But the world kept moving.

"He dies in 1630," Owen corrected. "It's 1606 in game."

"How do you know that?" Andreah asked.

"Why wouldn't I? Hated that guy for months. I wanted to kill him sooner, but since he's a historically based character I knew the game wouldn't let me."

Chris cleared his throat, and the two turned to look back at him as if they had forgotten about his presence. "That was true, until now. If you want to level before the battle, now is the time."

Despite the date, some things were accurate about this day, like the location. They had to travel all the way to Castelnuovo Scrivia, Italy. It took longer to reach Italy than it did the Canary Islands, or Paris. He worried the extra training would gather dust even with the game fudging the details to make this night happen when dictated.

The battle was so huge that one could have sold tickets to witness the depth of the brutality. And maybe they had. Ambrogio Spinola would have secured himself somewhere he could control the battle. This show, however, was not for them. It had been going on before the thieves' intrusion to the field. The Thirty Years' War, as it was so named, was long. This battle alone would not change the tide, but in war, the tide isn't the only thing at stake. Pride, honor, and revenge were always pieces to be won, *and re-won,* time and again.

The trio of thieves traveled with the Spanish reinforcements that were sent shortly after the Archduke was replaced with General Ambrosio Spinola to help end Spain's losses. The treachery only further unsettled Daniel.

The city in front of them was starting to show the damage upon its walls—only some of which done by the Spaniards, since nature herself bore down the hardest. A small fort had been won under the Don's control, and thus he gained the trust of any Knights who'd doubted him.

The details beyond that were slammed together in a way that was world-shattering to pull apart. Somewhere along the way, the rival commander believed that land wasn't solid enough, so skulls and bones were used.

"Amilia," Daniel called.

She doubted the ramparts were built on top of fallen soldiers to demoralize, but the sight certainly did. The worst part is that this morbid plan didn't even work. The ramparts stood ever crumbling from cannon fire.

"Amilia, you need to take a deep breath and tell me where we are," Daniel continued.

She looked over at him, then Lance, who stood close by with an equally concerned expression. The first half she was able to do, but the rest...

"The commander called this place *Nova Troia*," Daniel said. "Meaning New Troy. For his vow to hold it as long as the ancient Trojans."

"Charming," Lance said, with a tight expression.

"Do you want to go back?" Daniel asked.

"No," Amilia was quick to say. She glanced around and turned back to the boys with a greater focus. "I hate him as much as the rest of you, and want the peace of knowing this is done."

"Here," Lance said, and pulled off the wedding ring from his hand. They'd done this before to help ground Amilia, and it worked like the worry token Lance offered before. They'd tried similar things, but something about the weight of Lance's offer worked better than anything else.

"Thank you." She took another breath and glanced up the wall again. This time looking at each stone that offered a hand or foothold. "Up we go."

The broken bits made it possible to climb the chipped stones until they made it up the wall. Questions like what was next was lost to the carnage below. Two armies clashed, any civilians left in the city were lost. Or, hopefully, hidden.

Any time war started to feel modern, the harshness of it all was brought back to Daniel. This was hand to hand, pikes and clubs. The sort of battle that made you spit out blood with no reprieve. "The mission is to find and kill the Don. Other wars are not ours today."

Lance had one foot on the ledge as he looked out. Mentally, he mapped what could be used to jump down into the fray. Roof, window awning, scaffolding, ground. "Should we split up to find him faster?"

Daniel debated if it would be wise to clear this top level first, or simply a waste of time, before answering the question he was sure of. "No, we are in this together so we stick together."

That left the deciding vote with Amilia. "Together."

Amilia stood perched like a guardian angel on the scaffolding as Daniel and Lance made the extra leap down. During the first moments of the battle, they focused on defense. Correctly assuming the Spanish soldiers would help as they worked their way through the city. But their nationality would only buy them so much.

The ground was cratered. Shields pushed against the beating of swords from similar men in different tunics. They created a blockage that only showed signs of letting up once enough men were sacrificed.

A clean whistle broke through and Daniel looked up to Amilia, who had free run past the blockage. Ground, wall run, ledge. Daniel took a few steps back and made a run for it. His hands grabbed on the overhang and pulled himself up. Lance followed, and within seconds they were behind, and above, enemy lines.

When the boys dropped back down, one thing was clear to Amilia. Sword fighting was about passion. Lance's movements were fluid like a dance. The soldiers, who were just fighting because they were ordered to, quickly fell to the blade. Daniel's weapons were about closeness. He flipped off a wall to get close enough to sink in his daggers. Her bow was about patience. Being rash in battle might feel right, but the key was biding your time just long enough to send an arrow into someone's chest.

"Lance, behind you!" Amilia called.

He turned, pure instinct, and slashed. The attack was halted as the man collapsed with a bubbling neck wound. Lance give a quick salute up to Amilia before turning back.

"Getting a bit old for this?" Daniel teased as Lance fell back in line with him. He ducked as a halberd swung over his head.

"Watch it, Ortiz," Lance grinned.

Daniel smirked. He kicked his attacker back, who then stumbled into a Spanish soldier who finished the job. The advantage of this war was several front lines. There, leading the onslaught from the west, was the Don they were looking for.

Getting to him was a far loftier mission. Pikes and clubs were only part of their concern. If they got too close Santiago might spot the extra players on the board.

"How much time do we have left?" Lance asked in French. Even though it was doubtful that eavesdroppers could hear over the clash.

"Not much." Daniel glanced around. Forward meant a bunch of Spanish soldiers. The sides, however....

He ran over to a banister, then jumped to a smaller wall and pulled himself up. Lance and Amilia followed with their own free running feats.

Unfortunately, this level was not unguarded. Amilia fired an arrow. The close quarters gave her no favors. A single fist overpowered her more elegant weapon. Her vision flickered from here to somewhere else. Her grunt turned into a yell. Her knee found his gut. Her fist found his jaw, and when he fell, her boot crushed his windpipe. Daniel and Lance stood tense, weapons still drawn.

"I think I might need to retire after this." Amilia shook her head in an attempt to clear it. She moved past the weary boys. "Maybe the four of us should go on vacation."

"Compelling offer," Lance said, as he sheathed his sword.

When the siege was all over, what was left of the enemy garrison was allowed to retreat. Instead of tucking their tails and silently leaving, they marched out with flags flying and drums beating. To say there were a few people left on the streets would have been an overstatement. There was their trio, and maybe another couple tucked by the blacksmiths. Everyone else was either dead or a soldier.

Having a banquet with wine that poured as freely as blood was distasteful, and part of the reason they didn't partake in the Spanish victory. Another reason was that once poison was slipped into the drinks, nothing felt safe. All three of them were too conspicuous, so they bribed a server to deliver their silent weapon.

Once his hand was lined with gold the server smirked and looked up at Daniel. "Pleasure doing business," he said, before slipping out of the room.

"How will we know when it works?" Amilia asked.

"It won't take effect right away," Lance explained. "Which should give us enough time to lure him away from anyone less than excited about our plan."

"You mean the murder plan?" Amilia couldn't help but joke from her spot on the counter.

"Yes, that is what I was referring to."

When dinner died down, the officers started heading back to their new rooms for the night. Which left their target in the main hall, wondering if his meal agreed with him. Daniel walked up to the head table, pulled the large serving fork out, twirling it like any other weapon...which it could be, with such long and sharp prongs. When the movement finally caught Ambrogio's narrow focus, Daniel sat down at the table across from him.

Instead of exchanging a word, the two men just watched each other. Ambrogio's age seemed to catch up with him all at once. Rasping sounds escaped his throat as he struggled for air past the poison that took control. Muttered words formed on his dying lips, but the only ones Daniel could make out were honor and reputation.

"This was war, and now you are bankrupt," Daniel corrected. Amilia thought that would be that, but he went on. "Last time we met I told you I'd be the end of you."

"Just couldn't let nature have me, boy?" Ambrogio strained to speak. "I still have my honor and reputation. What do you have?"

Daniel glanced over to Amilia, who met his gaze as she spun around the ring on her finger. Then looked to Lance, who was carefully watching their target as Daniel took a moment to think of his answer. "I have them." Despite everything he still had both of them at his side.

Their current target was no longer a threat, but when the door opened, everyone tensed. The concern soon settled when it was the server they bribed earlier. "Quick, you can make your escape through the servants' kitchen before anyone takes notice."

"Party's over, let's go." Amilia headed out the door first, followed by Lance, then finally Daniel stepped to join them.

He took only a few steps before a knife at his throat stopped him. "Remember me?" the server asked from behind.

Daniel carefully exhaled as if even that would be too much to bare. "Maybe you could refresh my memory?"

"I already know the answer," the man said, with a growing hate in his tone. "I know that you don't. You didn't even pause for a second before you bribed me to do your dirty work. Like I was no different than any other tool."

A white hot pain erupted from Daniel's side. A gulp accompanied his swimming vision. The knife that was once at his throat was pulled from his side. Daniel fell forward with the help of a shove. He held his side, and turned to stare up at his attacker. But his face wasn't the concerning thing. It's what was said next.

"Fucking roleplayers."

"What?" Daniel said, too confused for any other remark. How much hate and bile was needed to blur the player's thought and make it real?

"Name's Elijah. It's nice to meet you again after all this time."

Daniel was breathing. He was breathing, he was terrified, he was alive. The wound itself might not be the worst injury ever, but it was unexpected. It had thrown him out of sync enough that he heard voices of those who weren't playing. They were arguing, they were surprised too. Owen couldn't quite make them out without further losing his connection with Daniel.

He needed to focus. Focus on the fact that he was bleeding, that he was being dragged by other men who must be employed by Elijah.

Elijah.

That name meant nothing to him. How had someone come to hate him so much when he knew so little about them?

"The great Daniel Ortiz isn't going to give up the ghost already, is he?" Elijah taunted.

'Screw you,' came to mind but it wasn't the wisest thing to say right then. Daniel lifted his head, but couldn't manage to get the glare off his face. If only he could place him. How had this guy even found him?

Owen expected that question to be equally hard, but by the time it was even thought, he knew the answer. fnVR advertised this event, and made Daniel's life available for everyone to see. Being in the spotlight had cast a shadow. Made this possible without any bone digging required.

"Where are my friends?" Daniel asked. No other questions mattered at this point.

Elijah sat on a desk, his legs spread, taking up more room as he watched Daniel on the floor in front of him. "Always with your friends," he said before making a tsking sound. "People like you are always so concerned with your own story. You didn't even look at me twice today. Destroyed everything that mattered to me without even a second thought because it wasn't relevant to your version of the world."

Daniel pulled himself to a standing position. It wasn't very graceful as he held his side in the process. When or how he did what Elijah accused was lost to him, but the timing wasn't. "So you wanted an audience?"

"I do have that now, don't I?" Elijah laughed. Daniel didn't share in his amusement. He just wanted to know where Lance and Amilia were. Elijah went on. "That was the original plan. But then I realized just because your world has a bigger platform doesn't make mine any less valid."

Daniel stayed quiet. He was sure words wouldn't change Elijah's mind. Whatever pain Daniel accidentally caused wouldn't be fixed with an explanation or apology. He could see it in Elijah's unforgiving eyes. He found himself staring at this short man, who wore a smile as bright as the pins on a coat he now wore. Daniel wanted to hate every inch, but was caught up in Elijah's point. It was such a cruel reminder that he hadn't taken a moment to wonder how his story intertwined with the world.

Snapping brought Daniel's attention to the moment. "Now isn't the time to get all introspective. I have a choice for you to make." Elijah gestured to the door, and Daniel glanced over expecting to see another guard...but it was just an empty hallway. "You first. I promise not to stab you this time."

Daniel forced a smile as he glanced back to Elijah. "Where are we going?"

"To church."

Where exactly that was, Daniel wasn't sure. But each step out of the hall, each step outside, changed the field. Unfortunately, it also meant reinforcements. Elijah picked up two guards along the way. Making it painfully clear he had plenty of back up. The church soon pointed itself out with a steeple that dotted the skyline towards the right. A clue which Daniel ignored as he continued walking forward.

"Now's not your moment," Elijah corrected.

Daniel paused. He stared ahead at the just-out-of-reach buildings. If he had just a few seconds to spare, he could use them to break the line of sight. But he'd been found once. Running would just delay this. If Elijah wanted to play the game, he would too.

Elijah took point, and Daniel glanced to the men waiting for him to fall in line. Once he did, they walked behind him. The church wasn't far, but it would need a lot of work before someone came here to worship. Stained glass littered the floor like broken jewels. Bits of red and yellow crushed under their boots.

If Spain hadn't needed so many soldiers, these mercenaries might have been easier to spot. Daniel wondered if any of the gold they'd given Elijah would end up in their pockets. They hung back at the door as Elijah strolled to the front of the church.

"Are you going to make me confess my sins?" Daniel asked.

Elijah stopped with a single foot on the altar. "That's clever," he smiled in a way that made Daniel want to grind his teeth. "But I believe everyone knows your sins. So, I asked myself, how do I stop a man like you in particular? What did Lance once say?"

Daniel glanced over at the name, but otherwise looked between the pews for anything that could give him the edge. There were people already inside. Scattered like wayward worshipers among the seats. When Daniel was on par with one, he noticed they weren't here to pray. They sat as still as the grave with weapons in their hands instead of prayer books. It made for a slow walk along the plank closer to Elijah.

"He said you can live your whole life with a man, but you don't truly know him until you threaten his life," Elijah continued. He was a few steps higher and now roughly the same height as Daniel. "Same can't be said for you, since it's always about them."

"If you are trying to scare me by claiming you have my friends, you showed too many cards, because I'm not buying it," Daniel said.

"Have? No." He held up a finger. "But soon."

"Will it be before I bleed out?"

Elijah's eyes narrowed, the first sign of doubt he'd shown. He glanced down to Daniel's side as if to judge how bad he was by the stain on his tunic. "Don't worry, I'll give your fans a good show."

The remaining stained glass shattered from both sides. With the colorful shards, Amilia and Lance came down like the rain. Each took out a guard that had escorted him here within seconds. Their ambush might have been a success if they hadn't walked into a trap themselves. Everyone in their seats stood and pulled their weapon. An army of swords, shields, pikes, and arrows.

"You never could choose," Elijah said, far too calmly for Daniel's nerves. "You always hesitate. Who are you going to save, hero? For once, *decide.*"

Daniel glanced over to Amilia, who had her bowstring pulled taut, unsure of who to pick off. Then over his over shoulder to Lance as he stood ready to counter the first person to move closer. Daniel's gaze then fell back on Elijah. "No."

Elijah managed to tilt his head before Daniel charged straight for him. The collision sent them both to the ground and triggered a free-for-all. Daniel groaned as he tried to be the first back on his feet. His side erupted in pain again, and he rolled to his back to suck in a lungful of air.

Despite Daniel's best efforts, Elijah got back up first, and went for the classy move of kicking him while he was down.

Daniel silently thanked whatever gods were still watching the place that it was his good side.

He rolled away before Elijah could take out any more of his annoyance and swung up to his feet. Daniel's expression twisted with pain and anger, making him look feral.

Daniel drew his arm back and threw a punch. Elijah leaned back enough to narrowly avoid it. Except that wasn't Daniel's real plan. With the closeness he gained, Daniel slammed his instep into Elijah's shin. His groan was oddly comforting, but not as much as the sound of Elijah's nose ramming against Daniel's hand seconds after.

He took quick stock of the church. Instead of drawing a weapon to use on Elijah, Daniel ran to the pews, or more accurately, on top of them. After a few he jumped on the back of an archer. The man screamed as Daniel's dagger bit into him. He tossed his attacker off. The motion caused the blade to drag down the man's spine until they crumbled onto the seat.

"I need this," Daniel said, grabbing the fallen bow and slamming the end of it against the man's head. As the archer sunk further, Daniel stole his quiver. Daniel popped back up and fired a shot at the nearest enemy. The arrow missed, embedding itself into a tapestry instead of the person attacking his friend. Daniel shook his hand out. He exhaled. And fired another.

This one sank into the back of an enemy's neck. Daniel worked like triage was flipped onto its head, and bought both Lance and Amilia some time. He lined up another shot before it went awry as someone bear hugged him from behind.

"If you refuse to decide, you can watch," Elijah said into his ear.

If Elijah expected him to watch in horror, or thrash around, Daniel didn't. He clasped both his hands together in front of him and brought them up. The leverage forced Elijah's grip to pop open. Daniel stepped sideways, and drove his elbow into Elijah's gut. He fell against the pew behind him.

Somehow, somewhere, there was a fire. Daniel stepped back to the aisle and could smell wood burning. A warm, golden glow flickered off stone walls. Daniel held his side as it started to look like the end of days.

The city was destroyed, and now it seemed a building meant for hope was also crumbling. With a creak, it did so. A balcony caved, and with a thunderous crack the burning wood came at them like an avalanche. Whatever choice Daniel could have made was now blocked off. He backed up, the little he could, and hoped both his friends were okay on the other side. Between the rubble he could see bits of the battle from the other side. A reflective shield here, fabric moving there.

"It's you and me now," Elijah said. He wiped his bleeding nose, and grinned when he saw it had stopped gushing. "God and the devil await whoever survives."

"The Greeks believed in fate, do you?" Daniel asked, as he turned around to face Elijah.

His eyes narrowed slightly, not understanding.

Daniel threw a small knife. It stuck in Elijah's shoulder as a distraction as Daniel moved closer. "My name means God is my judge," Daniel said, sliding a dagger between Elijah's ribs. He ripped the dagger to the side. Elijah wheezed, and leaned into Daniel for support. "Not you," Daniel said through gritted teeth before shoving Elijah away.

He stared up at the detailed architecture of the ceiling. By the time Daniel walked over, Elijah's eyes had closed for good. He was only a man, after all. Daniel fell to his knees at the altar, looking like he was ready to pray his own pain away.

Daniel closed his eyes. He could hear the crackle of wood, the heavy rustle of people trying to move the rubble to save themselves. It had been minutes and he realized that the blade was still clutched tight in his hand. "It's over," he whispered to himself. It was an exciting and terrifying fact that he didn't know what to do with.

"Daniel!" Amilia finally made it over to him and knelt down to his level.

"You're okay," Daniel said with a single breath. He didn't want to point out that she was risking herself further because of him. As if the same couldn't be said about many other moments, and many other people. Daniel only wanted one thing right now. He leaned forward, pressing his forehead against hers. Daniel was too afraid to see if she was injured, and while it wasn't the safest thing, he needed this precious moment.

"We both are," Amilia said. "Most of the mercenaries ran off when the building started crumbling. The rest left when they realized they weren't going to get paid. All the same, we really need to go. Are you okay?"

Daniel glanced up to Lance, who had a cloth around his nose and mouth to protect himself from the gathering smoke. "I'm alright, let's go." Daniel tried to stand, but getting up made his vision black out for half a second. "Okay, maybe I'm not."

"Don't worry, we've got you." Lance literally meant it as he scooped Daniel up. With the location of his wound, this was oddly the best way to be carried.

Daniel rested his head on Lance's shoulder. He breathed in then sighed, despite knowing he should be holding his breath against the smoke. Yet he simply didn't have the silence within him. "I feel like you are carrying me over the threshold."

"Two men married in a church?" Lance said, his words slightly mumbled behind the cloth. "How scandalous in this day and age, *amant*."

LOADING...EPILOGUE

One Year Later

"That is the worst shirt I've ever seen you wear."

"Isn't it?" Owen said proudly as he looked down at it. Over his chest was a loading wheel with the words, 'Pretending to care, please wait.'

"It's not even true," Andreah added.

She was still looking at the shirt when he looked back up. He didn't know what to say to that, or why it took her until after they got their coffee to say anything. "You are distracting me from my studies, *ma fille.*" He looked back at his phone to the French learning app.

Andreah combined a laugh and roll of her eyes that rivaled Owen's as she went back to her book. She managed to read a chapter before he was the one distracting her.

"Vous me plaisez," said the not-quite-real voice from his phone's speaker. He took a sip of his coffee topped with whipped cream and studied the words for a second before glancing up to Andreah and repeating it a bit less fluidly.

"What does that mean?" she asked.

"'I have a crush on you' according to this."

"Ooo, a crush, huh?" Andreah chuckled.

"I think it literally translates as 'you please me,' but I could be wrong." Owen waved his free hand in a fluttering 'whatever' before clicking next on the phone.

"What other very flattering flirts are you learning to use on me?" she teased, but wanted to hear more than she'd outwardly admit to.

The phone spoke again and Owen typed in a translation, but only smiled as he continued on. It wasn't that he didn't want to play along, just that most were fairly low-level flirts. Do you want to go out, do you come here often, and can I buy you a drink were already covered.

"On va chez vous ou chez moi?" Owen said, as their drinks were getting low. Despite hearing his phone say it and hearing Owen repeat it a little slower, she still had no idea what was just said. "Are we going to your place or mine?" he repeated.

"How forward," Andreah said in mock shock.

Owen grinned. "No, I'm serious, what are we doing after this?"

"Oh, my place is closer. We can head there. But first, I told Drew I'd pick him up something before we left."

"Alright." He glanced at the line, which objectively wasn't long, he just didn't want to stand in it twice in one day. "I'll wait outside."

It was one of those rare days where the weather was nice for the season and made people wish every day was like it. "Hey, I know you," Owen said to a bright pink-haired girl on the street. "Zoey, right?"

"Hey." Her surprise turned into a bright professional smile, with an underlying joy she simply brought to her always-on job. "Do you have a second for me to interview you, for old time's sake?"

"Um," Owen glanced back towards the cafe. "Okay, but quickly please."

Andreah stepped out with a bag, and the blogger who once interviewed them both looked even more taken aback at her luck. Owen wondered if her first question was about

Andreah, but Zoey recovered with the perfectionism he learned to expect.

"It's nice to see you both again. How are you two?"

"Well," Andreah said, leaving Owen curious if she was messing around, or just didn't want to talk.

Owen grinned as he bit his straw. He glanced back over to Zoey, and lifted his head to answer her properly. "We are good. Don't know if that makes the best story for you, but I'm quite comfortable where we are now."

Andreah smiled, and felt no need to explain further.

"Should I be listening for wedding bells soon?" Zoey asked.

"Oh geez," Owen said, making a face that the blogger wished she captured before he laughed at the idea. "It's a bit early for marriage, I might wait for Lance to show me some more pointers first."

"Speaking of Lance, you once said Andreah was your Amilia. Does that mean you have a Lance?"

"Lance is my Lance." Owen said with ease, knowing he could play it up for news or just do his own thing now. "So, I guess that's a yes." Owen winked in a way that made the blogger blush.

"One more, please."

Owen glanced over to Andreah, who shrugged. "Ah, okay last one," he said.

"You're out of contract with fnVR now, but can you tell us what you see in store for Daniel and Amilia?"

"Hmm." Owen took another drink, enjoying the sweetness. "I imagine three kids. Two boys, and the youngest is girl who ends up marrying Lance's only son. And the first time Lance holds his grandchild, he smirks over to Daniel and says, 'Look what we made.' Something like that."

"And, your plans? Do you want something similar?"

"Someone is cheating with the bonus question. But nah, nothing so traditional planned. The future is mine, so we'll see."

Author Note: DLC in video games is extra content, often in the form of outfit changes, extra storylines, or exclusive items. You'll find a similar vibe featured in the following ficlets. Some take place before the story, some during, others after. They offer alternative point of views, 'deleted scenes' or AU settings.

First Year Kisses

— The Start

They were huddled in the back room as they waited for the crowd and those aware of their thievery to clear out. The church had strict rules on tithing, and if the rich didn't want to pay their share, Daniel and Lance were more than happy to help out.

Daniel's focus was on the door, making sure only silence had followed them this way. Lance's was elsewhere. His feet wanted to sway forward before he realized this was not the place, or time. Hell, likely wasn't several other things too. While Lance controlled his actions, his attention was still drawn to Daniel's lips.

"I think we are alone," Daniel reported, and turned his head to Lance. Daniel missed what was going on, but ended up smiling at Lance's expression. It lit up in silent acknowledgment before flushing slightly from fear of being caught. "What?" Daniel asked, with a smile.

"Nothing."

That Daniel caught. There was a slight tilt of the head before he gave up trying to guess what. "*Menteur*," Daniel said.

"Very good, your French is getting better," Lance said, completely ignoring the fact that Daniel had just called him a liar.

"You're a good teacher."

Lance tried to hold his gaze, but couldn't. It was still long enough for Daniel to notice the same look he'd seen there before, an admiration Lance gave another. There had been shameless buster the first time Daniel caught it. But Lance's joke asking if he was jealous changed the tone, shifted their dynamic to an uneasy one, and the subject was dropped quickly. That had been weeks ago...

"You could kiss me," Daniel whispered. That pulled Lance's eyes back up. The words had been so soft he thought he had imagined them. Daniel held still resisting any nervous ticks. "Please."

Lance breathed out roughly, knowing that this was a first of many things. He leaned in, giving into that draw he felt any time they stood "too close" and granted Daniel's request. It was such a small sweet thing that washed his thoughts blissfully away.

When Lance pulled back a moment later, he found Daniel unable to open his eyes for a moment longer. "My god," Daniel grinned, as he got his nerve back.

"You should be careful using God's name in vain," Lance teased. He leaned forward again, this time resting his forehead against Daniel's. A move that was actually a disappointment for a split second before the tenderness of it won out.

"I believe that meaning is up for interpretation," Daniel countered.

"And what about thou shall not steal?" Any discussion seemed a secondary focus as Lance's hand made it along Daniel's jaw.

"Well," Daniel grinned. "I won't tell if you don't."

"Deal."

— The Middle

Being a thief meant getting in, doing the job, and then vanishing into thin air. The first two were easy but that last one was tricky. And far, far too much running most times. Daniel ran down the Spanish streets, heart pounding as fast as his feet moved. Quick on his heels was his fellow thief, Lance, and back further still was a pack of guards chasing after them.

Daniel made a tight turn, breaking the line of sight as he turned down an alley and a wound demanded he stop for a moment. He stepped into the limited darkness provided by the building's overhanging roof. Lance almost missed the turn, but caught it just in time. There wasn't a lot of room, forcing Daniel to be flush against the wall in order to share any of the shadow.

Even though Lance was inches away, his head was turned toward the alley's mouth watching guards as they ran past. The whole time, Daniel had his eyes on the man in front of him. His sight was completely filled by Lance, his strong jaw and sharp eyes that could be barely seen under his hood.

Daniel's heart continued to pound against his ribs even though he had stopped running. As the coast cleared, Lance turned to look at Daniel studying his face before recognizing a familiar wanting look. He took half a step closer so their hips, and lips, were flush against each other.

A noise rumbled low in Daniel's throat as both pleasure and pain rocked him. Lance's body had put pressure on the laceration low on his stomach, but the kiss relaxed him like morphine, causing his brain to jumble up the sensations.

Lance lifted his mouth from Daniel's, moving to whisper in his ear causing Daniel to blush at the words. "But first,"

Lance said, switching to Daniel's native tongue of Spanish. "Let's see how bad you are injured."

"I'm fine," Daniel insisted, but Lance ignored him, moving back enough to get a look at the injury. Daniel's tunic was cut, but his gear made it hard to see all of the damage. Lance pulled the tunic up to reveal a bit of Daniel's hip and stomach, deciding that wasn't good enough he pulled down on Daniel's pants line with his thumb.

The actual cut was about four inches long, but wasn't that deep. A simple bandage would fix him up, but for now, he'd have to go without. "Looks like you'll live to fight another day," Lance said, without pulling his hand away.

"Oh good," Daniel said sarcastically. "I was worr—" He felt a kiss on his hip, tensing up as his brain blurred these two lines again. Daniel swallowed trying to finish what he was saying. "—worried."

Lance stood back up, but his fingers gently trailed around Daniel's waist.

"You're being unfair, *amant*," Daniel said, and snaked his fingers up into Lance's hood.

"I love when you call me that," Lance said, with a near purr. "Admit you love every minute." He grinned, and grabbed the brim of Daniel's hood, playfully pulling it over his eyes. Before Daniel objected, Lance kissed him roughly, letting out a small moan as Daniel pulled on his short hair.

— The End

Action gets the spotlight. Pain can get the loudest voice. But when your action is to simply endure, pain is silent. Daniel witnessed this sort the most in Lance.

"I know the guild looks to me to lead, but we don't have to act like that here," Daniel said softly. Lance's hand was pressed to his lips in thought, or maybe even lack thereof, as they sat in a private hall. He seemed to consider it, but didn't show much change. "We might not be an *us*," Daniel continued, "but there will always be a *we*."

"Won't my family be proud," Lance said bitterly, his hands dropping in annoyance.

Daniel stayed silent. Lance was generally the most cheerful person in the room, but needing to crack didn't make him less of himself. "Did they write?" He asked, after a moment.

Lance looked up, as if the light could help him control the emotions he wanted to shed. The non-answer said everything that actual words could. Daniel gestured like he would take that very letter out of Lance's hand. Instead, he placed a hand on top. "They don't define you. You can have a legacy, an heir, without becoming what they think you are."

The encouragement should have helped, but in the moment seemed to do little good as he closed his eyes. Daniel wished he could hold him in the way he used to. When everything was new, and not so serious. Instead, Daniel's hand rose to Lance's cheek guiding their eyes to meet. "Even if you marry some fine French woman for love, or for children like the nobles do, it doesn't mean you filled the mold they tried to stick you in."

When Lance blinked a tear streaked down his face. "What does it mean then?"

"That you decided what *you* wanted in *your* life, and stuck to it. That is brave, and true. You've always been a role model for me because of that. And I suspect you'll guide me in many more ways over the years."

"Th-Thank you." It was a soft, unsure sound, but it made Daniel smile anyways. He leaned in, and gave him a kiss on the tip of his nose. It was a silliness that made Lance crack a smile himself. "You are ridiculous."

"Well, *someone* has to give you a run for your money."

Friends

— Reverse Death AU

"By the wishes of the crown, we gather here to end a sinful soul. Daniel Ortiz, has been convicted on counts of treason to the crown, and the church," Don Ambrogio Spinola spoke allowed.

Daniel had faced death before, but not like this, not with a noose around his neck. Not for love, nor had he ever walked in knowing for sure what was going to happen. It seemed, today, that God wasn't his only judge. On the outside, he was a piece of steel, unapologetic for his deeds. Yet internally he was shaking. Daniel's attention was pulled back as Ambrogio spoke again to ask, "Daniel Ortiz, do you have any last words?"

He paused, looking at the crowd for moment, but was quick to close his eyes to them. Daniel didn't want to see who was there, didn't want to see Amilia or Lance as he stood on the gallows. He knew his death would not go lightly, but it was the only way to grant their freedom for collective sins.

His friends would show up with the loyalty he had expected from them. Ambrogio's haste made it hard for Amilia and Lance to find the right moment to act. Lance silently got rid of as many guards as he could, as Amilia moved through the crowd getting as close as she dared.

Daniel had asked them to trust him, let him go, but his friends had trouble with that request. It was a shame he couldn't have put up a fight, or made a speech, anything to gain them more time. But there was no point. A price had to be paid to end the Knight's resentment.

He fell as Amilia called his name, and she shoved everyone out of the way. Leaving them appalled by the rashness of this small woman. She watched his boots just hang there. "Okay dear, take me with you," she said softly, not knowing what to do without him, and fell into a heap on the ground.

A knight that was guarding the front moved towards Amilia, but someone shoved him out of the way. A move that normally would have spilled more blood, if his hand wasn't out carefully trying to separate them. "Step away from her," Lance said, "You've had your sacrificial lamb."

Amilia took it all in as the pieces of her broken heart crystallized into a hate, not wild and rash, but vengeful and determined. Lance took her hands and pulled her back up to her feet. He had lost his best friend, he sure as hell wasn't going to leave her to the wolves.

She looked up to the Don and vowed, "I will kill you."

A comment that was much to Ambrogio's amusement. He laughed. "A girl such as you? Take me down? I think not."

Lance urged her to leave, but she refused to move again as the threats continued. "I will make you pay. You have no idea what fury you have unleashed," she swore.

"There is nothing here for you anymore," Lance insisted, cutting into her enough to pay attention, "Let's go. I will not see two of my friends sent to the gallows today."

Amilia weakly nodded, and they fled before the Don went back on the deal he made with Daniel. They continued to run far past what was needed, and ended up at the edge of town, too tired to continue with the weight of their broken hearts.

"This is your fault," she said grabbing Lance's tunic. "You are a thief! I thought you were to protect your own!" Her tone was hysteric as she beat on his chest with closed fists.

"I'm sorry this happened," Lance said distantly. His words did nothing for her as she continued to pound on his chest. "Amilia!" he yelled, catching her hands and surprising her with his sudden movement. "You need to stop. I'm hurting too, and trying to be here for you, but if you yell at me anymore I'm going to break as well."

Amilia ripped her hands away, stumbling backward as he didn't try to hold on at all. She looked over at him, filled with hate for anyone she looked upon. But it didn't last as she saw Lance's expression, suddenly understanding each better than she thought they ever would.

Lance waited a second before wrapping his arms around her. "He was the best part of my life too," he said, sounding like he was no longer able to hold back tears. "He did it so we could be safe. You have to hold onto that."

"There," Owen said, as he pulled off his headset, "I'm dead. Nothing can hurt me anymore."

Charlie's mouth opened, but couldn't think of a single decent thing to say. "Yeah man, you certainly made a choice there."

"Could you have said anything more middle-of-the-road?" Owen asked.

"I could try."

"Please don't," Owen said, as he got up. "There were two choices. The Knights would had made someone pay, and I refuse to watch either of them get hurt. So, self-sacrifice."

Charlie nodded slowly. They understood the choice, but actually going through with it was something else completely. Charlie exhaled, and decided to try again. "How about this; you are a really good friend. Fictional or otherwise."

"You flatter me."

"Eh," Charlie said seriously before finally cracking a smile.

The sly humor made Owen laugh and feel a lot better about everything. He refused to let it show that losing Daniel was a big deal, and enjoyed the help of hiding his true feelings under a seven layer dip of snark. "Ready to meet up with Emily?"

"Absolutely," Charlie said, as they stood up as well. "I low key love pretending our real lives are the lost seasons of Friends. But you know, with added diversity."

The woman they expected to meet was not the one that approached Charlie as they waited for Owen to come back from ordering.

"Can I get you a drink?" she asked, gesturing to the empty table besides Charlie's book.

"No, thank you." Charlie said, and looked down to read. It was all for show. This sort of thing was rare, but it happened enough that any stranger was always on their preferred avoid list.

"Can I sit down?" she pressed further.

"No." Charlie was louder this time because being proper wasn't working.

"I'm just trying to be nice. Won't you even give me a shot? I just want to get you coffee and talk. And we are literally at a coffee shop already."

Charlie closed their book. They really didn't want to be mean to the poor girl. She likely got her fair share of bullshit, but explaining the whole gender thing was not on their to-do list today. Among other Queer 101 vocab lessons. They just wanted to stop talking before she said the wrong pronoun and ruined the whole day with that bullshit.

"Excuse me," a new stranger—no, someone they knew— said as they stepped around into Charlie's view. "That's my seat," Owen said diplomatically.

The woman moved away with hesitation, and Owen confidently took the seat despite the two drinks in his hands. "Sorry babe," Owen said, "The line wasn't actually that bad so I just waited until our drinks were ready."

"That's okay..." Charlie continued to stare, as the confusion seemed to touch everyone except Owen. Their eyes slowly moved towards the woman, and Owen seemed to notice her again.

With both sets of eyes on her now, the woman laughed nervously and walked away without another word. Owen slid Charlie's drink over hoping the caffeine would reboot his friend.

"Did you just pretend to be my boyfriend to save me from awkwardness?" Charlie asked, ignoring literally everything else.

"Yeahh," Owen stretched out the word. "I hope I came off as believable."

"Almost too much so."

Owen smiled. "I know I paid for your coffee, but Charlie..."

"Yeah?" they said hesitatingly.

"We need to break up. I don't think I'm your type."

Charlie laughed. If they had dared take a drink before this, they might have had a spit take now. "Owen..." They felt speechless like earlier today and was left to wonder again. "Is there anything you won't do for your friends?"

He exhaled roughly. More than the situation called for and hinted back to events with Daniel. "I hope I never have to find out for real."

Fools

— Chapter 25 in Andreah's POV

Andreah had nearly spilled her beer as she watched everything unfold in front of her on the TV. She sat up, and thankfully didn't alert Owen of her shock. There he was. Daniel. The character she had been tracking across his adventures, pulling strings here and there with Amilia. She felt like a fool inadvertently bone digging her boyfriend's game. Worse, compiling video to sell him out without even realizing it. She felt sick. And scared. She grabbed her phone, as if it offered her something. She started three separate texts to Abby, ready to scream to her through messages about this. But she froze up, still not understanding what exact reality she had landed in.

Her eyes moved to stare at Owen. He didn't have any idea she was a bone digger, much less have any interest in Age of Shadows. What if he thought bone diggers were the scum of gaming?

Her eyes closed tightly, her thoughts deafening to whatever noise existed in the room. She knew this all along, at heart. That they didn't really know each other, that Owen didn't know her. They were dating but she held him at a distance, keeping his knowledge of her just above the level of a hookup. She decided to be everyone's flavor of the week, easily changing for anyone that would have her. Until whoever got bored first ended it. And just because she found a legit nice guy, she hadn't stopped being that.

Turns out they were both blind, to so much. Now she knew her latest project involved digitally stalking her boyfriend every day, and none of this would be easy to explain.

While gathering her things, she steeled herself to walk out quickly without hinting at anything Owen would catch. She nearly reached the door before he caught the movement. Her eyes danced around before she could figure out a way to dig herself out of the situation.

"Uh. I gotta go." She lied, eyes glued to her phone screen as if something was there to explain. "Sorry."

"I thought, uh, you were going to stay the night?" Owen asked, while taking a small glance down at her phone. Andreah tilted it casually away so that he wouldn't see. She didn't want to confront him about it right now. She just couldn't.

"Well, there's this emergency," she said, hastily tucking her phone away as if it was the only evidence of her lie. "One of the newbies ended up getting in a bad accident. I need to cover for 'em." As if there were more than just the couple random orders left at this time of day.

"Oh, okay. Stay safe." He swallowed her lie harshly, and she could tell he didn't want to.

At his touch, the small moment he held her hand before she could leave, she questioned if she should just blurt it all out then and there. She was a terrible liar, now an even more terrible girlfriend. She felt the world shrinking in on her, threatening to crumble everything she had here; Not just her work, but their relationship.

Once out on the street, Andreah's thoughts blurred together. She leaned over as if she had just gone on a long run. She didn't know where to go. She always thought, maybe if they got to that point, Owen would be the person she could go to when she was upset or stressed. But obviously that wasn't on the table this time.

She called Abby while walking fast away from his apartment toward the subway. The first time, she didn't pick up, but Andreah was relentless in the search for her best friend.

"Hello?"

"Abby. Daniel's Owen. Or, well, Owen is Daniel," she stammered, cutting to the chase.

"Woah, what?" Abby whispered, making Andreah wonder where she caught her.

"Ye-up. I don't know how I've been so close; It's been in my face. I'm a fucking fool. I don't—I don't know what to do. I can't breathe."

Abby took a moment to respond. "Are you still going to sell the story?" She was speaking more normally now, probably not around people anymore.

Andreah had already reached the subway, but couldn't go down without losing signal. She collapsed on the first few stairs. No more than a handful of people walked around this time of night, so no one could complain she was in the way. "Fuck. I actually like him, Abby. I just want to crawl into a hole and stay there forever."

"Then just, I don't know man. Tell him the truth? Pull yourself out of his game and tell him sorry."

"I've messed with his game too much to just abandon Amilia...and from what I know of his kind, the type of player he is, he probably thinks bone diggers are assholes. He'll probably like, write an exposé piece about me. Who knows, maybe I deserve it." Her mind was in a million pieces. "Do they have, like, video game themed revenge porn websites? I don't think he'd do that type of stuff, but who knows. I'm a shithead. Maybe not as bad as those girls who smash Xboxes but—"

"Andreah! Shut up. You're rambling," Abby and Andreah both took a moment to breathe. "It's going to be okay. I promise." The vow broke the protective wall of sarcasm and bitterness Andreah usually held and tears started blurring her vision. "Can you ease your way out? What did you change?"

"I don't know. I—I made Amilia into a glitch, she's trouble for Daniel and bad for the thieves. She's going to end up causing a war if they choose each other over duty, family, and all that shit. Maybe if I just..."

"Are you still there?"

Andreah stood up and started walking down the stairs. "Yeah, yeah. I'll call you back later."

She hung up and jogged to the train as it pulled in. Admittedly, she was involved with a lot of Daniel and Amilia's story so far. She'd been planning to really blow things up when it would bank the most for exposing who he was. This needed a new plan. This needed a firm commitment from herself to end the nonsense that had come between them. Maybe any pieces remaining could be salvaged.

"Fuck. Why did it have to be you, Owen?" she whispered, as she rested her head against the train's wall, softly knocking into it each time the track jiggled the cabin.

Author's Note: This is something super short I wrote on my phone, and I find it utterly adorable so I wanted to share it. It's set before the novel around the time Owen is just comfortable enough with his feelings to be playful about them online.

— Let's Dance

Daniel pulled his lips away from Lance. "I need to go to work."

"You are at work," Lance smirked.

"Loving you is work?"

The grin on the Lance's face only grew. A hesitant lick of his lips spelled out more than his words, and Daniel's eyes closely watching spoke further.

"I meant," Lance started again, "We're at the guild already."

"Oh, yes." He shook his head. Things had peaceful blurred recently between real life and the game, if they were ever separate in the first place.

"So, where are you going?" Lance asked. His tone was flat, if not slightly restrained.

"I meant what I said," Daniel said softly. Chest tight as he hoped to ease back into that bliss held moments before. "I'm going to a place where you shall be missed, if that isn't work, I don't know what is."

Lance leaned forward, softly kissing Daniel again. A goodbye kiss that lingered a moment too long to be considered such. "Do you intend to woo me, sir?"

"That is what one does with noble men, is it not?"

"You forget yourself."

Warning or not, Daniel ignored it. "No, I find myself. Bit by bit, each day, thanks to you."

Author Note: I once played with the idea of what a Bone Diggers spin-off would be like and as a thank you for buying this version I wanted to exclusively share what would have been the start of that hypothetical book.

— Player Too

Charlie was often told they were confused about many things in life: gender, sexuality, and what was or was not considered romantic. All were a solid pass, and topics that were personally sorted out long ago. The confusing thing was the blinds in their apartment.

"I swear to God. These make no sense," Charlie said, as they pulled on the strings that controlled the convoluted pulley system. "There," they said triumphantly, as the blinds came down to rest on the window sill. "Now we can watch the game without glare."

"My hero," Owen smiled. He had a small bi pin that caught the light and keep drawing Charlie's eye to it. Since Owen was in control of his own gameplay again he wore the small pride symbol while streaming and had simply neglected to take it off yet.

"He couldn't have died at worse time," the commentator recapped what had happened before the ad break. "Whoever wins this will have his, or her, name added to fnVR's roster of sponsored players."

"Their," Charlie corrected.

Owen glanced over, agreeing, but not knowing what to really add. "It's not that great of a prize. Whoever it is, they are going to have a rude awakening."

"I should have competed," Charlie said. One of the players on screen was climbing around the side of the building try sneak up on someone controlling the base that needed recapturing. "When I won, I could have demanded that fnVR finally patch Age of Shadows so that I don't have correct people on pronouns all the fucking time."

Owen's grin widened, and he didn't look back at the TV by time Charlie sighed and silently questioned the look. "Nothing," he was quick to add then shook his head. "It's just, that would be fucking cool. I should have tried to pull some strings when I worked for them."

"Is this where I say 'it's the thought that counts?'"

"No," Owen laughed. "This where you tell me I should have figured out my own shit faster. Like, wow, much VR, very betrayed."

"Are you memeing me?"

Owen shrugged a shoulder. "Maybe I could try to Courage Wolf you if it helps."

Charlie's eyes went wide with a breathless amusement. "Seriously dude, take a break from the internet."

"You should try though," Owen said, with a sobering tone.

"Try what?"

"Get fnVR to change their shit."

Charlie's mouth scrunched up to one side of their face at the idea. Their attention returned to the TV with a growing dissatisfaction. "You know, I really should," they seemed to say to the game instead of their friend. "I'm a player too after all."

ACKNOWLEDGMENTS

To Rachel Sharp, thank you for smoothing over the localization and being so aware of my characters you're able to tell me if something sounds off. You're brilliant and I love you for this reason and may others.

To Anne Chivon, indie authors don't normally get to experience a fandom, but you have given that all that love and more with this story. Thank you for your everlasting support, silliness, and overall company.

To John Lopez, thank you for your brainstorming sessions. Even years later I still had the screenshotted notes of all your help and support.

To everyone on Wattpad who read this story either as the chapters were still being posted weekly. or afterwards before the editing was complete. Every comment, every vote, every nomination for a community award meant so much to us and allowed for the paperback dream to come true.

ABOUT THE AUTHORS

Lovers of science fiction and video games, Tiffany Rose and Alexandrea Tauber met online to write stories heavily influenced by the fusion of the two. Connect with them on social media or their blog artoverchaos.com.

OTHER JOINT WORKS

HELLO WORLD (.EXE Chronicles)

When a technology company can buy your personal freedom Scott is a hacker ready to prove that a single voice can be a powerful weapon.

Scott's skills as a surveillance expert are useful when he's breaking down firewalls. But hacktivism isn't enough; he's going after the holy grail—UltSyn's Human Information Drives, human assets implanted with cerebral microchips. After digging deeper into restricted databases, he discovers that those who enlist with UltSyn get far more than they bargained for. Plunged into a world of human trafficking and corporate espionage, Scott is determined to find his sister, no matter the cost. But when the information reveals the people closest to him have been working for UltSyn all along, he has to find her—before UltSyn finds him.

Proof

Made in the USA
Columbia, SC
15 August 2018